The Cage-maker

STORY RIVER BOOKS

Pat Conroy, Founding Editor at Large

The Cage-Maker

a novel

Nicole Seitz

The University of South Carolina Press

© 2017 Nicole Seitz

Published by the University of South Carolina Press
Columbia, South Carolina 29208

www.sc.edu/uscpress

Manufactured in the United States of America

26 25 24 23 22 21 20 19 18 17
10 9 8 7 6 5 4 3 2 1

Library of Congress Cataloging-in-Publication Data
can be found at http://catalog.loc.gov/

ISBN: 978-1-61117-843-2 (hardcover)
ISBN: 978-1-61117-844-9 (ebook)

This book was printed on recycled paper
with 30 percent postconsumer waste content.

Foreword

Every family has its lore from past generations, the myths, legends, tall tales, and half-truths we grow up hearing about long-lost relatives. There is usually royalty of some kind, a Cherokee princess, a wealthy countess, maybe a duke who barely escaped the old country before the revolution. Southerners almost always have Civil War stories, about the heroes their family produced, the battles they fought, and the fortunes they lost. These are the stories we want to hear, not the one about great-uncle so-and-so who was an accountant and never traveled outside the little town where he was born. Most of us live pretty mundane lives, give or take a few colorful characters who occasionally appear to spice things up a bit, so we're hungry for the tales of adventure, passion, and high drama.

Many families have a family historian, the one we turn to for questions about our heritage who has spent long dreary hours researching the lineage. Genealogy can a tedious undertaking, and not everyone is up to the task. Genealogists look for stories beyond the ordinary, for the discovery that makes your heart beat faster. Such a find can propel you to dig deeper and deeper, to widen the search until you get to the bottom of the story. If you're lucky, you might uncover one or two really interesting characters who capture your attention or uncover a few papers or diaries to help with historical data. The day Nicole Seitz decided to learn more about her family tree was a lucky one indeed. It was a happy day for her as a writer, and it was even happier one for us as readers.

Imagine digging into the history of your family who came from that most fabled of all southern cities, the incomparable New Orleans, and finding a treasure trove of thwarted love, passion, greed, jealousy, adultery, insanity, voodoo curses, and even murder. Throw in a beautiful heiress, or two, who dies mysteriously; gory court cases and imprisonment; a rare genetic disease worthy of an Edgar Allan Poe tale; strange dances and rituals carried out in a hidden mansion; and a tragic love affair that goes all the way back to Cuba. All these elements add up to quite a story, as any writer can tell you. But how do you unravel all the mystery and put the pieces together to form a coherent narrative? Can the truth be excavated from a jumble of documents that may remain forever incomplete, from the frustrating fragments of long-ago lives that might never be truly understood? Or are the mysteries of the past destined to remain elusive and just beyond our grasp?

It was a quest that obsessed Nicole, the writer, for years. What began as a natural curiosity about the French ancestors who landed in New Orleans in the 1800s became the driving force that propelled her fertile and creative imagination. Here was a tale begging to be told, peopled with unforgettable characters of historical significance. It also had a complex narrative, splendid setting, and mythic themes of lost love, greed, and tragedy. If only there was a focal point to tie it all together, then Nicole could take it from there. Ultimately it was the discovery of a great-grandfather who made his living by creating birdcages that provided her with the unifying focus of what would become this book. It was all any writer could ask for.

Whenever and however a great story comes to a writer, the question is always the same: What is the best way to tell it? Because Nicole Seitz has written six critically acclaimed books of fiction, I doubt she had to ponder that dilemma for long. Great truths are often presented through the framework of fiction, which allows for the creative exploration of possibilities in a way nonfiction cannot do. In addition, most of Nicole's other works deal thematically with the traumatic intersection of past and present. Although the sins of the past may not visibly mark the present generation, the wounds are buried underneath where they fester unless exposed to the healing light of truth. The damage might even be considerable enough to be thought of as a curse. And the task of the writer of historical fiction—as opposed to a more factual rendering of events—is to tell the story. This is when it happened, this is where and how, these are the people who lived it, and this is what it did to them.

So Nicole tells us the story of a birdcage maker, François Reynaud. Although François is a fictional character, in the hands of a skilled storyteller such as Nicole, he becomes so real on the page that we as readers come to know him well. His cages are described in such loving detail that we can not only see them, we can also feel the passion of their creator. Once François is caught up in the dark and twisted lives of the Saloy family, his plight becomes the axis on which the plot turns. His melancholy, artistic demeanor is presented in stark contrast to the scholarly, scientific-minded Dr. Yves Rene Le Monnier, another central character of the story and one who is based on a real-life historical figure. Dr. Le Monnier is the outsider who is drawn against his will into the tangled web of the doomed Saloy/Carcano/Pons family. All good gothic novels demand such an impartial observer, going back to the tenant in *Wuthering Heights*. He stands in for the reader, who starts out observing but cannot turn away, despite the mounting tension and feeling of inevitable doom.

Through the letters and journals of Dr. Le Monnier and François Reynaud, Nicole brings to life a vast cast of characters—some who once lived, others who live in her imagination—who captured her attention and demanded that their story be told. It's a bold and ambitious undertaking because the plot is as intricate and detailed as the exquisite birdcage that becomes the central motif; the timeframe spans several generations; and the historical records are as numerous as they are necessary for authenticity. Then there's the matter of the family curse and what's to be made of that peculiarity. A less skillful writer might have concocted a melodrama from such a delicious brew of gothic elements, but Nicole resisted the temptation. Instead she artfully weaves a rich, complex narrative that beautifully blends the past and present while exploring the age-old themes of suffering, sin, and redemption. Throughout, the possibility of a curse lingers in the background like the foul odor of decay. Rather than ending in pat and easy answers, the question of the curse raises even more puzzling ones: Are the sins of the past ever truly behind us, or do they form a part of who we are and what we become? Are both the innocent and the sinner equally doomed by the past, and, if so, what is the hope of redemption?

Not content with concocting a rollicking good story while tackling some of the great spiritual questions of our time, Nicole Seitz takes it a step further and presents the reader a delightful surprise. Because she's a talented visual artist as well as an acclaimed author, Nicole chose to illustrate her book with sketches that bring the characters and scenes of a bygone age to vivid life. The illustrations are the crowning glory of a work that brought to my mind the great old books I came to love passionately when I first discovered the many joys of reading. I'm proud to add *The Cage-maker* to my collection and will display it next to its kinfolks of the gothic tradition, *Wuthering Heights, The Tenant of Wildfell Hall, Jane Eyre, Jamaica Inn,* and *The Fall of the House of Usher.* There it will feel right at home.

Cassandra King

Part One

"Like cages full of birds, their houses are full of deceit;
they have become rich and powerful."

Jeremiah 5:27

Blog post, ReVive or DIY Trying, June 2

UNEXPECTED TREASURE

As many of you DIY-ers know, I am a fanatic for bringing back to life treasures from the past that have fallen into disrepair. Usually, I find them at thrift shops or garage sales. People have no idea what they're throwing out! But this morning, a treasure literally arrived on my doorstep in the form of an enormous brown box. The UPS man was my Santa, bringing it all the way into my foyer, and after signing his electronic doohickey, I shut the door and began to salivate. What WAS in that box?!

The packing slip said it was from New Orleans, and I was wracking my brain, trying to figure out who in the world I know in New Orleans. Nobody! And then, I found a letter from an attorney.

> Dear Ms. Sinclair,
>
> The laws surrounding your adoption require absolute silence as to the identity of your parents and grandparents, but your birth grandmother has died and left a will, bequeathing this birdcage to you. I am sure this package comes as a surprise, but make no mistake; you are its rightful heir. I apologize in advance, but I am unable to answer any questions about this package, your family or your inheritance.
>
> Respectfully,
>
> _____, Esq.

Okay, people. I am officially freaking out. If you've been following me for any time at all now, you know I'm adopted, I don't hide that fact, and I'm not ashamed. I have the best parents anyone could ask for. And it's because of them I've never tried to find my birth parents, although I admit I've been curious.

Anyway, back to the point. I opened this box and unearthed the most unbelievable, gorgeous birdcage I've ever seen in my life. Just look at it! On its stand, it's taller than me, and its width and depth are four feet. I mean, who made this thing?! It's not even a birdcage; it's a replica of a house, a mansion. Did my grandmother live in a house like this? How did she get this birdcage? Why would she send it to me? I had no idea anyone in my birth family even knew of my existence!

Sorry to go on like this. Enough about my personal mystery. Back to business. The birdcage is pretty dirty right now. Looks like it was outside for a while, but I am bound and determined to clean it up and ReVive it to its natural beauty. I know it's vogue to turn birdcages into lights and spray paint them turquoise these days, but it would be a sin to alter this antique in any way except to its original state. Don't you think? Stay tuned as I post in-progress pics.

Trish

Blog post, ReVive or DIY Trying, June 3

CAGEY QUESTIONS

It's hard to explain the emotions I have, restoring this birdcage. I often get sentimental in ReViving certain pieces, thinking about the people who once owned them, imagining their stories, their lives. But this one is different. My birth grandmother owned this. With every stroke of my rag, the warmth of the wood shines through, and I cannot help but imagine my grandmother, looking at the birdcage, just as I am doing now. What was she like? Did she look like me?

I'm starting with the wood stand it came with. Don't you think it's going to be gorgeous when it's refreshed? For those of you interested, I'm using only a light-oil product to clean the wood. I don't want to alter this in any way as to lessen the original value. I'm estimating it to be at least 100 years old, but I'll have it properly appraised soon. True antiques should be unadulterated or else you run the risk of devaluing them completely.

Now, back to work.

Trish

Blog post, ReVive or DIY Trying, June 4

UNCAGED SECRETS

Okay, I'm nearly hyperventilating now, and I may have scared the neighbors by screaming so loudly. My daughter, Kelsey, is glaring at me from behind her iPod Touch. But people, I HAVE JUST FOUND A SECRET COMPARTMENT INSIDE THE BIRDCAGE! Did you hear that loud and clear?

I've been up all night and finished the stand (doesn't it look amazing?!) when I decided I had to start cleaning out the cage. I just had to. I started on the inside. There's dirt and grunge, pine straw and leaves, not to mention bird poop. After vacuuming the debris, I started to rub my rag over the bottom of the cage. I had to really press to get the grime to come up, especially in the corners, and then . . . wait for it . . . then I pressed on something and a secret panel opened up! I am not kidding you when I say I nearly wet my pants.

Friends—*gulp!*—the secret panel was NOT EMPTY. I'm so jittery right now, I don't know if I'll ever sleep. There was an old leather attaché case inside. I opened it up and found folders and files filled with letters and documents, photos and newspaper clippings, diaries and journals. Of who? I don't know yet!!

I think I need a sedative.

Here is the attaché case. Isn't it amazing? How old is this thing?

I cannot show you a photo of the contents because it all feels too personal still. This is by far the greatest treasure I have ever discovered, and I mean EVER. I may share some of it with you, but honestly, I need some time to process this. Please be patient with me as I take a little time off from the blog to sift through everything. I have a feeling what I'm about to read will tell me about my birth family . . . and Kelsey's ancestors. Am I ready to find out? Do I even want to know? Does the lawyer know there was a secret panel in this thing?! I have no idea. But it's mine now.

If you're the praying type, I could sure use your prayers about now. And your patience. My next blog post may be a while. In the meantime, go on out and find your own personal treasure. Remember: ReVive or DIY Trying!

Trish

My dearest Pauline,

So it has come to you—the cage and this letter. I realize many years will have passed since this writing. You are surely very different now, a young woman. The last time I saw you, you were chasing a butterfly on my veranda, all pigtails and sunshine. You will never know your mother, and what a shame. She was lovely. So young. I wonder how this not knowing her might affect you in the years to follow. Yet, I digress. You are reading this now, so you are of age and time has passed. I, no doubt, am now deceased. May this letter find you in a state of mind and body and spirit that is strong and able to ward off—

Forgive me. An old man is sometimes distracted by the flickering of the fire. Let me begin again. First and foremost, I have remained a long-time friend of your family's for as long as I can remember. There has not been a day in which our lives have not been intertwined, although for many years I remained unaware of the connection. It is the same as a mother and an unborn child. There is no knowledge of the other until the first breath and sound of wailing, though the intimate connection formed long before then.

Your inheritance is unusual, I admit. I have left you my research, all of it, so that you may see for yourself what is your history, that to which I devoted much of my life. I have put it in order as best I can. This was my story, and Francois' and Madame Saloy's and your mother's and uncle's. It is part love story and part horror and madness. All of it true.

This is your story now. Has your ancestry doomed you or are you set free? I pray for the latter, though you shall tell me in the next life.

Till then, with love always,

Dr. Yves René Le Monnier (Papa)

A photo of me for your remembrance

From the journal of Y. R. Le Monnier, M.D.

RE: NEW ORLEANS 1906

I can still hear her voice. She asked if I believed in curses. I'd been so sure of myself. Believed in no such thing. How could I have known the depths of my ignorance?

I remember in those days after Eulalie died, I was living in a netherworld—a time when I considered life to be as bad as it had ever been and as good as it could possibly get—but that was all about to change with the arrival of the girl. No longer was the "Doctor is in" sign posted to the door of my home on North Galvez as I was mostly retired except for the occasional examination of a friend, and yet she had sought me out completely unannounced.

"Please," she pleaded, "my brother is in a great deal of trouble. The woman has died and they're going to send him away!"

"Shhhh, now, wait just a minute," I tried to calm her. "Come and sit and tell me your name first, and your brother's."

"Carmelite Kurucar," she said, breathless. "My brother is Andrew Reynaud." She put her hands up to her face and pressed until she was more composed. I noticed a wedding band on her left hand and was surprised as the girl appeared very young. I reached into my pocket for a handkerchief and gave it to her.

Something about her brother's name struck a chord with me. I might have read it in the *Times-Picayune*. "Your brother, Andrew, may go where, exactly?"

"To prison. For murder," she said, shaking her head and dabbing at her eyes. "He shot a woman on Franklin Street, and she accused him of it before she died."

"I see." Yes, it was beginning to become clearer. I certainly had read about it in the paper. There were many murders in New Orleans, and I was accustomed to reading about each of them in detail, taking fair interest, but I remember taking notice of this particular case, as the victim lived several days after the shooting. Just long enough to identify her slayer.

I came and sat down next to the girl. She could have been the age of my granddaughter, had I had one. "I'm very sorry about your brother," I told her. "Truly. It is quite a predicament. I do have one question for you, though." She peered up at me with red, watery eyes. Her face was swollen with grief. "I don't understand why you've come to *me*. As a physician, I can no longer do anything to help this woman, I'm afraid. And I am no longer city coroner; someone else occupies that position now and will be conducting the autopsy and finding evidence that can be used in your brother's case."

She stood and walked across the room to where my certificates of medicine and service were hung among photographs of myself with the three mayors I'd served under as coroner, and with Governor Kellogg who'd appointed me to the board of health. She hung there, quietly for several moments, until she turned back around and faced me. Her redness had receded a bit, and I was able to see again the true beauty of the girl, her light brown hair, framing a smooth face of nearly the same complexion. Her eyes were a piercing pale blue and her lips so young and full and supple.

"Dr. Le Monnier, my grandfather told me you were the foremost expert on insanity in this city."

"Well, I suppose . . . I was, when I was working with the insane asylum . . ." I stood and ran my hands along my vest. "And I suppose I still may be. Yes. No, I don't think anyone in New Orleans shares my understanding of lunacy and other psychological ailments. Tell me, is your brother pleading insanity? Is this why you came to me?"

"It's what his lawyers want him to do."

"Ah, I see. And is he insane?"

"I don't know. Possibly. But my brother is claiming another defense."

"If I read the paper correctly, I believe the woman said he shot her in the back. I'm not sure what other type of defense there could be for that act."

"My brother," said the girl, steeling her face, "claims there is a curse. That ever since he received a large sum of money, his life has been cursed. That the money is cursed."

I raised my eyebrows and bit the inside of my lip. I could hardly see how that defense could stand up in court. I'd been witness to countless murder trials, and never had the mention of a curse saved a man's fate from the penitentiary or worse.

"Mrs. Kurucar, I'm afraid I don't know how to help you. I am mostly in retirement, and I'm afraid this isn't a good time for me at all. I'm quite busy with—"

"I will pay you," she said.

"No, no, it's not that, I—"

"Please, Dr. Le Monnier. It has to be you. You admitted yourself there is no one better."

I stood for a moment reproached by my own words. Her blue eyes grew large, like those of a child, tugging at the pant leg, but they were not about to convince me to come out of retirement. She could see my resolve, so she tried another tactic. She handed me a *Times-Picayune* article dated June 20, 1902, four years ago.

MISSING FROM HOME
Andrew Reynaud Has Been Away for Ten Days.
The police have been asked to look for Andrew Reynaud, a 16-year-old lad, who has been missing from his home, at 1415 Esplanade Avenue, for the last ten days. His people have searched all over in the hope of finding the lad, but no trace of him has been learned, and of course there is no end of anxiety among his people, who fear that some ill may have befallen him. When he left his home, Andrew said that he thought he would either go to Little Woods, or Bay St. Louis, or to South Africa. Perhaps he did go to South Africa, but so far there is no proof as to his whereabouts. He is 5 feet 7 inches tall, of good build, is dark complexioned, and has a scar on the right side of his head. He was dressed in a blue serge suit of clothes, with a white and black negligee shirt.

I looked up at her after reading, and she looked just past my head as if staring at a memory.

"Late one night," she said, "I heard a sound at my bedroom door and there he was, my brother, reeking of whiskey and urine. I didn't dare go and hug him, for he looked so different. He was still wearing the clothes he'd left home in, but now they were soiled and his hair disheveled. What could possibly happen in ten days to change a boy so much? Had he gone all the way to Africa and back? Had Mother and Father seen him downstairs? I was too afraid to ask him, and too afraid to go run and tell them he was home. I simply said a silent prayer of thanks that he was safe and still alive." She walked across the room and picked up a photograph of my beloved Eulalie, studied it, then set it back down.

"My little sister, Gladys, was still asleep, and so it was just the two of us, Andrew and me, staring at one another, my eyes threatening to spill over in tears. He came to me and touched my face, then patted my head with a sloppy hand and lumbered down to the floor beside my bed, curled up like a baby.

"I never did find out where my brother went for those ten days, although I suspect it was the Storyville District. I do understand why he longed to run away though. I, too, feel it. Can't you see? We need you, Dr. Le Monnier. Please say you'll help."

"Well. I . . ." She had won me over. "I suppose I could at least review your brother's case and examine him to make an assessment of his state of mind," I said. "The curse he speaks of could very well be the manifestation of Delirium of Persecution in which the subject believes someone or something is out to do him harm. It's a paranoia I've seen many times in patients, and if this is the case, it very well may be your brother's best defense."

"Thank you." She was silent and seemed timid all of a sudden. She looked down at her wedding ring and twisted it with her right hand. "I'm sure you're right. I'm sure that pleading insanity may very well save my brother's life, and I want that. I don't want him to go to prison. It's no life for a twenty year old man. I'm sure if he could take back the events of that awful night, he would. I know he is remorseful."

"Good then. I will be happy to call his lawyers and try to make an appointment to meet with the young man."

"I cannot thank you enough," she said. She looked at me for a moment longer and then turned to walk to the door.

"Is there . . . is there anything else, dear? Truly, I am sorry for your brother. I will do what I can. I am a man of my word."

She nodded and tried to show her gratitude with a small upturn of the corners of her mouth. "I don't know how to say this. Perhaps you'll think me mad, too."

Perhaps, I thought. "Please. Speak your mind," I told her.

She bit her lip. "I need you to determine if my brother is insane, Dr. Le Monnier, but more than that, I need you to tell me if there is, indeed, a curse."

"A curse. I see. I'm afraid that would be next to impossible, dear. First, one would have to believe in such things, which I do not, and second, how in the world could one prove that a curse exists? And why on earth, I say most respectfully, would you be so interested in said curse?"

"Because, Dr. Le Monnier . . ." Fright rushed behind her eyes. "The money has now come to me as well. I am in possession of a great deal of this same money. I need to know if I, too, will fall under its curse."

11

My mouth opened, and I took in a quick breath. I wasn't sure what to say to this creature, but I felt at once a deep sadness for the burden she carried. Finally, I managed a smile. "I am quite sure your curse does not exist, but I give you my word, I will do my very best to disprove it for you, so that you may feel more at ease and your brother may be spared a dark sentence. I believe it may be his only chance."

She seemed to breathe a sigh of relief and finally turned to reach for the door after giving me profuse thanks. She was almost to the sidewalk when it occurred to me to ask her a question.

"Mrs. Kurucar, you are quite young to be married, are you not? May I ask your age?"

"Sixteen," she said. "The same age as my brother when he began to . . . stray."

"I see. And you never told me. Who is your grandfather who referred you to me?"

She turned and faced me, standing in place as a carriage rolled by behind her, the horse clopping and biting at its bit. "His name is François Reynaud," she called out. "He was a birdcage maker on St. Ann. He says he knows you from long ago."

I stood, transfixed in bittersweet memory at the name I knew so well and also the guilt that came along with it. My mind flooded with the details all over again, and I found myself feeling off balance, as if I'd raced through the past decades in an instant, standing now with his granddaughter in front of me.

Indeed, my blood was beginning to stir. I felt my heart race and promised the child I would do my best for her brother, especially now that I knew who his grandfather was. And especially since I seemed to recall the cage-maker speaking of exactly the same things—a great deal of money and tragedies that seemed to follow it.

New Orleans Item, November 30, 1906

REYNAUD CHARGED WITH MURDER - SHOT WOMAN IN FIT OF JEALOUSY

Doris Sheldon Makes Dying Statement
"I Hate to Die," She Says.

Georgia Collier, the woman known as Doris Sheldon, who was shot twice by Andrew Reynaud, her paramour, in Franklin, near Conti street

Tuesday night, died in the Charity Hospital last night, and this morning the young man was charged with murder. When arraigned he pleaded not guilty, and was remanded without the benefit of bail. The woman succumbed from two wounds she received from a 28-caliber revolver in the hands of Reynaud. The first shot entered the small of the back and passed through the abdomen, perforating the right lung. The second shot entered a point a little above the hip line and passed through the abdomen. Before she died Special Officer John Exnicios, of the district attorney's office, obtained a statement from the woman. This statement was jotted down and will be used as the dying statement and will serve as part of the evidence against Reynaud. Special Officer Exnacios, with Corporal Geis, began questioning the dying woman.

"Do you think you are going to die?" asked the officer.

"I don't know," answered the patient, in a low, weak voice.

"Who shot you?" asked Exnicios.

"Andrew Reynaud."

"Why did he shoot you?"

"Because he saw me sitting on another man's lap."

"What did you do?"

"Nothing."

"Where were you when he shot you?"

"Going to the front door."

"Where was he when he fired at you?"

"About two feet behind me."

"Did you know he was going to shoot you?"

"No."

"What did he say before he shot you?"

"He kissed me good-bye, and then said, 'See me to the door.'"

"What did you do then?"

"I led the way."

"How many times did he shoot you?"

"Twice."

"Were you facing him?"

"No; my back was turned to him."

"Are you sure Andrew Reynaud shot you?"

"Yes."

"Do you think you'll die?"

"Yes, and I hate to die," moaned the poor victim, and the party left her bedside.

Mrs. Carmelite Kurucar

Since the woman was confined in Ward 45 of the Charity Hospital the house surgeon gave orders that no one was to see her. Her condition was such that a change for the worse would mean her death at any time.

Much to the surprise of the surgeons at the hospital, the woman lived all though Wednesday and Thursday. Yesterday evening the end was drawing near and Special Officer Exnicios was notified.

Reynaud told the police when he surrendered that too much whiskey caused him to shoot the woman with whom he had been living. After finding her seated on another man's lap Reynaud asked her to kiss him, saying he was going away. This the woman did. He then asked her to lead him to the door, and it is believed that the willingness of the woman in doing this and her apparent indifference cause the jealous passion to awaken in the man and he fired as Doris was leading the way to the front door.

From the journal of Y. R. Le Monnier, M.D.

RE: NEW ORLEANS 1906

It was evening now, and I thought of the girl, Mrs. Kurucar, as I moved to the hearth. For a moment, I imagined I'd supped with my wife and she'd already gone off to bed without me, but then I remembered. My wife had been gone seven months now. In the beginning it was impossible to sleep in an empty bed. The noises of the house were louder than I had once known them to be. I hated the sounds, and I hated the quiet equally. Day by day I awoke to the knowledge that my wife was dead and would never come back. How much longer would it be that I'd have to endure this empty house?

I had begun to make progress though, to dig myself out of the trenches of despair as I had urged so many patients to do before. I had applied myself heavily in service of commemorating the Civil War. I had run for the seat of vice-president of the Association of the Army of Tennessee, and was working to raise funds for monuments for each deceased Louisiana soldier. I had begun writing my own personal account of the Battle of Shiloh, that much misunderstood but pivotal battle of the war. I was beginning to feel my life might still have meaning, and there were days, moments rather, when I thought of Eulalie in a sweet way, sad nonetheless, but more along the lines of, *oh, how my Eulalie would love to be here to see this.* It was progress, I tell you. Real progress. I couldn't let the girl disrupt all of that. It would send my therapy weeks, if not months, in arrears.

I stoked the fire while wild light flickered and embers danced and flew. The heat on my face was welcome in this chilly room which served as my office. The cold was bone-deep in New Orleans when the damp air crawled through crevices in my home, and especially so, now that my skin was thinner and sagged a bit at the jowls. It was December, and I felt the chill down to the core of me.

My mind was tight and swimming and dull at times, ever since the child had set foot in my presence. There were voices and faces coming back, and often, several times I thought *I* was the one going mad, something which unnerved me, having always been the authority on insanity. Yet the mere fact that I considered I was going insane was the very thing that proved my sanity. *An insane mind cannot have sane thoughts about one's one own sanity. Can it?*

It reminded me of Andrew Reynaud's defense. I was to meet with the young man at the Orleans parish prison the next morning at 9 o'clock, but until then, there was much I needed to do. My curiosity had gotten the best of me, and I found myself compelled to refresh my memory.

I walked to the bookshelves behind my desk, ran my fingers along them and stopped momentarily at the partially-completed book that bore my own name, Y. R. Le Monnier, *General Beauregard at Shiloh.* It was a tattered notebook that had seen many a night and glass of whiskey as I poured out my heart and attention to the battle that still held my soul. I had been in that battle and also others, but Shiloh was my first. I'd found some freedom in writing of the Civil War, of setting things straight, discounting other less reliable sources, and someday I would publish it. Some so-and-sos had written accounts without ever setting foot on a battlefield. *Absurd,* I thought. I'd been there and that was all there was to it. The eyewitness must always be the author of the story. My wife had always fully supported me in my reasoning and imagined with me the day the book was finally finished. I would finish it. I would. I would not allow this diversion from Mrs. Kurucar to keep me from my duties to Shiloh. And yet, I had promised her I would do my best.

I had countless other notebooks filled with the eyewitness accounts of my patients over the years. In order to help the young girl, I simply needed to find the notebooks that contained the records of my time with the cage-maker. He'd come to me just over twenty years ago, but his story had become quite sketchy in my memory.

I put on my glasses and knelt before my file cabinet to thumb through my notebooks. I'd kept them religiously, as if ledgers could be one's own religion. Perhaps they were. They were sacred and real. They were part of history, a true love of mine. Included in the books were my own memoirs, journals of day to day life and opinions. There would be pieces of my life with my wife in here. I was both hesitant and expectant at the thought.

I flipped through one notebook and then another. And another. Entry after entry of patients I'd seen at the city insane asylum. More notebooks on the ones who were deceased. Notes about skulls and brain softening, bullet holes and causes of death when I served as city coroner. And finally, the last books strewn together with more cohesion. These were the ones from my private practice—clients and patients I'd known for decades. Illness, deaths, secrets and sins, all divulged to the trusted doctor.

I had been trusted, I realized this, and it was this fact that nearly paralyzed me. Must I keep quiet about the observations I had made? Surely client privilege and Hippocratic Oath would be enough to keep my mouth shut, and yet . . . yet I had made a promise to the girl. Her brother's life was in jeopardy.

As I flipped though my files in reverse chronological order, I erased the years. 1900, 1895, 1891, 1877 . . . Ah, yes. Here they were. I pulled them out and held them in my hands. I closed my eyes and could envision the cage-maker again, his dark eyes, his darker goatee.

For the purposes of preparing to meet with the accused murderer tomorrow, and also for my commitment to his sister to disprove the curse that bewitched him, I set out my notebooks on the sofa nearest the fire and donned my eyeglasses. I poured myself a brandy and threw a blanket over my chilled legs. I felt the heat of the fire like a slap across my face as I opened the first notebook entitled simply, "The Bird Cage-maker." Sadly, there were only a few filled pages.

From the clinical notebook of Y. R. Le Monnier, M.D.

THE BIRD CAGE-MAKER, 1877, FIRST APPOINTMENT

François Reynaud is truly the most pitiful creature, ravaged by unrequited love. He is quite insane and suffering from stupidity due to intense melancholy. I've

*entertained the thought of sending him immediately to the city asylum, despite
its horrible treatment of inmates, but he sounds completely lucid in his speech.
Only his forlorn eyes and wringing hands betray his mental state. I have set up
a regular schedule of sessions in which I will take his vitals, prescribe medication
and then settle in for a nice long listen. Monsieur Reynaud speaks of Paris and
also of some of my other patients. Perhaps he can give me more insight into them.*

From the clinical notebook of Y. R. Le Monnier, M.D.

THE BIRD CAGE-MAKER, 1877, SECOND APPOINTMENT

*François Reynaud is quite comfortable after having a small brandy. He sits, legs
crossed, staring out the window into a tree while gently tugging at his goatee.
He appears either genius or madman. At this point, I'm not sure which. Alas,
he has sat silently for so long that I am growing impatient. I clear my throat
and pour my own brandy. He is trying to find the courage to speak of it, he
says—to speak of her, but he cannot. He is beginning to weep and feels he cannot speak the words into the air.*

 Paranoid.

 *It is then he tells me he's written it all down and would rather I read his
thoughts. He hands me a letter from his pocket written in barely legible scrib-
ble as if he was up all night scratching it down, attacking the poor paper with
ink. He blows his nose in his kerchief as I begin to read silently. His attention
to detail and memory recall in his writing suggests high intelligence as well as
psychotic hypergraphia.*

Letter from François

SEPTEMBER 1877

Dear Doctor Le Monnier,

 It was like heaven to have my own studio. Never had I felt such freedom. Unlike the poor winged creatures doomed to spend their days in
one of my creations, I flew wild and free as I stretched my wire and shaved
intricate details in wood, as my brush delicately savored the surface, until
the end, when the cage was complete. Then I was spent and wistful. I celebrated with a crust of French bread, a bottle of Bordeaux and soon after,
by beginning a new cage.

I remember one day when I was to begin again. I stood in my studio at 47 Rue St. Ann and studied my drawing of La Maison de l'Opera. Something was not quite right, not quite as I remembered it. A window needed to move to the left. *Oui*. Is that it? I closed my eyes and tried not to hear the clopping of horse hooves in the street or the loud calls of men *en espagnole*. I understood it, I did. When one is immersed in Babel, languages of the masses, all words begin to make sense. It was in the tonation. The man in the street there was angry. He felt he'd been cheated out of money. A woman was trying to calm him down but he yelled to make her silent. He raved about his money again. It was all too much for me.

I opened my eyes again and startled when I saw a woman standing before me. My hand jolted across the page and the woman said gingerly, "*Pardonnez-moi.* I didn't mean to startle you."

"*Non, pas de problème,*" I replied. "I was just thinking about a sketch." I gestured. "My mind was far away, and I didn't hear you come in."

"It is magnificent," said the woman, regarding my drawing.

I could smell her, a gentle sophisticated scent that took me somewhere back in France. I knew this scent, like lilacs and pepper, yet couldn't place it. It was maddening.

"You have quite a talent for making birdcages," she said.

"*Merci.*" I stood and guided the woman to the cages perched around the studio, the ones completed and waiting like orphans to find a home. "May I show you a cage? This one perhaps? It is simple yet elegant." Her face was lovely. Smooth skin framed by dark hair and eyes with flecks of gold.

She smiled, and her brown eyes sparkled. She was extremely smartly dressed, and it occurred to me that I was standing in the presence of great wealth. It unnerved me a bit. I saw in her, not money, not food or peace of mind, not extravagance or gambling munitions, but the right to create. Money to me meant the time and space and raw materials for my Creator to work within me.

"Mmm, I don't think so," she said with regard to the simple cage. It was pointed into a dome at the top. "There is a beautiful one in the window here." The woman swayed toward it, her face changing to something akin a child's.

"La Maison de Rosimond," I said, smiling. "I know it well. I spent many days there, studying it before I left France. I drew every facet of the exterior and walked its hallways so that I could feel it. I must feel in order to create." I realized my pontification was sounding a bit insane, and perhaps this woman might not understand the motivations of artists. "*Pardon,*" I said, bowing slightly. "*Je m'appelle* François Reynaud. Welcome to my studio."

"Carmelite Saloy," she said. "Carma. *Enchanté.*"

I shifted. "Madame Saloy." My eyebrows rose, and I stole a glance at her ring finger. "You are married to Monsieur Bertrand Saloy, I presume?"

"The same." The playing field had been set. Saloy was one of the wealthiest men in New Orleans, a fierce landlord and real estate mogul. He recently moved with his wife into la maison de Le Monnier and had the audacity to build a fourth floor. It now stood as the tallest residence in New Orleans. Word had it he forced a grocer out and into selling the building to him. Saloy. I knew this name well. I was aware of the Saloy family back in Paris, yet none were as potent as this Bertrand Saloy of New Orleans. He practically owned the canals as well as had his hands in sugar and rice.

Madame Saloy stood before me in her exquisite drapery, a silk wrap over skirts of the palest color peach. I thought of champagne Rosé and swallowed hard. It had been a full two minutes since I'd thought of my drawing.

"I have seen the work of some of your contemporaries, Monsieur Reynaud, in the market. You French are so talented with your hands." She turned. Was she blushing? Was she speaking of her own husband, the hands of Monsieur Saloy, or could she, in fact, be speaking of mine? And in which way was she inferring I was good with my hands? I felt myself stiffen and excused myself for a glass of water. I offered one to the lady, but she refused.

"You have heard of my husband," she said, all business now. "You will know where we live on Rue Royale?"

"I believe I do."

"Good. I will look forward to seeing you there tomorrow at seven o'clock in the evening. Sharp." She turned, and I caught another whiff of her *parfum.*

"I'm sorry, Madame, I don't mean to be slow."

Madame Saloy smiled and showed her youthful cheeks covered in a barest swipe of rouge. "I want you to build a cage for me, Monsieur Reynaud. A model of la Maison de Saloy. A miniature of my home."

I was stunned and shook my head. "I'm sorry, Madame, I don't take commissions." The words spilled out without thought. "But I will give you a fair price on this one, la Maison de Rosimond, the house you admired in the window."

The woman stood still. Only her eyelashes closed once. I could hear my heart beating through my shirt. Or was it the horses outside in the street again? A commission. From the wealthiest couple in all of New Orleans. And me, an artiste, a free spirit who refused to be caged in by others. No. I could not consider a commission. Or could I? No. I would not consider accepting money in return for my freedom to create.

"Monsieur Reynaud." Madame Saloy placed thin fingers on my shirt sleeve. "I'm afraid I cannot take no for an answer. You are the best cage-maker in New Orleans. Your ability to render architecture in this medium of twigs and wire in miniature, is nothing short of . . . of miraculous. I assure you, you will be more than fairly compensated for taking on my little project."

I breathed in deeply. I was not sure if my intoxication was from her fingertips on my sleeve or of her scent. I closed my eyes to steady myself.

"Madame, forgive my . . . may I ask . . . what is that perfume you are wearing? I . . . seem to recall it from Paris."

"Eros," she said, but her voice trailed behind her. Madame Saloy was already in the doorway, and I could see the narrow of her waist in the sunlight glowing around her. She smiled with dazzling teeth. "Seven o'clock, Monsieur François Reynaud, cage-maker extraordinaire of New Orleans. I will show you around the house myself."

The door closed behind her, and I stood motionless in my empty studio, the sawdust on the floor, the cages and empty cityscape all around me. For a moment, I could only smell the scent that lingered and try to remember the lover who wore it in Paris. And as I turned back to my drawing of La Maison de l'Opera, the cage I was about to begin, I could not be sure if what had just happened had really happened or if the phantom of Madame Saloy was a hallucination caused by the fumes of opened enamel. I walked, as if in a stupor over to my upright piano in the corner. I needed something. To be swept away or to find my bearings. I wiped the dust from the keys with my calloused hands and then closed my eyes to play a tune I remembered hearing once in a smoky café in Paris. I felt a long way from home. Please help me,

François Reynaud

Madame Saloy

From the clinical notebook of Y. R. Le Monnier, M.D.

THE BIRD CAGE-MAKER, 1877, THIRD APPOINTMENT

Another session, another letter, I'm afraid. François Reynaud sits mum, drinking his brandy and stroking his facial hair while I sit next to him, reading his letter. He keeps his kerchief in hand. It is odd. Sane people do not write their thoughts for others to read, or do they? I am beginning to feel guilty that he is paying me for these visits. I am not the one doing any work. It takes little prying to get to his truth.

Letter from François

OCTOBER 1877

Dear Doctor Le Monnier,

My father was a birdcage maker, an active member of the royal guild of cage-makers in Paris. I grew up under my father's tutelage amongst the wood shavings and strands of wire, pliers and saws, hammers, and the melodious fumes of paint which held my imagination and made me soar into the streets, liberated by youth.

I was a great birdcage maker, not simply a good one. And I was not one of these poseurs who made the cages simply for money, although I did do it for money, it just wasn't the same. Money wasn't my motivation. What motivated a Frenchman like me was the act of creation. I was an *artiste*. Today, I would remain one, not sell my creative soul for the Saloys or anyone else.

I stepped into the path of a horse and carriage on Rue St. Ann and hurried to the other side. I was on my way to la Maison de Le Monnier. I would tell Madame Saloy face to face: *I would not be bought.*

There was a bustle on the corner of Rue Royale and Rue St. Peter. Night would be here soon, and children ran toward distant callings of mothers. Gentlemen or not so gentlemanly men were shuffling down the street to the saloon. An Irishman stood on the corner, looked at his watch, then returned it to his pocket and hurried past me. I stood there with head tilted up. I was trying to take in the enormity of la maison de Le Monnier. The fourth floor was blocking the purples and oranges of the sunset, blocking the sun. I noted every detail. I would not model a birdcage after this structure. I would not. Yet, I could not help but soak in all the architectural details. My mouth watered slightly, and I swallowed. Architecture had this effect on me.

The building was simple, for the most part. Gray or brown—it was hard to tell in this light—stucco over brick. There were balconies here and there with rounded ironwork and the monogram of Le Monnier in the middle. The monograms stopped at the third floor, for the fourth was added by Saloy. Did I detect an S anywhere? With a man like Saloy, I expected to see him leave his mark in some way. Perhaps adding a fourth floor was enough of a statement.

The turquoise shutters on the many tall windows were closed on the St. Peter side. I liked to carve shutters, liked to add them carefully with tiny hinges onto my birdhouses and if done properly, they would open and close like the real thing. I pictured the jar of enamel one would use to duplicate these shutters, then I pushed the thought away. I brought my eyes back down to the large door and clearing my throat, climbed the few stairs and raised a hand to knock.

I was about to make contact when the door swung open, nearly knocking me off balance. "Oh!" said a young mulatto housemaid.

"*Pardon,*" I said, "I didn't mean to startle you. I've come to speak with Madame Saloy."

"Right this way," she nodded, then turning, she said, "you're the cagemaker?"

"*Oui.*"

"Oh, I love birds. I had a cockatiel once. It was the strangest thing; I found it in an oak tree down by the river. Must have flown away from the market. It came right to me, and I took it home. Didn't have a cage, so it sat on my shoulder most of the time, until one day—oh, I am sorry, sometimes I carry on so." I had followed this woman into a center courtyard, hidden from the street. From here, I saw windows leading to the different floors and a main staircase made of walnut. I followed her up and around and glanced occasionally into the windows.

"These are rooms rented out. The Saloys are up on the top floor," said the housemaid. "I cannot tell you how many times I climb these stairs in a day."

The housemaid was extremely fresh, and I found her enticing and annoying at the same time. I tried hard not to look at her bottom as she mounted the stairs ahead of me. I counted the newels instead. The stairs ended at a landing at the top. The housemaid and I walked to the door at the end of the hall, and she rapped with her knuckles before entering to announce our arrival. I caught my breath from the long walk up and took in the grand apartment.

She was sitting on a velvet blue sofa in the parlor, her dress fanned out perfectly and draped to the floor. The sunset was coming in through the open window, and the light made her brown hair flame red. Madame Saloy was a peacock. The room was drenched in cream and gold with touches of blue and turquoise in the exquisite rugs and drapery on the tall windows. The furniture was in the style of Louis XVI, opulent, rounded wood, carved details of foliage. It felt very French in here, reminiscent of Paris, and it stirred something deep in me.

Madame Saloy rose to her feet. "Monsieur Reynaud, so nice of you to come." She reached her hand out and I took it, bowing. "Bertrand," she called, "we have a guest, darling."

I felt the presence of the man before I turned and saw him. Bertrand Saloy was large and imposing in the doorway. He was not fat, yet stout as a steam pipe. I remembered my hat and removed it before shaking Saloy's hand. I wished at that moment I might have changed my clothing after leaving the studio, but had not. Saloy had the eyes of a bulldog, small and solid, yet not much there, or perhaps, not much he was allowing to show. Saloy's reputation preceded him. He was known to be ruthless when it came to business, and he owned much of New Orleans. It had been said that he owned this very mansion after buying up the notes of the grocer Fisse and forcing them due.

Ruthless. The word hung in my head.

"Bertrand, this is Monsieur François Reynaud," said Madame. "He is the most talented birdcage maker in all of New Orleans. He has a little shop on St. Ann. I've asked him to make a replica of this house."

"A birdcage?" Saloy looked at his wife incredulously. Apparently, he'd had no such conversation with her, and I saw this as my chance to leave.

"I'm sorry for taking up your time," I said. "I'll just—"

"*Mais non,*" said Saloy. He held his hand up to me as he finished his conversation with his wife.

"What about the other cages, *mon cher*? The other filthy birds? Will you get rid of them?" Saloy asked.

Madame Saloy looked sly. "I'll move the lovebirds into the new cage, dear." She smiled at me and placed her hand in her husband's arm, "But I'll get rid of the others when you give up those nasty cigars."

There was silence, uncomfortable silence, and I felt the need to flee, yet the silence held me. Then Saloy broke into a smile and kissed his wife gruffly on her temple. He appeared old enough to be her father.

"A birdcage maker," he said. The words came out slowly with perfect diction. "Do tell. What kind of a living does a birdcage maker earn, *exactement?*"

"My father made a fine living in Paris," I retorted. "He was a member of the guild there."

"Ah, a guildsman. Carrie, bring Monsieur Reynaud a drink. We shall toast to old Paris."

"I—thank you," I said. I could not refuse a man making a toast to my beloved Paris. I took the bourbon and swished it in my mouth before swallowing. It went down smooth and hot.

"To Paris," said Saloy. Then he sat in a rather small plush chair and motioned to me to sit on the sofa. Madame Saloy moved next to me.

"Tell me, Monsieur Reynaud, do you own any property? Are you a real estate man?"

"Mmm, *non.*" I thought of the rent I paid for my house. I didn't even own my own home, nor the space I leased for my studio. I wanted to say I owned something, anything, but there was nothing. "I've not really a heart for business," is the honest shred that forced its way out.

Saloy stopped drinking and set his glass on the lamp stand. "Well then, you should find good company in Monsieur Reynaud, *mon cher.* My wife, she loves to spend my money on frivolous things like art and birdcages, isn't that right? It's that Latin blood in her. Her father was a hot-headed Italian, her mother a Spanish flamenco dancer." He motioned with his hands mockingly in a flamenco pose and straightened his back. "Would you dance for us, Carma?"

Her face reddened, and she straightened her skirts. I could see she was accustomed to his rudeness and was again uncomfortable. I took another sip of bourbon. It went down harder this time.

"Monsieur Reynaud, won't you let me show you around?" said Madame. "You'll need to know every bit if you're to make a replica." She looked at me and asked, "You did bring your sketchbook?"

"*Non,*" I said. I pushed to stand. "I'm afraid that's why I've come tonight. I've come to tell you I won't be making a replica of la maison Le Monnier, eh, Saloy."

"Oh, but you must. Tell him, darling. Tell him he must."

Saloy leaned forward and stood, pushing off his thick knees. He scowled at me. "I'm curious, why a Frenchman such as yourself, and an excellent *birdcage maker*—" he emphasized the words again —"would not entertain the wishes of Madame Saloy?"

"I do not take commissions, monsieur."

Saloy was quiet. Slowly he smiled, then laughed out loud. "You don't take commissions?! How on earth do you live, *cher* cage-maker?"

I was fighting offense. I moved to put my hat back on but held it in mid-air. "I do quite well," I said. "I simply prefer to maintain creative control over my work."

"Ah, an *artiste* . . . who likes to be in control, nonetheless! Carma, you do love him, don't you? My wife adores a sensitive man who can work with his hands, don't you, *cher*? It runs in the family."

"I'm sorry for taking up your time," said Madame Saloy. She was flushed and pushing me toward the door. "Thank you for coming." I saw something in her eyes. She was not as lofty as she was in my studio. She was fragile now. Vulnerable.

Saloy came to the door and placed his hand on my shoulder. "How much?" he said.

I shook my head and replaced my hat. "*Merci, mais non.*"

Saloy's grip grew tighter. "How much for your little *birdcage*?"

I breathed in sharply.

"Bertrand," said Madame Saloy.

"Five thousand dollars?" said Saloy. I was still. I could not believe what I was hearing. "Ten thousand? Hmm?" He was teasing. Or was he serious? Who had that kind of money to spend on a cage?

The sound of all that money, the thought of it, pricked at me and curdled my spine. It was enough to buy a new home, a real home. With ten thousand dollars, I wouldn't have to sell another birdcage for a very long time. I wouldn't have to worry about money. I could devote myself to my work for my work's sake. I was tempted, truly, which unraveled me. I thought I was a man of true conviction, yet something was taking over me. I didn't feel myself. Perhaps it was the good bourbon.

"*Merci,* Monsieur Saloy, *mais non.* I am grateful for your generous offer, but I must insist, *non.*" I held his hand out to shake. Saloy looked at the hand. His eyes had changed from those of a bulldog to those of a moccasin, slithering near the edge of the water.

"*Non,* I insist," said Saloy, taking my hand and squeezing. "You will be making a small fortune, and the way I see it, I am getting a bargain." He kept my handshake and turned to his wife. "What do you do with a woman who doesn't appreciate a steam yacht being named after her?

Hmm? The *Carmelite Saloy* is afloat and lovely on Bayou St. John, but does she care?" He turned back to me. "Fifteen thousand dollars for an exact replica of la maison de Saloy. Not another word. One of us has a head for business, and I'm telling you, you'd be a fool to pass this up. I am only looking out for your best interest, Monsieur Reynaud. Fifteen thousand to make my wife happy and to put food in your mouth. And we'll place it near the window for all of New Orleans to see."

I wanted desperately to walk away, to blink my eyes and be back in my studio, never having met this awful man, yet I was here, and Madame Saloy was looking at me with the sincerity and eagerness of a child. "Say you will," she smiled and I found myself saying, "*Alors,* very well. I will do it."

As I descended the stairs with the housemaid at my side, I felt strangely heavy as if my feet were moving without any help of my own. The night air nipped at me, and I turned to look one last time at la maison Le Monnier. The sun had gone down, but I thought I saw Madame in the flicker of gaslight in the window on the fourth floor . . . where part of my soul remained.

François

From the clinical notebook of Y. R. Le Monnier, M.D.

At this point, I'm afraid I can no longer read François' letters. He seems perfectly content with sitting in silence for half an hour while I read his thoughts, but I've much to do and have taken to catching up on other work while he is here. I do not feel guilty for François seems comforted simply being in my presence, sipping his brandy and staring out the window.

"Is this helping?" I asked him.

"Yes. Very much."

"But I'm doing nothing but reading."

"You're helping me to work through my thoughts."

I smiled ever so gently and said, "Is that so. Well, I believe you've discovered your own form of writing therapy, François."

I claimed him cured or at least on his way as he seems able to heal himself while getting his feelings out on paper. At his protest, I conceded to allowing him to continue to write his letters to me, only that he may drop them off through the slit in my office door, and need not pay for any more sessions.

After thinking this over in some bit of anguish, he has agreed to our arrange-
ment. Again, I shall not feel guilty for not reading his letters. The writing is his
therapy, no matter if his words get read by me or anyone, for that matter. The
intimate thoughts of a love-struck birdcage-maker can hardly be life-altering.

From the journal of Y. R. Le Monnier, M.D.

RE: NEW ORLEANS, 1906

The New Orleans Parish Prison was at times a soulless place but quite familiar to me. It was adjacent to the criminal court, and I'd spent countless
hours there over the past three decades, examining prisoners who were facing a life or death sentence and claiming insanity as their defense, witnessing for some. It was tricky. There were degrees of insanity, and some much
more obvious than others, though I took pity on each and every one. There
were the stark raving mad who spouted profanities, who could not control
their bodily movements, and stuttered and shook. There were those with
darkness in their eyes as if evil had taken over, or sadness so severe that all
they could do was cry and wail and gnash their teeth. Some were suicidal
and often this was not known until it was too late, of course, when they'd
wait for a private moment and slit their throats with a dull butter knife,
causing a public uproar in the newspapers. These were these obviously
insane. But it was the one who looked and seemed like any normal person
that was the trickier case, I found. And this was how I found the young
Mr. Andrew Reynaud.

Sheriff Uniacke had not much use for me, and yet he had to let me
in. It was his duty and mine to see that justice was served. Several years
after the epidemic of yellow fever in Memphis, I'd gotten in quite a public
row with the Sherriff's office, and I'm afraid I had embarrassed it. Everyone knew I'd spent time in Memphis, helping the poor people of that city
when so many had died, and I'd become a specialist on the yellow fever,
authoring a paper on the topic for the *New Orleans Medical Journal*. I'd
also become known as an expert sanitarian and had determined the best
disinfectant and sanitary practices to keep the disease at bay. In 1897, I advised the Sheriff as to how to protect the prisoners. He'd done as I'd asked
and used the disinfectants, but still, a few of the men had succumbed. I
was certain it was due to the visitors he let into the place and I'd suggested
sternly that quarantine was the only way to be safe.

The Sheriff rejected my idea and instead brought in the fumigation corps of the board of health, much to my offence. I was the physician, the specialist on the disease, and here he was, subjecting the men needlessly to illness. I'd written the Sherriff a stern letter and published a copy in the *Times-Picayune,* and the Sherriff, in turn, published his bitter reply. Three more men contracted the disease and died that season and both of us thought the other was the blame. It turns out that we were both wrong. Three years later, no one could have been more stunned than I was to read that the US Army Yellow Fever Commission determined the culprit to be biting mosquitoes. It had been there under our noses the whole time. And I'd not seen it. Sometimes, no matter how hard you look for truth, you are destined to miss it until it is too late.

"Sherriff," I nodded, as I walked in door.

"Dr. Le Monnier," he said. And that was it. No more words between us and believe me, no more words needed.

New Orleans Courthouse and Parish Prison

From the clinical notebook of Y. R. Le Monnier, M. D.

ANDREW REYNAUD, NEW ORLEANS PARISH PRISON, FIRST MEETING

A prison guard led me back to the meeting room, and I found Andrew Reynaud in prison clothes and handcuffs, seated at a table. For twenty years old, he looked a little older, as if hard drinking had aged him. I looked beyond the tired eyes and saw a quite handsome young man, dark complexion, dark unkempt hair that spilled over his eyes. He was certainly the brother of the attractive young Mrs. Kurucar. He sat with his clasped hands out in front of him and seemed to be contemplating his handcuffs, unlocking them with his eyes. When I said Hello, he lifted his face to me and what I saw was no murderer, but a scared boy. The prison was a terrifying place but could not compare to the horrors of the State Penitentiary in Angola.

"I'm Dr. Le Monnier," I told him as I took my seat across the table. "May I ask your name, sir?"

"Andrew Reynaud."

"Do you know what day it is, Mr. Reynaud?"

"December second, 'ought six."

"And can you tell me why you are in here?"

"For killing Doris Sheldon."

He certainly seemed lucid. I pressed further. "And did you kill her?"

He closed his eyes as if wincing in pain and then opened them and looked at me. "I didn't mean to."

"You didn't mean to kill her. You mean it was an accident?"

"Not exactly."

"Please. Tell me exactly then."

He picked at the skin around his fingernails. "Doris was my lover," he said. "She lived across the street from the saloon I kept."

"She lived in Miss Pansy Montrose's bordello house, Mr. Reynaud," I said. "Doris Sheldon was a prostitute, was she not, who went by the name of Belle Georgia Collier?" I baited him, and he took it. Rage flitted behind his eyes, and he banged his hands down on the table.

"She was my lover!" he yelled. "I lived there, stayed every night with her!" The guard came over and looked at me, but I waved him off.

"Okay. She was your lover," I said. "That must have been quite expensive."

He turned away and stared at the cracks on the wall.

31

"I'm sorry, Mr. Reynaud. I should be letting you tell your story. Please. I won't interrupt again. Tell me what happened on the night that Miss Sheldon died."

He took his time, the room filling with silence, and finally he breathed deeply.

"My mother died four years ago. It was the anniversary of her death."

"I see."

"I worked that night and could not bear the pain of remembering my mother. I began drinking with my customers. I was forgetting, and the bourbon was working, but just before midnight, I walked a man outside and looked up to Doris' room. She was there on the balcony." He winced. "She was sitting on another man's lap."

He clenched his fists. He was still jealous and angry, even after the woman's death.

"And this angered you," I said. He looked at me then, once more as the sad boy.

"Have you ever loved someone, Doctor?"

I blinked at the pain of losing my Eulalie. It was still too fresh. Heat filled me and I could feel my ears turning red.

"This isn't about me, now is it? Please, go on. What happened after you saw the woman sitting on a man's lap?"

"I ran over there. I flew up the stairs and opened her bedroom door. I went to go after the man, but he escaped my grasp and fled. I didn't even get a good look at him. Doris looked terrified, but she convinced me nothing had happened."

"And did you believe her?"

"She was sitting on his lap," he hissed slowly.

"And so you wanted to kill her?"

"I wanted the awful night to be over. I wanted my mother to be alive again, and nothing could bring her back. I had Doris, she was all I had, and now, I realized I could not even have her. Nothing was right. Nothing would ever be right again." He banged his hands as tears filled his eyes. "She calmed me down. She told me everything was all right. She smoothed me over the way she always did. So I calmed down. I never hit her. I would never do that. She told me to go back to work, and I said I would. She kissed me, and I told her to walk me to the door. She walked before me . . . and I pulled out my pistol. I shot her twice."

"In the back."

"Yes."

I took a deep breath. He'd certainly admitted his crime and so far, I saw nothing but his guilt.

"And did she die?"

"No. Not there, but I didn't know it. As soon as she fell to the floor, I was terrified at what I'd done. I thought for sure I had killed her and I fled the house by jumping from the balcony. I landed poorly on my ankle and hobbled away, but no one had seen me. I planned to hide. I planned to frame the murder on the other man who'd been there before me."

"I see. This sounds like very rational thinking. Poor judgment, of course, but rational, nonetheless."

"She lived. I heard the rumor that she'd been shot and was taken to Charity Hospital. I felt like I had another chance. I thought I could go to her and tell her how sorry I was. I believed that she would take me back. It was insane to think so, was it not?"

"So you went to see her?"

"Yes. She was lying in the bed and looked pale, but I thought she would be okay. The people working with her said she was not doing well at all, but I was convinced otherwise. I told her that I loved her. I told her I was sorry. She squeezed my hand and calmed me the way she always did, but then the police came. They asked her what had happened."

"And did she tell them?"

He nodded. "Everything. She blamed me. She said I shot her in the back."

"You did shoot her in the back."

"They asked her if she thought she was going to die and she said yes, that she hated to die. But I didn't believe her. I thought she would get better. She was still my beautiful Doris. She was alive. I hadn't killed her. But then, then the life left her. She quit breathing."

"And they arrested you on the spot?"

He didn't say anything more. He seemed to retreat into his own head.

"Mr. Reynaud, your lawyers are claiming that you are insane, that this is why you killed the girl."

"I didn't kill her. I only shot her."

"Yet she died from her injuries. Mr. Reynaud, you seem completely sane to me."

"I haven't been . . . right."

"How so?"

"Ever since I got the money, I've been . . . well, everything has been wrong. I cannot stop drinking. I cannot get enough women. I think of more and more things I can buy with my money. It is all I can think about."

"And where did this money come from?"

"From my mother. When she died, she left me a large sum, $30,000, plus a building on Canal Street. Two years ago, I was emancipated and gained access to it. I would walk into the bank and withdraw large amounts every week. I carried a thick wallet and threw my money around. I gambled nearly every night. I got into fights. I bought women. I could buy any one I wanted. Do you know what this feels like, Doctor? Can you imagine the power that I feel when I have this money in my pocket?"

I remained quiet. I certainly did not know how it felt.

"In March, I sold the building on Canal Street for $60,000. That was more money than I could imagine. I felt invincible and yet, I was under its spell. I had no more control over myself. I was no longer Andrew, I was a slave to the money, a slave to its power. I was a slave to the bourbon, a slave to the women. I did not own them. They owned me. I could not stop gambling. I could no longer sleep. At times, I would see my mother's face and she would tell me to stop drinking. At times, I would look into Doris's face and see my own mother's." He shook his head as a tear fell down his cheek. He lifted his shoulder and wiped his eye with it.

"I sued my father over a piece of property. I sued my own sister, Viola, for another. I turned on everyone I have ever loved, and it was all because of the money. Don't you see? The money killed my mother. She was thirty-seven years old. It killed her because it was cursed, and the curse has now befallen me. I am under its spell. You have to help me."

"Your mother, Mr. Reynaud. How did she come by this money?"

"From her aunt. Her aunt was married to one of the wealthiest men in New Orleans. Bertrand Saloy. I'm sure you know of him."

I stopped and put my pen down. Yes. I knew him. I found I could not speak for my mouth had gone dry. I motioned to the guard for some water, and he called another to bring me a glass. "Forgive me," I said after taking a sip. "Your mother's aunt was Carmelite Saloy?"

"Yes."

I tried to keep my professional composure, but my mind was racing. How could this be so? There was some sort of familial connection between the Saloys and the cage-maker? I tried to table my thoughts for later. "So

34

you have inherited the wealth of Bertrand Saloy. And I assume your sister has as well, Mrs. Carmelite Kurucar. Ahhhh." I knew it as soon as I said it. Yes. The child was named after her great aunt, Madame *Carmelite* Saloy. "I—"

"Ha!" he said, sneering. "Mrs. Kurucar, indeed. She's only a child. She ran off with the man, eloped from our father's house, so she would be emancipated and therefore, receive her inheritance. He's using her, can't you see? She's just a baby. Tell me, Doctor, have you asked my little sister what she's done with her money? Hmm?"

I was at a loss for words and needed to take control of the matter. "Mr. Reynaud, your sister tells me you think the money you've inherited is cursed. I admit I do not know how such a thing can be true. Do you care to enlighten me?"

"I don't know how it can be cursed, but it is. Nothing good can come of it. It only brings death. Doris is gone because of it. Mother is gone because of it. And I'll be gone soon because of it. Perhaps Saloy, himself, cursed the money before he left this world. Perhaps he haunts us from his grave, still missing the money. Perhaps he's here, laughing in the room right now, a specter tormenting my very soul with hot iron." He looked about him and for a moment, I saw it, the paranoia in his eyes. Perhaps he was, indeed, insane.

I put it all down in my notes and then rose and said good bye. I felt I'd had enough for the day and the boy had said all he could say. I would speak to him again, no doubt, but for the moment, I had quite enough to go back and examine. I had my notes from Mr. Reynaud to study and my notes from my ledgers.

From the journal of Y. R. Le Monnier, M.D.

RE: FIRST MEETING WITH ANDREW REYNAUD
AT NEW ORLEANS PARISH PRISON

I remained convinced there was no such thing as a curse. Andrew Reynaud was suffering from too much alcohol and sex. He was suffering delirium of persecution, brought on, no doubt by the grief of losing his mother. The money could not bring her back to life. No amount could ever do that, and so he loved the money and hated it, both.

This could be perceived as a curse on someone so young and naive.

If somehow, the money Reynaud had inherited went all the way back to Bertrand Saloy, it occurred to me to go back further in my notebooks, to my own dealings with him—before I even met the cage-maker.

Yes, I was just barely beginning to see it, this mystery, almost as if walking down the street into the glare of the noonday sun. You know there are things straight ahead of you, yet you're blinded to it all. Regardless, you keep on walking, trusting that the ground won't fall away.

My ledgers were calling me as were the unopened letters of the cage-maker. I should have read them. It would have been so simple, wouldn't it? There had to be more to the story. As it was now, my testimony in court could not save the boy. I had to have more convincing evidence. I had to dig deeper for I now understood that this young man's story, no matter how he had entered my life, seemed to be connected in some way to my own. And the answers lay written in yellowed unread letters and in my own handwriting from long ago.

An excerpt from George W. Cable's "'Sieur George's House," *Scribner's Monthly*, 1876

"In the heart of New Orleans stands a large four-story brick building that has so stood for about three-quarters of a century. Its rooms are rented to a class of persons occupying them simply for lack of activity to find better and cheaper quarters elsewhere. With its gray stucco peeling off in broad patches, it has a solemn look of gentility in rags, and stands, or, as it were, hangs, about the corner of two ancient streets, like a faded fop who pretends to be looking for employment."

From the journal of Y. R. Le Monnier, M.D.

RE: THE HOUSE ON RUE ROYALE, NEW ORLEANS 1876

I stood clenching my hands on the corner of St. Peter and Rue Royale while I watched the workers tear out the roof garden of the mansion and hammer their scaffolding into place. It was an old family home no longer in our possession, sold at the start of the Civil War. It shouldn't bother me, should it? I had witnessed the bloody battles of Shiloh and Stones River, tried to save lives and watched men die, but it wasn't until now, years later when they began adding the fourth story that I felt myself coming undone.

My wife, Eulalie, was expecting our first child, and I was finding it hard to concentrate, so excited was I to have someone on which to pass the family name and all the importance, prestige, and legends that came along with it. My father, my namesake, had passed away seven years ago, and with the man went his stories. I had a thriving private practice, meeting patients out of my home on Rue St. Joseph. But my history, the Le Monnier history, lay there in the foundations of this house on Rue Royale. I had longed to tell my child about his father and grandfather, his heritage, how we came from a long line of physicians, and perhaps one day he would be a physician, too.

I had imagined walking the boy (or it could be a girl, but in my fantasy this was not so) down to the house and pointing at it. "This is where your great-grandfather lived when he first came to New Orleans," I would say. "They had said it could not be done, that a house above two stories would not hold in the treacherous Louisiana soil. But my grandfather, your great-grandfather, had a theory: *If one built the house well enough, it would stand, no matter the foundation.* He bought the property and built up the walls past the first floor and the second, and then with confidence up went the third. The people laughed at him as he built. They called him a fool and said his house would fall down. Well, look there. It did not, and they were wrong, and no one will ever, ever call a Le Monnier a fool again."

And then there was Cable's story. George W. Cable had written in *Scribner's Monthly* the most vulgar fictitious rendition of the house, calling it a "fop." No longer did they associate the house with the prestigious Le Monnier name but instead called it "'Sieur George's house" for that fictitious yet hideous insane character who rented a room there, protecting a box of worthless lottery tickets.

I grabbed at my chest. I was breathing heavily. What would I tell my child now? I would have to amend my story. I would have to tell my beloved progeny that since the house had left Le Monnier hands vulgar people had had their way with it. First, the embarrassing article, and now, this. I could almost hear the people of New Orleans talking about it around their dinner tables and laughing again at the name Le Monnier.

A man walked by. It was Bertrand Saloy, the new owner of the house. He was portly and unattractive though dressed in an expensive suit. He was the fop. He was the laughable character in the house now. His wealth, his ungodly wealth, made him believe he could buy anything and do anything that he pleased. Was that so? *You sir, are a disgrace to our city,* I wanted to say. I imagined walking up to his face and declaring that he was ruining my story for my child. How dare he eliminate the tiled rooftop garden that my grandfather nurtured with his own hands? How dare he get so greedy as to tempt fate and build even higher than my courageous grandfather had done? The grand feat was that there was a *third* floor. This is what my father had always told me, something I took on with a great sense of pride. And now a fourth story to destroy the marvel of the third? Preposterous. My father and grandfather would be turning in their graves if they knew.

Monsieur Saloy looked my way and tipped his hat. "Admiring the building, are you?" He stepped across the street and came toward me. "You know, we're adding a fourth floor." He pointed. "It'll be the tallest building in all of New Orleans. We'll live up there. From the rooftop, you can see all of Vieux Carre and clear out to the Mississippi. *C'est magnifique.*"

I stood motionless, bottom lip dropped, unable to speak. I was stunned at this braggadocious clod and wanted nothing more than to slap him across his chubby cheek. I pulled myself together.

"I'm quite aware of the view," I said. "My name is Dr. Yves René Le Monnier, Jr.."

Saloy's beady eyes perched with the realization of the name and he grabbed my hand and shook it vigorously.

"Ah! Ha!" he exclaimed. "The Le Monnier mansion. Your grandfather, I presume?"

"Correct."

"Well, what an honor it is to meet you. You must come inside and have a look. Has it been a while?"

The prospect of going inside stirred me. I'd not been expecting this. I'd been content with gazing at the house and remembering things as they once were, remembering my grandfather's office on the third floor, that magnificent oval room. My grandfather had died before I was born, and so I only knew him through my father's tales. "Your heritage is here in this room, Yves," my father would say. "In this room, your grandfather would meet with all sorts of important people. He would heal his patients. He would plan for his meetings with the first grand lodge of Louisiana as Grand Pursuivant. I loved to sit in that room and look at all of his books, stare in wonder at the railing through the open shutters, with his monogram permanently affixed in iron."

I looked up and saw that the balcony railings were still there. YLM. My grandfather's initials still etched in iron.

"Monsieur, I asked you, has it been a while since you've set foot in the old house?" prodded Saloy.

"*Oui*," I said. "*Oui*, it has. I left for military school in Mississippi, and the war broke out. It was sold by my aunt while I was away."

"I see. The war. Well then, come on in and have a look around. I doubt you'll be able to recognize anything. We've changed it quite a bit already. Good bones," said Saloy. "The house has good bones."

I felt as if in a fog as I walked through the southeast entrance. Immediately, my skin bristled with a mix of memory and the affront of change. The house was laid out with shops on the bottom and living quarters above. In the middle was a paved courtyard with staircase going up and fan windows on the side. I ran my hand along the walnut rail and cypress newels as we ascended past the first floor where an apothecary shop was open to the streets. I remembered that shop as a grocer's and playing on this staircase when I was yet a boy.

"We've tenants on the second floor," said Saloy as we rounded the corner and climbed a little higher. "I can show you the plans when we get up there. They're quite grand, I think you'll see."

"Mmm," said I, touching the sleeve of Saloy's fine coat. "Might we have a look at the oval room on the third floor first? It was my grandfather's study. He was a physician like myself."

Saloy stopped, one leg on the step above us. He paused as he considered this request. "*Mais*, of course. It's our dining room now, but I'm sure my wife won't mind if you have a look."

As we stood at the door, I felt overcome by nostalgia. I was once again the boy before the war, the innocent young man who had never touched a dead body, never saved a life, and never taken one. But now that seventeen year old boy had seen twice that many years.

The wife, Madame Saloy, was sitting in the parlor when we entered.

"*Cher,* I've brought someone in at the moment to have a look at the dining room. This is Dr. Le Monnier. His family owned this house before the war."

"Built this house, if I may." She came forward after setting aside some sewing. She was a glowing halo of a woman.

"A pleasure to meet you." She straightened her gown and was lovely in it. Too lovely, I thought, to be the wife of Bertrand Saloy. She was quite a bit younger as well, though perhaps a bit older than myself.

"I ran into the good doctor on the street," said Saloy. "He was admiring the work on the roof."

"I'm afraid it's a lot of clanging and hammering at the moment," said Madame Saloy. "I look forward to the day when it will all be finished."

"We've another place on North Rampart," said Saloy. "When it gets too disruptive, we'll stay there for a while. In the meantime, this is home."

"Home. Yes. My father was born in this house," I spit out.

"Was he, now?" Madame appeared to have noticed the discomfort on my face and came to take my arm for a tour.

"I can't imagine that it looks anything like it did when your father was here, and I'm terribly sorry for that. It's often jarring to visit a place in one's memory and find it completely changed."

I turned to look at the beauty at my side and felt warmth spread across my chest like liniment. Yes. Yes, that was it exactly. How lovely of her to so eloquently describe the way I was feeling. I took an instant liking to the woman.

"It's quite lovely what you've done with the place," I said. "Especially the furnishings. In the style of King Louis XVI, I presume?"

"They are. A bit ornate for my tastes, but Bertrand is fond of them."

"I do love extravagant things," said Saloy, flirting with his wife.
I looked over the sitting room at the mahogany chairs with claw feet. I itched to tell my connection to the pieces. "My ancestor was first physician to King Louis XVI."

"No. Is it true?" asked Madame.

"*Oui*." I felt a bit flushed. I was not anticipating liking anyone who lived in this house. And now I found myself in a pleasurable state, wanting nothing more than to tell my whole history to these perfect strangers, much as I would my own son.

Over wine, I did just that. I told them how my ancestor, Louis-Guillaume Le Monnier, the botanist, was introduced to King Louis XV, and how he fainted in his presence. The King was so taken with his knowledge of plants and flowers, that he put him in charge of the Tuileries garden, and soon after, appointed him first physician to the king. From there, Louis-Guillaume Le Monnier was called on whenever there was trouble with the king, and in turn, became physician to his successor as well, King Louis XVI.

"He was in charge of the blood-letting when the King became ill. It was Louis-Guillaume who declared him fit enough to stand trial." I smiled a bit, tempted to tell this next bit of the story.

"And so it was said that the King's doctor, my ancestor was at the Chateau on the night the savage Marsellais ransacked the place. The old man sat quietly in his chamber as death and destruction commenced all around him. Suddenly, the door was struck by bloodied arms, and two men approached him. 'What are you doing?' they asked him.

"'Sitting in my chamber.'

"'Who are you here?'

"'Can you not see my coat? I am the King's doctor.'

"'Are you not afraid?' they asked.

"'I have no one to fear for I have done no harm.'

"'You are a good fellow,' they told him. 'But the comrades after us may not be so kind. Come, let us take you to safety. Do not be afraid.'

"'I've told you. I do not fear those to whom I have done no harm.'

"And with that the men led Louis-Guillame Le Monnier out of the carnage and safely to the Palace of Luxembourg."

Madame Saloy clapped her hands and smiled with delight, but I was turning away distracted, staring across the room.

I was taken aback by the boldness, dare I say, garishness of it. The walls were a pale blue with oil portraits all around, but above the thick white moldings the ceiling was a deep thrush blue with stars painted all across it. Stars, I say. Out of Orion's belt, hung a large crystal chandelier that sparkled with the light coming in from the balcony. I stood motionless for a moment, trying to remember my grandfather's desk, passed on to my father and now my own. It had been over there, on the wall, and there were two chairs over this way. The bookshelves were gone, replaced with a buffet table and stacked with lamps and dishes. I moved toward the daylight and spied my grandfather's monogram in the iron railing, the turquoise shutters thrown open to the air, but I had to look through three bird cages blocking the view of the corner of St. Peter and Rue Royale.

"My wife is fond of birds, as you can see," said Saloy, perhaps with a slight bit of embarrassment. "Filthy creatures. I'd open all the doors and let them fly free if I thought she'd forgive me. Alas, I don't think she would."

I, myself, was tempted to go open the cage doors and let the creatures go out the window. I wanted to throw the cages out with them and tear down the stars on the garish ceiling. I wanted the room back the way it was in my memory, but it wasn't to be so. Feeling I could remain there no longer, I bid Monsieur Saloy adieu and headed out to tell his wife the same, but he stopped me, his voice going low.

"You are a physician, *oui*? One who sees patients for . . ."

"For whatever ails them," I said. "Physical or psychological."

My father, Dr. Yves René Le Monnier

My ancestor, Louis-Guillaume Le Monnier, the botanist and King's doctor

"I see." He looked peakish for a moment. "May we pay you a visit . . . in a professional sense? My wife . . . it's rather delicate."

"Yes. Yes, of course," I said, relieved to be once more in my professional realm of physician. I felt less antipathy for this man and more removal of emotions. We set a time and date for the appointment, and I left my encounter with the Le Monnier mansion feeling strangely as if things were just beginning with the house instead of the sense of closure I had hoped for when I first entered its doors.

From the journal of Y. R. Le Monnier, M.D.

RE: NEW ORLEANS 1876

Monsieur and Madame Saloy came to visit me at my office the following Tuesday. Although they could have walked the five and a half blocks, they came by way of a brilliant black carriage and two stunning horses. I noticed their arrival, along with everyone else within eye and earshot, before they came to the door. I'd been staring out the window, pondering what it could be that was so delicate an issue, as Bertrand Saloy had put it. Problems in the bedroom, no doubt, but I chose to reserve judgment—there were still days when a physician found himself surprised.

Saloy walked his wife in as if she was a fragile porcelain doll. Had she wanted to come or had he forced her? I wondered. The look on her face was difficult to ascertain. She was dressed exquisitely in a dark morning dress with square neckline and red ribbon tied at her bosom, her figure in it quite sublime, yet not equal to her face beneath her bonnet. I walked out and met them at the door.

"*Bonjour* Madame Saloy, Monsieur." I shook his hand and showed them in. Shutting the door behind us, I told them that that we were the only ones here as my office assistant had stepped out and there would not be another patient for an hour. "You have my undivided attention," I said. "Please, sit; tell me what brings you here today."

They found their seats on a chaise lounge on the wall nearest the street. Madame looked down at her gloved hands while Bertrand stared out the window as if the thing he was here for had just escaped him and was just outside in the trees.

He pursed his lips.

"I, well, we're here," said Bertrand, "because we're having . . . mmm . . . marital difficulties."

"I see." I paused so that he could continue, but he did not. Apparently I was to read their minds.

Madame Saloy found her tongue and said, "The fourth story is coming along nicely, the walls propped up here and there. Still, we can look right through them, but I'm beginning to see how it will look when it is all done."

I bristled at the thought and pushed it from my mind. I was not here to stew over the adulteration of the Le Monnier mansion. Not now, anyway. "That is very nice to hear, Madame. Now, please. I realize this is difficult—a man and his wife approaching a near complete stranger and offering up their deepest marital issues. Monsieur Saloy?"

"Bertrand," he said. "If you will, call me Bertrand."

"Bertrand it is."

"We're having the difficulty in the bedroom, I'm afraid."

"I see." I'd known it. I was right. Now, to listen to the embarrassing details. Embarrasing for them, not for me. I had nothing at all to be embarrassed about. "Tell me, does this difficulty stem from yourself, Bertrand, or more from you, Madame?"

I tried not to blush as I said these words, but truthfully, I was human and I was a man before I was a doctor, and it seemed I always would be. I felt myself embarrassed for them.

"From me," Madame said quietly.

"Ahh." I stood and turned from them, composing myself. Turning back I said, "Are you ill? Is there anything ailing you at the moment?"

"No, nothing."

I nodded.

"Is there anything you can tell me that might be bothering you?"

I could sense the woman stiffening as she tightened her skirts around her knees. I looked at Bertrand and winked.

"Madame, might you feel more comfortable talking alone in my office? Your husband can wait out here. I'm sure he wouldn't mind. Would you?"

"No, no, not at all," said Bertrand, standing, appearing relieved. Madame stood, and he kissed her on her cheek.

"Very well, I will take great care with her. Bertrand, please help yourself to some coffee . . . or something stronger, should you like it. I've a whole library of books in the next room if you'd care to take a look."

Uneasily, we parted ways, and I got Madame Saloy situated in my office, closing the door behind us. She walked to the window while I took a seat behind my grandfather's desk, the very one that used to sit in the Saloy's garish dining room. I pulled out my notebook and pen.

"Now then, your husband seems to be a very reasonable fellow."

"Yes, he seems," said Madame, staring out at her horses and carriage.

"I'm afraid I can only help you if you want to be helped," I said.

"Yes," she said, turning to me. "Of course."

"Would you like to sit down?"

"I'll stand, if I may."

"Some sherry?" I found that it sometimes loosened up an unwilling patient.

"No, thank you. I—I lost one of my children. My son. Bertrand Jr. died three years ago when he was only five."

"Oh," the statement struck me through the heart. I thought of my own yet unborn child and how much I loved him already. "I'm so sorry. No wonder you're having difficulty. Grief can put strain on even the strongest of marriages."

"It is the grief, yes, but there's more. Our problems in our bedroom have their origin from long ago. Before I met my husband. It has to do with my name, Carmelite."

"Please," I said. "Go on."

From the clinical notebook of Y. R. Le Monnier, M.D.

MADAME SALOY, 1876, FIRST APPOINTMENT

Madame Saloy stands at the window, telling me of the source of her troubles. She is still lovely in her anxiety and seems quite sane, even saintly, if you will.

IN THE WORDS OF MADAME SALOY

"When your father and I came to New Orleans, we had little," my mother told me, "and what little we had, went quickly. There came a point," Mother looked down at her kerchief in her hands and picked at the edges, "when I'm afraid we didn't even have enough to feed your brother. You would be born soon, and I sat upon the front step, holding my middle, crying in despair as I watched him playing in the street."

We looked over and saw my seven-year-old sister chasing a dirty white cat across the sidewalk. "Don't touch it, Madeline," my mother warned. Then she continued quietly. "A woman came over to me, one of those nuns like the ones on Barracks Street, and offered me words of encouragement. The thought crossed my mind to give my child to a nun like this . . . to her orphanage. But I knew I could never do it. When she left I was resolved to raise you no matter what. It was the first time I'd felt hopeful since we'd come here."

I didn't know what to say. It had never occurred to me my mother might have given me away. It stung.

"And so I named you after a nun," she said.

"Her name was Carmelite?"

"No. No, I did consider naming you Ursula because they were Ursaline nuns, but it . . . wasn't right. Then I remembered stories my mother had told me of the Carmelite nuns in Spain who lived a contemplative life, quite severe, and who took on the sins and prayers of the people there . . . instead of their children. Carma—" she turned to me and touched my chin. "I needed redemption for my sins, strict, severe penance. So I named you Carmelite."

"For what sins, Mother?"

Her face turned to Madeline, and her eyes let me know she was far, far away, perhaps in Cuba, perhaps in Spain. There was no use pressing her. She had told me quite enough for one day.

"I was named after a nun," I said slowly, mostly to myself, "after a woman who devoted her life to God." The realization took hold of me. It made me feel different in some way, as if my name were some clue to my existence. The nuns in my school were strict and kind. I'd often studied them in their habits and wondered about women who would choose such lives.

I left Mother on the front porch and went in to begin peeling potatoes. The sun was high and there was much to do before our family meal. My father was down at the docks and would not be in until late, but my brother Antonio was coming for supper. He'd taken on an apprenticeship with a cooper, and I hadn't seen him in weeks. I'd missed him terribly.

I peeled the potatoes over a pot at the kitchen table, careful to catch the remains. Mother could use them in her garden. We tried not to waste anything in our household, for money was scarce. It had been all of my seventeen summers, but this didn't bother me. When being poor is all you've ever known, you do not know what you're missing. It was difficult for my mother, though. She'd had money back in Cuba, a nice house, clothes. Every now and again, she would speak of this or that luxury with lights in her eyes, and then catch herself. There were secrets tucked away with the memories, and I wasn't sure if I'd ever know them. Or fully know my mother.

I was thinking of my mother when I winced in pain. Blood ran quickly off of the knuckle of my left thumb, and I stuck it in my mouth to stop the bleeding. I held it there, staring at the potatoes, and as I did, something washed over me. *Blood. Washed in blood. Sins washed in the blood of Christ.*

I wasn't expecting it, wasn't looking for it, but I experienced the calling of the Lord as a pull, a chill, a deep down feeling of rightness in the world. In that moment, it was if the Lord was saying to me, "Carmelite, come."

It was decided in my heart before my head was even aware of what was happening to me. It was my purpose in life to become a nun. I was born to devote myself to prayer and chaste living. Relief and joy washed over me—me, a young woman who'd been raised by two passionate parents to believe that we are all bound for great things—and I stood to wash my hand in the basin. What could be greater than a life devoted to God? As I bandaged my thumb, I felt as if I could run to the convent right that very moment.

Deep down though, I knew it would be much more complicated than that. I sensed my parents' deep disappointment before they even gave it. My mother had long thought I was pretty enough to garner the attention of a prosperous man, and in turn, change all of our destinies forever. It was her dream for me, not mine, but hers. And I knew that my choosing to marry Christ instead of wealth would strike her with the gentleness of an open hand to the cheek.

And yet, I'd tell her over dinner. Surely my brother would come to my aid.

The table was set with white flowers from the garden. I had changed into a simple blue dress and had wrapped an apron around my waist for serving. Mother sat at the head of the table where my father should be, elbows sullen at her side. During this season we rarely saw my father for the fish were plentiful, and there was money to be made. Not all months were the same, and my father had to take the work when it came to him. My mother looked tired. She was a beautiful lady, her dark hair now becoming streaked with white. She need not act so old, I thought. She was trim and healthy. It was her spirit that had aged. Something was broken inside of her and lately it rendered her useless. I took care of all the cleaning and cooking while she looked on sadly. Madeline worked at folding the napkins.

My brother walked in the door, and at once I ran to him and threw my arms around him. He lifted me up and spun me around, kissing my neck. Antonio was much like his namesake, my father, much like his Italian roots—passionate, loud, excitable. I loved that about him. I had longed for his presence, something to shatter the dreariness of my life with mother. As he held me in mid-air I wanted to tell him the news immediately and not wait. I went to whisper to him what I was sure the Lord had called me to do, and as I opened my mouth, I also opened my eyes. There, standing in the doorway was a man, a stranger. I slid down and waited for our introduction.

"This is my sister, Carmelite," he said to the man. "Carma, this is Monsieur Bertrand Saloy. I've asked him for dinner. I hope there's enough?"

"*Bonjour,* Mademoiselle," said the man, holding his hand out for mine. I put my hand in his and curtseyed. "She is as lovely as you mentioned, Antonio."

My mind was spinning. Another mouth to feed, and a large one, at that. I would eat less meat and potatoes. I would set another place setting and move mother down from the head of the table. I would need to make room for this man as he was stouter than my lanky brother.

"Please, make yourself at home," I said.

"Oh," said Monsieur Saloy, "this is for dinner. I hope I am no inconvenience." He handed me a bottle of red wine, and I took it graciously.

"Why, thank you. Not at all." I eyed my brother and then scrambled for the kitchen. My mood had changed. It wasn't that I minded being hospitable to a stranger, it was only that I was so looking forward to spending time with my brother unencumbered, as we used to be. I would have to be more proper with this man in our home, and Antonio would have to entertain his guest. Truthfully, I would have been angry if I'd had the time to think about it, which I did not. I urged mother to go in and meet Monsieur Saloy while I finished with the table preparations. When I called everyone in for dinner, it occurred to me I would have to wait to tell my family the news—that I wanted to join the nunnery. Disappointment pricked at my side, but I shooed it away. It was more important at the moment to be a good hostess.

By the end of the meal, our guest had become quite comfortable, laughing, explaining the way he'd made his living. "I started out with two picayune I could rub in my fingers," he said in his strong French

49

accent. "I bought and sold bottles and rags right there on the corner of the market. It was not much, I assure you, but I was savvy. I watched all the wealthy businessmen. I am a quick learner, you see. And soon, I had enough to invest in a little real estate. *Je pense* I've a bit of the Midas touch."

His candor was quite unattractive, as were his features. He was perhaps thirty or thirty-five and had begun to grow a belly. His expensive suit could not hide it. His hair was unremarkable and dull, and his nose was quite large above full wide lips that reminded me of the fish father brought home.

"He's done quite well for himself," said my brother. "Carma, you should see the house he owns on Marais Street."

"Si," said mother, who'd become strangely animated due to the wine. Her cheeks were flushed, and she was smiling in a way I had not seen in a long, long time. "Si, you should visit Monsieur Saloy's home. That would be very nice."

"*Allors,* in that case, Mademoiselle, may I collect you tomorrow evening? We might . . . have a bite to eat and perhaps visit the opera first. Do you like the opera?"

My mouth dropped open. I did like the opera, very much. I used to stand outside the doors and listen as the productions commenced, unable to enter with no ticket and no one at my side. I used to watch the pretty women in fine dresses on the arms of gentlemen and would secretly dream of what the inside of the Opera house must look like. I would listen to the voices calling out through the walls and into my soul.

"Yes, I like the opera," I told Monsieur Saloy. And in an instant, I felt a ripping, a tear in the spirit, like the pulling apart of the temple veil, except it was inside of me. I was to become a nun. This wasn't right. I looked at my brother and mother, and then into the face of Monsieur Saloy. This had been planned, I realized. Monsieur Saloy was here for me. This was the wealthy man my mother had wished for. My brother had delivered him right to our doorstep. This was the end of me, the marrying off of me, that befell young girls in New Orleans like yellow fever. Just as it seemed life was calling me to some worthy adventure, I was to be caught and tamed and caged into married life.

But the life before me came with opera. It came with a fine house. It came with money. The other life that beckoned me brought chastity and poverty, but also true love and the joy of purpose.

I knew I had no choice.

"Why thank you," I told our guest. "Mother?" I asked.

"Si, Carma, you may go. You may go and have a wonderful time." She smiled and looked so hopeful. It occurred to me this was a foreign look on my mother's face, and I wasn't quite sure it belonged there.

"Then it is settled," said Monsieur Saloy, who looked at me just a little differently then, or perhaps it was me who was looking at *him*.

Yes. I swallowed. It was settled.

From the journal of Y. R. Le Monnier, M.D.

RE: MADAME SALOY, 1876, FIRST APPOINTMENT

"And so you married him," I said, watching Madame Saloy's face intently.

"Of course," she said. She moved away from the window. The horses were still in their place. Madame pulled off her bonnet and tucked the ribbons inside, laying it on the bureau. "And now you know why all of this happened. I'm afraid I damned myself the moment I said yes. My child was taken as punishment."

"No," I said, unable to bear it any longer. "No, of course it was not punishment. You've done nothing wrong."

"Dr. Le Monnier," she said as if the weight of Atlas had been placed on her shoulders. She tried to smile. "It is done. *C'est la vie.* Off to go out and spend more of this money which grows and grows. It is a curse. It is all I have, aside from my daughter."

I wanted to say something more, that I understood her feelings. That I was sorry that her son had died. That I was sorry she had chosen Monsieur Saloy over the nunnery. That I understood how unfair life could be. She was suffering from melancholy and an undeniable case of Delirium of Persecution as she felt God was punishing her. What could be worse?

Alas, I nodded and put my pen down.

"I can prescribe a slight sedative," I said. "It may help . . . with your husband, you understand."

She nodded and looked sedated already.

"Just be sure to take only as I have prescribed. You shan't have any issues, but do call for me if you do."

"Thank you, doctor," said Madame Saloy, taking her hat in hand once again. "It feels strange to let all of this out into the open, but in a way, I feel it's necessary. May I speak to you again . . . sometime in the future?"

"Madame Saloy," I said, taking the hand of this gentle creature in my own and lifting it to my lips, "I should like nothing more than to help you sort out anything you may have on your mind, physical or otherwise."

She took her hand and opened the door, putting a pretend smile on her face for her husband. Bertrand Saloy stood with an expectant look. "I think Madame Saloy will be feeling much more like herself very soon," I said, passing her arm to his.

"Thank you, doctor," said Saloy, shaking my hand. The two walked out of my office, but I felt myself thinking of them long after they were gone, how sad it was for a woman to feel in some way responsible for the death of her son. That would seem like a curse, indeed.

From the journal of Y. R. Le Monnier, M.D.

RE: NEW ORLEANS, 1876

For days and weeks and months before my son arrived, I found myself taking a leave of my office mid-afternoons for a brisk walk over to Rue Royale, checking on the progress of the fourth story. Flocks of people would be there on most days, bemoaning the project and fearing the house would topple. The building owners to the left and right elicited pangs of outrage and tremors of near panic. But I stayed quietly in my place on the corner of St. Peter and absorbed the shock of the new look. And it wasn't a good one. The gray stucco didn't quite match the rest of the home, and there were no balconies. It lacked the graceful beauty of the rest of the building (and how could it not?) which had been designed by Hyacinthe Laclotte and Aresene Lacarriere Latour, principal engineer to General Jackson during the Battle of New Orleans—a battle in which my own grandfather had fought admirably and received a hand-written note of commendation from the General himself.

I never did catch glimpse of either husband or wife Saloy, and yet I could feel them inside the house, well aware of what the people were saying. I imagined it was the way my grandfather felt as he was building up to the third story. I imagined he said, "to hell with them," most likely the sentiment of Bertrand Saloy.

I didn't want the house to fall down as the onlookers claimed it would. I found myself, despite the affront of the new story on my own history, inwardly cheering on Monsieur Saloy. I did not want him to fail. I did not want the house to crumble back into the Louisiana soil.

My wife had our son, Yves René Le Monnier III, on 24 April, 1876. We were smitten and reveled in watching the child sleep. We dreamed of his grand future, and I often thought of the day when he might be a bit older and I could take him to the Le Monnier mansion and tell him all about his past. But this thought led me to remember Bertrand and Madame Saloy's sad story, and I'd not heard from them in several months. As a physician, it was quite standard to follow up with my patients, but I felt it might be imprudent on my part, and justified my silence by the fact that the Saloys would return if my assistance was needed. Or another prescription. My days as secretary of the board of health were often busy as well, and I found I had no time to go calling.

Not to mention, I could not help but feel an actual pain in my chest whenever I remembered Madame Saloy's grief at losing her son. I could not bear the thought. It made me all the more protective over my own precious son. At times in the middle of the night, I would awaken with acute anxiety, feeling the need to sit in the dark and keep watch over him, my gaze like a cage, for if I didn't, something or someone might come and steal him away.

Partial letter written by François Reynaud to Y. R. Le Monnier M.D., of the year 1877.

UNOPENED UNTIL 1906.

I set my hat and coat on the rack inside the door. I'd carved it by hand in my earlier days, when I was courting Salome. Back then, we would walk along the streets of France and stop in cafés. We would laugh, and Salome would smile at me all the time, never ceasing. But that was back in Paris before we were husband and wife, before we had Felix, before we moved to New Orleans.

I washed my hands at the kitchen sink and dried them on a towel. My wife was moving around the kitchen like a cat, stealthily and silently, building my plate of food and setting it on the table. She slid into her seat before I did, but there was no food at her setting. She placed her chin in her hand and elbow on the table. She watched me cut my thin slice of beef and dip it in the *jus* and potatoes before filling my mouth. I closed my eyes and said, *"Merci, j'ai faime."*

"You are home late," said Salome. "Did you forget the time?" I could hear the irritation in her voice. She had already eaten without me. "We tried to wait for you, but the meat was getting too tough."

"I'm sorry, dear, but I . . . I had a meeting."

Salome's eyes opened wide. "*Oui, avec qui*? Did someone buy one of your cages?"

In the beginning, Salome was taken with the skill of her husband, my passion for my art, my all-consuming attention to detail, but then later, when bills began to pile up, I knew she had grown irritated with me. This move to America was my idea. Truthfully, it had been my father's dream to visit America, but he had died before that could happen. We were on our way to riches, I had told Salome, and she had believed because it was what she wanted to hear. I wanted to be a good husband, I did, yet I did not know how to be true to my artistic needs as well as to the family. It had seemed so effortless to my father, and yet, perhaps it was because my mother had worked so hard to make ends meet. She had washed and ironed clothes and quilted. She was always busy, and as a boy I was unaware of any financial strain, if there was any. In my eyes, my father was a magician, and my love and respect for him was unending. I'd wanted to be just like him when I grew up.

Salome looked at me and urged, "François, did you sell something tonight?"

It had been two months since I'd sold a cage, and there wasn't enough money for this month's rent. I set my fork and knife down and finished chewing. I picked up my wine and just before taking a sip said, "*Oui*. I sold something."

Salome's shoulders relaxed, and I watched her exhale.

"Darling, I realize how difficult times have been, *mais je pense* that's all going to change now."

"How so."

"I've taken on a commission. I . . . I'm not sure how I agreed, but before I could turn, the words were spilling out of my mouth and . . ." Salome took my hand and squeezed. I had not felt this touch in a very long while. Her hand was hot, and I could see warmth beginning to fill her eyes as well. She was looking at me in a way that reminded me of the Salome of old, the one with no lines around her eyes, the one with plumper cheeks. I felt my heart flutter, and a flash of heat came over me. I could not believe that pleasing my wife in this way would make me feel so happy. I'd not felt that I'd pleased her in a very long time. I had condemned myself to feeling a failure in her eyes, to remaining a disappointment.

"I met with the Saloys."

"The Saloys?"

"*Oui.* I am to make a replica of le maison Le Monnier."

"*Mon dieu.* The skyscraper?"

"*La meme.*" I felt a ripple coming up through my belly. I was over-come and was forgetting for the time-being my loathe for selling my creative soul. "Guess," I teased.

She was smiling now. "Guess what?"

"Guess how much?"

The years were erased between us. She shook her head, "Five hundred."

It was an exorbitant amount. I knew she was half-joking, that this was a fanciful sum of money one could only dream about. I motioned with my chin higher. Salome lifted her left eyebrow.

"Tell me," she said with all seriousness.

I pushed my plate to the side and took both of my wife's hands in mine. "Salome, *mon coeur,* Bertrand Saloy has agreed to pay me . . . fifteen thousand dollars."

Salome looked dire as if she had swallowed a bone. She shook her head.

I nodded.

She shook her head again. Then the tears began to fall. I reached in and lifted her off her feet and hugged her close, held my wife so tightly that I forgot the whole world except for her. She was kissing me with wet tears on my neck. She was breathing in the smells of my studio, of my life, and it seemed she could not get enough. She was kissing me on the lips, tasting my pleasure, and I knew our lives were changed forever and wondered why I was suddenly blessed with such good fortune. I would have to go to St. Louis Cathedral and say a special prayer of thanksgiving.

Salome and I moved hand in hand past Felix's room, where he was already fast asleep. Behind the closed door of our bedroom, Salome was a young woman again, slowly unbuttoning the fabric from her waist and stepping out of her skirts, teasing me. In the light of a candle, her bare skin glowed in all the right places, and I forgot my age, forgot my occupation, my station in life, my worries, my cares. Forgot everything but her and the moment that held me captive. While my wife looked down upon me, loving me silently so as not to wake our son, I heard in the back of my head, *well done, François. You deserve this bit of happiness.*

And I was happy until the candle blew out from the drafty window and the two of us, husband and wife, were asleep and tangled in one another's arms. Unaware a new day was about to dawn in New Orleans.

François

From the journal of Y. R. Le Monnier, M.D.

RE: NEW ORLEANS, 1906

I awoke at dawn to discover I was still on the sofa, head down and neck stiff. The fire beside me had long gone except for some slow burning embers. I'd read my ledgers and unopened letters of the cage-maker late into the night and apparently neglected going to bed. How many had he sent to me? There were too many to count. I'd dreamed of the cage-maker and the Le Monnier mansion in foggy blue wisps of light and darkness. Morning seemed blurry to me, and I wondered what was real and what was not—until I realized Eulalie wasn't there. Her disappearance still stunned me afresh.

I'd married Eulalie Deschappelles, the daughter of a prominent planter, in 1873 just three months after our first meeting. It was in the French market, and I clumsily backed into her, a perfect stranger, begging her forgiveness. She was buying flowers and turnips or some such, and for the life of me, I cannot remember what I was there to purchase. I believe I left empty-handed except for an address of her father and a smile on my face. I was different the moment I saw her. It was the first time I'd been truly happy in several years.

When the war broke out in 1862, I was a student at St. Thomas Hall Military Institute at Holly Springs, Mississippi. The school disbanded at the time, most of the town enlisting in Featherstone's 17th Mississippi Regiment. I was offered a first lieutenancy with the approval of my father, which he refused to give, so I stayed on as drill sergeant for Holly Springs until I could take it no longer. On March 5, 1862, I enlisted as a private in Company B, Crescent Rifles, Louisiana Regiment under the leadership of Colonel Marshall J. Smith. Several years later, after I'd fought so many battles it shall take some doing to put down on paper, I walked from Greensboro, North Carolina, all the way to my hometown, New Orleans. I was a new man, not merely privileged, but a survivor now also, and received my degree as a doctor of medicine from the Medical College of New Orleans in 1868. I traveled to Paris for more study but returned upon my father's death in 1870 when I began my private practice. I was alone in my father's death, in the grief of it, for three years. Until I met Eulalie.

I thought of my wife over a breakfast of eggs, toast and strong coffee, imagining her sitting there in her housecoat, scarf across her hair. I smiled despite myself when the memory became more real than my solitude. And I perused the *Times-Picayune* for tasty bits of news, arrests, and obituaries, which Eulalie and I used to share in the mornings. And then there was a knock at my door.

Still in my robe, I peered through the sidelight and spied the girl, Mrs. Carmelite Kurucar. She was back, no doubt, to see how it had gone with her brother, and yet the sun was barely up. Why in the world would she be here before the decent hour of eight o'clock? I tried hard not to be annoyed. She was just a child after all. I told her to wait a minute while I went and changed.

As soon as I unlocked the door for her, she burst into the room and hid herself. She peered outside the window and then then pressed her head back to the wall, closing her eyes and catching her breath.

"My dear girl, what is the matter?"

She shook her head. "It—it's nothing. Really. I just thought I'd seen my husband. That's all."

"Well it looks to me you are hiding. Do you have cause to hide from your husband, Mrs. Kurucar?"

"No. Of course not. I just wanted to be sure I was not seen coming here. I'd told Ferdinand I was going out to the market and did not want him to think I was lying."

"Yet, you're here."

"Yes. I want to see how it went with Andrew. Did you see him? Is he all right? Is he terrified?"

"Come," I told her, motioning for her to sit on the sofa. I moved the books and ledgers that were strewn about over to my desk, then came back and stoked the embers back up into a weak fire with a bit of the *Times-Picayune*. I sat across from the girl in my wife's favorite armchair.

"Why is it your husband is not aware of your coming to me?" I asked. "Is this not something a husband should know?"

I tried to take the scolding out of my voice, but I could not help but see her as the child she was instead of the woman she was pretending to be.

"He would not understand, I'm afraid. He and my brother are not fond of one another."

"I see. That explains your brother's comments."

"Then you did see him? Please. Tell me everything. How did he look? Oh, how frightened he must be. Is it very dangerous, this prison? Is it?"

"Your brother seemed to be faring quite well under the circumstances. He admitted to me that he shot Miss Sheldon or Collier, whichever name she was going by. These ladies of the night are often masked in mystery. My point being, he admitted his guilt. I'm sorry to say I don't think this will bode well for him in court."

"But did he talk about the money? Did he mention how he *feels* about the money?"

"He did. Indeed, your brother spoke of a curse, as you suggested he would. But I'm afraid I don't have enough of an understanding yet to make an opinion on his state of mind. Still, I do not believe in curses as do some of these unfortunate souls who walk the streets of New Orleans and leave trinkets on gravestones. One cannot live his life in fear of curses, for in doing so, one misses his blessings altogether."

The child put her face down and stared at her fingers. She breathed in deeply.

"Mrs. Kurucar," I said gently, unfolding my legs and leaning toward her across the coffee table. "Might you tell me about your marriage at such a young age? I admit, I am quite curious. If I'm rude, please forgive my asking."

"Andrew told you to ask me, didn't he? He never has liked Ferdinand. He believes he only married me because of my money, but that is a lie." She looked conflicted, and then her face softened and she stared up at me with the stupid grin of one in love. "I have never felt this way. Never dreamed that a girl could feel this way about a man. He is all that I think about, still, even after nearly eight months of marriage."

Eight months of marriage. My heart hurt. I'd spent 33 years with Eulalie by my side. Thirty-three years through good times and bad. What did this girl know of true love?

"How old is this husband of yours?"

"He's nineteen."

"And your father approved of the marriage?"

She looked into the fire. "He had no choice." Mrs. Kurucar stood and walked to the window. She checked to see if anyone was there, then came back and touched the porcelain cherubs on my mantel. They had belonged to my Eulalie, passed on to her from her own mother. "My older sister, Viola, will be nineteen next week. Last September, she got married, and Father put on a nice reception at our house on Esplanade." She came and sat so far on the edge of the sofa that I feared she might slip to the floor at any moment.

"It was difficult when Mother died. Father tried to do the best he could with us, but Andrew was unmanageable. He sensed freedom was just outside the door, and he could not wait to get his inheritance. The problem was, my father as his lawful tutor, held the keys. Not being able to take the arguments any longer, Father told us that when we were each eighteen, still minors, that he would allow us our emancipation. Andrew received his money at eighteen and Viola did as well. After they finished school."

"But you," I said. "You have your money and you are only sixteen. Are you not in school?"

"I was. I attended the Pinac Institute for many years, but no longer. I received my inheritance at fifteen."

"How so?"

"Dr. Le Monnier, what I'm about to tell you . . . may cause you to form a different opinion of me, I'm afraid." Her pretty eyes were uneasy, looking into mine.

"I'll be the judge of that. Go on, dear."

"When Viola left home, beautiful, eighteen, married and in love, not to mention having received a large fortune, I lay in bed at night, envious of her. Envious of her life. I still shared a room with my little sister, Gladys, and felt like such a child. I wanted to know what it felt like to be in love, to have people look at me with respect in their eyes. I wanted to know what it felt like to have a man like her Joseph look at me the way he did at Viola. And then, there was the money." She turned the ring on her finger. "I'm ashamed to say, I wanted my share of the inheritance. If I couldn't have my mother, the least I could have was her money. You see, it wasn't Ferdinand who took advantage of me, Dr. Le Monnier. It was I who took advantage of him. Did you know that in the state of Louisiana a minor can be emancipated when she marries?"

"I was aware of that. But I'm also aware that a parent or guardian must approve of said marriage. You've told me your father had no choice but to approve of your marriage. How is this so?"

"Because I was already married by the time he found out about it. I forged his name on the marriage certificate and then told my father that we'd consummated our marriage and if he denied me my emancipation and husband, no decent man would ever have me."

"I see." I rubbed my face and stood to get my blood stirring. "Forgive me, but would you care for some water? I'm finding myself parched." It had been several years since I'd had such clients and many more years since the insane asylum. As of late, I was unaccustomed to hearing such drama, not having spent much time in the presence of young girls.

"Yes. Thank you."

I went to the kitchen and rattled around, composing myself. It was still so early yet. When I returned, I handed the girl a glass of water and noticed her hand was shaking as she took it from me.

"I threw myself at Ferdinand," she whispered after I was once again seated. "He was unable to resist me. I told him that I was going to come into a large fortune when I married, and so in less than a month after we first laid eyes on one another, I found myself crawling down the side of the house in the middle of the night on a ladder brought by my betrothed."

For a moment I was beginning to feel like the girl's priest and was quite uncomfortable with the amount of detail she might confess. I needed to cut her off.

"So now you have the money, your inheritance."

She nodded.

"Your brother Andrew mentioned that you've done something with the money."

"I've given it all to my husband to invest," she said. "We're going to be partners when we go into business together."

"You gave it all to your husband?" She blinked as if confused. "Did you do this on your own volition or was this something your husband asked you to do?"

"I am his wife, Dr. Le Monnier. What's mine is his, and what's his is mine."

"And does he have anything of value that he offers back to you?"

She looked crossly at me and then blushed. "He offers me plenty." She cleared her throat. "Now, the reason I have come here. I need you to determine if there is a curse on this money, and quickly. For if there is, I've now unwittingly cursed my husband as well."

"What's yours is his," I said. Just as I was about to reiterate the fact that I was perfectly ill-suited for such a task, there was another knock at my door. What I saw on the young Mrs. Kurucar's face when it seemed she might be found told me there might be more substance to her fears than just some superstition and an invisible curse.

Partial letter from François, regarding the year 1877

I sat still, feet planted in my studio with both hands on my knees. Hypnotized, I watched floating dust swirling in the air, dancing for me. I swallowed. I closed my eyes and caught a memory of last night with my wife. I felt different today. Instead of yesterday's trepidation about the Saloy commission, I now felt confident, strong. I opened my eyes and viewed my studio, my true home.

The floor had been swept by the windows only, so that potential buyers could look at my wares and not shuffle up dust. The windows were not as full of inventory as they once were. When I first moved to New Orleans and leased this space, I found myself so full of energy, worry, and bliss, I would work all night. I could complete a birdcage in less than a week under duress or mania, and although I was beginning to feel something prick at my insides, the feeling a child has when going to a candy shop, I would take my time on this cage. Saloy and his wife were paying me well, too well—it still made me nervous—so I would do this properly. There was no need to rush.

All was quiet in my storefront, so I stood and picked up my sketchbook, a ruler, gum for erasing, and three pencils of varying thickness and value. I donned my hat and locked the front door which read, *F. Reynaud, Bird Cage Maker,* after sticking a hand-written note for such an occasion in the window. *Pardon the inconvenience. F. Reynaud shall return soon.*

New Orleans was strangely quiet this hour. It may have been due to the horses at Metairie Race Course. The sun and the moon shared the sky, and I thought this phenomenon odd. How was it that the rulers of night and of day coexisted at the same time? I saw a pothole at the corner of Orleans and Rue Dauphine and was careful to step over it. My brother, Leon, had slipped on the ice in Paris and cracked his head while visiting the dentist for an abscessed tooth. Leon's death had made me a more careful walker. In fact, I walked so carefully most of the time that it was exhausting and not very relaxing unless I knew my way. I would much rather be in my studio than out here in the lovely daylight, dodging loose cobblestones.

It was exactly 710 steps from my home on Rue Bourbon to my studio on St. Ann. There was a large black dog that threatened to bite me after 111 paces, but the dog was always tied to a sycamore tree. I had grown accustomed to the bark and knew it was coming, so I crossed the street preemptively.

Traveling to la maison de Le Monnier was not a trip I made regularly, though I did visit St. Louis Cathedral for mass and was quite familiar with Jackson Square as my little shop overlooked it. On yesterday's trip I'd traveled through the square and passed the church, taking note of some obstacles and potential hazards along the way. At the corner of Chartres and Royale, there was an old man who made me uneasy. He sat on a chair and stared across the street at the statue of General Jackson on horseback. His lips moved as if he was talking to someone. This man was there again, I noticed, just as he was yesterday. When I walked in his path, the man reached and touched my sleeve. I stopped and looked at him, a toffee colored man with a glass left eye. The right eye engaged and I felt my heart through my vest. "*Un picayune?*" He was asking for money. His legs looked tired and wasted away. I shook my head, no, and kept walking, a little faster, a little more recklessly. I did have change in my pocket, though not very much. I could spare it, I thought, since I'd been promised such a large sum of money, but no. I shook my head again, trying to shake a bit of the guilt and the feeling of unease that rose up my spine when the man touched my arm.

When I reached la maison de Le Monnier at last, I was breathing heavier and had forgotten all about the old Spanish man in the shadow of this enormous residence. I looked up in the window and for a moment, imagined Madame Saloy there, but the shutters were closed. I walked across the street and bought a small brioche from Cadet's Bakery. I sat at an outdoor table and poured myself a glass of wine I'd tucked in my coat pocket for this occasion. With a clear view of 640 Royale, I pulled out my paper and lost myself in lines, all the while memorizing every one and imagining the birdcage going up piece by piece.

After my wine glass was empty and several drawings were complete, I walked the perimeter of the building and measured it with my footsteps. I was scribbling down numbers in front of the door when it opened and out walked Madame Saloy. I blinked then smiled and tipped my hat. "Madame Saloy, *bonjour.*"

She was breathtaking, and I felt my heart once more.

"*Bonjour*, François. How lovely to see you. I was just thinking about you. I do hope you're here to . . . ah, yes, is this it?" Madame Saloy reached for the sketchbook, but I shook my head and put it down by my hip. I hated that I looked like a child now. "I'm sorry, but I don't like to show the drawings before the cage is complete. Mmm, how do you say . . . superstition?"

Madame smiled and set me at ease. "I would expect nothing less in this town. You may keep your drawings secret until the cage is complete. Now, please, won't you come in and sketch the interior? Or perhaps you don't need to do that. How silly of me."

"No, you are correct. I don't need to do the interior sketches, but I like to do it. It helps me understand the house. I try to know all that I can before I begin. I find that the cage begins to build itself and the work is not so hard this way."

"Then perhaps we are paying you too much if the work is so easy," she teased. But it was true, and the weight of her statement made me want to back out of this deal, to turn around again. "I am not serious, François. Please." She touched my arm, the same arm the old man with the glass eye had touched. It gave me chills this time, then a sweat broke out above my top lip. I wiped my face with my kerchief and asked, "And Monsieur Saloy? Is he in?"

"No," said Madame Saloy, "my husband loves the horses almost as much as he loves me." So I found myself following her through the door and into the courtyard. I was feeling intoxicated by her Parisian *parfum,* and the dazzling shimmer of her lavender dress with poufs in the back that made me think of the beautiful peacocks that roamed my grandfather's estate when I was a child. I did not feel my sober self. I was part memory, part present, and part head full of clouds, not so eager to get back to my studio. Not just yet.

At the top of the stairs, Madame Saloy's housemaid opened the door and welcomed us in. "Carrie, Monsieur Reynaud will be joining me for tea in the parlor."

"Yes, Madame."

I followed Madame Saloy through the foyer and took the same seat on the velvet blue sofa I held just yesterday. I put my hands on my knees. "I'm afraid I'm overstaying my welcome." I looked around nervously at the furnishings of this first-class household. The Saloys lacked nothing. Above the fireplace were gilded mantelpiece mirrors that reflected the light from the windows draped in silk curtains. It gave the room a sooth-ing glow and made Madame Saloy's face appear as smooth as the silk itself. I looked down and began tracing the intricate pattern in the rug with my eyes.

"You mustn't be afraid of me," she said. It struck fear in my heart. Could she hear what I was thinking?

"Of course not, Madame." I attempted a smile, but only the left side of my mouth found its way up, leaving me feeling ridiculous.

Carrie came and set the tea server on the center table and poured a cup for each of us. "Thank you," said Madame Saloy. She took a sip and set it back in her saucer, holding it primly at her breast. "Now then, I promised you a tour of the house, didn't I? I would imagine you're getting ready to begin the birdcage, *oui?*"

"*Oui*, Madame," I said. "I would be happy to see the bones of this lovely house."

We left our teacups steaming in the parlor and headed for the dining room. Madame Saloy motioned to the table set with white tablecloth, napkins and a fine set of ornate porcelain with five glasses at each setting and buffed silver. "Monsiour Saloy likes to entertain," said Madame. "One must be ready at all times with him. In fact, he may bring several of his cohorts home from the races this evening. They enjoy a hearty meal after winning—or losing a small fortune. Do you gamble, Monsieur Reynaud?"

I was caught staring at the delicate gas chandelier with teardrop crystals. The room was in an oval shape and the light through the windows and glass cast a dazzling prism all over the walls. "Me? No. Well, once, but the bet didn't go in my favor, I'm afraid. No, I leave all that to those who have money to spare." I hadn't meant to say it, but it had come out awkward and left dangling from my mouth like a corn silk in my teeth.

"Well, perhaps this little project may put more money in your pocket . . ." Madame Saloy looked down at my ring finger. "For your wife. I imagine every lady likes nice things. Tell me, your wife, what is her name?"

"Salome," I said. "She is . . . well, she came from a first-class life back in France. I'm afraid New Orleans is not quite what I had promised her."

"Oh, and what had you promised her?"

I felt my face blush at the intimacy of our talk. I needed to change the subject. I pointed to the doorway. "Is the kitchen through there?"

"Oh, yes, I forgot all about our tour," said Madame. "If you wouldn't mind, please begin without me. I must speak to Carrie about tonight's dinner. I won't be long." Madame Saloy sauntered off, and tentatively I moved into the kitchen with its luxury stove and cook top and hanging shiny copper pots. I loved to cook, an inheritance from my mother, and my mouth nearly watered.

Next a quick glance into some bedrooms with rosewood furniture sets. When I approached the door of what seemed to be Madame's boudoir, I turned away only to see her standing behind me. "Oh, there you are. Go on in. I insist," she said. "The bed is mahogany. It's a little too large and ornate for my taste, but its one of the first things Bertrand bought with his own money. It has sentimental value to him. Do you know how my husband started out, Monsieur Reynaud?"

I shook my head. I had always assumed that a man with wealth like Saloy had simply always had money. The Saloys in France were certainly well off.

"He started as a bottle and rag salesman." My eyes enlarged, and then I attempted a cooler gaze. "That's right," she said. "His father had practically disowned him when he wanted to come to America, and he arrived with nothing. Before I knew him, Bertrand was a young man going door to door. Eventually, he bought and sold a few more things, each time, saving his earnings. After several years, he bought his first piece of real estate and sold it for a profit. He's been in love with real estate ever since. This house, in particular, was a favorite purchase."

I tried to forget what I knew about the property from the *Times-Picayune,* how Bertrand Saloy took the grocer from the house by help of the sheriff. "My husband added this floor just last year. Look." Madame held on to my arm and pulled me toward the bedroom window. I felt inappropriate standing in this room with her and grew hot, imagining my wife walking in just now. "You see? From here, I can see all the tops of the buildings and clear over to St. Louis Cathedral. Just beyond, I can see your studio." She closed her eyes and breathed in the air from the window, then she closed it once more.

"But I have saved the best for last." Madame Saloy tugged on my elbow and led me to the music room where a lovely Pleyel piano sat shimmering in wait amongst walls of burgundy brocade.

"Do you play?" she asked me.

"*Un peu,*" I said.

"Please." Madame Saloy motioned for me to sit down on the piano bench. She took her place next to me and arranged her skirts. She was very, very close, and I felt moisture bead on my top lip again. In front of me was an open songbook, but I closed my eyes. I tried to forget the attractive lady next to me and let my fingers read the keys. I played lightly at first, almost bittersweet, and then the melody rose and captured me. I wasn't sure if I was writing this piece myself or if the music was writing me, but when I was done, I opened my eyes and realized where I was. Startled, I looked over at Madame Saloy and backed up on the bench a few inches from her. She was watching me with tears in her eyes.

She said nothing, then cleared her throat and stood. Turning to the wall, she wiped at her face and said, "You are a lovely piano player." She faced me once more and smiled, breathing deeply. "I had no idea you were such a talented man with music, as well as art. Now—" I could hear it in the tone of her voice. Something had happened as I played my tune. I wasn't quite sure what it was, but I could feel Madame Saloy retreating. I wanted to excuse myself before she was forced to hint at my departure.

"I really must be going, Madame. It has been a lovely visit, but I'm afraid there is much work to be done."

"Of course. What am I thinking, holding you here, when you must have so many things to do, cutting and, and . . . well, whatever it is you do in your studio."

"You are more than welcome to come and watch the birth of your birdcage whenever you like, Madame." I was saying it to be kind and to smooth over this transition out of her house, but as soon as I said it, I knew it was a mistake. I didn't work well with others around, and certainly . . . well, I couldn't imagine being able to concentrate with Madame Saloy and her scent to distract me.

"That sounds lovely," she said. "I may accept your offer."

I walked away from la maison de Saloy, and as a horse and carriage passed me, I realized I'd forgotten to keep count of my steps on the way back. I'd been thinking about the house and about her. Somehow I could not think about the house without the image of Madame coming right along with it. It was indecent, I knew, and a quiet sense of shame brushed my neck as I cleared my throat and headed back to my studio to busy my hands.

François

From the journal of Y. R. Le Monnier, M.D.

RE: NEW ORLEANS 1906

My hands shook as I set down François' letter and looked into the fire.

I was beginning to feel that this girl, Carmelite Kurucar, had certainly come to the right place. As a physician, I had the ability not only to look at symptoms, but to pattern together the history of a patient in order to make a more accurate diagnosis. It had helped me to save countless lives in Memphis when the Yellow Fever ravaged that land. I'd cured many at the asylum after listening to tales of melancholy and mania and identifying the patterns.

In this way, a physician is not so different from a detective, is he not? I was not a rash man, but one who studied a topic from all angles and only then offered my opinions. Once I did offer my mind on a matter, I never, ever retracted it.

Le Monnier House, Saloy residence, Royal Street

And I felt I'd known it all along. My notes and the letters of the cage-maker confirmed it. There was some connection to the house on Rue Royale, this so-called "curse," although Reynaud had never mentioned it. I wasn't sure how, but the Le Monnier mansion seemed to connect us all—the Saloys, the cage-maker, myself, and now this young man in peril, and his sister Carmelite Kurucar.

Madame Saloy, herself, had felt cursed by the money, and felt that the curse had begun with her denial of God when she chose to marry Bertrand Saloy instead of becoming a nun. But that was absurd. Was it possible the money could be cursed from the simple act of a woman choosing marriage over God? I thought not. It was time to visit the prison again—or a priest, one.

From the clinical notebook of Y. R. Le Monnier, M.D.

ANDREW REYNAUD, IMPRISONED FOR MURDER AND AWAITING TRIAL AT NEW ORLEANS PARISH PRISON, 1906, SECOND MEETING

Andrew Reynaud was waiting for me when I entered the small room at the parish prison. He jumped up and seemed to want to run to me, but his arms and legs were shackled. He'd become the ghost in Dickens' past, paler since I'd seen him last.

"I'd shake your hand, but . . ." I motioned with my head to his handcuffs. "Well, let's have a seat then. Mr. Reynaud, I wanted to have another chat with you, if that's all right."

"You've got to get me out of here," he said quietly under his breath so that the guard would not hear.

"I . . ." I shook my head. "Have you met with your lawyers?"

Andrew nodded. "They say a trial is several months away. I can't—"He looked up at me with tears in his eyes. "I can't wait that long. I'll die in here."

"You won't die in here," I said, but then remembered I wasn't here to comfort him but to garner the truth about his mental state. "What I mean to say is, why do you say that? Why do you say you'll die in here?"

"I don't know." He put his hands up to his face and rubbed his eyes, then pushed them through his shaggy hair. His eyes had taken to staring at nothing on the table between us. I was afraid I would lose him soon.

"I saw your sister, Carmelite. She's quite worried about you. I can see she cares a great deal about her brother."

The boy was softening, and his bottom lip quivered. "They're all I have," he said. "My sisters. My sweet sisters. Did she look all right? Is she feeling well?"

"Yes, I suppose."

"She's not pregnant, is she?"

"I haven't the slightest idea. She didn't show if she was. Would this be a problem . . . if Carmelite was to get pregnant?"

He shook his head. "My mother, she used to get so sick when she was expecting a new baby. As the oldest, I worried about her. Every time. As a child, I didn't understand when she would take to the bed, swollen and sad. It seemed as if something had taken her over. First it was Viola, though I hardly remember her birth. When Carmelite was born, that—that I remember. I could hear my mother's screams. I was terrified she was dying, and then I saw her with this little baby, smiling. She asked me . . . if I would help her take care of her, my baby sister, and I told her I would."

He bit his lip. "You don't have any whiskey, do you?"

I did. I had a small flask in my vest pocket that I kept for emergencies, but I didn't offer it to the boy.

"I'm sorry to say, no. But please. You were telling me about your mother. When Carmelite was born."

"I didn't take care of her. My sister. I can't protect her from herself. She's like me in many ways."

"In which ways?"

"Rebellious. Free-willed." He looked up at me with iron eyes. "Cursed."

There he went again, saying that blasted word as if it were just another adjective like *pretty* or *simple*. I shifted in my seat and shuffled my notes.

"I had a brother who died," he said. "Felix, Jr. He was named after my father. He died just 18 days after he was born. My mother was never the same after that. Neither was my father. I can never erase the image of my mother's face when she held him, dead, in her arms." He shuddered then went on.

"I was named after my grandfather, Antonio. Antonio Andrew Carcano. My father has always hated me because I'm too much like my mother's father and not enough like him. Not disciplined enough. Not rigid enough. But it's all his fault. He introduced me to bourbon. From the moment I could walk, I was in his saloon. My lawyers want to plead insanity caused by too much whiskey. That I shot Doris because I was drunk."

"I see." I scribbled in my notes. "How do you feel about that?"

"It's a demon. I need a drink right this very minute."

"How long would you say you've had this problem?"

"Since about sixteen. Carmelite's age."

I flipped through my notes to his sister's confessions. "She says you left home then . . . and were gone for many days."

He smiled, but not happily. "I told you my father . . . we don't see eye to eye. He said I was just like my grandfather, and he and my mother fought about me all the time. Finally, I said I was leaving. I packed a bag and walked to the door. I thought my mother would stop me. I thought she'd choose me over him. I thought she'd cry and beg me not to go."

"And did she?"

He shook his head.

"She let me go. Just like that. But not before she kissed me and tucked a wad of bills in my hand. Ten days later, I'd had more whiskey and women than I ever knew existed. I came back home, but the damage was done. My mother died the next year. My father said it was my fault."

I was beginning to understand. "And the night that you shot Miss Sheldon, it was the anniversary of your mother's death."

The truth stood there between us.

I leaned forward on my elbows and put my notes to the side. I looked deeply into Andrew's eyes. "I still don't understand one thing. Can you help me? You said that you had calmed down in Miss Sheldon's room. That she was walking you to the door when you shot her in the back. It seems to me that if you were angry or jealous of the other man, you might have shot her to her face, in the heat of the moment."

He looked up at me like a child. "She was letting me leave. I—I told her I was going to go away. She didn't try to stop me. Instead she kissed me and went to get the door for me. Just as my mother had four years ago."

"Ah."

So there it was. The poor boy was still wrapped up in his mother's skirts. Doris' betrayal brought back feelings of his mother's rejection long ago. I felt such pity for him in that moment that I wanted to reach over and put a hand on his shoulder, though I didn't dare. Instead I said, "Just one more thing, Andrew. I need to understand how you are connected to the fortune of Bertrand Saloy. I feel I've missed something."

"My mother's father," he said. "My namesake. Antonio Andrew Carcano was Carmelite Saloy's brother."

"I see." There was the blood relation. The guard came over to take Andrew back to his cell. As he was standing, I added, "And what about the house? Do you know of any connection to the mansion at 640 Royale?"

He turned to me, seemingly stunned that I would mention it. "Yes. My mother owned that property. It was hers until the day she died, the Le Monnier mansion." Realization donned on him. "Doctor Le Monnier . . ."

Both of us stood wide-eyed, studying the other, taking in the knowledge of our strange connection, and though I meant to tell him goodbye, I found that I had no words. I could only watch as the prison guard hauled the young murderer away.

Partial letter from François, regarding the year 1877

The police were hauling away a drunk man in the street. From my window in my studio on St. Ann, I had watched his charade for the past ten minutes, hand raised in the air, spouting bits and pieces of scripture in a brash Irish accent. The hatless man in worn jacket appeared to have drunk too much whiskey for breakfast or perhaps his stupor carried over from a late night. Whatever the reason, I was relieved the police were finally here, and I could get back to concentrating on the task at hand.

Today I was to begin Madame Saloy's birdcage.

Of course, it was Monsieur Saloy's cage as well—he was paying for it after all. Yet it was Madame Saloy who inspired the piece.

It would be grand. It would be even more magnificent than the mansion itself! I worked at building my confidence, then I opened my book of drawings and studied them. With precise measurements in scale, I set out to cut a piece of wood for the bottom frame. When four such pieces were cut, two for the front and back and two for the sides, I made sure they were straight and level, then repeated the process for the top of the cage, cutting four more pieces.

It was a laborious business, this, but I enjoyed it so. I forgot about anything happening in the streets of New Orleans. I forgot about my wife, and how she kissed me that morning in a way that was old and familiar. How she packed my supper of leftover meat and bread from the night before. How the night before she lay with me and squeezed out any thought of this birdcage or of Madame Saloy.

Madame Saloy brushed the front of my mind, then I shooed her away. I felt the rush of being engulfed in my creation, of being part of it. I felt the metal of my tools and created delicate, precise dovetails in the ends of the pieces of wood so that I could fit them together like lovers, as if they were made that way, so tight, that they might never come undone.

71

I could see the numbers in my head, 1 centimeter and 3 sixteenths. Four centimeters and 5 eighths. It must be exact. I was shaving away a miniscule sliver of wood with my eyes as close as I could get them when I smelled something wonderful. It was her. It was Madame Saloy with that amazing scent that whisked me back to Paris.

My heart stirred, and I turned and saw the bottom of a dress at my side. I looked up and found not Madame, but my wife, Salome, looking at me adoringly. My wife. The *parfum* Madame wore that I had remembered from long ago was my wife's! Yes, I'd given it to her when we were courting, yet had only remembered the way I felt when I smelled it, the lover who had turned me inside out with feeling. That lover had been my very own Salome? I thought back to last night. My mind raced over all that had happened since moving to America. Here she was smiling, my Salome, but I thought I detected dollar signs in the blackness of her pupils. I shook my head and leaned in for a kiss. I wanted to be closer to that scent. She hadn't worn it in years.

"To what do I owe this honor?" I asked. Salome had not set foot in my studio for at least nine months. It seemed to me that she has been angry with this studio, and with me, for that amount of time. So now I was working on commission. And Salome was here. I tried not to be suspect, but it wasn't easy.

"I thought you might like a piece of this apple tart," said Salome.

"How delicious. You can set it right over there."

Salome walked through the studio and looked around with the pie box in hand. She eyed my birdcages slowly and tested the dustiness of the floor with her shoe. "It's quite tidy in here, François. You've had much time to clean?" I closed my eyes. There it was. The jab I was expecting. She was insinuating I'd had nothing to do but sweep the floors. "It looks very nice." Salome set the box down on the table in the corner next to my food sack. She stopped and rested for a few moments, head down. "Is this the mansion, dear? The Saloy house?"

"*Oui.*"

She was quiet for a while, flipping through pages. It made me uneasy. Made me feel like she was intruding on my private thoughts. I shouldn't feel this way about my wife, should I? Perhaps I would feel this way about anyone fingering my drawings.

"It is lovely." I could hear a slight change in her tone. "Especially this interior. How did you manage to get such detailed drawings of the Saloy's household?"

"I sketched this earlier today."

"Oh. I suspect Monsieur Saloy was all too happy to show you about. He is spending quite a fortune on you, isn't he?"

I was quiet for a moment. I set down my tools. It was no use trying to work while she was here. "He wasn't there," I said. "He was at the races. Madame Saloy is the one who led me around."

"Ah, I see." I knew how this struck my wife. Here was a woman who once had a first-class household herself, now living the wife of a cage-maker. She was jealous of Madame Saloy and her wealth. She was envious that this woman lived in luxury and prestige.

"Seems you drew everything, except *le bidet*."

I turned to my wife and saw it on her face. Then I watched her struggle inwardly and shrug off that demon. She smiled again, a forced enthusiasm. "Is this it? Is this the cage?"

"*Oui*. It is beginning. The frame on which to build." I approached my wife and wrapped a hand in the small of her back. I let it sit there for a moment as my wife thawed, then I pulled her to me, inhaling her. "Thank you for the pie, *cherie*. I will think of you as I eat it later."

It is what she needed to hear. Salome leaned in and kissed me quickly on the lips, then pulled away. We were in my studio after all and someone might come in. But I wanted her there. Then.

"Will you be home for dinner on time?" she asked.

I smiled. I was grateful she had stopped by. I realized what a grand gesture this was, and saw how hard my wife was trying to show her love for me, even donning the perfume she once wore to secure my heart. "I promise," I said. "Tell Felix I'd like to play ball with him before supper, *d'accord*?

"*Oui*."

With that, Salome turned in a flurry of dark green and exited the studio. I was left standing, feeling my heart missing her already. There were moments when the love I felt for my wife all those years ago was raw and rich and new. In those moments, I liked to linger and imagine that things could always be that way, that I would always feel that way as I first did. But in my head I knew that I had distanced myself from Salome. That it was harder for me to break through the walls that had grown up between us. And right now, I needed all of my effort to go into fulfilling this commitment I had made to the Saloys. There was a lot of money at stake. I tried hard not to think of the money, but it was there, nonetheless, just as the thought of Madame Saloy was there in the back of my mind. Raw and rich . . . and waiting.

François

Partial letter from François, regarding the year 1877

It was not anything I would have expected. I could not have anticipated the way I would feel while creating the Saloy masterpiece. Of course, calling it a masterpiece was something I would only do in my own mind. It was impossibly pretentious, yet helped justify the way I felt—a deep love reserved for the brilliant artist, the Titian, the Michelangelo, the Bernini. It was as if the other cages had been in preparation for this moment. As if the Saloy cage was my *raison d'etre.*

The sides had begun to take shape. I drilled holes for the wires and had begun twisting them with my pliers after shoving the tips through the wooden base at the bottom and top. The cage lay on its side so as to retain its shape. The wood frame was not yet fully constructed, so the weight was horribly off-balanced. One false move would create a weakness in the wires that might never be recovered. I would have to start all over.

I pulled down my visor and lifted the blow torch to sauter two wires together. The blue-white flame trickled out as I pointed it toward the junction. My kerosene was running low. I would have to get more tomorrow. I set the tool down and looked out the window across the park. It was dark already. What time was it? I felt as if I was waking from a dream, one in which everything is pleasant and lovely, and then morning hits with stark reality.

I pulled out my pocket watch. Nearly ten o'oclock in the evening. I was late, very late, and my heart sank to the pit of me. My wife. How long had Salome waited there for me with my meal? How angry had she gotten as the minutes and hours ticked by? But worse, had Felix cried when he had to go to bed, realizing his father had not come home and played ball with him as he promised?

What sort of a man was I? I wondered. A selfish oaf who only looked after his own affairs? Who had no time for his family? Who would willingly break the heart of his wife and child over and over because of his work?

But weren't other men this way? Surely Bertrand Saloy was not home for dinner at the precise hour he told his wife every evening. Surely, traipsing off to the races and losing pockets full of money, coming home reeking of bourbon and cigars as he slobbered a kiss on his delicate wife, was worse than what I had done. I'd merely done my best at my work, to put food on the table, the very table Salome had probably sat at and cursed me tonight. No. I was not the evil here.

I took one last look at le maison de Saloy as it lay on its side on the wood table, surrounded by chips, shavings, wires, and tools. It would be there when I woke up, I knew. The fact that this cage would be there waiting for me was impetus enough to send me into the dark of New Orleans in search of home and rest. It wouldn't be hard to get there, I knew, for the moon was directly over my house at this hour. I could follow the pale sliver and count my footsteps, and if any trouble came my way, I would keep quiet and walk on by.

I passed Heyl's Saloon. I saw men tucked in to tables and bentwood chairs by the walls, others standing and patting one another on shoulders, possibly steadying themselves with a firm body. As I walked by, counting my steps . . . 107, 108, 109 . . . I heard the sounds of the revelry and stopped in my tracks. My wife would be in bed already. She might not be asleep, only waiting like a viper to attack when I pulled my trousers off. A man might need a drink to prepare for something like that. He might need something to calm his nerves.

I turned and just as I did, a man walked out of the bar and stood there for a moment, assessing the street. Then he lit a match and his cigar. I watched the puffs of white smoke swirling into the cool night air and the man's profile of face and hat as he mouthed the end of it. He was a beefy fellow, and his clothes were fit and fairly neat. The light of a lamppost hit the man as he turned back to the entrance of the saloon, and I realized I knew that face. It was Bertrand Saloy himself. I felt a kindred spirit at the moment. I'd been working hard on a replica of his very house all day. It had consumed me, all the details of this man's home, and now here he was in the flesh.

I moved to take off my hat and address him. Perhaps I would go in and buy the man a drink. After all, he was supporting my family these days. My mouth opened to speak, but before I could, Saloy had wrapped his arm around a sensual quadroon dressed in red and yellow, as if she were on her way to a ball. The woman giggled into him and kissed him on the cheek, and as I tried to take a few steps back, Saloy's eyes caught me. He squinted.

"Is that you, cage-maker?" he said, a brusque warning.

"*Oui. Bonsoir, monsieur.*" I stood frozen. I had lost count of my steps. I had promised myself I would stay quiet and avoid trouble—it was my personal motto—and now I was here, standing face to face with what I assumed was an adulterous Bertrand Saloy, my very own benefactor.

"Thinking of spending my money on wine and whiskey, are you?" he asked.

"*Non, monsieur.*"

Saloy was quiet for a moment, then he whispered in the woman's ear. She turned and sent a slithery glance toward me that appeared to suggest some relationship between the two of us as well. It made me feel flush. Perhaps this was no mistress but a whore instead. She took a moment in Saloy's ear and then kissed him on the lips. Saloy turned quickly and shooed her away then approached me with arm extended. He scooped me up in a side bear hug as if we were old friends.

"Come, cage-maker. Have a drink with me. The night is young and our women are already in bed without us. You do have a woman, don't you? If not, I know of some ladies who would be more than happy to know you." He was jovial now, and drunk, and as I walked into the saloon on the arm of Saloy, the light and noise accosted me along with the fog of smoke. It took the first several sips of my drink to burn the images of Madame Saloy out of my brain. I was drinking with her husband. The man who kept women on the side. Did Madame Saloy know? Would she care? Of course she would care. What woman wouldn't? With a few more sips, the thought of Madame grew bright in my head. How could this man ever consider the company of another woman when he had someone like her at home? It didn't make sense. I felt keenly protective of her, and the bourbon hitting my soul made me daring enough to take Saloy out of the saloon and challenge him to a duel.

But that was ridiculous. I smiled when prompted and shook hands as Saloy introduced me into his corral. And then I had another bourbon and laughed at their seedy jokes. One who met us for the first time would never know there was a difference between me and Saloy. In the distant back of my mind, I realized an onlooker, passing by this saloon as I had done earlier, might not know there was a grave difference between us—this rich, adulterant, swindling benefactor, and the honest, humble, hard-working artiste at his side. No, from outward appearances, sans the sawdust on my jacket, no one would ever know we weren't exactly one in the same.

François

Partial letter from François, regarding the year 1877

It was not something I had to see with my own eyes—I knew she was angry, could feel her anger, even as I lay looking at the black backs of my eyelids. I could smell her, my wife, in the stillness of the morning. Her perfume lingered from the night before, and it swelled my head and heart and body with an assortment of emotions. The past was gone yet here still. My wife and Madame Saloy, both here in this bed now. But it was all wrong.

I opened my eyes and looked about the bedroom as widely as I could without moving my head or stirring. Salome was next to me, her back shunning me. I thought of rolling over and wrapping my arm around her waist, moving in close to take her from behind, but in my mind's eye I could see she was lying there waiting, eyes open. Yes, perhaps I should be a man and pretend that I did not slip home in the wee hours of the morning, just love her as a husband should. The problem was the anvil sitting on my forehead, the nasty taste of stale bourbon and cigars in my mouth. I rolled over, away from my wife and sat on the edge of the bed. I would come clean before she could ask it of me.

To my feet I said, "I had drinks with Saloy last night." I threw the sentence out there in the open space and let it bounce around aimlessly, waiting for her to pick it up. She did not. "I lost track of time and then ran into him on the way home. I felt compelled to accept his offer of a drink. It was the least I could do."

"The least you could do," she said. Salome pressed herself up and sat behind me. I could feel her stare at the back of my head, so I rubbed my neck. "The least you could do indeed." Salome rose and walked out of the room. I closed my eyes so I wouldn't have to see her in my peripheral vision. Then I moved to the side table and poured water into the basin and washed my face. I would look in on my son and hope for a more receptive audience. Once my head cleared, I would take the time to play ball with him as I'd promised, and then I would return to the studio where the Saloy cage was already calling.

I threw the baseball to my son Felix, a brown-sugar-haired boy with big eyes to match. He resembled me in so many ways, in his slight build (even at seven years old, I could tell he'd be no taller than my own five feet and ten inches), but also in his hands. The boy had been able to catch a ball for several years now, and was quite good at making houses from a deck of cards. That kind of precision, that sort of hand-eye coordination, I knew was passed down from my own father, through me and now, to my son.

Felix was an artiste in waiting.

Felix caught the ball and ran over to me. He didn't like to throw the ball back, but instead, would come close enough to roll it on the ground at my feet. No matter how hard I had tried to get the boy to throw the ball to me, my son would refuse. Perhaps it had something to do with being careful. Perhaps he'd rolled it so many times, the task was ingrained in his brain, his lucky talisman. Perhaps he couldn't catch well if he could also throw. This is what I told myself and truthfully, it made me feel better. Although the Creator bears many gifts, one cannot be great at all things. One must pick and choose *the* thing at which to be great and then do it with all one's heart.

"Would you like to come with me to the studio today?" I asked.

"*Oui!*" The boy jumped in his spot and then ran to me. He wrapped his arms around my legs and I melted. "Good. Good. Let's go tell your mother you're coming to work with me. You can help me with my new cage."

"May I hammer the nails?" asked Felix.

I smiled and mussed the hair on top of the boy's head. "We'll see, *petit*. But first we must get past your mother. Don't beg; just be a man about it. She'll respect you more."

Salome softened a bit with the prospect of having the house to herself, so not only did she agree to the boy coming to work with his father, she sent us in with a large basket of leftover dinner. There was nearly an entire chicken and diced potato hash. I carried the basket in one arm and my son's hand in the other. I noted that Felix stepped whenever I did and stopped whenever I stopped. I wondered if he kept count of our steps as I did. When it came time to pass the ferocious dog, it was Felix who pulled me to the other side of the road first.

"That dog will not scare us today," I said to my son.

"*Non.*" The dog, tied to the sycamore tree, erupted in a fit of fury as we crossed its path on the other side of the road. It seemed incensed that it was tied down and unable to reach us. As we walked on, farther away from the creature's barking, Felix looked up into my face and said, "I am sad for the dog."

"*Pourquoi?*"

"It is not free," said Felix. "It can never run free. It is always tied to the tree."

"But if it ran free it might bite us. I imagine it would like to eat a little boy like you."

The boy walked on and looked straight ahead. "Maybe," he said. "But I don't think so. I think it would just run and run. I think it would never stop running. It doesn't really want to eat us."

I squeezed my son's small hand and smiled. "You are a very smart boy, Felix. I think today you are ready."

"What am I ready for?"

"I think you may be ready to become my apprentice."

The boy was silent for a moment, and I realized he did not know what that word meant, nor would he ask.

"An apprentice is someone who learns everything about making cages. It means, if you pay attention I will teach you everything I know, and someday when you are bigger, you may be an even better birdcage maker than I."

Felix stopped and turned to look at me. A bit of fear was in his eyes. "Maman says you are the finest cage maker in all of New Orleans. She says you are working for the king. I don't think I can be better than you. Never."

I set the basket of food down and picked up my boy, holding him close and staring into his eyes. "*Pourquoi?* I will teach you everything I know."

"Yes. But you will always be better than me. Because . . ."

"What is it?" I asked, searching my boy, and trying to reassure him that he would someday surpass his father, just as I had surpassed my own. This was a natural and welcome progression.

"I don't want to work for the king. I am afraid of kings."

"Ah, I see," I said. I set Felix back on the ground, picked up the basket and the boy's hand and continued walking. After a horse and carriage strode by, I squeezed his hand. "But do you know what comes along with a king?"

Felix shook his head and kept walking.

"The queen," I said. "Along with the king must come the queen, and the queen, my son, is someone you *would* want to work for. She's a lovely person. Now come. We have work to do. We mustn't keep her waiting."

François

From the journal of Y. R. Le Monnier, M.D.

It was a rainy afternoon, and I'd found myself unable to stop reading the cage-maker's story. I'd gone in hoping to see some talk of curses, when all I got was talk of his cage-making. It figured as much, I chuckled to myself. He was an interesting fellow, and I noted that I would have to seek him out and speak with him if he was still alive. But for the moment, someone else had piqued my interest. It was his son, Felix, now the father of Andrew Reynaud and Carmelite Kurucar. What sort of man was this to have married into money? What sort of man to raise a murderer and a girl-child who elopes at fifteen?

I found him quite easily in the city directory and took the chance that he, like me, had given the soggy day over to staying inside. I donned my jacket and hat and fixed my umbrella after shutting the door, but the wind nearly knocked me off my feet. The umbrella inverted and lifted up to the sky, drenching me, and as I bent to retrieve my hat, I was overcome by the foolishness of my actions. What was I thinking, venturing out on a day like this one? I was no longer a young man. I could slip and break a limb or worse, catch pneumonia.

When I was safely indoors, I went to my room and changed into dry clothes. I made myself some hot coffee and scolded myself for being so rash. What had gotten into me? What was it about this curious case that had me attempting to traipse about the mud and cobble stones of New Orleans on the slight chance I might meet Monsieur Felix Reynaud? Was it that the story being told by the cage-maker was becoming more real to me? Was it becoming more real than my very existence in that empty house? Did I care so deeply for the boy, Andrew, or did I believe so fervently that he was not insane that I felt I needed to do something, learn anything that might corroborate his suspicions—and Mrs. Kurucar's—of a curse?

Or was it that I was beginning to wonder seriously about the existence of curses, their origins, their ends, when before I'd thought them nonsense?

Any number of these made me question my own sanity.

The coffee would make me feel better, and if not, I had a bottle or two that would bring me back into full view. I would not read any more of the cage-maker's notes for the day—that was resolved. Instead, I would work on my book about the Battle of Shiloh. It was long overdue, and I'd neglected it so. There were still those out there who were distorting the truth about that day of retreat, and a distorted truth in my book was an out and out lie. Yes, there were lies being told about Shiloh, and this was enough to gather me to my desk.

I sharpened my pencil and sat there, hand poised above my notes. The empty page looked so bare. My mine wandered. I took a sip of my coffee. I glanced over to the fire. I'd need to start one if I was going to spend time in this drafty room.

After getting a small flame on the logs, I stared into the fire and thought of the Battle of Shiloh. I thought of the men who lay all around me. I thought of the blood on my hands from young soldiers like me. I remembered the fear in my heart that I had never loved a woman. I would die there in my first battle of the war and would never, ever know the love of a woman. Now, I was thinking of the love of a woman, my Eulalie. I was thinking how grateful I was to have loved and been loved. And now, I was staring at the stack of the cage-maker's letters on the sofa. They were pulling me closer like a moth to the flame.

I picked up my letter opener and sat down in my wife's chair. I would read about the cage-maker and about Madame Saloy. For the moment I cared nothing of curses, but only of the longing of a man for a woman, for that is all I knew at this stage in my life—a deep longing for a woman I would never, ever hold again this side of heaven.

Partial letter from François, regarding the year 1877

"In the words of my father," I said to my son, "No one *needs* a bird cage. And this is true, for the most part. Unless of course you have beautiful chickens and need a place to hold them before supper." The little boy smiled, and I ruffled his hair. I held him on the shoulders and walked him around the studio, stopping a moment or two at the bird cages in the windows and on display.

"Since no one really needs a cage, the only people who buy them are those who have the money to do so. And why do you think they buy the bird cages?"

"To put birds in them?"

"*Oui*, for the birds, but why do you imagine they want the birds?"

This seemed to stump the boy. Then he turned and said, "They hop around. And sing."

"*Bon, oui,* they sing. And they are beautiful in all shapes and colors. And so I think, the only reason a person would want a bird cage is to find some facet of beauty to hold on to in an ugly world. You will find out soon enough, *mon petit.* Everyone, even Papa needs something beautiful to hold on to."

"Is it cruel to the birds, Papa? They cannot fly about." The boy's face wracked with concern.

"Well, some birds are not meant to fly."

I thought for a moment, remembering the peacocks on my grandfather's farm in France, how they beveled back and forth in the yard and flounced around with their tails puffed up in glory. "My father also told me this, Felix: Never fool yourself into thinking you are a hero or creating something that betters the world. You are not. Yet you are, in some way, making the life of one person a bit more tolerable at the sacrifice of some other more negligible beast. The Bible speaks of a sparrow and a man, and the man is worth much more than the sparrow. My father believed that the glory in cage-making is ours alone, Felix. Not God's, but ours."

"Is this what you believe?"

"I've not always agreed with my father. He was a good man, a talented one, but he never saw the true beauty of his craft." I stopped and bent down on my knee, turning the boy to me and looking him in the eyes as if about to tell him a grand secret. "I've always felt the Creator at work within me when I make the cages. When I fashion the bars with my pliers and sauter joints. Watching it go up, piece by piece, is magical. Very special. My father, your grandfather, and I were both gifted at cage-making, *oui,* but gifted in different ways when it comes to faith. My faith is simple. Expect God to be there when you use your creative gifts, and he will show up without exception because *he* is the one who gave them to you. Use those gifts and you will know that God lives and dwells within you."

My son looked serious and a little frightened. I knew I'd gone too deep for him, and I straightened to standing and coughed to fill the air with noise. "I have seen that you have marvelous hands, Felix. A gift passed on from your grandfather to me and down to you. Let's see what you can do with them, *d'accord?* Would you like to hammer?"

The boy's eyes grew large, and he bounced up to the top of the stool as I propped him there, his legs dangling.

Less than an hour went by, father and son busy working on the Saloy cage, when the door opened and pulled us from our hypnotic tasks. A woman's voice said, "How wonderful to find you here. And who is this handsome young gentleman?"

I turned and smiled toward the door. I whispered to my son, "This, Felix, is the queen I was telling you about." I stood proudly and announced, "Madame Saloy. Madame Saloy, please meet my son, Felix. He is helping me today."

*Bonjour*s were said all around, and Madame came in closer and shut the door, leaving the dust and sounds of Rue St. Ann muffled. She kept her eyes on me, an intense stare that made me catch my breath.

"May I offer you something to drink, Madame?"

"No, I simply wanted to come by and say thank you for dealing with my husband last night. Oh, forgive me from staring," she said, pointing her gaze now to the floor. "I'm just afraid to look around too much or I might spy the cage you are making for me, and I know you're a bit superstitious."

"Truly, I'm not the least bit superstitious if you'd like to have a look."

"Thank you, but no. I have to admit I do like surprises. I think I shall wait until you are ready to share it with both myself and Bertrand."

She turned and walked to the window, seemingly watching a group of Negro children chasing a dog down the street.

"Son, I have some drawing paper and a pencil on the table there. Would you please make a drawing we can take home to show your mother? Make it a grand drawing of the cage you're helping me build."

Felix ran to the table and quickly began sketching. I came closer to Madame Saloy and noticed the brocade in her dress, how the sheen of the design flashed in the sunlight. She stayed with her back to me and said, "I'm afraid my husband likes to stay out late some nights."

"All men do, I suppose, at some time or another. I was out, after all."

She turned to me, something in her eyes, a glistening, a strength and vulnerability at the same time. "Yes, but you were on your way home from work. I'm afraid my husband spends more time in Storyville than with his own wife."

The truth was there before me and it itched at my ribs, felt like an anvil of weight that had dropped in an otherwise pleasant room. She knew of his infidelities, of his sport at courting the ladies of ill-repute. "I—"

"You needn't say anything, François. I am sorry for confessing such private matters. I simply wanted to let you know that . . . well, that I am grateful you were there last night. Bertrand told me what a gentleman you were. Although I'm afraid the word he used was not 'gentleman', but some other crudity meaning you remained faithful to your wife."

I remembered the girls who laughed and drank among us, and how each of them seemed to know Monsieur Saloy. I felt a strange sense of relief that I didn't have to keep the indiscretions of Madame's husband from her after all. I also felt an unusual intimacy with this woman I'd only met days ago.

"I am at your service whenever required, Madame," I said bending at the waist and swooping my hand in a grand motion.

She smiled and said, "Your son looks much like you. Same eyes. Same shape of the face."

"Today he became my apprentice, isn't this so, Felix?"

The boy looked up from his drawing absentmindedly. "He is a bit like his father in that he becomes absorbed in his work."

Something strange came over Madame's face as she watched my son. "Then I will leave you two to whatever it is you need to do," she said. "I did want to invite you, however, and your wife and son, of course, to a little Independence Day soirée next week. If you have no other plans. My daughter, Berthe Therese, also has her birthday on the fourth. She'll be turning sixteen. It won't be too much. Some fireworks and cake."

My mind flew with all the information I had gathered about the Saloys, and I was caught unfamiliar with them having a child. Not wanting to sound ignorant, I said, "My family and I would be honored to be your guests. Are you sure it is . . ."

I wasn't able to get the right words to come.

"I am positive that Bertrand wants you to join us. It was his idea after all."

This surprised me, and then it did not. Perhaps Bertrand wanted to show himself as a family man as well, after last night.

Madame left the store after speaking more kind words over my son, carefully avoiding any gaze toward the cage beginning to take shape, and when she left, I felt myself happier than I had been all day. I whistled and told my boy all about the house where we would be spending our Fourth of July, how grand its rooms, its furniture and draperies.

And I couldn't wait to get home that evening to tell my wife, Salome, that we were invited guests to such a prestigious affair as the personal birthday party of Saloy's own daughter.

In a matter of days, our lives had gone from humble and unwavering to brimming with excitement. The rush in my veins made me dizzy with my own self-importance. *It's my cage,* I told myself. *My cage-making changed everything.* I did hope that one day Salome would see how my hard work had paid off. For all of us.

François

Partial letter from François, regarding the year 1877

I spent the days following my Fourth of July invitation working as fast as I could. I had new vigor, and although it was unrealistic, fancied having the birdcage finished. I imagined presenting it to the Saloys in the presence of all the guests at their Independence Day celebration. It was fantasy mostly —I didn't consider myself quite that vain, but I couldn't help my mind rummaging over the possibility.

Salome, as I had hoped, was excited to visit la maison de Saloy, and had already begun fretting about her appearance. I had heard the complaints and couldn't help but take it as a personal slight, that my wife had nothing decent to wear. This, of course, was completely my fault. If I earned more money, then she would have finer things, we would live in a better home, etcetera. *A chair maker or sugar handler does something useful,* she would say. *Something worthwhile. But a cage maker?*

What did she know? She was right about one thing. Cage-making had not been lucrative . . . until now. Money was tight, and new dresses were a luxury Salome had not been able to afford since she had lived in Paris under her father's wing.

In the corner of my studio, I had a small porcelain vase nestled among my books and papers. It was four inches in diameter with blue designs of flowers and birds painted along its sides. It had been my mother's. I could still remember it perched on her dressing table as she brushed her long brown hair. It held her hairpins, and she would let me hold it as I sat on the floor while she was putting her hair up. "*Un autre,*" she would tell me, holding her hand out. "Hand me another." I would reach my small fingers into the vase and pull out a pin. She would then tuck lock after lock into the back of her head until she'd been transformed into a magnificent sculpture. I thought the sculpture was beautiful. That she was beautiful.

Some days when I was building a cage up stick by stick, wire by wire, I would think of those hairpins and the beautiful sculpture I was soon to behold.

Here in my studio on Rue St. Ann, the little porcelain vase no longer held my mother's hairpins but a small roll of bills I kept for an emergency. I'd begun saving ever since setting foot in New Orleans. I wasn't sure for what reason. I set my ruler down and swiveled my stool. I spied the blue and white vase, hidden in the shadows, and rose to retrieve it. *Salome deserves a new dress,* I thought. It was no emergency, but I felt like splurging. I had quite a sum coming to me when the cage was complete. I would replace the bills soon enough.

I would surprise my wife this evening over supper. I played the scenario in my mind and saw her squealing with joy and smiling at me with lovely crinkles in the corners of her eyes. I saw her making sweet love to me with wild abandon as we once had before the birth of Felix.

I was lost in my thoughts when a strange man entered the studio. I set the vase down quickly and moved to the front of the store to greet my customer. The man shut the door softly behind him and removed his hat. "Are you Reynaud?" he asked. "François Reynaud the cage-maker?"

I felt my face redden at the flattery. Someone else had now learned my name. Perhaps it was Madame Saloy who was sending new business my way. "*Oui. Je m'appelle* François Reynaud."

The man held his hand to his coated chest and said, "M'name's O'Sullivan. I work for Bertrand Saloy. I come to tell you that the party is off. The one for Independence Day."

"Oh? Oh." In a moment, my excitement was dashed. Was Monsieur Saloy playing with my head? Was there actually a party, but now my family had been uninvited? My blood ran. It was about that night at the saloon, was it not? Saloy was angry I had seen the type of man he was.

The man stood there, expectantly, his wide girth filling the space. He seemed to want to speak, but was uncomfortable.

"*Pas de problème,* Monsieur," I said, dismissing him. "Thank you for delivering the news."

I turned back to my table with the bones of the Saloy cage beginning to take shape. Perhaps Monsieur Saloy would back out on his promise to pay me the full amount. No. It was certain. I should have gotten more money up front! I was feeling like a fool, and a silent curse was about to exit my lips when I realized the Irishman was still there and hadn't moved a muscle.

"Is there . . . something more? Something I may do for you?" Perhaps he wanted a cage. Or a tip. Imagine the gall of this man expecting a tip for bearing an un-invitation.

The man fiddled with his hat in his hands and looked down at it. "It's . . . just that Madame Saloy. Well, she's . . . a-and rightly so."

"She's what? What is it with Madame? Is she ill?"

"Ill . . . no, well. It's her daughter, Miss Berthe Therese. She was on her way back home from the country. She was staying with a relative for the hot summer months, but . . . well, the wagon broke a wheel. The horse got panicked and run. The driver, he . . . well, he'll be all right, a broken leg, but Miss Berthe . . ."

My eyes grew large. "Madame's daughter. Is she going to be all right?"

The man's head shook. It shook so hard that I didn't need for him to answer. The man fidgeted and put the hat back on his head. He backed out slowly and nodded goodbye. "I'm sorry to bring you bad news. There'll be no party on the fourth of July. It was her birthday." The man turned, and I could hear him mumble as the door was shutting, "Would have been sixteen . . ."

François

From the journal of Y. R. Le Monnier, M.D.

RE: NEW ORLEANS, 1907

Yes. Yes, it was coming back to me. That poor child, that poor woman, Madame Saloy, losing her only daughter after already suffering the loss of her son. She was childless—her children stolen from her, which was a worse fate than had she been barren and never conceived at all.

My heart ached. It churned for her, for no one can bear the death of a child and survive to be the same again.

No one can.

I threw down the cage-maker's letter. I wiped my brow and pulled my housecoat tighter. I felt feverish, sweating and freezing at the same time. Perhaps I was getting pneumonia. I was so foolish to venture into the rain yesterday, and now I was paying for it.

I was reminded of the time I caught fever after the battle of Franklin, 1864. I shivered and burned up in the cold air, sweating and moving myself along as no one else could move me, and Col. John Bell Hood was too persistent to allow rest. I'm not sure how I survived then when so many perished. Youth and dumb luck, I suppose. By now, I'd used up my portion of each.

I rinsed my face and pulled the *Times-Picayune* to my bed. I would climb back in and read from the warmth and safety of the covers.

"Don't call on me today," I warned the world before I pulled a blanket up to my chest.

I became interested in a front page story from Pittsburg, in which a man had murdered his wife and stepson and the next day, the townspeople led by clergy, tore into the prison and pulled him out. They left him hanging from the local bridge but not before holding a prayer meeting. Vigilantes playing the role of God, and not particularly well, I might add.

I looked for news about Andrew Reynaud's murder case, but could find none. His lawyers were still working on the angle of alcoholic insanity, for he did seem to be a dipsomaniac, and I had to admit, I was curious to see if it would work in court. I recalled the story of the French Revolution, as the Marsellais ransacked the King's Chateau, they absconded his treasury of liquors and wine. Their dementia from alcohol, although not relieving the mob from the guilt of its massacre and atrocities, could explain in part, the depth of its madness and depravity.

Andrew's lawyers claimed it would be a quick trial before jury, but the getting to trial part seemed to be a much longer process than imagined.

A painful, lonely Christmas had come and gone, and the New Year had danced in just a week ago. I wasn't expected to meet with Andrew for another two days' time. So far in my examinations, I'd found him to be a sad boy, becoming darker as his stay at the parish prison wore on. The longer one sits in a state of incarceration, the more pronounced any strange thoughts may become. It was why I'd once abhorred the admittance of patients to the city insane asylum for no more reason than a husband putting his wife away as a nuisance or a parent putting in a difficult child with fits. If they were not insane before they entered the door, they may very well be just after.

After reading the financial pages, I closed my eyes and fell fast asleep, having a fitful dream of one of my old asylum patients. I was in the middle of doing the autopsy of an Irishwoman named Sarah who had once sat naked in her cell, her occipital bone jutting out. Right in the middle of the procedure as I studied closely her atrophied organs and softened cerebellum, her dead body splayed out on the cold metal suddenly sat up and screamed, "I told you I was ill!"

I awoke, startled by a noise, and as I prayed it was no caller at my door, I realized the sound was only some distant happening on the street. How long had I been out? I sat up and rubbed my face. I was not so cold any longer. Perhaps I wouldn't fall ill after all.

I sat up and took the paper in my hands once more. I would force myself to get out of bed and get on with my day. I would admit, since Eulalie had left me, I'd had days of melancholy in which getting out of bed was impossible, but today would not be one of them. I was determined to be strong.

I threw my feet over the edge and down into my slippers. I fixed my glasses and went to turn off the light when something caught my eye. It was a name. A jolt in my nervous system. I sat back down and held the paper closer to my eyes, my hands as still as I could muster.

There was a judicial notice, a succession.

It was for Carmelite Reynaud, wife of Ferdinand Kurucar.

Carmelite Kurucar, the sister of Andrew, the girl-bride was dead at sixteen years old?

No. I clutched at my heart. I closed my eyes and winced in quiet rage. I could envision her pretty face, pleading to me. *The curse,* she'd cried. *Is it coming for me?*

I stopped breathing for a moment when down was up and in was out and curses were real—and this one, it seemed, had claimed another life.

And I, the doctor, had been too late.

Letter from François to the Saloys, 1877

Cher M. et Mme. Saloy:

I was sorry to hear of the terrible accident that has befallen your family. I offer you my most sincere condolences in your bereavement. As a token of respect, I am sending a wreath made by my wife, Salome, and although it cannot bring your daughter back, I do hope it shows the respect we have for you.

Yours very truly,

F. Reynaud, cage-maker

Partial letter from François to
Dr. Le Monnier, regarding the year 1877

I stood awkwardly at the foot of the steps of la maison de Saloy, holding the wreath made of wisteria and red roses clipped from the garden of the widow Terrebonne three houses down from my own. Salome had stolen them in the evening, and when I saw her enter the house, arms filled, she had given me a look. Understanding passed between us, and I'd not reprimanded her for it. Her intentions were good, and I loved her very much in that moment.

I touched the notecard tucked into the wreath and reread it. Did it convey how deeply sorry I was? Did it express that I'd thought of nothing else since I'd heard of their misery, and how desperately I wanted to be sure that Madame would survive her grief?

The door opened and the housekeeper appeared. She was not so cheeky this time, and it appeared she'd been crying. Her eyes were swollen and red. "Why, thank you, monsieur," she said. I pushed the wreath forward and into her hands, but the woman stood still. Was she afraid to take the flowers upstairs? Were they gaudy and inappropriate?

"She's here," she said. "If you'd like to see her."

"Madame?" I asked.

"Berthe Therese."

I felt a chill and turned to look behind me. I watched children running in the street. "Ah, well I—"

"Madame Saloy is with her. Alone. I'm sure she'd like to see a friendly face."

This was quite odd, I thought, and although I would like to see Madame and know she was all right, I didn't fancy being with the body of the girl. I'd never done well around bodies. It seemed others had no issue. Other men regarded them with the same reverence as a piece of furniture. Ladies touched their hardened faces. It unnerved me, and I thought for an excuse. I could find none suitable. I could not pass up the opportunity to see Madame without her husband nearby.

"Merci," I said, and I passed through the door and followed the girl into the courtyard and up the stairs. There were pieces of laundry strung up and heating in the sun. On the top floor, I entered the Saloy residence and felt a palpable silence and sadness in the air. I waited at the door as the housekeeper went to retrieve Madame Saloy.

She came from the direction of the bedrooms and when I saw her dressed in black and face pale from sorrow, a lump formed in my throat.

Her eyes found mine from across the room and for a few moments, neither of us could speak a word. Then I set my hat on the rack and approached her carefully, as one might approach an injured bird, fallen from a nest. I reached out my hands and touched hers. She responded by closing her eyes. "I'm truly sorry," I said.

Madame nodded almost imperceptibly and put her arm in mine. She led me to the parlor, and the lovely blue sofa on which she had spun my heart not long ago.

"She was all I had left," said Madame looking at her lace kerchief. She dabbed her eyes. "She loved horses. She loved any living creature, and we thought sending her to the farm in Baton Rouge was the best thing for her. She could be around all the animals she wanted and we wouldn't have to worry about . . ."

I was unsure what to do. I wanted very much to put my arm around her and pull her close to me in sympathy, but I could not. I froze. It seemed I only had met this woman. She had gaily come into my shop. They had commissioned me in their home. I had worked on her cage day after day, and now this. The intimacy of being thrust together at her most vulnerable time made my head swoon. I found the courage to reach over and place my hand on top of hers.

"Please know that if you need anything. Anything at all."

"Thank you, François." She looked at me with eyes glistening with flecks of gold. "I am no stranger to grief."

"No. No I suppose none of us are."

"I lost a son four years ago."

I was struck with such force that I squeezed her hand then pulled away. I thought of my own son at home with his mother, and breathed in deeply, closing my eyes. "*Mon dieu.*"

"His name was Bertrand also. He was so young." Madame stood and walked to the window as if she expected to see him down on the street, playing with the other children. "It was the fever that took him."

The fever. The dreaded yellow fever that plagued this town. I had known many acquaintances who had succumbed in the short time I'd been here.

I could take it no longer. I rose, walked to my benefactor and stood there, inches from her back. I looked down on her hair pulled back in a fashion reminiscent of my mother's, hairpins all tucked in. "What can I do?" I asked meekly. "What can I possibly do?"

My voice quivered, and Madame turned quickly. She buried her face in my chest and sobbed silently. She clutched my coat as her body shook. I could not move, could not breathe, could not bear it. I didn't dare touch her and stood there, arms to my side. I looked behind me to see if the housekeeper or Monsieur Saloy was there, but we were alone.

When Madame grew still, she pulled away and turned from me, wiping her eyes and nose.

"It means so much that you are here," she said. "Please. Won't you come see her? She is still so lovely."

I would follow this woman anywhere. I knew it in that instant.

Madame led the way to the bedroom on the right. I remembered it well, its rosewood furniture set, its pale pink walls. I simply hadn't known it belonged to Berthe Therese. The child was laid upon the bed as if she were only sleeping. Madame went around to the other side and sat in a chair next to her daughter. She reached over and stroked the girl's silken hair and face. I stood in the doorway, unable to come any closer.

"I know it seems we have so much," she said. "But I would give it all away. It's a curse," she whispered, pulling her hand back and tucking in the sheet. "It cannot bring her back. Or my son. It mocks me, the money, remaining and thriving while the people I love are gone." Madame Saloy looked frankly at me. "What I wouldn't do to have never touched his money, for it cannot bring me comfort now. Can it?"

I looked at this woman in her fine mourning clothes in this wealthy home with exquisite furnishings, and the sight of the dead girl before me made my stomach fall.

"Please know that I will stop working on the cage," I said. "It is all right. You needn't—"

"No!" she said, pushing to stand. Madame Saloy stood tall and pushed her skirts aside as she rounded the bed and moved toward me. "You must continue your work, François. I—I long to see something beautiful again. I need to see this house, this monstrosity as something lovely, filled with the sweet song of birds. Please, François. Please continue your work for me." She was pleading, and my heart broke.

"As you wish. I will do whatever you require of me. I am honored to—"

Madame Saloy leaned up on her toes and lightly kissed my left cheek. I backed from the room and walked toward the door for my hat, a man on a mission. There was something I could for Madame after all. And I would do it. I would make the cage even lovelier than it was to be before, because a woman like this deserved to have beauty and song in her life. For a woman like this, there was truly nothing I wouldn't do.

Aside from betraying my wife.

I spied the wreath on the dining room table along with several other arrangements. I said my goodbyes and headed down the stairs with a new sense of purpose and importance to my work. In fact, I'd never felt such worth in all my life.

Madame Saloy was the reason I forgot my insecurities, my frailties, and simply, blessedly, felt like a man with important work to do. In fact, I never counted a single step or cobblestone the whole way back to Rue St. Ann.

François

Letter from François, regarding the year 1877

Dear Doctor Le Monnier,

The funeral of the Saloy child, Berthe Therese, was unlike any I had ever attended. It wasn't the mass at St. Louis Cathedral or the sheer number of attendees that stunned me. It wasn't even the first time I had been to the funeral of a child, witnessing the end of a life taken too early. What was remarkable about this funeral was the immense size of the tomb in Metairie Cemetery and the money that had set it erect.

There were seven marble steps leading up to the tomb entrance. Flanking the stairs on either side were two marble torch-bearers and another female statue on top of the tomb, carrying a book in her left arm and clutching a cross to her chest—carrying knowledge but clinging to faith. Upon the flat stone of the tomb entrance were etched the names of both of the Saloy children, the young Bertrand and now Berthe Therese. The names were so small in comparison to the majestic entombment that it seemed to swallow them up, as if Forever was housed within.

But the tomb was too small for Madame Saloy's grief. She sat rocking slightly in a chair that didn't budge as the marble door was put back into place. Both of her children lay there behind the steps and statues and stone. I watched as she lifted the black kerchief to her face. I couldn't see her eyes from here. She was next to her husband, Bertrand, while I stood several people behind them, holding the hands of my wife and son.

I turned and looked at Felix, a boy too young to be particularly moved or sad on this day. He'd been fidgety in the church and was peering around at all the grievers, studying their pain as if it was the most marvelous curiosity.

I pulled my son close and draped my arm over his chest. I felt for the boy's heart and closed my eyes to the *thump, thump, thump* of it. Suddenly, I had the great urge to flee. To grab my boy and run far, far away from these people and this city where children sometimes expire, but I held firm. I had a job to do. It seemed the birdcage was the only thing to which poor Madame had to look forward.

She would survive. She must. I would see her smile again. I would see to it that she did smile again.

I stared at the back of Madame's head, at her locks pulled up and hidden beneath her hat. To her left was another woman, another hat nodding and bobbing with her sobs. I wondered who she was—family or friend. *Perhaps she would like a cage also,* I said to myself, then horrified at my shameful, inappropriate thoughts, I cleared my throat and turned my head, shaking it as if to dislodge the evil there.

The woman sitting next to Madame Saloy turned to see who was grieving so loudly and when she noticed me, she nodded in agreement as if she, too, understood my pain.

My face flushed. What if someone could hear my thoughts! When had I become the kind of man who could stand at a funeral, watch people weeping with great loss, and wonder which of the lot of them might be my next bill of sale?

"Pardon," I said to my wife, handing Felix to her. I needed to remove myself from this scene. Needed some air. I moved up a gravel walkway and turned my face to the lake. I wanted something to take my mind off of things. I needed to work on that blasted cage, but I remained here, stuck instead in the Saloy's grief.

I looked to a tree and began counting the leaves, and it calmed me. It did. Until, of course, the ceremony was over and Madame came to touch me on the arm.

"Thank you for being here, François. You are so kind."

"I'd be nowhere else," I told her.

Madame attempted something other than a frown, which, at this point seemed otherworldly in courage. Her eyes were red and her skin so pale against the black that surrounded her.

"I'd like you to meet my sister, Madeline Pons. Madeline, this is the talented cage-maker, François Reynaud."

"Madame Pons," I said. "I wish we were to meet under better circumstances."

"Yes, of course," she said.

I could not help but see a small resemblance in the cheekbones, the shape of the face, but seeing her sister made me realize just how well her family features had come together on Madame Saloy's face. I tried to think of something to say, but nothing sounded appropriate in my head. "Yes, well, I remain your servant. Truly, I am sorry for your loss."

"François?" Salome moved in beside me with Felix.

"Madame Saloy, Madame Pons, I would like to introduce you to my wife, Salome, and our son Felix, whom you've met." I nodded at Madame and watched to see her expression as she took in Salome. Madame Saloy was nothing but gracious under the circumstances, as was my wife, but it was while I was studying them that I noticed Madame Pons, the sister, studying *me*. I caught her eye and knew I had betrayed my feelings for Madame Saloy. In an instant, Madeline Pons, the sister, had read quite enough in the looks that passed between us, and as my stomach rose into my chest, I looked away from her gaze, from the one that claimed, *I know you and your little secret now, François.*

And I hold none of the sweetness of my dear sister.

Thankfully, blessedly, we were interrupted just then by a man wearing glasses who claimed to be a physician.

"Dr. Le Monnier," said Madame Saloy. "How kind of you to be here."

"I could not stay away, dear lady. I realize it's been a while, but I want you to know—" here, you took her fair hand in both of yours— "that I am here for you, if ever you'd like to speak again. I can imagine this time is quite difficult for you, losing—" you choked. "Losing another child."

"Thank you, doctor. I may take you up on that."

"She'll be just fine," said Madeline Pons, taking her sister's arm and pulling her away only after she'd given me the evil eye.

François

Saloy tomb at Metairie Cemetery

From the journal of Y. R. Le Monnier, M.D.

RE: NEW ORLEANS 1907

The dead girl's eyes haunted me for twenty-four hours. I saw them when I looked in the mirror as if she were standing just behind me. I saw them when I poured my coffee or stared off into the fire. I saw them in my fitful sleep, those beautiful eyes, never to open again. Carmelite was a child. Sixteen years old, and now she was gone forever.

Had she been cursed? What had I done? What had I not done?

I was pricked at all sides with the feeling that I should have done something, anything to save the girl, though I had no idea how she had died. I'd not seen an obituary at all, no notice of her death, only notice that her money was at stake. According to the judicial ad, her father, Felix, and his eldest daughter, Viola, were petitioning the court to be administrators of her estate. But what about the husband? Where was he? I had too many questions that needed answering. I would visit Andrew in prison a day earlier than planned.

The sheriff was civil but close-lipped as I pleaded my way into the prison unannounced.

The men were at breakfast, he explained, and if I were brave enough, I might have a go at finding him there. He didn't seem the least bit interested in pulling Andrew out and into a guarded room for my protection. Undeterred, I accepted his challenge and walked with a guard back into the cafeteria where dangerous types sat hunched over metal plates, clinking tin cups and laughing maniacally. I'd been used to the sort back at the asylum, but I admit, my brow began to sweat.

Andrew Reynaud was sitting at the end of a table where two men beside him were arm wrestling. The guard put his stick between them and shouted, and they withdrew their arms. Andrew seemed confused when he saw me. He stood up and extended his hand.

"Doctor, it is Wednesday already?"

"No, no, I came a day early. How are you doing?"

"Fine, I suppose. Considering."

"Yes, I am so sorry. I cannot imagine what you're going through."

"Please. Have a seat."

I sat across from him on a bench beside one of the arm wrestlers who was eyeing my pockets as if they had bills or whiskey. I glared at him and he backed away. It was a look I'd mastered at the asylum out of necessity. Sometimes a look speaks louder than words.

I studied Andrew's face for grief but found it not much more grieved than usual.

"It's hell, is what it is," he said. "I wouldn't wish this on my worst enemy."

"I saw no obituary on the paper, and so I was hoping you might be able to tell me how she died. Again, I am so very sorry."

Andrew looked at me as if I was the insane one. His eyes turned angry. "We've been over this," he hissed. "How many times to I have to tell you? I don't want to relive it any more than I have to."

"I'm sorry, I—" It was in that moment that something dawned on me. Something I should have picked up on as soon as I saw him.

"Are we speaking about Doris Sheldon?" I asked.

"Look, I'm not sure what game you're trying to play here, but—" A light bulb seemed to switch on for him. "Ahhh. Ha! Good. Very good. I'm losing my mind, which is the purpose of this visit. Right? My lawyers are still trying to get me to court, but the longer I'm here without a drink, the more sane I get. Maybe they'll slip me a bottle before the trial, then I can show them who I really am. You think that could work, doctor?"

I bit my lip. The boy knew nothing of his sister's death. Suddenly, I questioned myself. Had she really died? Was I in some delusional state? I pulled out yesterday's folded newspaper and set it out before me. I read the words again to be sure of what I was about to say, then I realized I mightn't say anything at all. Andrew was staring down at my paper. I simply turned it around to face him and pointed.

I watched as his eyes squinted then raced back and forth. I watched as he slowly picked up the paper and read and reread the words. His eyes changed and filled with tears, then anger. He couldn't speak.

"I take it you'd not known about this. I am very sorry to be the bearer of bad news."

"No," he whispered. "I don't believe it. Not her. Not Carmelite."

I folded my hands and clasped them, leaning my elbows on the table. The two men beside us had long gone though I hadn't noticed when.

"Andrew, I came here today because I read this and had no idea anything had happened to your sister. I hoped you'd be able to tell me what had happened."

Andrew dropped the paper and put his hands over his face. He rubbed his eyes until I thought he might rub them out. Then he shouted, "She's dead?!"

"You didn't know?" I asked.

He put his hand in front of his mouth and stared at the paper. With muffled voice he said, "Are you telling me my sister is dead?"

"I'm afraid so. Or it appears so. Does it not? I have to admit, I don't understand this. No one has notified you of anything?"

"Bastard!" Andrew slammed his fist down on the table. Rage contorted his face. "You see? You see this? He's after her money. I've known it all along."

"Her husband? Carmelite's husband?"

"No!" he said. "My father!"

"Your father," I stated. And suddenly I regretted very deeply staying in on that rainy day. I should have done what my heart told me I needed to do. I needed to meet the man who had raised a murderer, the man who now had lost his child.

"Your father is after her money?"

"Yes, yes, can't you see? No obituary? He didn't want me to know he's going after the money. Viola's in on it, but poor little Andrew's safely tucked away, now isn't he? He can't do anything from prison. He snarled his lips and cursed him. "I'll show him. I'll show him he can't put me away like this."

"But Andrew," I said, feeling as if I were in a dream. "Your sister is dead. Do you only care about the money? About your hatred for your father?"

"My sister . . . is dead?" he asked. His face changed into that of a sad little boy, as if I'd only just revealed this fact. "How? How did she die?"

"I don't know. I was hoping you might. Was she ill? Was there anything she suffered?"

Andrew pressed his temples as his eyes searched his memory. "No, no, I don't know. I don't think so." He stopped rubbing. "Was she . . . murdered?"

My eyes lit up. I shook my head as I honestly knew nothing.

"Oh, god," he cried. "It can't be."

"Andrew. I know this is a strange thing to say and a very poor choice of timing. But your sister, she came to me."

"Yes. She wanted you to help me."

"Yes, yes she did. But she also asked me for something else." His eyes searched mine. "She asked me to investigate the possibility of a curse. On the money. Just as you had said."

"A curse. On the money. It took my mother. It took my Doris. And now, it's taken my Carmelite." He seemed to stop breathing, and I watched as he turned purple.

"I don't believe in such things," I said emphatically. "I don't."

"Then why do you bring it up?" he pleaded.

"I—I'm not sure," I said, putting my head down and closing my eyes. "I'm not sure why I brought it up. I need—I think it's time to speak to your father."

"Or maybe her husband killed her. I never trusted that stupid boy. He was only after her money."

I stood and eased my way out from the table. I called a guard over and motioned that I was ready to go. Regrettably, I'd gotten nothing from our encounter, but I'd sent the boy into some sort of mental state, and his paranoia and delusion of persecution was becoming more pronounced.

"I'm terribly sorry about your sister," I said. "If I learn anything, I'll be sure to let you know."

I walked away from the man, knowing how helpless he felt. He'd been put away and stripped of any freedoms. In taking the life of his lover, he'd given away his rights to watch over the affairs of the ones he truly loved. And now, another one was dead.

From the journal of Y. R. Le Monnier, M.D.

RE: NEW ORLEANS, 1877

A Frenchman died in my care on September 29, 1877. He'd been working on a ship and had mistaken a glass of carbolic acid for claret wine. I was called in to give him antidotes, but there was no hope. He expired two hours later, suffering a painful, horrendous death. It never gets easier to watch.

Exhausted and in need of a stiff drink, I refused the offer of a ride home and decided to walk. I wanted to stroll by the Le Monnier mansion, now the Saloy house, and see how it looked at night. I also wanted to wind down so as not to wake up my poor wife and the baby when I returned home. Little René was not sleeping through the night yet, and both Eulalie and I were out of sorts from fatigue.

Although I was not a believer in ghosts or anything of the sort, as a believer in God and all that was good, I recognized there was also real evil. I hurried past the LaLaurie house at 1140 Rue Royale, for I never dawdled there. It gave me chills. My father had told me the story of that house, and it had never left me. In the 1820s and 30s when my grandfather lived in the mansion on Rue Royale, there were many prosperous neighbors to build up houses on the same street. One such couple further north seemed to be the epitome of New Orleans hospitality, and in fact, my grandfather had been to their house for a party. Little did he know what secrets were held in that house, for years later after my grandfather's death, it was discovered that Madame LaLaurie had been mutilating and torturing her slaves in an upstairs room. One of them was pushed off a balcony to her death, and scores of others were found tied up in a wretched state when suspicions were aroused. No one knew the number that had been murdered in that home and ghost or no, I chose to steer clear of blatant evil whenever possible.

As I found myself getting closer to the Saloy house, I watched as the home's full beauty shone in the moonlight. The fourth floor was imposing and stood much higher than all the rest. It was late yet, but there were lights on in the upstairs apartment. The Saloys were awake. It had been two months since they'd buried their daughter, Berthe Therese, and I could only imagine that it was hard to sleep experiencing that sort of grief.

Part of me felt like a peeping Tom, but the other part was overcome with sadness. Was I here to look at the house that still held a part of my soul, or was I here in hopes of seeing that Madame Saloy was all right and surviving?

I realized, strangely, it had become the latter. I felt sympathy for these people, more sympathy than antipathy for their abominable fourth story.

I watched a shadow move in one of the upstairs windows and hoped I was not standing in any light where I would be seen. I willed Madame with my mind, *come see me for help, dear one.* But I was not sure if she had heard. I walked away, tired now and ready to sleep. I said a short prayer for Madame and her husband Bertrand, and for the poor French sailor who'd gone to his grave this evening, as my heavy feet found their way home.

The next morning in my office, I sat waiting for my first patient when I heard a knock at my door. My wife answered it, and my heart leapt thinking it might be the Saloys, but there was only a strange man standing there.

From the clinical notebook of Y. R. Le Monnier, M.D.

THE BIRD CAGE-MAKER, 1877, FIRST CLINICAL MEETING

An unexpected visitor arrived at roughly ten thirty. He put off his hat and showed thick black hair and a neatly groomed goatee. I stood and came forward to him as he put out his hand. "*Bonjour*," he said. "I hope I am not disturbing." His voice was thick with French accent. "I met you two months ago at the funeral of the Saloy child, Miss Berthe Therese. My name is François Reynaud."

"Yes," I said, recognizing him slightly. "And how do you know the Saloys?"

"I am a cage-maker. I am making a cage for them, a replica of their home."

"The Le Monnier mansion?" I asked, eyebrows raised.

"*Oui. Mon dieu.* Le Monnier? Is it the same, Dr. Le Monnier?"

"Yes, my grandfather. Tell me, what brings you here today?"

"Well, I—" He looked over to my wife and put his head down.

"Eulalie, would you please go make us some coffee?"

"Of course," she smiled sweetly and walked off, leaving us alone.

"I do have a patient coming in soon. It seems they are late."

"I see. I am sorry to have bothered you."

"You're trembling," I said. "Are you ill?" Tears welled up in his eyes, and he looked at me desperately.

"I am sick in the heart," he said. "And I don't know what to do. I have become so nervous. I cannot sleep. I cannot eat."

"Oh, my, maybe you should have a seat." I went to go grab my stethoscope.

"No. It's not that. It's . . . the other heart sickness."

I stood there, trying to take in this man, this dark creature. "Love?" I asked.

"*Oui. Je pense.*" And then he broke down crying.

What I was able to glean from him in the next several minutes was that he had been hired to build a cage for the Saloys for quite a sum of money. He had taken it on reluctantly, but soon found himself thinking of Madame Saloy all the time. He put it off to brotherly love as Monsieur Saloy was quite an ox. But soon, he realized he could not stop thinking of her, even when he was with his wife. He was torn by this sin, being somewhat of a religious Catholic, who knew the dire consequences of what he was telling me.

"You must help me," he said. "You must give me something that makes me go back to the way I was. Now that Madame has been grieving for her daughter, it is all I can do. I cry when I think of her. My wife does not know what is wrong, but she knows something is very wrong. I don't know what to say."

"I understand these are very real feelings, Monsieur Reynaud, but . . . tell me. When will this cage be done?"

He looked at me with alarm and whispered. "I've just finished it last night." He put his hands on his face. "*C'est complet*, and now . . . now I must give it to them."

"There now, you see? You can hand it over, and the work will be done. What you need to do is remove yourself from the lives of the Saloys. Then you may be able to get back to some semblance of your former life."

"Yes but—" he rang his hands. "I do not want it to be over. I do not want to remove myself from her." He looked at his shoes. "I thought of breaking the cage this morning. I thought of dropping it on the floor, my beauty, my creation I've worked so hard for. I thought that if it was broken I would need more time to fix it, and there would be more time for me to . . ."

"To see Madame Saloy."

My goodness, I was trying not to form judgments in my mind. I did not know this man, and I only knew Madame Saloy from our brief encounter, but he certainly seemed amorously insane.

"Tell me. Does Madame share your feelings?"

"I don't know." He shook his head. "I cannot live this way any longer. I cannot live so torn and tormented."

Was the man before me suicidal? I thought of placing him down at the asylum, but something held me back. "Please, Monsieur Reynaud, I assure you it may help you to talk about this with someone. Me, perhaps. I would be very interested in having you come back to me on a regular basis if you like. You may come and sit and talk about these things until you are feeling better. I may also be able to prescribe something for you, to settle your nerves."

A small glimmer of hope came into his eyes, and he put his hands out and shook mine vigorously. "*Merci, merci*, Dr. Le Monnier. I would like that."

My nine o'clock appointment finally arrived, and Monsieur Reynaud said goodbye and shuffled down the steps and into the street. He looked back behind him and waved to me, then headed down St. Joseph Street like a man unsure of which direction to go.

Partial letter from François, regarding the year 1877

On the day I was to present the birdcage to the Saloys, there was a rumbling in my ears as if a train was coming. I was completely distraught, hammer in hand, considering doing the unimaginable. I was a creator, not a destroyer, but something had changed in me. There was a desperation that ran through my veins, the likes of which I had never known before.

The wood was polished to a deep shine, and the cage stood there looking so beautiful in my studio, I almost had to avert my eyes. It sat on a four-legged frame I had carved to match perfectly, exquisitely. It was majestic with its turquoise shutters and towering four stories, and seeing it there before me made me weak. I was not only seeing the cage, I was experiencing the memories. Of her.

I could envision my first meeting with Madame Saloy. I could remember my eagerness to tell the Saloys I was no man to be bought. I saw the eyes of Bertrand, so steadfast in his mockery of me. But now, what would these eyes show? Would they still mock me? Surely, the cage was not worth the amount of money I would be paid in the end, but I had put everything into it, I could say honestly—blood, sweat, tears, and soul.

The Saloy carriage arrived at half past nine. Large black horses breathed swirls around me. The coachman descended and faced me. I stood still. For a few moments I did not move, could not speak. How was it that this day had come?

"It will take the two of us," I told him. My heart was pounding. He followed me into the studio, which looked so dark as my eyes tried to adjust from the sunlight. "Please be careful."

"Of course, sir."

The Negro's eyes took in the Saloy's cage. "You done this?"

I nodded.

"Sure be something." Those were the last words he spoke to me as we lifted the cage and carried it outside into the sunshine, laying it on a blanket in the floor of the carriage. The stand was next. I retrieved it myself, and then locked up my studio. I closed my eyes and said a prayer to God to help me. I was not sure he heard me for I'd never felt him so far away.

I had thought long and hard about the circumstances of my presentation. Would it be a quiet, private moment when no one but Madame Saloy was home? Would it be just the two of them and Carrie, the housemaid? Or would it be a much grander affair, a party, a celebration?

Honestly, I couldn't imagine which would be worse. All of them ended my contract with the Saloys. Each of them severed my ties with Madame.

Salome had kissed me on the cheek before I'd left home that morning. I could see she was looking forward to the final payment, but there was more than that. She was eager to see me done with this cage, this creature that had crawled up under my skin. She could see this cage was different. I told her the pressures of working under commission were just too much for me. It was the precise reason I did not take commissions, nor would I ever again, I told her. I hoped she bought this excuse, poor as it was, and that she could not surmise the true source of my melancholy.

Miss Carrie met the coachman at the door. "They're all upstairs," she said.

"All?" I asked.

"Mmm hmm. Pretty much everybody. Miz Madeline, Mister Antonio, all the children. Where's the cage?"

My heart jumped. All of her family would be there. This was to be the big presentation, the great unveiling. I firmed my shoulders and entered the carriage again. Behind the curtain, I wrapped the stand in a blanket and covered the cage. It would be a complete surprise. I wanted to see her face the instant she saw it. I felt as if I would see her true feelings then. Not only of the cage, but of me.

"Out of the way!" Bertrand bellowed at his nieces and nephew when we walked in the door of the fourth story. His eyes were large like a child's. It was clear he was excited to see my work after so many months of waiting. I looked around for Madame Saloy, but saw her nowhere. I panicked a little, but hid this feeling as Bertrand showed us where we would set it up. We entered the oval dining room and moved over to the windows where the other bird cages had been shoved to make room. The children followed us in, giggling. "Back, back!" Bertrand scolded. The children pressed themselves up against the walls in obedience. There was one boy and five girls. The adults entered the room and stayed in the doorway.

"Monsieur?" said Bertrand holding out his hand. I shook it.

"The day is finally here," I said, attempting a smile. "Is Madame absent?"

"No, no. Carma!" he bellowed. "The cage is here. Come in, come in!"

I stood there next to the coachman by the window. We had set the cage on the stand, yet both were veiled and not an inch could be seen. I tried to catch my breath. I waited, head turned toward the door. "You've met my brother-in-law, Antonio Carcano?" said Bertrand.

"I'm not sure I've had the pleasure," I said. I left my post and moved to the large dark man. He was clearly Italian or Spanish, and rough as a man who works outdoors. I shook his hand. "Carmelite's brother," he said to me.

"I see. Very good to meet you."

"Antonio works at the Spanish Fort. He's the bridge keeper."

"Is he? What an interesting position." The man refused my offer for idle talk and stayed quiet.

"And Carmelite's sister, Madeline," said Bertrand. "Carma! What is taking her so long?"

Madeline took me in. "We've met," she said. "At the funeral."

"How do you do," I said.

"I do very well," she said. "It appears you do, too."

The look in her eye unnerved me. What was she implying? How did I do well? In my cage-making? With the money I would be given? With her sister?

"Ah, there she is. It's about time. Come in, let's have a look!" Bertrand held onto his wife. I could not approach her. She was precious like porcelain, wearing a dainty yellow dress that made me feel as if sitting in sunshine. It was so different than the black she'd been mourning in. My mood lifted instantly, and I marveled at her magical powers over me.

"*Bonjour*, Madame," I said, tipping my hat, then I set it on the table, remembering my manners.

"Quiet, quiet, everyone," said Bertrand as he got their attention. "Now. I hired Monsieur Reynaud several months ago at the request of my beloved wife, to build a birdcage for us." Suddenly, his tone changed. "No one could have anticipated that we would lose our—" his voice cracked. "Our sweet Berthe Therese." All heads went down, and Madame closed her eyes. "But this cage is something Carma has been looking forward to. And I'm now very happy I hired you, François, because . . . well . . . let's get on with it."

106

"Yes, of course. It is my pleasure. Madame? Monsieur Saloy? May I present to you, La Maison Saloy."

Slowly and carefully I pulled the blankets off the stand and cage, and I heard audible gasps. All I cared about was Madame's reaction. I watched her from across the room in Bertrand's arms. Her eyes opened and eyebrows went up. She broke free from him and walked slowly toward the cage around the table as if in a trance, fixated. The rest of the room grew silent as she reached her hands out and touched the wood frame. She bent to her knees, and appeared a little girl playing with a doll house. Her lips parted and I barely breathed. She ran her fingers along the bars, along the window sills, the shutters, and chills went down my spine as if her fingers were touching me. Then she stood, and her hand rested on the fourth floor outside the window of the room that was her daughter's. She saw it then, the thing I'd added just for her. It was a hand-carved and painted rocking horse with an angel riding its back, sitting there in the room where Miss Berthe Therese's bed would have been. Tears streamed down Madame's cheeks, and I found I was tearing up myself.

"Oh, François," she cried. Then she finally looked at me. I handed her a kerchief from my vest, and she squeezed my hand when she took it. "It's the most beautiful thing I've ever seen. Ever." She turned. "Bertrand?"

He came forward and stood in front of the cage, hands down at his side. He put a hand on Madame's hair and leaned forward, adjusting his glasses. I could hear my heartbeat in my ears as he looked over the cage. I could see he was impressed, but what would he say?

He said nothing. Bertrand put his hand out to shake mine, then cleared his throat.

"Isn't it lovely?" asked Madame. "Look at this house, the details. And did you see—"

"Yes, I see it." Bertrand reached in his coat pocket and drew out a check. He unfolded it and handed it to me. "That's quite a talent you have," he said. Then he retreated, and the others rushed over to see. "Don't touch it!" Bertrand warned the children before he left the room.

The rest of the event was a blur. There were cakes and cookies offered with tea, bourbon for the men. Madame and her sister kneeled down like children, pointing and petting the cage. At one point, Madame pulled me aside and kissed me on the cheek. I must have melted or flown away. When we parted, I was so sullen, I was nearly in tears. "Why are you so sad?" Madame Saloy asked me. "You're brilliant! I could not be more pleased with your work."

I shook my head. "Nothing pleases me more," I told her.

"Then what?"

"I—it's just that I, well, I've enjoyed getting to know you . . . and Bertrand. Now that the cage is finished, this chapter is *finis*. It's—"

"Over? Don't be silly, François. She put her arm in mine and walked me to the door. "You are not just a cage-maker to me, you know this."

I looked in her eyes, one to the other. Could she be saying what I thought she was saying? Did she love me? Did she return my feelings?

"You have become a friend. Cage or no cage, you're quite stuck with the Saloys."

If I could have run through the apartment screaming and flailing my arms, jumping out the window with joy, I would have, but instead, I stayed still and intact.

"We're having a little party for Madeline's oldest daughter next weekend. We'd love for you to bring your family." She turned. "Isn't that right, Madeline?"

She was standing nearby, acting as if she hadn't been eavesdropping, but it was apparent she had been. "What?"

"I've just invited François and his family to Carmelite's party."

"Carmelite?" I asked.

"Ah, yes," said Madeline. "Each of us, Antonio and myself, named our first-born daughters after our sister, the great and beautiful Carmelite. She's the bright light of the family, you know. The one who did well for herself, the savior of the Carcanos."

I sensed bitterness behind her words and looked to Madame. She pursed her lips. "Madeline," she scolded then turned to me. "The party is here next Saturday at three. I do hope Salome and Felix can come as well?"

"Of course," I said. Then I left the home, the house, the cage. I'd become so intimate with it all, I could imagine exactly where Madame was standing in the cage as I walked away, over cobblestones and sidewalks, past houses and cafés, saloons and markets, as I swam back to my studio that now stood empty and bare. I dusted off a bottle of Bordeaux from my cabinet and poured a glass. I sipped and sat at my piano, something I'd not played since I'd begun the Saloy cage. There was a check for a hefty sum of money in my pocket, but more than that, I was rich with emotion. I would see Madame Saloy again. I would stay in her life, it was clear now. And as my fingers hit the keys it was as if all of a sudden the birds began to sing for the first time, anywhere. Ever.

François

From the journal of Y. R. Le Monnier, M.D.

On my way to see poor Carmelite's father, the birds sang the strangest songs. I'm not sure what tuned my ears in to them, but I found it hard not to listen. First there was a chattering as if the sky itself was excited, then birds swooped down around me into trees, and one called to the other and back again. I felt as if they were speaking to me. What were they saying? *Watch it. Watch it. Over there. Over there.* I shook my head and swatted at nothing. The birds were not speaking to me! I pulled a flask from my pocket and calmed my nerves.

What would I say to this man who didn't know me from Adam? I would tell him I was monitoring his son for signs of insanity. That I was there on official business, assisting in his son's defense. But in asking him about Carmelite's passing, I would have to tell him about my relationship with her—how his daughter was the one who had approached me on Andrew's behalf.

I stopped in the middle of the street, cobblestones all around me. Would he think I was there collecting the money she'd never had the chance to pay me? Ridiculous. I was not going there to ask for money, nor would I accept it. I had taken on the assignment as a favor to the girl, and as a man of my word, I would honor it. It was no fault of her own that she was . . . well, no longer.

After an invigorating forty minute walk, the sky turned a brilliant blue as I rounded the corner of North Robertson St. and approached the house of Felix Reynaud. It was a narrow two-story Victorian with a balcony off the front. I climbed the brick steps, knocked on the door, and waited, looking about me. I knocked again, harder. There was no answer, no movement on the other side of the door.

"He's at work," said a voice, thick with German accent. I looked to the house next to me, to an old man sitting on the front stoop. He was smoking a pipe. "He's not home."

"At work," I said. "Yes, of course. He . . ." I looked left and right down the street.

"It's that way," he motioned. "On Gravier. The Continental."

"Oh yes, I remember it well. Thank you."

I turned and met the street again. The walk had been brisk. I was no longer a young man, but cared not. I would waste no time. I was intent on getting face to face with this man. First I would give my condolence, and then I'd try to get to bottom of the death of his daughter, young Carmelite. How could she die so soon?

The Continental Hotel was nicely kept with marble floors and columns and a long counter where one could register for a room. My eye scanned the lobby for Monsieur Reynaud. I'd never met him nor seen a photograph, yet I felt as if I would know what he looked like from knowing his father, his daughter, his son.

"Pardon, Monsieur," I said to the bellman, "I am looking for Felix Reynaud."

He looked confused for a moment. "Reynaud, Reynaud . . . no. Sorry."

"Are you sure? Someone told me he worked here."

He grimaced. "You can check the saloon. Maybe they know him there." He pointed me to a set of grand doors that led to a room filled with café tables and a long bar. A large mirror stretched along the wall behind the barkeep, lined with rows and rows of liquor on dark wood shelves. At this time of day, there were only a few drinkers in the establishment—a business meeting, no doubt, between two well-dressed men, and another lone fellow smoking a cigar and reading the *Times-Picayune*.

"What'll it be," said the man behind the bar. He was wiping wet glasses clean. It appeared I'd caught him at an off moment for he seemed annoyed that I might like a drink.

"Nothing for me, no, I was just hoping you could tell me where I could find a man by the name of Felix Reynaud."

The man with the newspaper set it down and looked at me.

"Who's asking?" said the barkeep.

"My name is Dr. René Le Monnier. I've . . . private business with him." The man studied me with steely eyes, and then he looked back down at the glass he was holding and finished wiping it clean. He stacked it neatly on the others, careful not to topple them. He threw the napkin over his shoulder, and I thought I'd lost him, that he was ignoring my request. But suddenly he reached behind him. He brought over a bottle of scotch and pulled two shot glasses from beneath the bar. He poured the drinks and shoved one to me. The other, he lifted to his lips. It wasn't even noon.

"I'm Felix Reynaud," he said just before he downed the liquor. My eyes opened. Yes, I could see it, the lock of dark hair at his forehead, the mustache thick above his full lips, a brow of consternation.

I found myself unable to speak. "Go ahead," he told me. "It's on the house. This is my saloon."

I could not insult the man. I picked up the pale shot of amber and let it burn my throat. Fumes wafted to my ears, and I felt my courage returning.

"Mr. Reynaud, it is a pleasure to meet you. I . . . I know your son."

"My son?" He turned and rinsed his shot glass in a tub of water and set out to dry it again. "And how do you know my son?"

"I've been visiting him at the prison. He's planning on pleading innocence due to insanity. I am a bit of an expert on the matter."

"Insanity?" He scoffed. "My son is a drunk."

"Yes, well."

"And he deserves to be in there. He's been trouble since the day he was born. Is this why you came to see me? Did Andrew send you here? Some sort of familial study? Perhaps insanity runs in the family, I see."

"No, nothing like that, I assure you." I licked my lips and felt the warmth of the scotch in my belly. I reached into my pocket and pulled out the *Times-Picayune* ad, the one regarding Carmelite Kurucar's estate. I set it on the bar and turned it for him to see. "I am also acquainted with your daughter, Mrs. Kurucar."

He swallowed and seemed to hide something behind his eyes. Was he tearing up?

"Come," he said, sighing. "Let's have a seat." He walked around the bar and pointed to a table in the corner as far away from the patrons as possible.

"My daughter," he said slowly. He squeezed his eyes shut as if in pain. "My daughter is dead."

I was surprised at how much it affected me to hear those words. I felt my heart racing and pulled out a kerchief to wipe my brow. I adjusted my seat. "I gathered that much from the newspaper," I said. "I'm very sorry. What happened to the poor girl?"

He shook his head. "I don't know. I don't know. She seemed fine, healthy, a spitfire, really. Last spring, she ran off with that boy and married him, Ferdinand. I was angry, as any father would be, but I never thought . . ."

"Was it an accident?" I asked.

"No, no, it was last Thursday. She was at her home on North Rampart Street. I had just come to visit her. I was trying to make peace with them both. We are family, after all. Soon after, she . . . she took to her bed, complaining of a stomach ache." He closed his eyes. "I was not with her

111

when she passed, but Ferdinand was. He described how she convulsed and writhed in pain. I cannot—"

"My god," I said. "Have you done an autopsy? I know the coroner—"

Mr. Reynaud held up his hand and stopped me. "It's too late, she's already . . . . The doctor had said it was something like ureic convulsions."

"Uraemic convulsions? I see." My mind was reeling. What had happened to the child? Had she been ill? Could she have been poisoned? "Forgive me, but I am trying to make sense of this. I saw the young girl just last week and she seemed the picture of health."

"Last week?" he asked. "What business would you have with her?"

"She had come to me to help your son, her brother. She was concerned for him." I studied the man for emotion. He sucked his teeth and looked out the window at a passing carriage and great black horse. "May I ask, why you've not told Andrew about his sister's death?" I said. "They seemed quite close."

"I . . . I have no son," he told me. "My son is dead to me. My daughter is dead. My wife is dead. I only have Viola and Gladys now, and Viola has her own life with her husband." He cleared his throat and stood when a man walked into the saloon through the door on Gravier. "I've got a customer," he said.

"Yes, of course." I stood and watched as he poured the man a glass of bourbon and took his money. In passing, I put my hat back on and waited until I caught his attention. I could see his eyes on me in the mirror.

"I am very sorry for the loss of your daughter," I said quietly, putting a hand on the bar. "But I will not give up on your son. He seems a decent boy."

I turned and walked out of the saloon, feeling his gaze heavy upon my back. When I reached the street, I shuddered. Was I further from knowing the truth of the so-called curse that befell this family, or closer? Perhaps I'd gained no ground at all. The child was still dead, her brother still in prison, and darkness seemed to shroud New Orleans like a mother mourning in the bright light of day.

New Orleans Item, 1877

CITY INTELLIGENCE HELD TO BAIL.

Bertrand Saloy and J. B. Morales were yesterday brought up before Recorder Baldwin for examination on the charge of assaulting and knocking several chips off from Max Block. Saloy was considered rather innocent, and discharged, but Mr. Morales was required to find bail for his good behavior for the next six months.

From the journal of Y. R. Le Monnier, M.D.

RE: NEW ORLEANS, 1877

In reading the *New Orleans Item* one morning, I was struck dumb. Bertrand Saloy had been arrested for assaulting a man in the Second Municipality. The other fellow involved received a stiffer sentence, but Bertrand had gotten off easily due to his money, no doubt.

It was understandable, was it not? He'd lost his only daughter. Grief reshapes a man into a slightly less recognizable creature, sometimes for the better, but more often than not, into something less desirable. I'd read how he'd become more overt in his court cases. It seemed he was taking everyone to court or shoving them out of their property. He'd become much more visible and definitely less benevolent and benign.

How was Madame Saloy faring in all of this? I didn't have to wonder long for my cage-maker, François Reynaud, paid me an unusual visit. It had been quite some time since I'd seen him in person. Usually, I only heard the clatter of his letter as it dropped through the mail slot every Thursday at 3 pm sharp. He told me he was suffering melancholy from creator's block—now that the Saloy cage was complete, he found he could no longer find the inspiration to begin a new cage—something which had never happened to him. My face reddened as I thought of the stack of unopened letters in my drawer. I had no idea what had gone on with this man or with the Saloys in ages. But I pretended as well as I could.

"Perhaps you'd like a stimulant," I offered. "It may spark your creative juices again. I've got one that is served in a tea."

He declined and explained that he'd begun to take tea with Madame Saloy in her home on Rue Royale at least once per week. Bertrand would be out at the horse races or doing business, and there François would be, in Bertrand's home, having tea with his wife.

"I sincerely advise against these meetings," I told him, but to no avail. François claimed that Madame had become more and more withdrawn, and he felt it his duty to look after her, to be sure she would not fall in to the pit of despair.

"I must tell you that I dislike Madame's sister, Madeline, very much," he said. "We attended a party for her daughter, and I studied the woman. She seems to have two faces, one for her sister, very flattering and pleasant, and another full of jealousy behind her back. Her home was very humble and her children, ill-mannered. They flocked around Madame Saloy and begged her for candy and trinkets. And the worst part—Madame succumbed to their requests.

"Madeline made it very clear with her eyes that she didn't approve of my being there, nor did she like the way my son took up with her brother Antonio's daughter, Carmelite. Although they'd only just met, they played together as if they'd grown up side by side." He paused and smiled a little. "Madame made sport of the way my Felix was fixated on her niece. She said if she didn't know better, it seemed to be love at first sight." He fiddled with his fingernail then seemed to forget he was sitting before me, lost in his thought.

"We've gotten a bit side-tracked, I'm afraid," I said. "About the sister, Madeline. Do you feel you must protect Madame Saloy from her?"

"In a way, I suppose I do. I don't trust her. I've not seen her since the party, but I hear about her nonetheless. Madame, it seems, feels sorry for her sister and has offered to pay for schooling for each of her children."

"That seems a familial thing to do, seeing as she has all this money to spend."

"But it's the way her sister plays the pauper. I believe she's using Madame's grief for her own gain."

"That sounds a bit extreme," I said. "Imagine if someone were to offer to pay for your son's education."

"She has," he whispered. "Madame offered the same to me—can you believe this? I—" His face flushed, and he stifled a smile. "But of course, I would not accept it. She is mourning the loss of her child. She will do anything to help another child. It's the only way she has to deal with her suffering."

I pushed back in my chair and smiled at François. "And now, who has become the doctor? That's very astute of you."

"I cannot help it. I am getting to know her more. I am learning to understand her more than I understand myself."

"And your wife?"

"What about her?"

"What does she think of these teas you're taking with Madame Saloy?"

"She doesn't know about them. Nor will she."

114

"Philosophically, morally, you have no issue with this deceit?" I asked him.

"Deceit?" He looked at me as a child might when not getting the ice cream he so desired. "There is nothing deceitful about our relationship. It is pure. You know that. She needs me." He was long gone into deceiving himself, and it was apparent that nothing I could say would change this. I continued to listen but I made a marked attempt to remain detached, to give fewer pieces of advice that would only be ignored. The insane do not know they are insane. They believe they are justified in every thought, every action. To impose rational order or absolute truths into such a skewed reality only makes the doomed messenger an enemy.

I worried he might show up again in person, but he did not. Instead, François reverted to the letter-through-the-slot therapy which suited us both as I began to get much busier in my private practice. I also became involved with the insane asylum and was hired to be the attending physician there. My letters from François became fewer and farther between, and compared to the others in the asylum, he was beginning to look quite sane.

And then there was the yellow fever.

In 1878, I left Eulalie and our son for Memphis. There was an outbreak of yellow fever so severe that hundreds were dying. I understood this disease more than those around me for I'd given talks to the board of health about it. I'd written in publications about it. I had to be the one to go, knowing full well I might not come back, just as I had done in the war. It was my duty.

It was a sacrifice well worth it, for I did return and was able to ease the suffering of many in that poor city. I came home to New Orleans with even more knowledge of the disease and how to fight it. I was becoming quite prominent in important circles. I was very well-liked and respected in town—as my father and his had been—and soon found a component of society wanting me to run for city coroner as my father had done.

As a child, I had always respected my father and the work that he did. This is why I went to medical school and chose to practice medicine like my ancestors had done. But being coroner was never something I aspired to do. When I was old enough to read the newspaper, I followed along with my father's inquests into murders and other unfortunate deaths for the sole reason of wanting to be near to my father. To know him more. I loved him with all my heart and longed to see him, for he stayed away much of the day and night.

One evening, when my father awoke to a knock at the door summoning him to the scene of a crime, I begged him to take me with him. I was ten or eleven at the time. My mother was still sound asleep, and my father only relented because he didn't want my whining to wake her.

I rode with my father through the night air to a place by the river. There were three men there with lanterns. They shook my father's hand and then held the light of fire over the swollen, water-logged body of a Negro man. I wanted to turn away, but I couldn't. I watched as my father touched the man. When we arrived at the coroner's office, the men lifted the corpse onto a hard metal table. My father asked me to leave the room, but I could not do that either. I stood there and watched with part curiosity, part horror as he studied every inch of his naked body. The cuts, the contusions. And then the scalpel to open him up.

I do not know why my father allowed me to see this. Perhaps he thought I was old enough. Perhaps he was so deadened to the sight that he could not understand its impact on virgin eyes. I never thought I would be able to shake what I had seen from my mind and had nightmares for a week after. My mother was angry with my father and secretly I swore I would never, ever take on a job such as that when I got older.

And yet, at age thirty-seven, I found myself adding my name to the ballot. Le Monnier for Coroner. Just as it had been with my father. I won the position but not without a contest. My opponent, Dr. Beard, went to the papers claiming election fraud, and I found myself fighting for the title I never desired, simply because he was insulting my honor and the honor of those who carried my name before me.

In 1881, the nameplate outside the door of the coroner's office on St. Louis Street between Burgundy and Rampart read *Dr. Yves René Le Monnier II.* I opened body after body. I determined causes of death and wound up sitting on the witness stand for cases too numerous to name. At home, Eulalie and I were smitten with the small boy who'd stolen our hearts, our son René, now a bright, precocious four-year old. I had repeated the previous generation and saw myself in the lad. Would he someday grow up to be a doctor like his father, his grandfather, his great-grandfather and so on? Would he, too, become coroner and spend his days piecing together mysteries of the dead? Did I want that for him? Would I wish such a thing on another?

It was hard for me to shake the anxiety I would bring to bed with me. I was afraid I would lose my son. It was irrational; I knew this and realized perhaps the patients at the asylum were having some regretful effect on me, their fears and sadness leaving some lingering residual on my skin. When I closed my eyes at night, I saw images of my son and of the corpses I dealt with. Sometimes I could not stop my mind from replacing the face of one of those bodies with the face of my own son. I began to take bromides to aid in my sleep. The demands of my job were beginning to wear on me. Eulalie spoke to me sweetly of her concern—I was working too much and too hard, spending too much time at the asylum.

But then the very worst imaginable happened.

From the journal of Y. R. Le Monnier, M.D.

RE: NEW ORLEANS, 1907

I could not take it any longer. I shoved my notes onto the floor and stood, feeling dizzy. I needed to get out of the house. I would not read another word this day. I'd been writing my book on Shiloh and researching my old notes, old letters, trying to determine some more information about a curse that lingered on Andrew Reynaud's family. I'd not left the house in two days. What was I doing, rehashing all of this misery?

Donning my coat and hat, I locked the door behind me and headed to the newsstand three blocks away. I would take my paper in the café and not return home for a very long time. If ever. I was sick it of it there, the rooms filled with their dark emptiness.

I paid the boy my money and took my folded newspaper down the block to the café. With a strong cup of coffee and a beignet, I meandered along the pages, trying desperately to forget anything about my research, anything about the past. A section of my paper flew to the floor with the breeze and skittered across to land beneath a chair. As I reached to get it, another man's hand was there as well. I looked to my right to see who was attached and there, before me, was an old man, but not just any. Age or no, I would recognize that face anywhere.

"*Bonjour*, Dr. Le Monnier," said François Reynaud, the birdcage-maker. He was here before me at long last. My mouth dropped open. Decades dissipated between us.

"*Bonjour*," I said, stunned. We did not shake hands. How could I shake hands with a ghost? I wondered if my mind had conjured him.

"I hope you don't mind, I followed you here. It has been many years, has it not?"

"It has indeed," I said, though in my mind it felt as if he'd never left. I'd spent my recent weeks reading his intimate letters from thirty years ago. He'd been living and breathing before me for days.

"I think it is time for us to talk," said the cage-maker. "I know my granddaughter, Carmelite, came to see you."

"I am very sorry for your loss," I said. "She seemed a lovely girl."

"She was. And you are no stranger to loss, yourself," he told me. I stiffened and closed my eyes. *Go away. Go away,* I wished.

"I know she asked you for help with her brother," said the cage-maker, "but I assure you, there is more you need to know. I believe my granddaughter was afraid."

"Yes, she seemed to be," I said. "She had mentioned her belief in a curse on your family or on the money which your family received from the Saloy fortune."

"There is no curse," he said.

"There isn't?"

"No. There cannot be. If there was such an evil, the culprit would be myself. I'm the one who became involved with the Saloys. If there is a curse, one birdcage altered the future for my family. It doomed us. And now my granddaughter is dead."

"It sounds as if you do believe in a curse."

His eyes searched mine long and hard before he spoke. "I need to tell you about my son, Felix."

"We've met," I told him. I spoke with him yesterday at his saloon."

"So you've seen him," he said. "You . . . know he can be difficult?"

"A bit. He seems to harbor some strong feelings about his son and the predicament he's in."

Monsieur Reynaud looked down at his hands. "He's after the money," he said.

"The money," I repeated, dumbfounded.

"His own child is dead, but my son is after her money."

"How can you know this? He's upset," I stated. "You're upset. Every man grieves in his own way." I gathered up the newspaper and pushed to rise to my feet. "I'm sorry, but I'm afraid I've got to be getting back."

I reached my hand out to shake his. He took it and held it for an extra moment.

"Yes, I understand. May I call on you again?" he asked. He was taller and thinner than I'd remembered. There was no curse. This man had told me as such. I felt the deep pull to break away from him, from his family. I wanted nothing more to do with them, with their insanity. I wanted to put away my notes, his letters. I wanted to let Andrew lie at the mercy of the courts and let God judge him for what he'd done. I wanted the bird-cage-maker and all of his problems to just go away from me. I was tired. I needed to go to bed for a long time, to my lonely bed without my wife.

I was tired of other people's dysfunction. I'd spent my life embedded in it. When was there time for peace?

"May I?" he asked again. "My family . . . is in trouble. Please. You helped me so many years ago."

"I couldn't have helped you. I did nothing."

"Of course you did. You listened. You read my letters."

"Look, about that. I have a confession to make—"

"You have nothing to confess," he said. "It was narcissistic to write my life down. Yes? Yet you allowed me to. And for that I am indebted. But this time, I need you to do more. I need you to help me catch my granddaughter's killer."

I swallowed. "You believe she was murdered?"

"I do," he whispered. His brow furrowed as anguish came across his face. "Yes, I believe she was murdered."

I stood there looking at this man, this man I wanted so much to bury along with his past. I wanted nothing more than to have my peace again, and yet, here he was destroying it. I was angry. The child, the sweet girl Carmelite could not have been murdered. If she had been, I would not be free until I knew what had happened. Why, oh why had they come into my life?

"I suppose you could call on me in a few days. I—I need to think. To rest a bit."

"Thank you," he said, reaching for my hand and shaking it again with both of his. As we touched, I felt the unusual bond between us. God only knew why our paths had crossed the first time and why, after all these years we were forced to meet again. But there was a reason. Of this, I was finally convinced.

From the journal of Y. R. Le Monnier, M.D.

RE: NEW ORLEANS, 1882

I knew too much about the Saloys.

For years I had planned on taking my son to the mansion on Rue Royale and walking him through the home his great-grandfather had built and lived in, where he had run his successful medical practice, served as Grand Pursuivant of the Perseverance Lodge. In my daydream, my son was old enough to understand what I was telling him. He would look into my eyes, and I would gather him up in my arms. Together we would see how far we had come, marvel at the strength of our fine name, Le Monnier. I would explain away the fourth story as if it was of no consequence at all, and my son would be satisfied. But I knew the Saloys too well now, partly from my time in treating Madame Saloy, but mostly from the stories of their birdcage-maker, François Reynaud. I found that every time I felt the urge to take my son there, I would stop myself. It was too awkward. I could not show up as a stranger anymore. I didn't want to intrude. I didn't want to get into some long conversation.

No matter how many times I started and stopped, I would never get the chance to fulfill my fantasy. In December of 1882, one year after I had become city coroner of New Orleans, my five-year-old son died from yellow fever.

It was the same yellow fever on which I was an expert.

My experience with the disease was of no help to me, but instead a painful thorn in my side. The fact that I was a respected doctor meant nothing to Death. I was completely and utterly helpless to protect my own child from its evil ravage.

There was hardly anything left of me.

With the loss of my son, I became inhuman for a while. I was dismantled and put back together in some awkward fitting fashion, never again to feel whole.

It had been a difficult few months leading up to it. On Halloween, a 19-year-old man was coming in on top of a train and hit his head on a bridge brace. His body was put in the depot at 8 PM, but I was home with my son, helping to put him to sleep after being frightened by all of the ghouls in the streets. I refused to come in or to have his body moved until morning, and the newspapers had their way with me. Two weeks later, I became the newspaper's hero as my medical research in a post mortem exam helped save an innocent boy from being charged with a murder he did not commit.

Alas, after suffering the fever, my son, Yves René Le Monnier, III died on December 22, and I could hardly bear it. There was nothing I could do. So I returned back to work on Monday, Christmas Day. I chose to go to the insane asylum where people's problems seemed to them worse than mine, where I had no desire whatsoever to console a crying, mourning mother for they were all mad. Every single one of them. Insane.

On that day, I recommended a 35-year-old black male, Willis Brothers, to the State Insane Asylum for acute mania. He was too damn happy.

And oh, how I pitied him.

To say I was changed was an understatement. I became a shell of myself with the only solace found in thrusting myself into my work. I was of no use to Eulalie. I could not bear to see her crying. I do not know how she stayed with me in those days. I must have been as cold as the metal gurneys on which the asylum took out its corpses. To this day, I am ashamed at this. My love, my Eulalie, suffered alone.

In those days of grieving, I couldn't care less about the Saloys or about François Reynaud. We received flowers in each of their names and their condolences in the form of hand-written notes. Madame Saloy's words struck me with unusual depth. It was I who should have been consoling her over the loss of her children—not her, mine. Perhaps I understood her more in those days. If I'd not been so self-consumed, perhaps I could have told her so and provided some comfort. But alas, I could not. I would not allow myself to feel for anyone or anything for quite some time.

It is a strange thing, being coroner, and having bodies of people brought to you that you once knew. I remained city coroner for three more terms, facing death in a most blatant way. I became numb to it. I stared it down in the faces of my cadavers and dared death to ever affect me again.

In the hot August of 1889, seven years after I'd lost my only son, I was in my office when my assistant came in to tell me that the bridge keeper at the Spanish Fort was being brought in. This rang a distant bell for me, but it wasn't until I saw his lifeless face and read his name that I remembered who he was. Antonio Carcano. He was Madame Saloy's brother, dead now at the age of 59. He died from phthisis pulmonalis, a complication of tu-berculosis, but they brought him in to me to be sure there was no foul play. He'd been quite a rough character, jailed several times for gambling mostly. At one time, he'd been arrested after chasing a hotel-worker with a kitchen knife, trying to murder him over some unpaid debt.

This was the first time I'd allowed myself to think of the Saloys in many years. I no longer saw the birdcage-maker and only rarely wondered what had become of him. Seeing Madame's dead brother before me made me suddenly think of her in a new way. I had survived the death of my son. I had allowed a length of time into my life so that I could once again find it in my soul to have sympathy towards another human being. And I knew it was time for me to show the poor woman, Madame Saloy, that I cared for her and for her loss. I was still human.

Yes. I would pay the grieving woman a visit.

The Le Monnier mansion was in a state of disrepair, at least, this is what it seemed to me in the first moment I saw it. A very dark cloud had come up from the west and had cast the structure into a shadow while all the build-ings around it shone in the gleaming sun. It was as if sadness had overtaken the home. The Saloys' sadness. My own. I forced myself to walk up to the house and enter the door. I curled around the winding staircase, shudder-ing from the haunting sound of my son playing and jumping upon the steps. He was not here. Of course, he never would be and never had been, but in my mind, he'd been there hundreds of times. *I played on these very steps, René,* I would tell him. *And so did my father. All of us Le Monnier men walked and played along these stairs.*

No. It was not to be.

A knock at the door on the fourth story produced Madame Saloy herself. She was worn. I estimated her age to be mid-fifties now. She wore a modest housedress and hair held back loosely. I could still see the beauty she had always been, but now, there was a sweet grief that had taken up residence in her eyes. They lit up when she saw me.

"Doctor Le Monnier, what a pleasant surprise. Please come in."

"It has been many years, I'm afraid."

"It has, indeed. You are looking well. How is your wife?"

"Eulalie is fine."

"I am so sorry for your loss. I imagine you have been through quite a lot."

I took her hand in both of mine and squeezed. I searched her eyes. "Thank you, dear woman." We were silent for several moments as I conveyed to her my empathy, my deep understanding. We were two people who had suffered the loss of a child, and in her company, I was wholly understood.

"Won't you sit down? I shall get us some tea."

I sat on a blue sofa and looked around the room. Everything was lovely and well-kept. I listened to her clinking around in the kitchen and then heard something else. Songbirds. I rose from my seat and followed the sound to the oval dining room. Over by the light of the window stood the most magnificent birdcage—an exact miniature replica of the Le Monnier mansion. How had I not seen this before? How had I listened to countless hours of François Reynaud describing this cage and his delivery of it to the Saloys and never, ever once desired to see it? It was truly a sight to behold and I found myself holding my breath. I felt the strange desire to bend down and imagine myself walking through it all, as a child would. I felt a cold chill come over me, a covetousness that struck me with such force that I stumbled.

"It is lovely, isn't it?"

Madame Saloy had found me and set the tray of tea on the table.

"I'm stunned at how precise it is," I told her. "I know the cage-maker, François."

"Yes. François." Madame smiled in a sad little way. "He is such a dear friend."

"I had heard him speak of this cage, but I admit, his words did not do it justice."

"Do you know it was his last cage?" she said.

"No."

"It's true. Had I known it would be, I would never have asked him to do it."

"I'm afraid I haven't seen him in years," I said, feeling I'd been down in the abyss, unaware of life above me.

"He's a cook now, at Gaillardanne & Debat. He checks in on me every now and again."

"I see." I wondered . . . did the cage-maker love Madame Saloy still? And did she ever return this love? Did his wife yet know about their taking tea together? Madame poured me a cup, and I gathered my nerve to say what I had come to say.

"Please accept my most sincere condolences for the loss of your brother."

It seemed to dawn on her as she looked at me that I was now city coroner and must have come to this knowledge in a most terrible way. I watched as the thoughts shifted behind her eyes. She nodded finally.

"My brother. Yes. I pray he gets some rest now. He was always a wild one. He was . . ." Her eyes began to tear, and I reached into my pocket for a handkerchief. "Thank you. Oh, Antonio. We were very close when we were younger. I believe I told you much of that changed when I met Bertrand. When he introduced me to Bertrand." She was whispering now.

"Your husband, is he here? Is he well?"

"He is not here, and he is not well. Physically, I imagine he'll live forever, but he spends his days in the courts now. I hardly remember the man I once cared for. In his grief he turned to destroying things. Lives, people. He has become so powerful in his wealth that I'm afraid it has gone to his head."

"I'm sorry to hear that."

"Though not surprised, correct? You could have told me, good doctor, years ago what my husband would become. For heaven's sake, I could have told you. We are beasts, he and I."

"You are not a beast."

"We are trapped in this world, in this house, in bondage to our fortune. We both willed it so. After our children died, I all but welcomed it. I allowed my husband to become treacherous in business, but now we are too far gone. There is no returning." She took a sip of her tea, and I found myself feeling guilty for not having come here sooner.

"I should never have stayed away," I said. "I could have helped you through your grief. Please forgive me."

"There is nothing to forgive. You suffered your own loss. It is the way of this world. We come into it alone and go out again even moreso."

The birds began a sad tune, and our eyes turned toward the cage.

"Look at us there," she pointed. We stared at the two beautiful birds, trapped behind the bars of the cage, singing a funeral dirge. Was she speaking of the Saloys in the cage or was she speaking of herself and of me there?

I backed away. I needed to go. I would not be caged here. *I release this house, here, now,* I said to no one but myself. "Madame, if there is anything you need, anything I can do at all to help, please, don't hesitate to ask."

I gave her a card with my address and telephone number on it as I had moved since she saw me last, then I said my goodbye.

My spiral down the stairs was a blur. I forgot about my son and my younger self playing on the steps. I forgot everything but the birds in the cage, and when I exited the door onto St. Peter Street, I breathed in so deeply, I nearly fainted.

I was free of that house, free of that sadness. From here on, a new day began for me. I would never be confined to the trappings of the Saloys again. They had no more hold on me. I barely felt the ground as I made my way back to North Galvez Street, flying off in freedom, trying hard not to look back.

From the journal of Y. R. Le Monnier, M.D.

RE: NEW ORLEANS, 1907

I should never have looked back. I could feel someone was following me, hear their footsteps falling in tandem with mine. I knew that another soul was trailing me, and it might be dangerous to slow down to look, but I could not help it. I turned, not because I was so curious as to who it was, but because my nerves were jangling about in me, haunted by the death of Carmelite Kurucar. A part of me hoped it was her, alive, coming to seek my assistance again. I would give it to her. I would. And this time, I would discover the curse in time to prevent her death.

Upon turning slowly, my eyes fell upon my stalker. It was not the girl. That would be asking too much. Instead, it was the birdcage-maker. François Reynaud. Oh, how I did not want to see him.

"Pardon, Dr. Le Monnier, I pray I did not startle you."

"No, I . . . just heard footsteps and—"

"I would have called out to you, but I was gathering my thoughts."

"I see. And have they gathered?" I could hear the annoyance in my voice and tried to clear my throat.

"*Oui.*" François took off his hat and held it solemnly in his hands. He looked up at me with tired eyes. "May I have a few moments of your time? It has been several days, as you requested."

"Yes, yes, of course. For you, François, what I wouldn't do." I did not like the insincerity that was coming out of my mouth. Perhaps I was tired, too. "I've got some free time now if you would care to visit. My house is just around the corner."

We walked on the sidewalk together for a short while, quietly, both in thought. I found it odd to be with this man whom I had known before Eulalie had borne our son. Before we lost him. Before François had become a grandfather and buried his poor girl. In front of my home, I could still see-hear her, the young Mrs. Carmelite Kurucar calling for me, telling me that her grandfather was none other than the one now standing before me. That he had recommended me to her as someone who could help. Someone who would help. My throat grew tight.

"Please. Come in. Make yourself at home."

"This is very nice," said François. "Different than your other home on St. Joseph."

"Ah yes, I haven't been there for many years."

"I know. When you moved, I stopped delivering my letters."

"Because you were healed?"

"Because I was tired."

We went on with small talk like this until I was able to stand it no longer.

I sat down in my leather chair by the fireplace and begged him to take the sofa across from me. But there on the coffee table were my notebooks and files, and many of his own letters unopened until recently. A small stack still sat bound and ignored. I shuffled them stealthily over to my desk, then sat again, a single notebook and pen in hand, just like old times.

"Now," I said. "Carmelite, your granddaughter. What can you tell me?"

"I believe she was poisoned."

"You what? Poisoned? By whom?"

He covered his mouth as if the mere speaking of his thoughts may solidify them into the truth and cause harm. "I—I'm not exactly sure. It could have been her new husband, Ferdinand. He is young and impetuous. I never liked the boy, to be honest. But why would I? He had nothing to offer my granddaughter. She, however, had everything to offer him."

This sounded so much like the disillusioned young cage-maker swooning after the heart of the wealthy and married Madame Saloy, that I had to catch myself not to bring it to his attention. "So you believe her husband, Ferdinand, poisoned her."

"*C'est possible. Peut-etre.*" The man looked anguished and clenched his teeth. "Truthfully, I'm afraid it was my son who killed her."

"Her father? Felix Reynaud?"

126

He nodded but could make no sound. I took a deep breath. It was all coming back to me. The paranoia, the desire for a woman he could not have. His life was fiction, fairytale, and now, I was afraid the birdcage maker was inventing another tale.

"Why would your son have reason to kill his own daughter?"

"The money," he said, tilting his head. "It all goes back to her." Then he shut his eyes hard and ran his hands through his hair. There was complete silence between us until I realized he might be unable to speak.

"Did you . . . write it down for me? Is there a letter you'd like me to read? Something in your pocket?"

"No, no," said François. "I am an old man now. I . . . I will speak my mind.

"Sometimes I see her, Madame Saloy, alive again in my dreams. On those mornings when I'm first aware of the daylight, I hold my eyes closed for as long as I can so the memory of her will not fade away. Yet it does. I open my eyes and realize I must face a new day without her friendship. It's been many years since she's passed, and still, I think of her. My wife, Salome, has become very kind as of late, and I find myself enjoying her company. She appreciates the rich meals I bring home from the restaurant, and she's grown plump and pleasant. Happy, she seems.

"In all my years, I would have never wanted a cent of Madame Saloy's fortune. I had seen what it had done to her. I had seen what it had done to me. Once I had received my payment for the Saloy birdcage commission, I changed. How? It is hard to say. I am not proud of this fact, but it is the truth, regardless.

"I reveled in the idea that one of my creations had garnered that much money. I raised the prices of my other birdcages and even though many showed interest, I did not need to give away my goods for I did not think I needed the money. I imagined I had reached the higher plateau, the one to which my father had always aspired. This, in turn, led to the downfall of my business, and it is why I became a chef at Gaillardanne & Debat.

"When my cage-making business failed, I told myself and my wife that I no longer wanted to make birdcages anyway. That it was time for me to move on. In reality, I was devastated and lying to myself.

"I was broke.

"I was a complete failure.

"There is something to be said for the Great Humbling, however. I believe the Lord Almighty is gracious when he removes our stumbling blocks—in my case, pride and fortune. Having survived, it makes one all the more aware of others' struggles with the same. I watched in horror as my son, married to Madame Saloy's niece, stood to inherit a vast fortune of her estate. Was it terrible enough that she had left this world, than that my own son would be tempted with her fortune all the days of his life?

"My son, after all, had married into the royal family. I could not help but feel responsible. The two of them met when they were children under my watch. It was at the birthday party of Madeline's daughter.

"Years later, as my business was failing and young Felix was now in his teen years, he began to sneak behind me. Salome and I nearly fainted when he came to us one day with the young girl, Carmen Carcano, and introduced her as his wife. They had eloped! I was beside myself with his betrayal, not to mention the fear of what her father, Antonio, might do. The boy had robbed his mother and me of the joy of a wedding, of blessing the union between these two—which, I might add, I would not have done as they were much too young to be married.

"Strangely, and however distantly, my lines had crossed with Madame Saloy's, and our stories would be forever intertwined because of this marriage. It was this thought that consoled me in my moments of rage toward my impetuous son.

"Shortly after, Antonio's wife died of a mysterious illness. Her daughter Carmen was devastated, and it became clear to me that my son was a tremendous comfort to her in those days. It was a good thing he was there for her. But as only a father might see, he was there for the money, too. He would wait until the Saloy fortune sifted his way. It's a hard corner to stand on: that of loving your child and at the same time mistrusting his motives. When Felix's wife died years later, I watched for signs of sadness, which there were, but I also noted something else."

François looked at me as if I lacked understanding. "Don't you see? His wife died a very wealthy woman. In her passing, he thought he would get the money he'd eyed for so long, but he didn't. She left it all to the children and only left him as the children's tutor. Their schooling was taken care of, their clothing, their needs, all of it, but there was nothing bequeathed to him. My son watched as his oldest daughter inherited her mother's money as soon as she married. He watched as his only living son squandered his portion and wound up in prison. And he could not bear to see another one of his children receive the money he so desired."

"I cannot believe that—"

"You must consider it, Doctor. Trust me. It has been abysmal trying to accept this myself, but I'm afraid I cannot ignore the facts."

"And which facts are these?"

"That my son's daughter is now dead. That his wife remains dead. And her mother before her . . . all of suspicious causes."

"What, pray tell, was suspicious about the deaths of his wife and mother-in-law?"

"There was nothing much more than a stomach ache, if even that. The doctors could not tell us why they had died. And it's just as it was with poor Carmelite."

His eyes searched mine, and I thought of a thousand illnesses that could cause stomach aches and liver poisoning, but none of them that would run in the family. And how many did I know that would lead to death?

"Poisoning?" I asked him. "You think they were all poisoned?"

"Possibly. It's possible. Don't you think?"

"Perhaps. But wouldn't the coroner find it?"

"There was no autopsy," he said. "Not on Carmelite. Nor on her mother. Nor on her grandmother."

I scratched my head and stood. This was a bit much to take in. I could not see the correlation. Why would this man kill all the women in his life? Why leave his oldest and youngest daughters? It didn't make sense. With her dead, he would have no right to Carmelite's money anyway. Would he? The husband would be the recipient.

I looked at the man bent over in pain before me. Was he a madman? Was he quite insane as I believed he once was? Was he now obsessed with his son instead of Madame Saloy? What sort of man accuses his son of something this treacherous?

"I'm sorry, François, so sorry for your loss, but I'm afraid there is no real evidence that your granddaughter was killed, nor that her father has done it. It seems to me you may be jumping to conclusions in your grief."

He reached for the newspaper I'd only just brought in from the café. He flipped until he reached a certain page, then handed it to me. "There," he said, his eyes now vacant. I took the paper and looked at the article before me.

SUCCESSION OF CARMELITE REYNAUD,

WIFE OF FERDINAND KURUCAR,

Civil District Court for the Parish of Orleans, Division "B" – No. 81,301 – Whereas Felix Reynaud and Viola Reynaud, wife of

Joseph Gracia, have petitioned the Court for letters of administration on the estate of the late Carmelite Reynaud, wife of Ferdinand R. Kurucar, deceased, intestate, notice is hereby given to all whom it may concern to show cause within ten days why the prayer of said petitioners should not be granted. By order of the Court. Thomas Connell, Clerk, James Legendre, Atty

"You see?" he said, defeated. "It has started. He's after the money. That horrible cursed money."

"Is this in session today?" I asked. "Is a judge seeing this case today?"

"*Oui.*"

I bit my lip. I had not yet enjoyed my paper. I'd not properly had breakfast, and yet here was this man, and here was this case. I thought of sweet Carmelite sitting where her grandfather was sitting just weeks before. *Help us,* she'd pleaded. *What can you find out about this curse that haunts us?*

Carmelite's brother was in jail for murder. She was dead. And her father was now petitioning to control the money she left behind. I knew it with a sigh. There was no other place for me this morning than the court building. I needed to see this happening with my own eyes. Only then would I understand if, and to what to degree, François' son, was the monster he so claimed. Perhaps François, himself, had succumbed to the money's curse. Perhaps each of us, if given the right circumstances, would fall.

Times-Picayune, 1890

DIED

SALOY – On Tuesday night, December 31, 1889, at 11:45 o'clock, BERTRAND SALOY, aged 77 years and 8 months, a native of France and resident of New Orleans for the past fifty-four years.

Partial letter from François, regarding January 1890

I felt as if I was spellbound. I could not believe what my eyes were seeing. As I held the paper, my hands began to shake. It could not be so, could it? Bertrand Saloy was dead?

My heart was flooded with emotions. Alarm. Disbelief. Sadness. Then . . . Madame Saloy. My eyes began to water at the thought of her own grief. Yes, he'd been an ogre at times, and an adulterer, but yet, he was her husband still. I felt deep in the pit of me her loss and knew I had to run to her at once.

"Salome," I said, setting the paper upon the kitchen table. "You won't believe it. Monsieur Saloy has died."

"From what?"

"It does not say." My wife was silent for a few moments as she nibbled at her toast. She'd aged quite beautifully and her face was full. She read the paper. She pushed it away and went to the sink to wash her plate. As she stared out the window at the house next door, she added, "That's quite a lot of money he's leaving behind. Can't take it with you, can you."

I stood there, staring at her apron strings tied loosely behind her, then headed to the other room to dress. I would see Madame before I went in to the restaurant. I needed to see her to know how she was faring. It did not need to be spoken. My wife understood this was something I had to do.

"Is there anything I can do?" I asked Madame Saloy. I stood, hat in hand at the top of the stairs, out of breath. She was walking out of her door, and I had just climbed all those stairs. I was not a young man anymore, now in my fifties, and found that seeing her there took my breath away even further, even though she was well sixty or so. The beauty of some women knows no bounds of age.

"Oh, how kind of you to come." She stood there at her door, her beaded purse hung at her wrist. Her face was pale and reddened around the eyes. She'd been crying. For an instant, just for an instant, I had the urge to run to her and grab her up, kissing her with the passion of one who truly loved her, something Monsieur never could do. And yet, I didn't. It would be foolish, even I knew this. Never once had my love for her crossed that sacred line, but the thought occurred to me: *Perhaps now was the time.* Perhaps now, twenty years into our relationship, a man like me might steal just one kiss.

She may have seen it in my eyes, my conflict. Her husband was dead. I was there to console her. She considered me a friend. A friend. Was that all? Perhaps that would all change with her husband gone.

"Madame, I'm sorry—"

"Thank you." She closed her eyes. "He was in court, of course. It was his heart. I'd seen it coming for weeks. I'd warned him to let this go, but he wouldn't."

"The court case?"

"Yes. He felt swindled. But he always felt this way. Never one to forgive a debt, and now I'm afraid—" She began to cry, and I could not bear it. I went to her and would have wrapped my arms tenderly around her had it not been for the girth of her hat.

"There, there." I held each shoulder and stroked her cheek with the back of my hand.

"He was upset," she cried. "It was the anniversary of our son's death. He shouldn't have added this stress to his heart, but he did it anyway."

"Shhhh, I know. What a fool." As soon as I said the words, I wanted to swallow them back again. "He suffered so, the poor, poor man," I covered.

"First Antonio and now months later, Bertrand." She pulled away and blotted her eyes. "I'm off to speak with his lawyers," she said. Her eyes searched mine. "I believe he's . . . left it all to me."

She appeared shocked as if she'd never considered this happening. Her burden appeared so great at this moment, that I imagined her bones to be fragile as a bird's. How could she possibly handle all of his affairs, all of his money, without breaking?

"Let me walk with you," I said. "Let me help you through this."

"She doesn't need your help," said a voice behind the door. It opened and there stood Madame's sister, Madeline Pons. She'd been listening to the whole affair. She scolded me with her steel-gray eyes. "Thank you, I've got it from here. We'll get along just fine to the lawyer's office."

"Yes," I said. "Of course."

"Madeline, this is our bird-cage maker, François Reynaud," said Madame Saloy.

"Yes, I know dear," she said. "We've met many times."

I should have been alarmed at Madame's statement. I'd known her sister for two decades. An introduction was the last thing we needed. But that poor, sweet woman—surely her grief had muddled her mind.

"If you need anything at all," I called after her as they descended the stairs.

"She's in good hands," said her sister, effectively cutting me off. I stood there for a few moments, eyes closed, a tear trying to escape. I could still feel her in my hands. But there was always something coming between us, Madame and me. Bertrand was always there, and now that he was gone, it seemed she was surrounded by her protective and most unpleasant sister. "I mean her no harm," I said weakly to no one. "I only want what's best for her."

My feet were leaden as I left the Saloy house. How they made it to Rue Dauphine, I do not remember. They must have known the way.

François

From the journal of Y. R. Le Monnier, M.D.

RE: NEW ORLEANS, 1907

I walked with François Reynaud to the courthouse and stared at the familiar marble floors and white-washed hallways as we made our way into the room where his son, Felix, was waiting. I could tell by the look in his eyes, he was surprised to see us there, and not pleasantly so.

"You shouldn't do this," François whispered to him, leaning down to his ear.

"It is not your affair," said Felix, staring straight ahead at the judge who was settling into his position and shuffling papers. Felix was no longer wearing the apron and rolled up sleeves I'd seen him in at the Continental Saloon. Here, he was cleaned up and dressed in his best suit. We took our seats in the chairs directly behind him and his attorney. I wondered for a second if young Carmelite's spirit might know what was taking place. Was she here? Was she aware at all what was happening after her death? That her father was suing her husband, and her grandfather was angry with his son? Of course not, I consoled myself. Of course, not. The child was blissfully at rest. At age 16.

My hackles went up. Why did the child have to die?

Her widower, the young Ferdinand, was sitting on the opposite side of the room. He was olive-skinned, and I wondered about his blood. From where I was sitting, I could see his shiny brown hair and strong jaw line, barely needing to shave. My goodness, he was so young. Too young to be sitting here, grieving the loss of a wife.

Over the next forty-five minutes, Carmelite's grandfather, the birdcage maker, and I sat watching a spectacle of both parties attempting to press their points.

"She inherited the money from my late beloved wife," said Felix Reynaud in a tearful plea on the witness stand. "It should rightfully return to our family. Her younger sister, Gladys, whom she loved so dearly, still needs much care." Little Gladys, his oldest daughter, Viola, and her husband sat nearby in support of their father, but, of course, there was no sign of Andrew. Carmelite's brother still sat in the parish prison, awaiting his sentence for murdering his lover. It was a mixed up, disturbed family, and as I sat there listening to it all, I wondered how I'd gotten involved in the first place. There was often less drama in the insane asylum.

A notary, Mr. Edward Rightor, took the stand and was sworn in. "Can you tell us what happened when you went to take inventory of the deceased's estate?" asked the attorney.

"Yes, of course." The young man looked over toward Ferdinand. "Mr. Kurucar took me around his house at number 839 North Rampart and described a few items that had belonged to his wife. A chair in the study. A wardrobe of clothing. Some jewelry. I wrote it all down and asked if there was anything more. He claimed there was not. I asked him if there was any money in bank accounts or other that had belonged to his wife. He said there was not."

"And what was the total worth of Mrs. Kurucar at her passing? What did Mr. Kurucar lead you to believe?"

The notary looked down at his notes and then turned his attention toward Felix as if he was speaking directly to him. "Ferdinand Kurucar, the husband of the deceased, stated that the sum of her belongings amounted to $1061.53."

"Lies!" said Felix Reynaud, standing.

Judge King pounded his gavel. "Sit down, Mr. Reynaud."

Felix sat, but could hardly be still. His lawyer, Mr. Legendre approached the bench. "Your Honor, I'd like to call Ferdinand Kurucar to the stand."

A hush came over the court. After Ferdinand was seated and looking around at all the people before him, his face turned sheepish and he seemed like just a boy.

"Mr. Kurucar, were you married to Miss Carmelite Reynaud on May 20, 1906?"

"I was."

"And did she die just days ago on January 6, 1907, less than eight months after you were married?"

His eyes went to the floor. "Yes."

"Thank you, Mr. Kurucar. I know this is difficult. It's unpleasant to be talking issues of fortune just days after your wife has died. However . . ."

he looked around the courtroom as if summoning everyone closer, "we must. Now . . ." Attorney Legendre walked back to his desk and picked up a sheet of paper. He moved just to the side of Ferdinand and stood facing the people of the court. "I have a few more questions for you, Mr. Kurucar if you would oblige. He put his glasses on his nose. "Did you on May 18, 1906 receive from your wife the entire sum of her paraphernal estate which totaled $30,008.40 for the purpose of investing it for her?"

Ferdinand shifted in his seat and looked to his attorney, Mr. Lemle. "Do not answer," he told him.

"And did you also in that month of May 1906, receive from your wife for the purpose of investment, $3199.89, given to her by her father, Felix Reynaud?"

Again the look between client and attorney. Mr. Lemle shook his head and Ferdinand stayed quiet.

"Mr. Kurucar, might I remind you that you are under oath of this court and you must answer these questions truthfully? Now, is it also true that that same month, May of 1906, less than one month after you eloped with the young Miss Reynaud, that she was given $2,050 by her brother, Andrew Reynaud, and jewels worth $500, all of which she handed over to you for investment and safe-keeping? Is this true, Mr. Kurucar? Is any of this true?"

Mr. Lemle stood up. "Do not answer, Ferdinand. You do not have to answer these questions."

"He most certainly does have to answer, Mr. Lemle," said Judge King. "And he will answer, otherwise he'll be in contempt of this court! Now, son, I will allow you one more chance to answer the questions posed to you by the plaintiff's attorney. Mr. Legendre . . ."

"Thank you, your Honor," said Mr. Legendre. "Mr. Kurucar, what say you of the amounts aforementioned in the sum in excess of $35,000? What happened to all this money your dear wife received from her inheritance and gifts from her family members? Did she or did she not give it all to you for investment and safekeeping?"

He paused to let Ferdinand speak, but he stayed close-lipped, staring at his lawyer.

"Will you answer these questions about the whereabouts of this fortune?" asked an inflamed Mr. Legendre.

"No," said Ferdinand.

"Ah, so he can speak."

"Very well," said Judge King, "Ferdinand Kurucar, you are now in contempt of this court. You will be delivered to the Parish prison for a total of ten days."

A wild murmur overtook the room, and the bailiff approached Ferdinand. I sat there, stunned, as I watched him hand-cuffed and led out of the room.

"I'll get you out of there, don't worry," I could hear his attorney saying to him as they led past us.

Another family member in jail, this time, the cage-maker's grandson-in-law.

François, the birdcage maker, looked at me imploringly. I could see the mystery in his eyes. The anguish, too. He was as concerned as I was. Had the young man killed his younger wife? Felix turned around and whispered, "You see what a scoundrel he is? I told you. I know what I'm doing. Best leave this to me."

Back in my home, I was haunted. What had happened to the girl? What had happened to the money was all anyone could think about, but I could not help but wonder, how had she died? If the husband was hiding something, if he would go to such drastic lengths to hide her fortune, might he also go to great lengths to hide his guilt with regard to her death? And what of the cage-maker's suspicions of his son Felix? Was he capable of murdering his own child in order to access her money?

I grabbed some water and rinsed the rotten taste from my mouth. This family, the Reynauds, was tainted and dark. No wonder the sweet girl had come to me with worry over a curse. I could see its stain on each of them.

The child bride had given her whole fortune to her husband just as soon as she'd received it. Why? Did she think the curse would affect her less if her husband was in control of the money? And why did she leave no will? Perhaps she didn't think she'd die at such a young age. She had her whole life in front of her. I stared out the window at a light gray mist now falling over the road. Carmelite Kurucar died intestate, no will. Something about it sounded so familiar.

With bourbon in my head and more in my hand, I ran to my files and pulled out the pages from sixteen years ago, 1891. There it was. Carmelite's namesake, her great aunt, Madame Saloy, had died leaving no will. Yes, it was true. History in this strange family was repeating itself. But why?

Partial letter from François, regarding April 1891

My heart was overcome with desperation. Madame's house had become a near fortress, protected on all fronts. The door remained locked and when I attempted to knock and enter, I was constantly turned away by a doctor or housemaid or Madeline Pons herself.

"I need to see her," I would plead to no avail. Madame Saloy was ill and in dire straits. It was all I could do. I was out of my mind with worry. Finally, on a day when I lay in wait and watched her sister, Madeline, leave the premises, I knocked on the door. I knocked again, louder and louder, until someone was forced to open it.

"I'm afraid you can't come in," said the housemaid. "She's not having any company."

"But have you told her it is I? That François, the cage-maker, is here and wants to see her for the hundredth time?"

"I'm sorry, sir, but I've had strict orders—"

I could hear no more. I pushed the woman aside and pressed up the stairs as quickly as I could, against her protests. By the time I got upstairs, I entered the Saloy's apartment on the fourth floor and nearly fainted from trying to catch my breath. I headed for her bedroom and kneeled at her bedside, panting. She was so pale. There was no rouge adorning her cheeks, barely any color at all, save for the pink of her lips. She was asleep and I hesitated, but I knew the housemaid would be there any moment. Now was my chance.

I leaned over and touched my lips to hers.

A lifetime of waiting, over.

I held my lips there and felt the soft warmth of her beneath me. I held my breath but could feel hers as she stirred. Tears dripped down my cheeks and onto her own. I wiped her face gently and leaned back to look at her. She opened her eyes and appeared confused for a moment, as if her eyes were adjusting. Finally, just the smallest hint of a smile spread across her lips where mine had been.

"François," she said softly.

"*Oui, mon cherie*, Madame."

She reached for my hand. "Please. Call me Carma."

"Carma," I repeated. Inside I swooned with this new level of intimacy. All these years she'd been Madame Saloy to me, and now . . . now she was Carma, my love.

"You should take back the birdcage," she told me. "I won't be able to enjoy it much longer."

"Shhhh, don't say that," I said. "Of course you will. It's yours. I made it for you."

"I can sense . . ." Her words drifted off and she closed her eyes.

"Madame. No, please." I shook her and grabbed her other hand. "Carma." She smiled again.

"It's time," she whispered. "I'm not scared. I am ready to let go of it all."

"But you can't—"

"There he is!" I turned and saw the housemaid standing with a man at the bedroom door.

"Sir, you mustn't be in here," he said. "Madame is very ill. I insist you leave at once so she can rest."

She did need her rest. I could see that. I wanted to do nothing more than to crawl into the bed and lie beside her, melt into oblivion with her, but I was too damned alive.

Reluctantly, I left her side, but not before looking in the dining room for the bird cage. She had given it back to me, and I wanted to see it one more time. I wanted to see if I might pull the cage into her room so that she could watch the birds and listen to their song. So that she could spend her last waking moments looking at the cage I made for her, thinking about the man who made it. She would see in the craftsmanship the love in each wire, in each carved piece of wood. She would have a constant reminder of my devotion to her.

I stood in the entry to the dining room, and my mouth fell open. The cage was gone and every hint that it ever existed. No bird feather on the floor, nothing.

"Where is it?" I shouted. The housemaid appeared. "Where is the bird cage?"

She looked frightened, and the doctor came toward me. He put his hands on me and shoved me to the door.

"Where is it? Where's the cage? Madame's cage?"

"I'm afraid you must leave now or I'll call the police." The doctor muscled me out of the apartment, and I banged on the door until I realized Madame would be upset with the noise. With my tail between my legs, I slunk down the stairway, and as my eyes overran with tears, I realized I might never see Madame alive again. They would be vigilant to keep me out. They had stolen her from me, just as they had stolen the cage.

I stood on Rue Royale and stared up into the window where the bird-cage had sat. I imagined it there. Where had it gone? Had it flown out the window? Had Madame given it away? Of course, she hadn't. Madame had just told me I could have it. She wanted me to have it. She wouldn't have told me that if she had gotten rid of the cage already. I stood there watching the window as if my stare might make it reappear. I allowed myself to remember the hours and days and weeks spent building that magnificent creation. Those were some of the happiest days of my life. Now they were gone. Now the cage was gone. And now Madame would be gone from me forever.

Yet I had kissed her. I had felt her lips. She had smiled at me and told me to call her Carma. I filled with warmth in spite of myself and touched my heart where Carma lived.

Then I remembered my wife and how Salome had asked me to bring home a tin of biscuits for her card game. I headed to the store as any dutiful husband would. This mundane task was a blessing for my troubled mind. I counted my steps along the way and lost myself in the numbers.

François

Times-Picayune, April 21, 1891

MASS To be said TUESDAY, April 23, at 8 o'clock at St. Louis Cathedral, for the soul of Mrs. B. SALOY

From the journal of Y. R. Le Monnier, M.D.

RE: MAY 1891

She died just sixteen months after her husband's passing. On the morning that Madame Saloy's death was announced in the *Times Picayune*, the stock market went wild. She was that important. Her money was that important. And yet, she left it to no one. No will. The courts would be wild with this news.

I was saddened but not surprised it had happened. I'd seen Madame Saloy at her husband's funeral and later checked in with her. I could see she was ill, yet she refused any of my attempts to treat. It was cancer, a slow kill. She may have suffered for quite some time, but the passing of her husband—or the inheritance of his fortune—may have finally done her in.

My first thought was the house on Rue Royale, the Le Monnier mansion. What would happen to it now? It was selfish, I realized, but I could not help myself from fantasizing that the house might one day end up back in Le Monnier hands.

My next thought was the birdcage maker. I knew he was probably on his knees by this point. How would the man live without the hope of one day securing Madame Saloy's heart? With her dead, what would a cage-maker who no longer made birdcages have to live for?

Part Two

"The greatest disturbance of the mind is to believe things because we want them to be."

Jacques-Bénigne Bossuet (1627–1704)

Blog post, ReVive or DIY Trying, June 9

BIRDCAGE MYSTERY UPDATE

Well, I imagine you've given up on me or at least found some other DIY blog to follow! I hope not. It's been a week, and I wanted to give you an update on the antique birdcage that was gifted to me by the UPS man. First, I'm almost done with cleaning the cage itself. The wires glisten shiny black now, and I'm using Q-tips to get the grime out of the hard to reach places. It's truly stunning, right?! I mean, seriously!

Okay, I know you all are waiting to hear about the contents of that attaché case I found in the secret compartment. Thank you all for your comments and emails about my unusual inheritance and for sharing your own stories about adoption. Because of you all, I don't feel so alone when I am reading these old files, notebooks, and newspaper clippings. I can't say that I have any better understanding as to who my grandmother is, though. In the beginning there is a note to a "Pauline," but so far, I have no idea where she fits into the picture. I feel as if I have opened up a time capsule. Documents and diaries from the 1800s and early 1900s are coming to life in my hands. I feel a strange tug on my heart as I read very personal stories about love, a doctor, a birdcage maker, and a wealthy family. There's even a murder! I care about these people, having no idea if any one of them is blood related to me. It's all very mysterious, and I wish I could share more with you, but right now, I just need to keep reading and let it sink in.

I haven't been to a thrift shop in a week!!! I would have imagined I'd be having withdrawals by now, but this mystery is just so engrossing, I've hardly suffered at all.

JUST BECAUSE I'M NOT SHARING NEW PHOTOS DOESN'T MEAN YOU SHOULDN'T! For the next week, would you please share with me your own photos of your latest secret finds and great DIY treasures? Just respond to this post in the comments section. I love you guys. No, really. Please bear with me and stay tuned.

Trish

Partial letter from François, regarding 1891

I stood on the corner of Bourbon and Conti and rubbed my clean shaven face, pulled my watch from my pocket and felt its weight. Should I cross the street and continue to the courthouse to testify for that woman, Madeline Pons? I remembered her attorneys' plea for decency, how my "appeal to the truth would be greatly appreciated." I wasn't being bought, but I did hope to gain something in return for my loyalty. I waited until a milk-runner on horse and buggy passed, and with heavy heart, crossed to the other side.

I had never trusted Madame Saloy's sister. She didn't seem to be cut from the same cloth. Madame was warm and hospitable, gracious in the most difficult circumstances, while the sister, Madeline, clung close to her, a moth to her money.

Perhaps, it occurred to me, this was precisely what the sister thought of me. How was it that a cage-maker had entered the close-knit circle of the filthy rich? It did seem unlikely.

I cared little about the money. What would it do for me? Bring Madame back? Nonsense. I put my watch back in my pocket and quickened my pace—but only slightly. I was dragging my feet, dreading this appointment at the courthouse.

Everything about this affair made me ill. A woman's character was being called into question by members of New Orleans society who ought not to judge the credibility of others. They were questioning her character because a great fortune was at stake, money that had belonged to the Saloys. I did not want to give testimony about Madeline Pons because she had been the sister of my beloved Madame Saloy. And the fact that there was need for testimony on this day meant that Madame was gone, something I had not yet swallowed. She had been everything to me. I thought of the tomb at Metairie Cemetery, once the grounds for the horse races where Monsieur Saloy threw away so much money. Now, the place held both of them along with their children, entombed in marble, never letting go.

I held on to my stomach and cursed myself for not taking a spoon-ful of Hood's Sarsaparilla before I left home. I passed an open café and watched as children danced around puddles in the cobblestones of the street. I came to a group of Negro men who were waist deep in the ground, digging beneath the sidewalk. A shovel-full of mud landed straight in front of me, so I stepped around it. But there was no getting around this: *Madame Saloy was dead. My love. Gone forever.*

I shook my head and removed my hat, slicking my hair back, and then replaced it absentmindedly as wetness stung my eyes. I was remembering her, the way she smelled, the way she laughed and made me feel a worth that no other woman on earth had been able to make me feel. Not even my wife.

I stepped gingerly over cobblestones, careful not to twist an ankle. I was getting older. My son was now grown and had given me a grand-son, Andrew. Madame had been so happy for me. Wasn't it just yesterday I was sipping tea in her parlor and telling her how smart the boy was? I remembered the glint of sadness in her eyes as she congratulated me. She had suffered cruelly from the loss of her own two children. Madame Saloy would never be a grandmother. She'd been robbed of it. Bequeathed so much money yet robbed of so much of joy. Where was the fairness in that?

And now I felt the one robbed of joy. It wasn't fair. I was beginning to break a sweat, but it was not for my stride. I was hardly moving. I wiped my top lip and brow with my kerchief and placed it in a breast pocket. *Oui.* I would testify about Madeline Pons, the sister of Madame Saloy, as the courts tried to decide whether or not she was suitable to be the executor of such a large sum of money. It wasn't really about the money anyway. With Madame it had always been about the simple things in life. The smile of a child. The sweet song of a bird in a gilded cage.

My mind was made up. I had decided I would testify on Madeline's be-half no matter what I felt about her. Quite frankly, she had what I wanted. She had in her possession the one object that existed as a tie between my-self and Madame Saloy, the one thing in this world that could summon her spirit like nothing else. Madeline, I was sure, now held the birdcage that I had once made with my very own hands, every detail painstakingly wrought with love and care for the gentlest person I had ever encountered. Yes. I would testify, and then Madeline would willingly offer me the bird-cage once more. She had no need for it. No need at all.

Would I lie in order to retrieve Madame's cage? Well, lying was an awful word. No, I would not lie; I would simply steer clear of anything that might cast Mrs. Pons in a dim light. Let her handle the estate for all I cared. Let her wrestle her children and take every last penny of that damned, exorbitant Saloy fortune, but give me what I was rightly due. I had no more Madame Saloy in my life. The least I could have was her cage.

As I approached the Civil District Court building, I saw images in my head of Madame Saloy, laughing and looking young and beautiful and then silent, lying in bed, the life seeped out of her. I wanted to create something with this sullen mood, to build a birdcage with my hands again, a memorial to her, but I no longer had my studio on Rue St. Ann. Those days seemed a lifetime ago. I pictured myself going into the restaurant this evening to cook, but the thought of fresh butter and cream, things I loved, made me feel queasy just now, and I found myself leaned over in the bushes beside the courthouse, holding my hat and retching.

In all the years since I had first met Madame Saloy, I had never truly allowed myself to imagine a world in which she was no longer a part. I certainly never thought I would outlive her. If only I could get my hands on that cage, I might have something to remember her by. Her last wish for me to have it would be fulfilled.

I used my kerchief to tidy my face, and then forcing back all emotion and memory, I pressed down my suit and opened the door to the court-house, preparing to utter my truth.

François

From the clinical notebook of Y. R. Le Monnier, M.D.

RE: ANDREW REYAUD IN NEW ORLEANS PARISH PRISON 1907

"Tell me the truth," said Andrew Reynaud. He was withering away before my eyes. Several months into his imprisonment, I could see it was taking a toll. "They're going to find me guilty, aren't they."

His words were not a question. They dripped out of his mouth like tiny tombstones.

"I believe they are," I told him. "I'm sorry, Andrew. I've done all that I could. Your lawyers are not convinced that my testimony could save you. After all this work, they're dropping the plea of insanity."

"But the curse!"

"The curse is more real than the insane defense at this point, however no court would ever touch such a thing."

"You could call in a priest."

"And he would say what? That God curses those who turn away from him? That evil is real and lurks, and the demon-possessed can be exorcised? This is a court of law. You drank too much. You squandered your fortune. You murdered your lover. The jury will have no mercy on young man who was given so much and who wasted it all."

My words stung, and yet I could not retrieve them. He sat there, wounded.

"Andrew, I am very sorry for your sister's passing. I cannot tell you how it haunts me that I could not protect her from this curse that you believe exists."

"It does exist!"

"I've met with your grandfather." He got silent and looked to me, searching my eyes. "He believes your sister was met with harm."

"By the curse."

"By the hands of your father. Or, of her young husband."

"What do you mean? He thinks she was murdered?"

"Is that so hard to believe?" It was ludicrous, really, the young murderer not believing that another could be murdered.

"Do you believe it?" he asked me.

"No. I don't think so. I don't know what to believe. Her husband, Ferdinand, is hiding something. Hiding her money. Your father has taken him to court. Your brother-in-law, as we speak, is sitting behind bars in this very jail for contempt of court. He would not answer to the whereabouts of your sister's inheritance. If evasion could make one guilty of murder, I'd say he was well on his way."

"But can you prove it? What does the coroner say?"

"The coroner had nothing to do with your sister. She was declared and cremated before any autopsy could be done."

"So we'll never know the truth."

"It appears we may not." I got up and turned from the boy, wiping my forehead with my handkerchief. "How one is all right with never knowing the truth . . . this is what I wrestle with day after day. The truth . . ." I turned back to him and leaned on the desk. "The truth is evasive and lives on its own timeline. It is not known in convenient time when it might save the life of a young man waiting in prison. Often, it does not show itself until much later." I sat down and looked at my wrinkling hands. "The truth does not show up until you've exhausted yourself, trying to save everyone including your own son, and then the damned disease you've been fighting all along is discovered by some unsympathetic third party to be caused by the pesky mosquito, which was there before your very eyes all along. And you could not see it. You could not to save his life."

"I'm trying to follow you," said Andrew.

"The truth," I said, pounding on the table, "is here. Right now. It sits in front of us as clearly as the nose on our faces and yet—yet we may never, ever see it. This, my son, is the greatest tragedy I have known."

I stood and put my hat back on. I walked to the door, head hanging low.

"Thank you," I heard. I turned and looked at him incredulously.

"What are you thanking me for? I failed you. I did nothing. I failed your sister. I failed my own son."

"But you cared enough to try," said the boy. "It ought to count for something."

Partial letter from François, regarding 1891

"It ought to count for something," she was telling the judge. "I loved my sister."

I sat in the back of the courtroom while the judge eyed the witness, Madeline Pons, with caution. Should this woman be the executrix of such a large succession as her sister's estate? I had my own opinion, yet admittedly it may have been tainted by the sadness of losing Madame.

Madeline turned her knees from one side to the other and attempted a look of sincerity and intelligence, at which, I thought she failed both miserably. She wore nicer attire than usual, and I suspected I may have seen this particular dress on her sister at some time in the past. It was peacock blue with a square neckline and seemed to glisten like a jewel out of place in this courtroom.

The attorney, Mr. Elliott, approached her and handed her a newspaper. "If you will, Mrs. Pons, please read for us the first column of the *New Orleans Bee*."

Madeline looked blankly at the man and then held the newspaper up to her eyes. She squinted. "I cannot," she said. "The words are too small."

Mr. Elliott looked around at the room, giving a sly look as if to say, *or is it that she simply cannot read?* "Mrs. Pons, is it true you've had no formal education?"

"I—well, I, no, but I can certainly read if that's what you're asking."

"Seven-hundred thousand dollars is a substantial amount of money. Being the administratrix of such a large succession is not a simple task. Do you think you are qualified for such a role?"

"I do," she said, bristling only slightly.

"Then why don't we try this? Hmm? It's a copy of *Les Droit Civil Francaise*."

I shifted in my seat. No matter what I thought of her, I was uncomfortable watching this spectacle. Madeline started and stopped, slogging her way through two or three sentences. Mr. Elliott looked pleased with himself. "Thank you. That is all for now." Madeline returned to her seat, holding her chin up unnaturally high, and another woman was called to the witness stand.

"The court now calls Mrs. Tony Bango." Mrs. Bango raised her right hand and was sworn to tell the truth, the whole truth, and nothing but the truth. She sat in the witness chair and tried not to look in Madeline's direction. Mrs. Bango had a pinched face, suggesting she'd just eaten a lemon. She smoothed the ruffles on her full skirts.

"Mrs. Bango," said Mr. Elliott. "Have you met Mrs. Pons?"

"I have," said Mrs. Bango. "I met her about four years ago at a house on Bayou Road."

"And what, pray tell, was the occasion there four years ago at the house on Bayou Road?"

Mrs. Bango was as still as a cat before breakfast, tail flicking. Her head turned slightly and she said, "There were voodou dances carrying on." The room broke out in a murmur. "I watched Mrs. Pons participate in the gyrations of the waltz, though I, myself, did not."

"So you did not participate in the voodou dances?" asked Mr. Elliott with puffed out chest. He grasped his jacket and jerked down to straighten it.

"I assure you, I did not," said Mrs. Bango. "I had my three children with me, a fact that would not have been had I known of the novel character of the place." She leaned forward and seemed to whisper, "Some of the people there removed their dresses and danced in their undergarments."

The room erupted and Judge Rightor tapped his gavel for order.

Mr. Elliott allowed the room to quiet and then excused Mrs. Bango with, "Nothing further, thank you. You may step down." I watched Madeline who seemed calm except for the fingering of her sleeve and the slight biting of her top lip. I couldn't help but picture her stripped down, dancing in her undergarments, so I turned away. I always attempted at decency. I wasn't always successful, but there was always a genuine effort.

Monsieur Drolla, one of the attorneys for Madeline Pons, approached the bench. "Your honor, if I may call on Mrs. Pons once more?"

After she was situated, Monsieur Drolla said, "Mrs. Pons, did you meet Mrs. Bango at a house on Bayou Road about four years ago?"

"I did, yes."

There was a moment of silence all around. "And would you please tell the court . . . did you participate in the voodou ceremonies alluded to by Mrs. Bango?"

"No sir, I did not," said Mrs. Pons emphatically. "I did not participate in any voodou ceremonies whatsoever."

Counsel looked at her to see if that was all she wanted to say, and she nodded. "Very well, please note that Mrs. Pons has said she did not participate in any voodou ceremonies. Thank you."

Mrs. Pons held up the fullness of her rich turquoise skirts as she stepped down and sent a nasty glance over to Mrs. Bango. I wished I was sitting at a different angle so I might see Mrs. Bango's reply.

Monsieur Drolla then brought up a string of positive character witnesses for Madeline Pons, one after the other. A real estate agent. A deputy tax collector. A cigar-maker. A grocery store owner.

Mr. Elliott stood once more. He was pencil thin in a dark suit and not a hair to his head. His spectacled eyes looked flinty and small through the thickness of the glass. I wasn't sure which side I was pulling for. In the course of the past hour, I had found myself turning empathetic to Madeline. Imagine having people about town getting up in front of the others for one purpose only: either to reinforce one's character or to tear it down. The process left a sour, musty taste in my mouth.

"The court will now call *Miss* Bango," said Mr. Elliott. A slightly pretty, buxom young girl walked to the stand and put her hand on the Bible. "Miss Bango, are you the daughter of Mrs. Tony Bango?"

"Yes sir, I am," she said.

"Would you please state your age?"

"Fifteen summers."

"Thank you. Now, Miss Bango, did you accompany your mother to the house on Bayou Road about four years ago?"

"Yes, I did." She paused and looked at her mother who nodded her on. "I was eleven at the time."

"And did you see Mrs. Pons there?"

"Yes sir."

"Thank you, Miss Bango, you're doing just fine. Now tell me, did you see dancing going on at this house on Bayou Road, the house where it is alleged voodou ceremonies were taking place?"

"Yes sir, I did. I saw many ladies taking part in the dancing."

"And was Mrs. Pons one of those ladies?"

Miss Bango fiddled with her fingers and then clenched them. She looked straight into Mr. Elliott's eyes. "Yes. I did see her dancing. I saw Mrs. Pons dancing . . . with a Negro named Leblanc."

"That is a lie!" called out Madeline Pons, and the courtroom erupted. Her counsel hovered over her and quieted her down while Judge Rightor banged his gavel for order.

Miss Bango was quickly exchanged on the witness stand for her mother once again, and Mrs. Tony Bango sat perched on her chair, eager to talk.

"Mrs. Bango," said Mr. Elliott, "you have testified that Mrs. Pons danced at the house on Bayou Road along with other ladies, is this correct?"

"It is correct. I saw her with my own eyes. I can show you right now how it was done." She pressed to standing.

"That won't be necessary, thank you," said Elliott. "But if you please, would you tell the court why the people were dancing at that house? Was it for pleasure perhaps, or was it because of witchcraft?"

"I do not know," she said. "It was strange. One went there to the house to win something, but nothing was won. It was all a fake. I had gone there because I had been invited. If I had known what kind of place it was I would not have taken my children. Everybody present was bound to do what the voodou minister wanted, and no one could get out because the doors were locked. I was frightened, and that woman—," Mrs. Bango pointed to Madeline, "just danced!"

The courtroom broke into whispers and Judge Rightor turned serious.

"Your honor." Monsieur Drolla stood from his seat. "We, the counsel for Mrs. Pons, came here today prepared to give a $1,000,000 bond, signed by ten responsible citizens in the sum of $100,000 each, for the administration of this estate."

At the talk of such sweltering money, even the judge seemed to flinch. He took a moment of consideration. He looked at counsel, at Mrs. Pons, and then back down to the papers in his hand.

"Are there any other witnesses to the character of Mrs. Pons?" asked the judge.

"Just one, your honor." Mr. Elliott moved toward the front of the room. "The court calls Mr. François Reynaud."

My heart sank. I had hoped I wouldn't be called. Hadn't they heard enough? Why had I come? I felt a feather stuck in my throat and coughed to clear it. I moved slowly and counted my steps . . . 1, 2, 3, 4 . . . there were 18 all together after getting situated and sworn in to the witness seat. I saw how pocked the judge's face appeared from this close angle. I swallowed hard and turned to stare into the round glasses of Mr. Elliott.

"Please state your occupation, Mr. Reynaud."

"Cook. I work as a cook at Gaillardanne & Debat on Rue Dauphine."

"Would you please tell the court how you have come to know Mrs. Pons?"

"*Oui*. I know of Mrs. Pons because of her sister, Madame Saloy. Some years ago, I was a cage-maker. I had a studio on Rue St. Ann. Madame Saloy admired my work." I stopped and turned to look at the clock at the back of the room. Not even a minute had passed. It felt like an eternity.

"Go on, please. How do you know Mrs. Pons?"

"I became friends with Madame Saloy. I met Mrs. Pons at her home on several occasions."

"And in your dealings with Mrs. Pons, did you ever see her act in a way that might imply she is incapable of being the administrator of her sister's estate?"

I knew what I was saying in my head, but I wanted to make sure it came out right. "I saw that Mrs. Pons trusted her sister with her own children. Madame Saloy educated two of them, and it seemed she made sure they were well taken care of. She had lost her own children, you see." I was overcome for a moment, remembering her sadness and my own. "Madame Saloy appeared genuine in her love for her sister and her children. She was genuine in her love for everyone she knew."

"But did *Mrs. Pons* ever act in a reckless manner in your presence?"

"Reckless?" I thought of how the birdcage had gone missing after Madame Saloy's death, and how I hoped it might be returned to me. Who had taken it? Did Madeline Pons have it? Might she think kinder of returning it to me if I testified on her behalf? "I never saw her imbibing or dancing or doing voodou, if that is what you imply."

The attorney glared at me, but I went on. It was obvious Mr. Elliott had hoped to get more salacious comments from me. "Madame Saloy was a dear friend," I said. "It is my hope that her affairs are looked after by someone quite capable."

"Do you believe Mrs. Pons to be quite capable, Mr. Reynaud?"

There was nothing I could say. Nothing to put into words the betrayal I felt that anyone had to take over the affairs of Madame Saloy. That she was gone in the first place. I had known Bertrand Saloy, the husband, and had remembered all the business dealings and law suits, the real estate, canals, railroads, and on and on associated with him, and honestly couldn't imagine taking on such a monumental task as managing that estate. So quietly, I simply mouthed the words, "*Oui. Je pense.*"

"What's that? Speak up."

"Yes," I said. "I believe Madeline Pons is quite capable of just about anything."

"Thank you, Mr. Reynaud. That is all for now."

"Arguments for this case are to be heard next Friday," said Judge Rightor, his brow knit tightly. "For now, this court session is adjourned."

I sat still as Madeline and her children stood. I heard the whispers and saw the venomous looks between Mrs. Bango and Mrs. Pons, and by the time I left the courthouse, I was feeling strangely tired. This day had taken too much of me. I was grateful that I had no more dealings with the Saloy fortune, for I could see the darkness it was summoning already. I had testified, and it was all over. Perhaps I might retrieve the birdcage, but the rest was up to the courts to decide.

As I walked out into the afternoon sun, I saw images in my head of Madeline dancing with a Negro at a house on Bayou Road, and I had the overwhelming sense that I'd been duped.

François

Times-Picayune, May 1891

AUCTION SALES.

BY THE CIVIL SHERIFF

JUDICIAL ADVERTISEMENT.

IMPORTANT SALE BY THE CIVIL SHERIFF OF THE ENTIRE CONTENTS OF THE PREMISES NO. 640 ROYAL STREET,

CONSISTING OF

Elegant Rosewood Parlor Set-Mantel-piece Mirrors-Pier Glass Mirrors -Crystal Gas Chandeliers-Mahogany Bedroom Sets-Imitation Rosewood

Bedroom Sets-Armoires-Extension Tables-Carpets-Rugs-Window Shades-Sideboards-Chairs - Étagères-Safes-Center Tables - Jardinières and Stands-Lace Curtains-Lamps-MusicBox-Statuettes-Car Receivers, etc.-Iron Safe-Revolvers-Bird Cages, etc.

ALSO,

Fine Porcelain, Glass and Crockeryware, Including a Large and Assorted Lot of Wearing Apparel and Underwear-Sewing Machine Awnings, etc.-Napkins-Sheets-Table Cloths-Towels-Tidies, etc.

ONE LOT BOOKS.

Stove, Range, Cooking Utensils, Washtubs, etc. Also,

ONE PLEYEL PIANO,

As Well as

ONE BUGGY, ONE NEW YORK BRETTE, ONE COUPEE, and ONE PAIR MAGNIFICENT CARRIAGE HORSES.

Various Sets Harness, Horse Blankets, Feed, etc., and Other Articles too Numerous to Detail, Usually Found In a First Class Household.

Succession of Carmelite Carcano, Widow Bertrand Saloy.

Civil District Court for the Parish of Orleans

BY VIRTUE OF AN ORDER OF SALE OF date May 4, 1891, to me directed by the Honorable the Civil District Court for the parish of Orleans, in the above entitled cause, I will proceed to sell at public auction, on the premises hereinafter designated, on SATURDAY, May 16, 1891, at 10 o'clock a.m., the following described property, to-wit, AT THE PREMISES,

NO. 640 ROYAL STREET THE ENTIRE CONTENTS, FURNITURE, FIXTURES, etc., of said premises.

Also

HORSES, BUGGY, CARRIAGES, ETC.,

HARNESS, ETC.

The whole as per inventory taken by Chas. T. Soniat, notary, of date April 8 to 29, 1891,

and on file in the above succession. Terms-Cash on the spot.

CHAS. W. DROWN,

Civil Sheriff of the Parish of Orleans.

From the journal of Y. R. Le Monnier, M.D., 1891

When I read in the paper that there was to be an estate sale of Carmelite Saloy's belongings at her home on Royal Street, I almost became giddy. It was not a proper response, for I felt very solemn about her death and would never have been happy for it. But something crawled up under my skin when I read of the sale. Perhaps it was that I would be able to walk along the walls of the Le Monnier mansion again unencumbered by the owners. Perhaps it was that a part of me felt that the home might be put up for sale once again. If I happened to be in the right place at the right time, then some benevolent force would see fit to return the home to its rightful heir, Le Monnier, for some petty price, or better yet, for none at all.

I realize it was all fantasy, but admittedly, my dealings with the home had been fantasy for many years.

On the morning of Saturday, May 16, 1891 I arrived at the Le Monnier mansion, one hour early at 9 o'clock. To my horror, I was not the only one. There was a line of people all the way down St. Peter and Royal streets as far as the eye could see. Panic set in, and I looked for a way to cut into the line and get a little closer. As I scoured the crowd for a friendly face, I found one, quite close to the door. It was François Reynaud, the cage-maker. How long had it been? Many years! He was so near the front, I wondered if he'd camped out and slept in the street the night before.

"François!" I called to him. He turned and perked at seeing me.

"*Bonjour*, Dr. Le Monnier." Then at once, his mood turned darker. I could read the grief on his face.

"I'm so sorry about . . . I know you cared for . . . I am sorry, François."

"It seems wrong, doesn't it? All these people here, waiting to pick over her bones?"

"Ah, with wealth comes a wealth of other issues, isn't this true?"

"I want you to know I'm not here for her things," he said. "I've never been after her money."

"Of course not. I would not have asked why you were here. I'm here, too, you see. And not for her things, either."

"I only want the birdcage," said François. "She gave it to me the last time I saw her, but when I went to look for it, it was gone. I suspect her sister has it, though I'm not sure." He pulled out the newspaper and pointed to the advertisement. "It says here in the list of items that there are birdcages for sale. Birdcages." His eyes looked hopeful.

"Perhaps you will find what you are looking for," I told him.

"So may I ask, what brings you here?"

I breathed in deeply and turned my eyes up to the balcony. There, in front of the open turquoise shutters, were the letters of my great-grandfather's initials permanently forged in iron. I waved my hand and presented the whole structure to him. "This home is my heritage," I said.

"This home?" His eyebrows rose.

"Indeed. I told you my great-grandfather built this place, did I not? Well, it is true. I have long desired to have it back in my possession. In my family's possession. This home is . . . very special to me. With my father gone, my grandfather, my great-grandfather . . . not to mention my son—the Le Monnier mansion is the one thing I feel is truly mine in New Orleans. It's a connection to a rich family history."

"I feel the birdcage is mine as well," he said. "I made it with my own hands."

"My great-grandfather made this house with his own hands."

François looked troubled. "I . . . I can only imagine how you feel." He looked around at the crowd and then down at his shoes. "All this time Madame was living there, you . . . were wishing you were there instead."

"Not at all. That's not what I'm saying. I'm just here because of the small fantasy that the property itself may one day come up for sale and then I might have a fair crack at it."

"Hey, we're moving!" said a man behind me. People began to push one another, and the Sherriff came round and opened the door. After explaining our rules, we marched up the stairs dutifully and in good form. As we entered the apartment on the fourth floor, I saw François crumble. "*Mon dieu*, it smells just like her still."

I held him up and said, "Come on. Let's find that birdcage."

We looked in room after room, checking with other people to be sure they didn't have it. Even the oval dining room which once held it was void of the cage. Indeed, we never did find it, though François frantically searched and asked around. In the end, I left empty-handed. No one miraculously offered the home to me, and François went home with not a birdcage, but something else that had belonged to Carmelite Saloy. It was her hairbrush, carved from ivory. I watched as he lifted it to his nose and inhaled the remnant of her scent then searched for hairs that may have lingered.

It was then I decided he was the most pitiful creature I had ever seen, and guilt pricked at my sides for never having cured him. He was walking grief. Unrequited love personified. I went home straightaway and grabbed up Eulalie, kissing my wife with a passion I'd not mustered since our little René had passed away.

From the journal of Y. R. Le Monnier, M.D., Re: 1908

I decided I couldn't watch it happen to the boy. Andrew Reynaud's murder trial was finally here, and I found that I wanted no part of it. I'd given the attorneys all that I could with regard to my findings—that Andrew could have been considered temporarily insane due to alcohol—but I'd advised them as well that this was a risky plea. So on the morning of May 12 I sat, mouth dropped open, at the headline that glared at me:

CURSE OF MONEY REYNAUD'S DEFENSE
Heired Saloy Fortune, and From Moment of Possession Until the Time He Shot Belle Collier Down, His Life Was One Continuous Squander and Spree.

The article detailed the courtroom drama, the witnesses who described the debauchery of Andrew's six months prior to the killing. It was just as he had told me—after receiving his share of the sale of Kirby's Ten-Cent Store on Canal Street, he wasted over $34,000 on whisky and women. The attorneys tried to prove that his being addicted to alcoholic stimulants caused him to be insane that Thanksgiving night.

But then the prosecution provided its crucial witness, a Doctor Van Wart. He claimed that Andrew was quite sane based on his observations and research into the family history—his main source being Andrew's own father. It looked as if a mistrial might be declared as the jury was still out. Andrew's fate now rested in its hands.

I slammed the paper shut and put my hand over my eyes. The attorneys went with the defense that Andrew was cursed by the money, not that the money, itself, was cursed. But of course, they couldn't. There was no way to prove that the same money that caused Andrew to kill Belle Collier, in fact, also caused his younger sister, Carmelite, to die. No, the courts would never hear of this. And yet, I knew that this correlation existed. Not only did the money connect the two tragedies, but something else connected them as well—the father. Felix Reynaud was a constant in both of these cases. He'd practically nailed the coffin on his own son's insanity plea. Might he also have framed the young Ferdinand to look guilty of murdering Carmelite?

I imagined the look on François' face as he sat in the courtroom watching his grandson's trial. All the man had time for these days was walking to and fro, room to room in the Courthouse, from one grandchild's case to another. If anyone was cursed, it was the old man, the birdcage maker, who had to watch it all.

I got up and retrieved my hat and walking cane. I decided I could not sit still in my home, waiting for the newspaper to come out tomorrow to tell me the news. I needed to be there in court to hear the verdict when it came back from the jury. I needed to be there for Carmelite who was there, no doubt, in spirit, watching over her brother from the grave.

The courtroom was filled with people, many of them ladies who were there in support of Belle Collier. These were women of all colors, dressed in their finest, a gaudy barrage of femininity. The room had an air of a circus come to town. There was much chatter and laughter between the ladies of the night and the gentlemen who filled the rest of the benches. As most of the witnesses were from the restricted district, either saloon keepers or patrons, the waiting was a lively affair. It did not seem as if the fate of a man lay in the balance.

I found François Reynaud sitting near the back. He was unshaven with gray stubble around his usually sculpted beard. His legs were crossed, arms contorted, his hat hanging off the toe of one shoe. A woman in purple taffeta giggled in front of him to a young blushing man who was admiring her attention. François was watching them both, biting his fingernail.

I took a seat next to him and touched his leg to let him know I was there. He unfolded and greeted me with a look.

"Any word?" I asked.

"No. Nothing."

I looked about me. How long would we have to wait? I could smell liquor from someone's breath behind me. I turned and caught a man tucking his flask back into his coat pocket.

After a while, it seemed the sentries were forming at the doorways. Was the jury coming? The judge? A hushed murmur moved over the crowd as the judge walked in and took his seat. Just then an old woman came and sat beside me. I didn't look at her but smelled her perfume. The couple in front of us whispered back and forth. "Three dollars he's guilty," said the man. The woman nodded.

"Guilty," said the voice beside me. The old woman crossed her arms and squinted. "As are we all." She pulled out a handkerchief and blotted the corner of one eye. I turned to look at François who had heard her comment. I watched his face contort when he saw her. He shook his head. Then the verdict was read.

"Andrew Reynaud, you have been found guilty on all counts of the murder of Doris Shelton, also known as Belle Collier." Cries and cheers were heard all over the room. "You will serve a sentence of life in prison in the Louisiana State Penitentiary, effective immediately."

I reached over and touched François' back. I was unsure if he might be having a heart attack. His mouth was dropped open and his eyes fixed on Andrew being led away. He didn't seem to be breathing. Slowly, he pushed up, and I helped him out of the bench. François headed straight for the door as I held his arm. I squeezed and said, "I am so sorry, François. So terribly sorry."

People were filing by us in the hallway, but François had slowed to a stop. I tried to urge him forward so we wouldn't be quite in the way, but then I saw it. His eyes were locked on those of his son. Felix Reynaud stood leaning against the white wall. His eyes were glistening. He looked at his father with pleading eyes but neither man spoke. Finally, he turned to me and said, "Did he . . ." I nodded and said, "Life." Felix looked down slowly as if a piece of dust was sifting to the floor. "I'm sorry," I added. I wondered if François would take this time to reconcile with his son in their shared misery, but deep down, I knew he suspected his son of causing much of it. François began walking again, so I followed.

We made it out into the daylight which smelled delightful and was beautiful and crisp to the eyes. It was much too happy outside for the storm that had raged inside the courthouse. François stayed silent for blocks and blocks. We walked, me holding him up by the arm, and I never dared asked where we were going. Finally, I couldn't keep my silence any longer.

"That woman," I said, "the old one sitting next to me. Do you have any idea who that was?"

François stopped and looked at me under the brim of his hat. His eyes cleared as he said the words slowly as if explaining to a child, "She was Madeline Pons, Madame Saloy's sister. She's part of the reason for our suffering."

"What do you mean?" I asked him.

"Voudoo," he said. Everything around him seemed to go quiet. Even the birds ceased to sing.

"You can't be serious."

"*Oui.* Have I never told you the story?"

"You've written many stories, François, but I'm afraid you may have left that one out."

"No, no, I'm quite sure I told you about Madame's sister."

He looked at me, and I could tell he quite knew I was lying and had not read his correspondence. "Yes, of course," I said. "I think I remember such letters, but it's been many years, you understand. Perhaps you can refresh my memory?" My mind was racing. Young Carmelite Kurucar had asked me about a curse. Andrew had claimed there was a curse. And now, after each was either dead or imprisoned, it came to my attention that voodou may have been involved—perhaps a real curse, so far as one can believe in them.

My skin crawled as I led him to a small café. I would buy him coffee. He would tell me this tale. And soon I would have to track down this Madeline Pons, for she may be more important than I once understood her to be.

Partial letter from François, July 1891

"Madeline!" I banged on the doorway of her home on Seventh Street. It was a humble place with some of the neighbors failing to keep up their yards. I stood there for a moment, waiting, and then knocked again. "Madeline? Mrs. Pons?"

The door opened a crack, but it was not Mrs. Pons who answered. "She's not here," said a young woman. I recognized her from the courthouse. "Carmelite?" I asked.

"Yes, hello, Mr. Reynaud."

The girl was not as pretty as her cousin had grown up to be. The other Carmelite, or Carmen, now my daughter-in-law, seemed to have stolen her beauty.

"Look at you. It has been many years, has it not? You've become a lovely young lady." I grinned at her. "I was hoping to speak to your mother." I peeked in the house around her to see if I might catch a glimpse of my cage.

"I'm not sure where she is or when she will be home, I'm afraid."

"Oh, I see." I put on a very sad face and said, "And I've come all this way."

The girl looked a bit hesitant. "Well, it is possible she may return any moment. Would you care to come in and wait? I could offer you a glass of water."

"Oh, yes, that would be lovely. I am parched after this walk."

She led me into her home and offered me a seat in the living room, yet I had investigating to do. I stood and looked around as if I were studying the photographs on the walls, the ones that included Mr. Pons before he'd left Madeline a widow, and the knickknacks and books on the shelves. I could hear her in the kitchen getting a glass. I hurried across the hall to the dining room, but did not see a cage. I peered down the hallway to the bedrooms, but I knew I could not go back there without being caught. When she brought me the glass of water, it occurred to me that honesty might be the best tactic in this situation.

"Thank you, dear." I swallowed nearly the whole glass-full, emphasizing how parched I had been. I smiled again, mustering all the charm I had. I'd recognized the fact that I was considered quite handsome in most circles, and drew upon this truth, gazing into her eyes.

"Do you remember the first time we met?"

Her eyes lit up. "Yes. I believe I do. It was at Auntie's house. I must have been, what, five? Six years old?"

"*Oui.* Just a child. I remember how excited you were when you would get down on your knees and peer into that large bird cage I had created. The one that looked just like the Le Monnier mansion, your aunt's house."

She clapped her hands together. "Oh, yes, I remember! I was lost in those tiny features, imagining myself a tiny person, walking about in it. It was quite spectacular. Do you still make birdcages?"

"*Moi?* Oh, no, I'm afraid. I've got little time these days, now that I'm cooking in Gaillardanne & Debat, but I miss it so. I do."

I rubbed my goatee and turned, looking about for my courage. "Tell me, Carmelite, do you happen to know where that birdcage is? It's the strangest thing. It seems to have disappeared. Madame Saloy told me she wanted me to have it . . . right before she passed away."

"Oh." She looked saddened and frightened at the same time. Had I said too much? I imagined myself before a wayward deer. One false move and she would scamper away in fright.

"Oh, how thoughtless of me. I neglected to tell you how sorry I am for your loss. Your aunt was someone . . . I considered her to be one of my closest friends." I hung my head and cleared my throat. The emotions were simply too raw.

"I am sorry for your loss, as well," she said. "My aunt was the most loving person. She taught me everything I know. If it were not for her, I would never have been able to go to the Pinac Institute. All those books above . . ." She pointed to the shelves. "Aunt Carma gave them to me."

I sighed. "I only wish I had what she wanted me to gift me. I . . . I think it might be the slightest bit easier to handle her loss if . . . well. I can see I've kept you too long. It appears your mother is out for a bit longer, wherever she is. I'll just be going."

"Please wait . . . Mr. Reynaud." I turned, my heart racing. Was she going to divulge the cage's whereabouts? "I, too, know what it is like to have something special to remember her by. You see, she gifted something to me just before she died as well."

"She did?"

Quietly, the girl walked to the dining room and reached up high over the hutch. She pulled down carefully a box, dark wood with an ivory inlay of Madame's monogram.

"Oh, how beautiful," I said. Tears welled in my eyes. "And she gave this to you?"

She nodded.

"How special you must have been to her. Is there anything in it?"

She looked up at me with that same deer-eyed look. She pulled the box closer to her and then turned to go put it back in place. "I haven't quite examined it yet. It's . . . too soon. Too hard."

"Yes, I see." But I knew she was lying. "If you do happen to catch wind of where my birdcage might be, would it trouble you to let me know?" I pulled out a calling card for the restaurant and handed it to her.

She turned and looked down the hallway for a moment before turning back to me. I knew in that instant the cage must be in a back room. Sweat broke out on my brow.

"Of course, I will let you know." She didn't look in my eyes but down at my jacket. Yes, she was lying. I handed her my empty water glass and left the girl and the home where I knew my birdcage to be. Why was she hiding it from me? Why was everyone trying to keep the single thing that belonged to me out of my hands? It was enraging, and I pulled at my hair as I counted my many steps home. How close I had come to the cage!

Maddening! Now, not only did I not have my cage, but I wondered, too, what Madame Saloy had given her niece in that box before she died. It is a funny thing, grief. It can go from sadness to bewilderment to rage—even jealousy—from one moment to the next, tossing and turning you like a bottle in the waves.

François

Partial letter from François, July 1891

I caught up with Madeline several days later as I lay in wait outside her home on Seventh Street. I had become like a hunter. I would wait for her either to come or to go. Then she would be forced to give me answers as to the cage's whereabouts.

She was arriving on carriage. I waited to approach after her driver had helped her to the ground. "Mrs. Pons," I called. "*Bonjour.* Might I have a word?"

She appeared deep in consternation and caught off guard by my presence. "A word . . . Mr. Reynaud?"

"Again, I am so sorry for your loss. Madame was—"

"My sister, yes. I know."

"I realize you are very busy with the affairs of her estate, and I wouldn't dare ask if it weren't terribly important. I'm looking for her birdcage. The one I created, the replica of the Saloy home, the Le Monnier mansion."

"A cage."

"*Oui.* She wanted me to have it."

"Did she? I haven't seen or heard anything of the sort."

"Well, I'm informing you now." I couldn't keep the edge from my voice.

"Mr. Reynaud, I am much too busy to be dealing with birdcages. I assure you, it was probably sold at the estate sale."

"But I was there. It was not sold. It was not there. It was not there even before Madame died. It was missing."

"Missing. Mr. Reynaud, the only thing missing is your missing the fact that I have too much on my mind right now for such trivial matters."

"Trivial? It is not trivial." My feathers flared. "That was my finest work. I spent hours upon hours upon hours crafting every piece by hand." My offense was plastered across my face.

165

Madeline seemed to soften. "I wish I could help you, but you have no idea what . . ." She began to tear up. "I only want what is best for my sister's estate, and I'm afraid it's gotten much more complicated. That's all I can say at this moment." She turned to her bag and reached for her key. "I do hope you get whatever it is you're looking for."

She opened the door and began to step in.

"So you have not seen the birdcage?"

The driver was still standing there, ready to step in if I made a scene.

"Good day, Mr. Reynaud." The door shut, and I heard the lock fasten. I eyed the driver to see if he may know anything of my cage. He simply glared at me, then went back about his business with the horses.

The next morning when I opened the *Times Picayune,* I realized what had been on Madeline's mind. It appeared her family was now the center of an enormous and embarrassing scandal. How trivial, indeed, my bird-cage must have seemed to her.

François

Times-Picayune, June 19, 1891

A TERRIBLE CASE

A Widow's Estate Claimed by the State on Peculiar Grounds

New Orleans, June 19 – About a year ago, Bertrand Saloy died, leaving an estate valued $700,000, which he willed to his wife, Carmelite Carcano. About three months ago, Saloy's widow died, and the estate was claimed by her sister and brother (deceased) and their descendants and put in their possession by order of the court. Today in the Civil District Court, Attorney General Rogers and associate counsel Girault, Firrar and Wynne filed a petition of intervention on behalf of the State of Louisiana, which claimed to be the sole heir of the estate.

The State alleges that Carmelite Carcano, widow of Bertrand Saloy, was an adulterous bastard, the offspring of the illegitimate connect between Dolores Morales and Antonio Carcano, late a resident of this city, now deceased. Petitioners allege that Mrs. Saloy's mother was married lawfully to Jaun Gestal in Havana, Cuba while she lived in open concubinage in New Orleans with Antonio Carcano. Detectives just returned from Cuba have discovered that Delores Morales had several children in Havana with Jaun Gestal before eloping to New Orleans with Mr. Carcano. Carmelite

Dolores' family tree in Cuba by Y. R. Le Monnier, M.D.

Carcano, widow of Bertrand Saloy, Madeline Carcano, widow of Antoine Pons, and Antonio Carcano, now deceased, were the fruit of the said illicit and adulterous connection, and not being legal or lawful descendants, the estate has been put into their possession illegally, and for these reasons, the State is the only heir at law.

From the journal of Y. R. Le Monnier, M.D., Re: 1908

"You have no legitimate reason to question me anymore," said Ferdinand Kurucar, the young Carmelite's widower. "I've been to court. I've explained the whereabouts of Carmelite's inheritance. I've suffered the indignity of serving time in jail for trying to conceal money that was rightly mine. My wife gave me her money. It was mine to do what I wished with it. And now, her father has got more than his fair share of it. So, no. There is no more need for questioning. I am simply trying to get back on with my life. Now if you will excuse me." The young man turned his light on and began to inspect with a magnifying glass a gold ring. I had found him working in his father's jewelry store on Conti Street.

"I'm not here to question you about the money, Mr. Kurucar," I said. "I simply wanted to ask you about the manner in which Carmelite died."

At this, his face went sallow as if he was remembering that very moment. Then he looked around him to see who was there to overhear. He ushered me out the door where we stood on the sidewalk, watching passersby.

"Had she appeared ill?" I continued.

"No. Not especially. Occasionally she would complain as all females might, I imagine, but I had no idea she was dying, if that's what you mean."

"And was it sudden? Can you tell me what happened?"

"I'm sorry . . ." he looked down at my card, "Dr. Le Monnier, but I don't understand why you are here. Who are you representing? Felix Reynaud?"

"I'm only here representing your wife, sir. I'm not a lawyer. She was a friend. The grandchild of a friend, really. I was just so shocked to hear she had died so young and what appeared to be so suddenly."

"Right." He went to his shirt pocket and pulled out a cigarette, offering me one. I shook my head, and he lit up and inhaled deeply. "Honestly, she was happy for the first time in quite a while. She seemed to be in a good mental state. She'd never been settled after having received her inheritance or, for that matter, after marrying me. Her father remained upset with her and had refused to speak to her for many months. But just before she died, they had made amends. We had invited him for dinner. She made roast beef and the most delicious pie." He smiled, remembering. "It appeared that we might finally have a normal life together with everyone getting along, but that was not to be the case. About a day or two after that supper, she complained she wasn't feeling well and spent much time disposed in the bath. I found her on the bathroom floor. She must have fallen and was writhing. Shaking. She looked so frightened, and I was terrified. I took her to the bed and called for the doctor, but she was gone before he could get there."

"Oh. I see. How awful for you."

He hung his head and kicked at the ground. I gave him a moment. Finally, I said, "And what did the doctor say was the cause of her death?"

"He said uraemic convulsions."

Uraemic convulsions, exactly. But what were her kidneys responding to? What were they working so hard to expel from her body?

"Thank you, Mr. Kurucar. I can understand you've suffered a great loss. I imagine the money is no consolation at a time like this." I was baiting him and wondered how he might react.

"The money? Ha. What can it give me? My wife is dead. I've been to court and to prison. I'm a widower at age nineteen. If you ask me, this money has bought me nothing but trouble."

"Of course. Again, I'm terribly sorry for your loss." I shook his hand before he went back into the jewelry store.

Walking down the street to catch the cable car, I mumbled to myself. "Yes, thank you, Mr. Kurucar. You've been most helpful indeed."

Later that afternoon, I decided to pay a visit to the Soldier's Home on Bayou St. John. I'd been surgeon for the home when I was a bit younger, and remained interested in the care of our veterans housed there. One of the most serious issues was the threat of attempted suicide. On my recommendations, improved care had been implemented to stave off this beast such as increased access to fresh air and the outdoors, more frequent visitation, and better diet.

As former vice-president of Camp No. 9 of the Army of Tennessee, the Soldiers Home was a special cause. Many of my former camp members were now living in that very home. I checked in with the medical personnel I knew, made my rounds visiting the soldiers, some friends, others I'd never known before. And when I went to leave, I remembered I hadn't signed the visitor's book. Staring at my signature, I thought to look through the log simply out of curiosity. There were many names I recognized. Some noble men and women visited their veterans who lived in this place, and others came to visit simply to fulfill their honorable duty as a citizen of this state.

There, on the page before mine, was the name F. R. Kurucar. Ferdinand had been here. Did he have a relative he was visiting? I thought back over every veteran I remembered, for there were nearly two-hundred by now, but the name Kurucar did not present itself.

I set the log down. What did this mean? Could I deduce anything from this coincidence at all? I supposed I could. Logically, a visitor to the Soldier's Home, simply for the sake of honoring his duty, could not be all that evil. Perhaps this Ferdinand was telling the truth. Perhaps he had no idea how his wife had died or what had caused her death. Perhaps he *had* been caught up with the money and tried to hide it when they came for it, but at that young age, might I have done the same thing?

I'd hate to think it, but nothing compares with the folly of youth.

As I picked up my hat and headed for the lawn, a bird flew so near me, I had to duck for it to miss my head.

I dropped my hat. When I bent to pick it up, it hit me. Yes. It had to be. I knew what I needed to do now. I should have listened to the cagemaker all along. By the time I stepped up into the cable car, my mind was racing nearly as quickly as my heart, and I felt the desperate need for a stiff drink.

From the journal of Y. R. Le Monnier, M.D.

RE: NEW ORLEANS, 1908

The saloon was not far away. I walked down Royal Street, eyeing the Le Monnier mansion as I passed her by. She was showing her age and had been neglected. Patches of plaster had fallen from her sides, exposing brick underneath and lines like spider veins crawling up the edges. The turquoise shutters had faded, and one had a broken hinge, leaving it hanging crooked. I stared up at the monogram of my great-grandfather in the iron railing and said a little prayer of forgiveness. Might he forgive me for letting our namesake come to this?

I pushed myself forward, bent on the task at hand. By the time I made it to Gravier Street, I was ready. Fortified. No drink necessary.

I entered the Continental Saloon. I found Felix Reynaud behind the counter, serving his customers. It was early yet, only past seven, so the room was still partially empty, not as it might be later when the revelers came out. I caught his eye as I sat on a barstool. He looked at me and said, "What'll it be?"

As if he didn't know me. As if he didn't know why I was here.

"Bourbon. If you'll join me."

"Bourbon," he said. "I'm working. As you can see."

"Then I'll wait until you're finished," I said.

"Gonna be a long wait. Late night."

I looked about me. Was there no one else working in the saloon? Of course, there was. A Negro was clearing a table, and another person was clanging about in the back room. He came out wearing an apron and carrying two bottles of liquor.

"Oh, I don't have that long, I'm afraid. Might you ask your friend to watch the bar for a few minutes? I'd really like to speak with you."

"I don't see what there is to speak about. My son is in prison for life now, Dr. Le Monnier. There is nothing you or I can do about it."

"I'm not here to talk about your son. It's your daughter I'm concerned with."

"Well. You're too late there," he said.

"Yes, because she's dead."

"Son of a—that's no way to speak to a father!"

"You're right," I said. "But it is the way to speak—" I leaned in closer to whisper, "to a murderer. I think it was you who killed your daughter, Mr. Reynaud. You saw her just before she died."

Felix Reynaud contorted into an enraged beast and grabbed me by the arm, jerking me from the bar stool. He held his grip as he told the man behind the bar, "Watch over for me, John." He dragged me into the back room where patrons couldn't watch with bottles and boxes surrounding us. A cockroach ran across the floor. He shook his hand off of me but I could still feel his fingers.

"Are you insane?" he hissed, just inches from my face. "Who do you think you are calling *me* . . . Oh. Oh, I get it!" he sneered. "This has to do with the house, doesn't it? The Le Monnier mansion. My wife owned it and wouldn't sell it to you. You'd do anything to get back at her, wouldn't you? Wouldn't you." He thought for a moment, his finger still pointed at me. "Yes . . . even killing her. Even killing her daughter. *My* daughter. It was you, wasn't it, Dr. Le Monnier! You killed my daughter! You poisoned her! You said yourself you saw her just days before her death!

I was stunned. There seemed to be as much circumstantial evidence against me as there was against Felix Reynaud. Was it preposterous that he was guilty? For a split second I felt as if the earth shifted, and I was unstable on my feet. I wasn't guilty. I'd had nothing at all to do with Carmelite's death, nor her mother's.

"'That's enough," I said. "You have proved your point, Mr. Reynaud, but I will get to the bottom of this. I will."

"You will not to show your face here again, do you hear me? I don't care if you're friends with my father or with my son. I don't care if you're friends with the Pope. You're not welcome." He stood, arms folded and firm. I brushed off my jacket and paused for a moment. I was ready to leave. Ready, but something was holding me back. Something was still bothering me.

I turned to face him again. His face was bright red, his ears in flames. "You know, it's funny. Interesting, I mean. When I spoke to you, I never said that I thought your daughter was poisoned. Yet when you were accusing me, you said I was one who had killed her. That I was the one who had poisoned her." I laughed a little. "I'm a doctor. I've seen just about every ailment there is, which is why the deduction that Carmelite was poisoned is an easy one to make. For me. But you, you're a saloon-keeper. What would you know of the effects of poisoning on a body? Unless of course . . ."

"Get out. I won't say it again, and I won't be as nice the next time. I promise you that."

As I walked home it became clear to me. Yes. It was just as François had told me. His son, Felix was the murderer. He had poisoned his own daughter for . . . for betraying him by eloping with Ferdinand, and so that he could get her money. I felt vindicated and yet I'd nowhere to go with it. With Carmelite's body already interred, there was no way to prove that she'd been murdered at all, nonetheless, who had done it.

And I was sure who had done it.

As I passed the Le Monnier mansion one last time, the shadows had turned a deep indigo, and the house looked smooth with all blemishes concealed in the darkness. For a moment, I saw it as I once had when I was just a boy, as a childhood home, a safe place, a wonderland. Yet his words, Reynaud's words, echoed in my mind. *You would've done anything to get back at her, wouldn't you?*

It brought it all back. It was strange. I hadn't remembered those feelings in so many years. I had all but forgotten the time I requested to purchase the Le Monnier home, my birthright, and was shut down by Carmen Reynaud, the new owner of her aunt's property. I was disappointed, yes. She wasn't using the property as her main residence, and could easily have let the property go back into family hands had she wanted to. But I could not pay her exorbitant price, and she wouldn't budge. For what reason? Did she need the money? She had more money than she knew what to do with, and I simply wanted the Le Monnier home restored to its familial glory.

I caught my breath and rubbed my sore arm. Suddenly, I did feel like a drink— a warm toddy to put me to sleep so that for a few short hours I might forget how helpless I felt and always had felt to see fairness, justice, and retribution served.

From a letter from François, regarding April 1892

"Fortune comes with a price, does it not," said Salome, holding on to my arm. "Look at this place! No one would ever know that its walls drip with shame." She stopped at the gate and turned to look at me. "Adultery defiles families for generations to come." She was referring to the headlines calling Madeline Pons and her siblings, Madame Saloy and Antonio Carcano, "adulterous bastards," but she was speaking about me. She had long thought I had crossed that line with Madame Saloy, but I had not. She was wrong about me. I'd stayed faithful to my wife. Faithful to my family. But my words would never convince her.

As the parents-in-law of one of the Saloy heirs, my wife and I had been invited to Madeline's new home for a dinner party. The residence was an exquisite Victorian courtyard mansion on Esplanade Avenue. The celebration was in honor of the fact that the collateral heirs of Madame Saloy had been victorious in their dispute with the State of Louisiana. The Louisiana Supreme Court had ruled in the heirs' favor, saying the State had no right to remove Madeline as administrator of her sister's estate. It also meant my son's wife was about to inherit a formidable fortune as was each of the heirs.

The house on Esplanade had been baptized with a fresh coat of white paint. There was a wrought iron gate to enter and then steps that led up to the covered porch with ionic columns. One entered the house from the porch through the main glass door that was part of a square tower at the left corner turned at an odd angle. Fourteen foot ceilings with tall windows and intricate moldings around the fireplace and stairwells made my head swoon. I could envision drawing the bones of the house and planning out each and every piece. It would be a magnificent cage, the tall tower presenting a wonderful challenge of engineering. I stood there, mourning the loss of my studio and of my cage-making business. Perhaps one day I could take it up again. Perhaps one day I would stumble upon the greatest cage I had ever created, the Le Monnier mansion. I looked around at all the people, estimating the square footage, and imagining how many rooms there were upstairs. My birdcage, no doubt, was in one of them, and one day, perhaps even tonight, I would discover it.

Salome seemed overwhelmed by the majesty of the place. She stared up into the ceiling at the detailed medallions holding crystal chandeliers and held on to my arm tighter as if she were about to fall. It was a far cry from Madeline's former home on Seventh Street. She must have spent a fortune on this house. And if so, one could only imagine what was in store for the rest of the family.

My son, Felix, and I had been getting along quite well considering the tension that had once come between us after his secret elopement with Carmen Carcano, Madeline's niece. Since then, both of her parents had died, poor girl, and she needed all the family she could get. It had always struck me that Madeline favored her own daughters over Antonio's only child, and I wondered how equitable her distribution of the family fortune might be.

Madeline stood in front of a grand round table with a towering arrangement of flowers. She held out a champagne glass while a man next to her called out, "Here, here, quiet down!" The guests soon hushed and gathered around.

"Thank you, Paul," Madeline said to the man. He was squirrelly and dark, sporting a mustache, and seemed quite pleased to have been of service. He most certainly wasn't her husband for Antoine Pons had been dead for several years now after an accident in Mexico.

"Welcome, everyone, to my new home." The guests began to cheer and clap, so Paul raised his hands to hush them once more. "In a few minutes," she continued, "we're going to dine on a wonderful supper together, but before we do, there are a few things I'd like to say." You could hear nothing now. There was no movement, no breathing for that matter.

Madeline's face grew solemn. "It has been nearly a year since my dear sister left us. She was a lovely girl, kind, and honest in every way, and she fell in love with a man."

I felt my face flush and hoped no one could see.

"A wealthy man, Bertrand Saloy." More clapping ensued. "Both Bertrand and Carma are gone now, and have left a void in our family that will never be filled. And yet, they have left us so much.

"This last year has been most trying in every way. First there was the grief, and then it was the courts. The cases. The appeals. The constant struggle for what is rightfully ours. But . . ." She held up her glass and closed her eyes. "No matter what has been said and done to this family, no matter how jealous people tried to taint our good names with evil ones, we have been victorious." She opened her eyes and smiled. "We are victorious!" The room erupted with joy, and I could not help but watch my son, Felix, remaining still and firm as his young wife jumped and clapped her hands. Hands in pockets, he seemed to be studying the whole situation, assessing it, much as his father was doing. We were not blood relations to this family, and at times it was surreal that we were considered parts of it at all.

Oh, how I longed for Madame Saloy to be here for this moment, to see me in her sister's home as part of her own family. Madame's family. How did I get here? My head swam with my champagne and thoughts of yesteryear. Oh, yes, it was a long history.

Madeline leaned over and whispered to Paul who quieted us all down again.

"My dear mother," said Madeline, "God rest her soul, was no earthly saint. This much has been established in the courts and in the newspapers recently, and yet, I say, who here is a saint? Is there one here among us?"

No, I thought, because she is gone. Madame is forever gone.

"It came as a deep surprise to find out that my mother had a family before ours in Havana. A dastardly, wicked surprise. Even more so to discover that many of her other *grandchildren* in Cuba, your distant cousins are, as we speak, making their way to New Orleans to claim their share of my sister's estate."

A murmur spread through the room as the realization occurred that more grandchildren meant more collateral heirs and smaller shares.

"Please, please," said Madeline, "let's stay on task. I feel it necessary to explain to you what my mother was like. You all knew her . . ." She turned to look at her daughters and Carmen, "as your grandmother. She was devoted to us all in her own quiet way, and I can tell you as a mother, she was second to none. She loved my father, Antonio Carcano, a hard-working Italian fisherman, and although I did not know her previous husband in Cuba," she winced, "I imagine he must have been most vile for her to flee for her life and begin again with a new love, a new life, here in New Orleans.

"My mother knew something that I am just beginning to understand, and that is that life sometimes offers us new beginnings, new chances to start fresh and to put the past behind us. And so, dear family, sweet friends, that is what I intend to do. Beginning tonight at this moment, we are all to forget the sting of what's been said of us in the papers. We are no longer *adulterous bastards* nor were we ever. I forbid any of you to consider that title again." She lifted her glass high above her head. "To new beginnings!"

"Here, here! To new beginnings!" shouted everyone, glasses raised. The music began again. There was a black man sitting behind a grand piano, and his music lifted us, carried us, pulsating like blood through veins to a grand dining room where tables and chairs were set for a small army. The night was young and before the end of it, I would sneak upstairs and scour the many bedrooms unnoticed, never finding my beloved birdcage. Was it really gone? Had it been sold? Would I never see it again?

My heart ached with grief. I watched as Madeline made her rounds to each heir with news of an inheritance alongside her new young mustachioed attorney, Paul Fourchy. By midnight, most everyone would be drunk not only with wine but with the intoxication of great wealth and the possibilities that came with it. I, of course, would be quite sober and empty-handed.

But my son would end up with a wide smile on his face and the same twinkle in his eye that I'd first seen when he was just a boy, beholding the Saloy home for the first time, the Le Monnier mansion on Rue Royale.

François

From the journal of Y. R. Le Monnier, M.D., Re: 1908

François had offered me the address where Madeline Pons lived on Esplanade Street, but he did not want to accompany me on my visit. He'd said that being in Madeline's presence had long been a draining event and one

Madeline Pons residence, Esplanade Street

he wished to subject himself to no longer. I simply felt the need to look into the matter more deeply, for if Madeline had indeed been involved in some sort of voodou worship or witchcraft, then the curse to which everyone in the family referred might have an origin. Might it then also have a point of reversal?

As I walked down the tree lined street of Esplanade, past grand mansions and sculpted hedges, I felt disoriented. How was it that a coroner, a New Orleans city physician and doctor of psychology was acting as some supernatural detective for a family to which he did not even belong? Was there sense in this? How did this happen? Did I cease to have free will at some point? I would much rather be working on my book about Shiloh. There was much to research and more to write. And yet, here I was, arriving at 937 Esplanade in the crisp February air. It was a massive Victorian structure with neglected white paint, now flaking like a shedding crepe myrtle. I entered the wrought iron gate and ascended the stairs to a porch flanked with ionic columns. The once blue ceiling was dingy and caked with spider webs. A look to the right showed a swimming pool with brackish water that hadn't been swum in for years.

Who took care of this place? Why was it so neglected?

I crossed the porch and stood at the door. It was at an angle attached to a tall square tower. I rang the doorbell and peered into the glass. Inside was dark with light streaking in across wood floors through the shuttered windows.

The door opened and there stood a black woman perhaps a little younger than I, but only a little. Her hair was frosted.

"Can I help you?" she asked. She was dressed in an apron and wiping her wet hands with it. Her eyes were kind, and she smelled of bacon and biscuits.

"Good afternoon, my name is Dr. René Le Monnier," I said, taking my hat off. "I've come to pay a visit to Mrs. Pons. Is she home?"

"A doctor?" She looked frightened. "No, we don't need no doctor."

"Oh, I'm not here on official business as a doctor, I merely happen to be a doctor. May I see Mrs. Pons?"

"She ain't here."

"I see. And would you happen to know when she might be back?" I looked over her shoulder and spotted a grand piano sitting empty and quiet.

"She . . . no, sir, I don't. Went out on her rounds a while ago and sometime take all day long."

"Charity, have you seen my glasses?" I thin shrill voice called out from the darkness. "I swear I had them a minute ago." The woman turned and tried to shut the door a little more, but I could see her, Madeline, walking around in her nightgown. Her white hair was unkempt and her feet wore nothing but socks. On top of her head was a pair of reading glasses.

"Madeline, there you are," said Charity. "How long you been back?" She turned to me. "Musta come home when I was cooking. I get awful caught up when I's in the kitchen." She was trying to cover herself but it wasn't working. Why would she lie to me?

"'Scuse me just a second." Charity closed the door and whispered something to Madeline. When she opened the door again, Madeline had disappeared. "Doctor, she say come on in. Miss Madeline gone be down in a minute. I can get you some coffee?"

"Thank you, yes, please." I took off my coat and handed it along with my hat to the cook. She disappeared to the kitchen and left me standing there in the foyer, looking around. I longed to turn on a light or to open the shutters, but it was not my place. I could see the house was grand indeed, and I could only imagine its previous life when Madeline was younger. What parties she must have had here. What stories these walls could tell.

Charity brought me a cup of strong chicory coffee and sat me down in a chair before a black fireplace with white moldings and mantel. A large mirror framed with ivory hung above it. The fireplace was cold and might not have been lit all winter.

When Madeline returned, she was wearing a gold housecoat and matching slippers. She had a sleeping bonnet on her head and had put streaks of rouge on her cheeks. She smiled like a child.

"Madeline Pons, please let me introduce myself. I am Dr. René Le Monnier."

"Le Monnier. Le Monnier." She was staring into my eyes, searching for recognition, yet she couldn't reach it.

"I'm retired now but was once city physician. My grandfather built the Le Monnier mansion on Royal Street."

"Yes. Yes, Le Monnier. The mansion. I own that, I think. I own many buildings. Thirty, thirty-three . . ."

She was going on almost incoherently, and I immediately recognized a confused mind. It seemed dementia from age might have been setting in.

"You say you're a doctor?" she asked.

"Yes. No longer in practice, but—"

"I'm not crazy," she said, her face changing into something darker. "I have all my wits about me, I tell you, and you can tell my daughters to stay out of my business. I am perfectly fine. Perfectly well."

"Your daughters? I'm afraid I don't know what you're talking about."

"My daughters. They sent you here."

"No, no, I assure you, they did not. Mrs. Pons, I am only here because I was a friend of your great-grand-niece Carmelite Kurucar and her brother, Andrew Reynaud."

"Carmelite, oh . . . and Andrew is . . ." She looked as if I'd just informed her of their fates, and her eyes filled with tears. "It's just so sad. Antonio would have been so sad."

"Yes. I am sorry."

"And my daughters sent you here?"

"No, Madeline." I leaned forward. "I hope you don't mind my asking, but why would you think your daughters sent me? I can promise you we've never even met."

She looked into my eyes back and forth as if one or the other held the truth. Then she started. "They're trying to put me away." Her voice was small and innocent. "They think I cannot handle my money anymore. Or this house. They want it all."

"Oh," I said, but that was it. I could not find the proper words.

"My daughter, Carmelite, she'll never forgive me. I sued her for the box my sister gave her before she died, and it's a good thing. Do you know how much money was in it? Nearly fifty thousand dollars! So they're after my money now. It's always about the money." She reached up and held her housecoat closed at the breast. "I own many properties. Ned and I ride around every day, collecting rent, and everything is just as it should be. Paul says everything will be just fine and that my daughters are unnatural and . . . *evil.*"

She said this last part in a different voice, and I had to ask, "Paul? Who is Paul?"

"Paul . . . is my friend. Well, and my lawyer." She squinted at me. "Does Paul know you're here?"

"Paul, no, I don't believe so."

"Oh. Well. I don't think this is a good idea. Paul will be back soon and I—" She turned to look down the hall, then peered back at me. "Did you say you were from the newspaper? Because I don't think I should do interviews when Paul is not here."

180

I looked at the poor woman and smiled sadly. She was demented and a bit paranoid, and whoever this Paul person was, he seemed to have control over this woman and possibly her finances. Things were deteriorating between us quickly, and I'd promised François. I was losing time.

"Mrs. Pons." I reached over and touched her hand softly. She stared at it. "I'm going to ask you what may seem to be a very strange question, but I hope you'll indulge me. A friend of mine, someone whom you know from many years ago, has been looking for something that once belonged to him. It's . . . it's quite personal to him. I wonder, have you any knowledge of the whereabouts of a very large birdcage? It was created to look like a replica of the Le Monnier mansion—the Saloy residence on Royal Street."

Her pupils seemed to dilate and swallow her eyes whole with darkness.

"A birdcage," she whispered. "I . . . yes, there was a birdcage."

"Oh, splendid. And do you know where it is? What happened to the cage?"

She seemed to go into a trance, and when she came out, she pushed to standing. "What? Who sent you here? I told the judge I didn't dance! I didn't dance! Paul?" The old woman escaped from my presence in a flurry of gold, and the cook, Charity, came running in from the kitchen.

"Madeline? Madeline, come in here and sit down." She threw me an evil look. "What you said to get her so upset? I told you we ain't need no doctor. Now, up outta here. Wore out your welcome." She picked up my coffee cup from the table and walked me over to the door.

"Charity," I said. "I can see you care a good deal for Madeline. And so I have to ask, is she—"

"She be just fine, Mister, and don't be telling them daughters of hers any otherwise. You hear me?" She shooed me out of the door, and I stood there in the chilly air. I was without coat and hat and when I turned to knock again, the door opened and Charity shoved them on me without a word. When the door was shut again, I bundled myself up for the walk home. I turned back around and stared up at the vast white house, the odd tower like the skewed corner of a medieval fortress. Something was amiss in that house. Prosperity had turned to loneliness and paranoia. Madeline was no longer of sound mind, assuming she ever had been.

I passed mansion after mansion as the cold air entered my nostrils and burned my sinuses. In the days before the war, these same beautiful houses held slaves and pinned them up like cattle in the courtyards. Now the courtyards were empty, yet the houses still like cages full of birds.

The birdcage? Yes, I was convinced Madeline knew of its whereabouts, and I wouldn't be at all surprised if she wasn't hiding it somewhere in that gargantuan house. Nothing conclusive though. Just as nothing in my investigations into this entire family had been conclusive. There was no conclusive evidence that Carmelite Kurucar was murdered, nonetheless who had done it, although I highly suspected her father, Felix Reynaud. There was no conclusive evidence that Andrew had murdered his prostitute lover as a result of a family curse and not simply from ill motives and alcoholic addiction. There was no conclusive evidence that a curse existed at all.

But something Madeline had said intrigued me – she may be the current owner of the Le Monnier mansion, a structure I had long given up hope of acquiring. For this, hard evidence would exist.

My mind spun. Was Madeline the owner of my family home? Was she the sole key bearer to retrieving my heritage? And might she, under the proper circumstances, be willing to part with "one of her many properties" that she surely was gaining no pleasure in owning? If her own home was any indication of her ability to keep up house, I worried about the condition of my grandfather's beloved mansion. How far had it fallen into disrepair?

The questions pricked at me, and I found myself turning around and heading straightaway for town hall to look up the chain of title and current deed holder of 640 Royal Street.

From the journal of Y. R. Le Monnier, M.D., Re: 1908

I had never been one to sulk and suffer in prolonged depressed states, but I found myself now squeezed in the middle of one, a vice of despair pressing in on all sides.

I lumbered to the mantle on leaden legs and lifted a photograph of my dearly beloved wife.

"Eulalie," I said. It was all I could manage. I took her back to the sofa and lay her across my heart as I sunk down into the cushions, my head back, eyes pinched closed.

The house on Royal Street, the Le Monnier mansion, did not belong to Madeline Pons after all. The chain of title I'd found listed clearly a string of owners beginning with Pierre Pedesclaux, and then passing into my grandfather's hands and those of François Grandchamp. Next, Le Monnier bought out Grandchamp and after his death, the house went to his daughter's hands. She sold it to Jean Fisse, the grocer, during the war. Bertrand Saloy then bought it up at a Sherriff's sale, and passed it to his wife, Carmelite Saloy. Later, it went to her niece, Carmen Reynaud, and finally . . .

The house was owned by none other than Felix Reynaud. The man I'd just accused of murdering his own daughter.

"It is hopeless," I told Eulalie. "Dear, what have I to live for?"

Eulalie was gone. The light of my life snuffed out. Our only son was a distant memory, a dream woken up from and desperately sought to recover, to no avail.

What was I doing here, anyway? Was I here in New Orleans, a childless widower with no familial legacy and no tangible ties to the former glory of the Le Monnier name, simply to be at the beck and call of the strange cage-maker and his cursed family? Is this what all my life had come to? I remained haunted by the fact that my efforts to identify the source of yellow fever was too little too late. It had claimed my only son not long before mosquitos had been discovered to be the culprit. Is this how things would go with the Saloy heirs? I would search for the seat of their mystery only to be too late once more?

I could not bear it any longer. I looked about the room. This house on North Galvez Street reminded me of Eulalie. She was everywhere. I was nowhere.

In that instant I made a decision, hastily yet firm. I would leave New Orleans. I would slowly take its tentacles off of me one by one until I was free. I felt something akin the mania of madmen, something close to happiness. As close as I'd felt since Eulalie had been laid to rest.

It struck me then. The cage-maker. Did I not owe it to him to tell him I was leaving? Of course, I did not! What sort of thinking was this? This man had been the cause of my chaos as of late, and yet . . .

As a dog with his tail between his legs, I acquiesced. Why must I tell the cage-maker? Perhaps it was the girl's face that came back to me. That poor deluded heiress Carmelite Kurucar, his granddaughter. Perhaps it was his grandson, Andrew, who now sat behind bars at Angola.

No matter. It would not be a long goodbye. It would be for my sake, not his, for closure of this open-ended, never-ending family saga of his. The closure would be for my sake. This is what I told myself.

Gaillardanne & Debat was a small, dimly lit ten-table restaurant on North Peters Street. A black man at the piano played softly while patrons dined to candle-light. A delicious odor of onions and brown butter wrapped around me and whet my appetite as I sat near the window. I was used to dining alone these days, yet tonight, especially, the empty seat felt like a slap in the face, a glaring reminder that all whom I cared about were dead.

Can the old birdcage maker cook? I wondered. I ordered a glass of claret and escargot and sweetbreads. My mouth and my soul entered another realm altogether as I dipped crusty bread into the rich béchamel. Good heavens, this man could cook. Was he an artist in every sense of the word? Was there nothing he could not do with his hands?

I waited until the meal was done and my dishes carried away before I mentioned who I was to the waiter and that I was there to see François Reynaud if he was available. A few moments later, François smiled as he greeted me and with the apron around his waist and flour across his cheek, he almost looked like he did when I first met him years ago, strikingly good-looking in a rugged, dark, French sort of way. He shook my hand and sat in the empty chair across from me.

"*Bonjour*, Doctor. What a pleasant surprise. Did you enjoy your meal?"

"Immensely. I dare say this is the best meal I've had in years in this town."

"You are only being kind."

"François, you know me. Am I ever only kind?"

He smiled and then turned serious. He was studying my eyes. "Why have you come? Is it because of Madeline?"

"Madeline? No, I—"

"Did you hear what happened with her?"

"Happened with Madeline? No. What it is?"

The cage-maker looked down at the table and wiped at a tiny crumb of bread. "It gives me no joy to say this. None at all. You know how I've felt about Madeline all these years, but I do not wish her ill."

"Is she ill?" I asked.

"*Peut-être*. But the courts will decide that. Her daughters have sued for interdiction. They're trying to put her away in a madhouse."

"No."

"*Oui*. I'm afraid her own daughters have turned on her. All except one. Antoinette is there, living with her in the house on Esplanade. Her sisters claim she's holding her there against her will."

"Holding her mother in her own home against her will?"

"Apparently."

"That seems ridiculous. I just met with her last week. She didn't seem completely well, but it wasn't the mention of Antoinette's name that caused me concern, it was her other daughters and that of her lawyer, Paul Fourchy."

"Her other daughters are claiming there's a scandalous relationship there between him and her."

"That seems preposterous. She's quite old now. But maybe he's after her money."

"Everyone is after her money. In fact . . ." He looked around him to see if anyone was listening. "This morning she was kidnapped."

"Kidnapped? By whom?"

"Her grandson, Walter Pons. He was waiting for her when she got back from driving."

"How do you know this?" I asked.

François pointed to the black man at the piano. "That's Ned, Madeline's coachman. He works here nights. Would you like a word?"

By all means, no. I had only come there to tell François I would be leaving. That I would no longer be drawn into this dastardly family drama, and yet . . . I could not resist the temptation to find out the facts from an eyewitness to a kidnapping.

"I'll leave you two to talk while I get back to the kitchen," said François after making our introduction.

Ned the coachman sat uneasily across from me. He kept his eyes down and hands in his lap.

"Can you tell me what happened with Madeline today?"

"You police?"

"No," I said. "I'm a doctor."

"A doctor," he said. His eyes shifted up to me and back down again as if he was troubled to speak with me. Afraid almost.

"I'm only a friend of the family. You can trust I have no ill motives."

It took him a minute. Finally he leaned in on his elbows and said. "We just come back from making rounds. Miss Madeline and me go 'bout every day to collect her rents. Miss Antoinette been going with us most days now. She was there when we got back."

He licked his bottom lip and looked to the side to be sure no one was listening. This time, his white eyes searched out mine. "Her grandson, Walter, done jumped up in the carriage after Miss Antoinette got out. He pointed a pistol at me and told me to get in and drive. He told Miss

185

Antoinette he'd kill her if she done anything to stop him. She run on up then in the house screaming and carrying on."

"And what did you do?"

"I got up in there and turned round to check on Miss Madeline. She be shaking and having a fit. But he had that pistol on me and say, 'Damn you, turn around and drive from here or I will kill you.'

"And then what?" I asked.

"I drived! He made me go on up to Ms. Veasey's house over on North Rampart Street. That be Miss Madeline other daughter. When we get there, all them women come on out and start making a fuss over Miss Madeline, Oh, Mama, this, and Oh, Mama, that. It was sick, what it was."

"And where is she now?"

"She still over there far as I know."

"Were the police called?"

"I reckon, but I ain't talked to 'em."

I sat there thinking to myself that this was a matter for the police. The police would handle all of it. They would sort it out. I had no need to get involved. None at all.

"You gone go over there and tend to her, doctor? She be awful upset. Terrible, shaking and all. They gonna kill her, I guarantee. Got a lotta unnatural greed in this family. Unnatural is what it is. I hope you gone go and make sure she ain't dying over there. You gone go?"

It was all I could do. I wanted to say no, I will not go over there. I have no business with this family. And yet, I did not. Yet, I could not. Why was I sitting here, talking with Ned, Madeline's coachman? How had this been orchestrated? Why, God, did you see fit to involve me in all of these affairs that had nothing to do with me?

"Yes," I said finally, stunning myself. "If she's still there tomorrow, I'll go by and check on her."

Ned grinned and reached over to shake my hand. "Thank you, Doc, thank you. Miss Madeline, she ain't the nicest person, ain't the smartest, neither, but she . . . she what I got. You understand?"

"Yes, Ned. I believe I do understand."

From the journal of Y. R. Le Monnier, M.D., Re: 1909

In June of 1909 I was struck by a street car while trying to cross over Canal. I was on my way to the old Le Monnier mansion to have my final look. My

Madeline Pons' lawyer, Paul Fourchy

mind was full of bittersweet nostalgia or else I surely would have gotten out of the way.

I spent the night in Charity hospital under observation, but was not broken, only badly bruised with a hip partially dislocated.

Two weeks later on cane, at the age of 66 years, I finally left for Shiloh. Although I still owned my house on North Galvez Street, in my heart I had left New Orleans for good. It was a bitter divorce. Every memory I'd ever had was there. Memories of my beloved wife Eulalie and of our dear son, René. Memories of my parents and grandparents and of the house on Royal Street that would never be mine. Memories of the court cases, the dead bodies, the insane asylum.

Of the birdcage maker and his family. The Saloys' wealth. The Saloys' curse.

They were memories I was willing to leave behind. All I wanted now was to be left in peace, far enough away from New Orleans that no one could come calling. No one would ask anything of me. I would retire to work on my book, *General Beauregard at Shiloh*. I would spend my days doing something worthwhile, retelling the facts of the war for posterity, recounting the truth as I knew it to be.

I bought the house near Amite City sight unseen. It was recommended to me by a former Confederate soldier and fellow member of the Association of the Army of Tennessee. At each meeting, a roster of newly deceased was read with reverence, and it was there I learned of the demise of Robert Anderson. He'd left a large estate ripe for growing and hunting along with a nice plantation house 75 miles northwest of New Orleans. My heart stirred as I imagined escaping the drama here and helping the family of a fellow soldier at the same time.

I named the place Shiloh before I ever laid eyes on it, but as soon as I saw it I knew I'd found a savior of peace, just as the name implied. It was a two story white structure with double porches on the front for enjoying the breeze, and it overlooked a lane of oak trees on either side of the drive. It was in good shape, aside from occasional peeling paint and dust indoors, but I approached the house like a father to a child. I carefully, lovingly, brought it all back to life. When my furniture was settled and the mirrors cleaned, I sat down at my desk and looked at the notebook before me. It was finally time to relive the war and get it all on paper.

Why would a man want to relive his battles? As a doctor of insanity, I had studied such matters. Not only can the battle of one's life be the most trying and dark time, but often, it can be the most exhilarating. The closer one is to death, arguably, the closer one is to living. I wanted to revisit the Battle of Shiloh, not necessarily to remember the gruesome images of it all, but to remember the adrenaline in my blood, my heightened sense of mortality. So often over the years since, I had grown bored with life and rarely felt a jolt of solid fear to keep me on my toes. I understood this to be true with other veterans, and it is why we clung together in organized groups.

On my desk, I set three priceless Civil War relics. One was a silver dollar presented to me by General Johnston near the end of the war. Another was a musket I collected at the battle of Shiloh. And the other was a pistol hand-carved from the leg bone and blood of a Confederate soldier, made by a patient whiling away time in Camp Chase Hospital, Columbus, Ohio in 1865. It was left by the previous owner of my plantation in a case in the wall beneath the stairs. I saw fit to hold on to it for inspiration—that useful things can be made from resurrected bones.

Day after day, year after year, I poured over my books and research, reading claims and counterclaims of the Battle of Shiloh. Occasionally when I felt especially enlightened, I imagined taking a trip to Pittsburg Landing in Tennessee to walk the grounds and remember those fateful two days, but I never did get around to it. I would pull out my maps and lay them out on the table, using tiny metal replicas of Union and Confederate troops to recreate the scenes moment by moment. In my mind, I'd gone back to the war. Back to its bloody fields, the sunken road, the Hornet's Nest. Back to the sounds of musket fire and horses whinnying, the clomping of hooves, the shouting of soldiers and generals. Back to my heart pounding within me, wondering if I would ever make it out alive. I would, of course, but the feelings came back as real as if they were happening again.

For days at a time I could not sleep and would stay up by the fire, reading, pontificating. We could have won that battle. We should have won that battle! It was not General Beauregard's fault that we were forced to retreat. He could never have continued on with the advances that Johnston had made the night before since the Union forces from Ohio had reinforced them overnight. Often, it was this rebuilding of defenses overnight that caused the downfall of an army, or of a man.

One morning, after reliving the war for several years alone in that house with no wife to keep me grounded, I awoke completely defenseless to the world around me. I'd had a sleepless night, tossing and turning, remembering Shiloh, the little church where the Union forces had taken refuge, their tents all around it. It was there where we surprised them. I could see the white cross off in the distance and although I knew my orders where to kill or be killed, I kept my eye on that cross. If God was indeed for these Union soldiers, then what force could go against them?

It was this sort of maddening thought that pursued me as I fled out onto the porch to catch my breath. I was staring off into the trees, imagining our soldiers emerging from behind them. I could hear the ambush, smell the burning muskets and iron in the air from spilled blood.

And then the girl suddenly ambushed my thoughts. "Dr. Le Monnier," she said, scaring me out of my wits, coming from out of nowhere. Had I had a pistol, I would have shot her dead right on the spot. She was not a girl but a Union soldier come to kill me.

When the fright wore down and my heart pounded loud in my ears, I realized who she was and was pulled out of one war in my head and straight away into another.

From the journal of Y. R. Le Monnier, M.D.

RE: SHILOH PLANTATION, AMITE CITY, APRIL 28, 1913

The curse arrived at my doorstep in the form of a pretty young girl. I inspected her. She was no more than a child, a buxom one at that. How had she found me?

"I'm sorry to have bothered you . . . my name is Gladys. You knew my grandfather, François Reynaud."

"The cage-maker?"

"Yes."

For a moment, I was too stunned to move. Blood drained from my face, and I was acutely aware of the beating of my heart. This had all happened before, every bit of it. The girl coming to me. The granddaughter of François. The plea for help. I'd come to Shiloh for peace and quiet. I'd left New Orleans exactly because of this family. They were mad. Each of them. I had to get away! And yet . . . here she was this young beautiful girl. I shut my eyes and opened them again to be sure was actually there.

"Tell me you're not Carmelite's sister," I said. "Tell me you're not Andrew's sister."

"But I am."

"No."

I got up and walked inside. I shut the door. I knew it was rude, even as I pressed up against it, trying to catch my breath. I needed solitude. I came here to finish my book! How could I ever be rid of the battle of Shiloh if this damned family wouldn't leave me alone?! Another grandchild of the birdcage maker had found me. Another one had sought me out like a reluctant general shell-shocked and wounded. *Retreat, retreat!* is what was going through my head. It was only the girl's crying that brought me back to reality.

Somehow I had left reality. I feared for my mind. I feared for my sanity.

Gladys was crying outside my door. I waited for a few moments, hoping she would stop, hoping she would leave, but she continued this sad whimper I couldn't bear. Slowly, I opened the door. I could almost predict why she was here.

"I'm sorry, dear, I don't know what got into me. I'm just not myself these days. Please, come in, come in."

I ushered her to a chair near the fireplace. She sat and lifted a handkerchief to her eyes.

"Now tell me, why did you come here?"

"You're the only one who can help me."

"Help you? How?"

"You've got to save my daughter."

"Your daughter? Surely you're not old enough to have a child. How old are you?"

"Fifteen."

I rubbed my rough chin. "Fifteen, I see. And are you married?"

"Yes. To Walter Maestri."

"You are Carmelite and Andrew's younger sister, are you not? If my memory serves me . . ."

"I am."

"And how then, did you become married at such an early age? Your sister, if I recall, did the same. So strange for girls this young. I see no reason—"

"After Mother died, my father me put in a convent school in Bay St. Louis. He didn't want the responsibility of me. But I hated it. I had to get out." She stood and walked to the window and stared outside as she told me her story.

"It was Mardi Gras, and we were allowed to leave as a group and go to New Orleans. We were there to pray for the souls around us, for the souls of the depraved. That's when I met him."

"Your husband?"

"Yes." She came back to me and stood by my chair, playing with her kerchief. Then she sat again, soft as a whisper. "He was so handsome. He was dressed as a devil and teased me, telling me how beautiful I was, telling me he wanted to marry a girl just like me. He would come up and whisper it in my ear, sending shivers down my spine, and then, just as a sister was about to turn around, he would dart away, back into the crowd.

"He did this repeatedly as we walked street by street past floats and colors and music. Finally, I could take it no longer.

"'Come with me,' he said. 'Marry me. Tonight.' He grabbed my hand and I turned and ran, never looking back. We ran and ran until we could not run anymore. We were laughing so hard, I nearly cried. I'd never felt such freedom.

"In the back alley, I saw Walter for who he truly was, a beautiful young man with brown hair and brilliant blue eyes, broad shoulders. He pulled me close and kissed me as my mind was spinning. What had I done? I had escaped the convent. The sisters would be so angry. Father would be so angry. I got scared and pushed him away, crying. When he found out I was fourteen, he said I was too young to get married. It had all been a game to him. He didn't want to marry me. I was embarrassed and ashamed, and suddenly I wanted to make him sorry. That's when I told him I was wealthy, or that I would be as soon as I married."

"And you actually married him?" I asked her.

Gladys nodded. "After a bottle of bourbon. That very night I said 'I do' to a lifetime with this man I'd just met. We went to Judge Maher at the Court of Algiers."

"Ah. The Marrying Magistrate. Somebody should shut him down."

"Father was furious. But I received my inheritance a couple weeks after. We moved in with Walter's parents on Esplanade. Soon, I was expecting a child."

I breathed in deeply. I tried hard not to be moved by her story, but I was. The scoundrel had taken advantage of her. "You said you needed help for your child. What sort of help?"

"I don't want her to inherit my money," she said. "It's cursed."

"Cursed." Déjà vu swept over me and made me dizzy.

"It's true. I know it now."

"And how do you know this?"

"Because terrible things happen to the one who holds the money. And terrible things have happened to me. Please help us. Please."

I took my glasses off and rubbed my eyes. I was no priest. I was no lawyer. I was nothing of the sort and yet . . . yet, they all came to me, each one to the good doctor. What had I done to deserve this family? Was I the one who was cursed after all?

I closed my eyes once again, hard, and then opened them. Just to be sure the desperate child was really there.

From the journal of Y. R. Le Monnier, M.D.

RE: SHILOH PLANTATION, AMITE CITY, APRIL 28, 1913

Gladys was another troubled heir of the Saloy fortune, another unnatural heir who had fallen prey to the supposed cage maker's curse.

As if curses could be real.

I remembered her older sister, Carmelite Kurucar, and her plea to know if there had been a curse on the money she'd inherited after eloping with her own young lover. Carmelite was long dead and the brother Andrew was serving a life-sentence in the Louisiana State Penitentiary. If one was the believing sort in such things, it might certainly appear as if there was a curse on the money. But I'd read over and over the ledgers and letters. Although many unfortunate things had happened, there was no way to prove that it was because of a curse. Science was proven until disproved. For me, curses were the other way around. They were disproved until proven to be so.

She had asked me to help her. "But how can I help you, young lady? Look at me. I am an old man. I walk with a limp. I no longer practice medicine, and as well, I have no time to go traipsing off as your detective. I'm afraid I wasted many a year doing just that for others in your family. I am tired, can't you see that? I am too tired and too old, and quite honestly, I'm not fit for company. I've gotten quite used to being by myself."

When I was done ranting and wildly waving my arms, I felt silly. The pretty girl sat still on the sofa, her black hat cocked to one side of her head. She stayed so quiet, it unnerved me.

"I understand you are worried about your so-called cursed fortune entering your daughter's hands, but why have you come to *me*?" I whined. "Why must you each come to me? This is what I do not understand."

"My grand-aunt Madeline," she said. "She's the one who sent me here."

"No offense but Madeline is quite insane."

"That's what they say, but I don't know if I believe it. They've fought for years in the courts, her daughters have, trying to press her interdiction. Madeline is cursed as well if you ask me. The money has done her no good. She is chipping away at reality. Her family is at war. Her health is declining."

"I don't mean to be insensitive, but I do not care about your great-aunt Madeline. She had quite her way with me a few years ago. She deserves what she's getting if you ask me."

The girl looked at me in horror.

"Forgive me," I sighed. "I am not myself." I got up and walked to the corner bar, pouring myself a whiskey. I stared at myself in the pocked mirror and cringed at my white hair and unshaven face, my sagging jowls. Who was this man? Who had I become? I offered the child some water but she declined. I waited until my chest was warm before telling her what had to come next.

"Several years ago, your dear great-aunt Madeline was kidnapped by her grandson Walter. Do you remember this? It was in the papers. It was clear what was happening. The one sister living with the old woman seemed to be closer to the money than the others. So her sisters were furious. How dare she get so close! What if the old woman were to leave all the money to Antoinette with nothing left over for the other children?

"With this reasoning, they set up Walter to take her by gun point. They housed her in her daughter Alice's house under the guise of caring what happened to her. Meanwhile, their mother headed for a steady decline. I'm surprised she's still alive from what I saw that day. She was confused and upset. She took me to be a newspaper reporter when I actually lied and said I was there on official doctor business. I talked the sisters into believing I was on their side. That I would make up my report in a way that supported their hypothesis that she was insane and needed to be put away."

I finished my whiskey and coughed. Then I turned and filled the glass again. This time I took a chair across from the girl, setting my cane to the side. I studied her for a moment. Youth was so unbelievably beautiful. If I could drink her in, I would have.

"As soon as her daughters were away, I felt the shrewdness of the woman come alive again. The light in her eyes shifted and someone seemed to be behind her pupils.

"'Help me get out of here,' she told me, 'and I'll make sure you get your hands on the Le Monnier mansion.'

"How had she known my deepest desire? I wondered. 'But you don't own it,' I told her. 'Felix Reynaud owns the Le Monnier mansion. I've seen the deed. You cannot lie to me.'

"'Oh, but I am not lying. Fill out your doctor's report in a way in which they'll be forced to let me go back to my home on Esplanade, and I, in turn, will reward you handsomely. Trust me when I say I, alone, hold the keys to the Le Monnier mansion.'

"I did not know what to do. What to think. Was it possible this old woman held some power over her nephew, Felix Reynaud?"

"'I suspect that Felix may not be all that he says that he is,' I told her, sensing an ally. If she knew I suspected Felix had murdered his daughter, she'd have more ammunition with which to play her hand.

"And yet, is anyone truly who they say that are?' Madeline said to me. We talked for a good while longer, and I decided to stay and fight for her. I worked with her lowdown lawyer, Paul Fourchy, who was obviously after the old woman's fortune. I did everything Madeline wished of me, even prescribing sleeping medications and other drugs for anxious worry. It was taking a toll on her, but after several months—and mind you, I was bound on leaving New Orleans and coming to Shiloh the night before I'd even met with her—it was taking a toll on me, being at this widow's beck and call, her own personal advocate in the courts. Her own personal physician. And did I take a cent for it? No, I did not. And why, might you ask?"

I looked at the girl and our eyes caught.

"Why? Because, young Gladys, I had convinced myself that if I were to do her bidding and get in her good graces that she would somehow work her magic and talk Felix Reynaud into selling me the Le Monnier mansion. It's all I've ever wanted, you know."

"And did she?" asked Gladys. "Did Madeline work her magic? Are you now in possession of the Le Monnier mansion?"

If my head could have exploded, it would have right then and there in my living room, all over the rug. But it didn't. Instead, I calmly turned and walked to her side. "In a manner of speaking," I said. I left her and walked out to the back of the house. I opened the door and left it ajar for her, taking in the cool, crisp air. My head felt better instantly. I closed my eyes, listening to the sound of the birds. It was a sound that once soothed me, and now, they were like clanging symbols. I waited, possibly for several minutes, before she timidly called after me.

"Dr. Le Monnier? Is everything all right?"

She emerged from the kitchen and daylight fell across her smooth cheeks, making her glow. "You were about to tell me about the Le Monnier mansion."

"Yes, I was." I smiled and took a sip of my drink then swirled it in my hand, watching the amber liquid form a whirlpool and then settle down. "See for yourself," I told her. Gladys walked to my shoulder and looked in the direction I was pointing. There, just between two glory maple trees, was a table etched of finest walnut, and slightly covered with leaves and straw, a nearly five foot tall replica of the Le Monnier mansion.

"A birdcage?" she asked me.

"A birdcage, yes."

"I don't understand."

"What's not to understand?" I tried not to laugh. "The old woman told me she would make sure I got the Le Monnier mansion if I did all she needed me to. In the end, after she had used me up, this was delivered to my home. There was a note bound to it. It read:

Congratulations, Doctor Le Monnier.
You are now the proud owner of the Le Monnier mansion.
From my family to yours.

Madeline Pons

From the journal of Y. R. Le Monnier, M.D., Re: 1913

Having the young girl Gladys at Shiloh unnerved me. Shiloh was my peace. Gladys was disturbing that peace. She spent much of her time in the back of the house tending to the dastardly birdcage. It was a large doll-house for her, and child that she was, she fussed over it. She swept out the cage and found a scarf woven of scarlet yarn which had been Eulalie's, and begged me to use it to line the cage. I was incensed. Over my dead body! I insisted. But in the end, when asked if I could remember Eulalie wearing that specific scarf, I agreed I could not, for she was a more subtle, tasteful type of woman than one who went around bearing red.

"Have you told my grandfather that you have his birdcage?" she asked me.

"No, I have not." I shouldn't be asked to explain myself by a child, but there it was. "I don't know why I haven't told him, except that I left New Orleans for good. There was no use contacting him again. I would only get drawn into his affairs once more, and that, I'm afraid, would be most unbearable."

"You could have sent it by messenger."

I looked at her. The gall of her youth. "I could have, I suppose, but . . . well, to be honest, I couldn't part with it. It was given to *me*. Although Madeline meant it for harm, having the birdcage allowed me to have some part of the Le Monnier mansion, even if it was not the part I desired."

She looked at me.

"It was selfish," I said. "I know. Please stop looking at me like that."

To appease her, I allowed Gladys much freedom. She hummed as she worked in the birdcage, and I sat there inside at my desk, listening to that abominable noise while trying to accurately portray General Beauregard's demeanor on the evening of our surrender. I needed to rebuff a publication by Col. Johnson's son, who had not even been there. I wrote,

> The report of General Polk was written in September, 1862, when he had no access to the reports of others, and therefore he was liable to error; but Johnston's book was published in 1878, when he had full access to all reports on the battle of Shiloh, and therefore his misstatements are unpardonable.
>
> Colonel Johnston wanted his father, though dead, to have won the battle of Shiloh; he brooded over it, and, with forgone conclusion, wrote his book and declared, mirabile dictum, that had General Beauregard not ordered the retreat, the victory won by his father would not have been lost.
>
> Of all I have ever heard or read concerning the battle of Shiloh this is one of the most singular assertions, and may I not, in the very words of Col. W. P. Johnston, repeat, "There is just enough of truth in all this to mislead."

I would get a few words in the ledger, and then find myself distracted with the sounds of *Her Bright Smile Haunts Me Still*. I would fly out to scold Gladys and then stand hypnotized watching as the girl filled the bottom of the cage with a nest of sorts made of purple hyssop and red yarn. I couldn't care less what she did with it. It wasn't my house. It wasn't the Le Monnier mansion of my forefathers, but every single turn of carved wood was a stab at me, directed by Madeline Pons. I should have burned it when I received it and at the moment, could not remember why I had not.

François had been right about Madeline all along. Poor sap, and I never truly believed him. Until I encountered Madame Saloy's sister myself.

Every now and again, Gladys would come into the house inquiring after me, a red rose from the garden now stuck in her hair above her ear. "How is it coming?" she would ask me.

"The book?"

"No, not that. Your helping me."

Foggily, and I'm not sure why this was the case, I would have to ask her forgiveness. "I'm sorry, but how is it that I am supposed to be helping you?"

Patiently, as if speaking with an old man who was losing his faculties, she would respond, "You're devising a plan for me to get rid of the money before it can be passed down to my daughter. You're working on a way to break my family curse."

"And why have you not gone to a priest?"

She stared at me as if the answer was obvious.

"And where is your daughter now?" I knew I was asking this question more than once, but I could not remember her answers. It was as if our conversations were gaseous and never took on the solidity of fact. Perhaps my thoughts were too embedded in the War. I worried, admittedly, about my state of mind, and thought that the girl could not have shown up at a worse time than she had.

"Pauline is with her father and grandparents. They're doting on her, no doubt. They want only the best for her. That's why this will be extremely difficult. You cannot conquer someone's will easily when they are convinced that their will is right."

"And you are convinced that getting rid of this fortune that you've inherited is necessary to break this curse? You do know I don't believe in curses."

"Yes, I know," she said to me matter-of-factly. "It is why I am here. You don't believe in the curse, therefore you cannot see that you've been pawn to it all along."

"Me? Pawn to the cage-maker's curse? That's preposterous. I've never accepted a dime of the Saloy money. Except, of course, in my natural business dealings with the family."

"And with my grandfather." The girl took my hand and slowly walked me to the back porch. She lowered me down the steps as I held on to the rail. Then she pulled me closer and closer to the bird cage. My heart ached looking at the miniature replica of my childhood memories.

She pointed. "Down there."

I looked, but could see nothing.

Gladys lifted her skirts a little and knelt. The door to the cage had been propped open with a hyssop branch and inside, two turtledoves had made nest of the yarn.

"Glad it will be of use to someone," I said.

She smiled at me and then leaned down further, just below the door. Her hand felt the wood and suddenly, what seemed to be a secret panel opened up. She reached inside and pulled out a box made of cedar. On top were the initials of Carmelite Carcano Saloy. I bent and took the box from her, rubbing dust off of the top and smelling the sweetness of the wood.

I opened the box and beheld a small book bound in leather, once white, now faded ecru. I lifted its cover and read in black ink, *Diary of Dolores Morales Carcano*. Carcano . . . Carcano. Was this the mother of Madeline? Of Madame Saloy? Beneath the book in a swatch of red velvet were two diamond necklaces and a ring made of sapphires and emeralds. I tried to catch my breath. I couldn't believe Madeline had left jewels in this birdcage. Should I return them to her? What about the book? Of course not. She had given the cage to me as an insult and injury. No. I would not return a thing.

I closed the box lid. Did I truly want to read the words of this woman? A part of me was titillated at the idea of sneaking into someone's innermost secrets, but another very large part was uninterested in reading anything associated with Madeline. Was it worth the time it would take to read her words? I doubted it. I needed to get back to my desk and work on *General Beauregard at Shiloh*. I needed to come up with a plan for the dear girl Gladys (after her interesting discovery of jewels, I was viewing her in a much more benevolent way), for how she might dispose of her fortune.

A tempting thought. Might it come to me? Might the money given to me eliminate her fear of a curse on her daughter? I was not afraid of any curse, for it was not real. Surely, I could make good use of a fortune like this one. I could have a monument built for every lost Confederate soldier in Louisiana. I could donate money to the Soldiers Home and make sure they had enough reading materials and medicine. My mind began to reel with the possibilities of the money, when slowly,

I remembered where I was. I was standing on the back lawn of Shiloh in front of François' bird cage, holding a cedar box filled with a diary and jewels.

The jewels. Family jewels. Gladys would want them.

I swayed and looked about me. The money. The money was getting its grip on me, too. I would have to be careful. There did seem to be some sort of seduction taking place. I turned to tell this to Gladys and to offer her the jewels at the same time, only when I did, I could not find her. Had she wandered back in the house while I was daydreaming? I saw the yarn of my wife's scarf wrapped with purple hyssop and now lying under two turtledoves within the Saloy cage. I took the box with me back into the house and opted to pour myself a glass of wine as I settled in to read the book. There was no use trying to work this afternoon. The girl had made certain my mind was elsewhere.

I sat in my most comfortable place, the side of the sofa where Eulalie used to recline, and wrapped my legs in a light blanket. Sipping on my wine, I could hear Gladys humming a sad tune from somewhere in the house. As soon as I opened the cover of her ancestor's diary, the words began to pull me in. At some point, the humming must have ceased. Gladys, it seemed, had let herself out to return to New Orleans alone.

She must have, for I never saw her again.

From the Diary of Dolores Morales, Havana, Cuba, Sunday, August 22, 1829

Dear Diary,

I held tightly to Juan's arm as we crossed the threshold of the Cathedral this morning. I had tried to be early to Mass, but it was not to be. My new shoes were beautiful yet hurt my feet with every step. I'd convinced myself I could wear them while getting ready and the pain would go away. It hadn't. It had only made me slow and my husband annoyed with me. It was all I could do to get from the carriage to the front door. Now there were people all about us, waiting. There were some nods of acknowledgement and a few turned heads. Did they mistake the look of anguish in my eyes as remorse? Two ladies ducked behind fans and whispered.

Juan stopped and removed my hand from his sleeve. He squeezed it and left me standing there in the aisle as he went to the confessional. He was older by twenty years, and his gait was beginning to show it. I felt something for him but couldn't determine what it was anymore. I looked about. I could feel all eyes on me now, so I made my way to the other confessional. I could face the priest easier than these stares. I pushed the curtain aside, ducked, and stepped in.

"Father." I made the sign of the cross and opened my eyes to see his shadow behind the screen. "Bless me, Father, for I have sinned. It has been two months since my last confession."

"I'm listening."

"It's . . . I have been unfaithful to my husband."

"I see. This is not the first time you have confessed the same?"

"No. I'm sorry, Father."

"And did you not say the Act of Contrition at your last confession?"

"I did, Father."

"And yet you did not repent."

"I need to confess another sin," I said, the words rushing out of me. Silence filled the air. I could see his eyes looking down through the screen. Was he praying for me already? Or judging me? "I am . . . with child," I whispered.

"I see. In that case you must tell your husband. Indeed God has gotten involved in your affairs. You must make it right now by telling the truth."

I knew that what the priest was saying was true. I felt it deep in my chest. I took a breath. Yes. I would tell Juan tonight.

La Casa de Gestal was a plantation on the outskirts of Havana. Juan had done well for himself, for us. He had several house slaves, many more who worked the fields, and Zula, an old freed mulatto who chose to stay on with him. I could never understand why a woman who had been manumitted might forego her freedom by staying with her former master, yet it happened quite often. Perhaps there was nowhere else to go. Perhaps she was too old to begin a new life. Perhaps she liked being under the full control of another.

I did not. I had seen my mother's unhappy marriage, one of duty and no other reason, except possibly for my own sake. I had vowed to love Juan before God, and yet, in his home, I felt trapped. Part of me realized this was my own doing. Juan was a reasonable man, just older. He didn't have the energy that I did to go and do and be young and free. It was the reason I needed a man like Antonio. I could come and go as I pleased with him. I could be wild and free and dance for him with abandon.

I looked at Zula. The old woman had always seemed to disapprove of me, even before I had started seeing Antonio. She sat now on the front porch smoking a large cigar. She wore a blue kerchief over her nappy gray hair. She fanned herself with a bright pink fan and rocked in her chair. I sat in another chair at the far end of the porch, watching the lights flicker out in other houses. I stood up. My heart was pounding. He would be going to bed soon. I needed to tell him now so that I could leave under the cover of night.

I walked past Zula, and she reached out with gnarled hand and touched my arm. A bolt of lightning ran through me, and I stopped. I looked into the old glassy eyes, faint ghosts in the evening shade. She removed her chewed cigar with the other hand, and I stood still. The woman rarely ever spoke to me and certainly never initiated talk. She licked her dry lips and with deep, aged voice she said, "*Ten cuidado. Con el pecado . . . viene una maldición.*"

Be careful. Sin comes with a curse.

How could she know? Had she known all along? A chill went up my arms in the heat of the night, and I swallowed. The old woman stuck the cigar back in her mouth and commenced to staring ahead again and rocking. For a moment, I wondered if I'd really heard anything at all. I firmed my shoulders and opened the door. I knew I would find my husband in the study, keeping company with his birds. He had two lovebirds he kept in a cage. It was cruel to keep them there, I thought. Although he was reasonable, what kind of a man could keep those beautiful birds in a cage instead of letting them fly wild and free?

Yes. I was doing the right thing. I would tell him the truth, and it would all be over soon.

"Juan," I said. He was sitting in his favorite chair, reading a book near the window. Green palms waved wildly behind his head in the breeze.

"What is it?" he asked.

I thought of sitting, but could not move. The lovebirds had grown still. "I need to speak with you."

"I'm listening." He set his book down on the table beside him.

I decided to just get it out quickly. "I've been unfaithful. I've been with another man."

I tried to gauge the look on his face. Would he be angry or hurt? Instead, I saw something like stone.

"Yes, I know. Everyone knows. Do you really think Father Fernandez keeps your little confessions between himself and God?"

I felt as if I'd been slapped. I firmed myself and continued. "I'm expecting a child," I said. "His child."

He clenched his fists and then hung his head. After several moments of silence he said, "You have other children. Have you thought about them?"

"I have. It is more than I can bear. And I'm sorry. Truly."

"Do you love him?"

"I do." The silence grew up around us until it threatened to smother me. "Juan," I said. "I cannot ask you to forgive me. I will meet with Mr. Jose tomorrow and we can begin to draw up divorce papers."

"No," said Juan, standing. He came close, and I thought he might hit me, but he passed by and walked on to his lovebirds. "I do not believe in divorce. You are alone in your sin." He turned to me and spit in his hands. "My hands are washed of you. I will not have the shame of divorce follow me. Instead, you will leave Havana and take your shame with you. You will elope with your lover just as everyone expects you to do. You want to play marriage with your Italian lover? Then go play being married. Just know that you are living a lie and that no matter where you go, your sin will follow you."

He walked to my side and got close enough that I could feel his heat. I wanted to reach for him. I wanted him to brush this shame from me. He leaned into my ear and said, "May your sin follow you and your bastard child." Then he walked out on to the back porch. Out of my sight. Out of my heart.

From the journal of Y. R. Le Monnier, M.D., April 1913

I caught the 7:20 train to New Orleans carrying a partial manuscript with me of *General Beauregard at Shiloh*. There was much more to write and research, though I wanted to solicit a publisher or two to gauge interest. That, and I sought feedback from a couple of comrades who fought there alongside me.

The real reason I had come back to New Orleans was the girl, Gladys. I could not shake her. I could not help but feel that this poor innocent child who was now the mother of a child herself, was about to find them both at the mercy of this beast, her inheritance.

I had let her sister down. A sweet, healthy child-bride, Carmelite, had been snatched away by the reaper while on my watch. And what had

I been watching? Her drowning brother, Andrew, on a sinking ship. He sat to this day damned behind bars, his own father having nothing to do with him.

If only I had my son living, I would do everything and anything to protect him. But I could not have this luxury. It was a cruel hoax. At least, I could help the girl.

After giving her matter much thought and reviewing all of my ledgers and letters regarding her grandfather, the cage-maker, and the Saloys themselves, it occurred to me that they had each, in their own way, turned from God and bowed to the idol of money. God, in his mercy, might very well lift this supposed curse of Biblical proportions if only they were to turn back, to repent, to change their hearts and ways.

I had devised the perfect solution for young Gladys, so that she would be free from the pull of the money as would her daughter Pauline. I could not wait to tell her. It had come to me when I was almost asleep one evening, listening to the mockingbirds outside my window, calling, mourning. I'd woken up refreshed and infused with new wisdom. It all made sense. I'd strike out to find her posthaste.

My first order of business was to check on my home on North Galvez. How was it faring after my long months away? I smelled Eulalie when I opened the door, and then the mustiness took over me. I threw open the windows to air out the place and found myself feeling strangely as if I had come home, but then again, as if too much had changed in me to ever be able to call this home again. Perhaps it was time to sell the old house. Yes, perhaps.

I walked to the back to check on the small garden which no doubt had died and become brittle as a witch's smile, and upon opening the door, I was dumbstruck. There, stretching from one side of my fence to an old rose bush of Eulalie's, now black and thorny, was a gargantuan spider's web. A labyrinth of massive proportions, intricate in detail and deadly. The sight of it was too much. How dare it take over my garden. How dare it! I reached for a broken branch from the oak tree which had overgrown with Spanish moss, and struck the spider and its web wildly, thrashing it here and there until there was nothing more than an old man swinging his punches into the empty air.

Had there been anything there at all?

I examined the branch for evidence. Yes, there were silken threads all about it. My blood was pounding, and I felt myself gasping for breath. Death and pestilence had taken over where life had been. Where *my* life had been. I turned and felt an urgency I had not before. Gladys! I needed to find her and execute our plan quickly. I did not believe in curses per se, but I did believe in evil. One could look at how my formerly tended garden was now overrun with decay once my eyes had been turned elsewhere. The weeds had cropped up and were thriving on the corpses of my beloved begonias.

I knew the child lived on Esplanade, yet I had not asked her number. Better to find her grandfather, François, and inquire of her whereabouts with him. After all, I'd not seen him for quite some time, and although I did not quite count him as a friend (for in true friendship it was more of a two-way street), I was strangely drawn to him, needing to see how he was faring, the old forlorn sap. His story had become part of mine. I felt it was time to tell him I know of his cage's whereabouts, though I did not know how he might respond. I would have to accept whatever consequence awaited me.

As I was nearing St. Roch Avenue, I came to a procession in the street with the wailing of sad trombones. The road was too thick with people to pass, and I would have to wait. Yet, I could not. Turning to the right, I would head to the start of the trail and cross just in front of the funeral. People stopped and gawked at the passersby. Some held their hats over their hearts, their eyes closed in reverence for this perfect stranger. I did not have time for reverence. I felt I was racing against the clock. I could not move fast enough to get to the front, and when I finally got there, blocks and blocks later, I found myself at St. Roch's Cemetery. Had I walked so far or had I been spirited here? I'd been deep in thought, and the trip had been a blur.

The black iron gates seemed to beckon me to peek through and spy on the solemn affair. How morbid I had become, I thought. A former physician and coroner was no stranger to the cemetery. It almost felt like an old friend or business acquaintance. I stopped and succumbed, walked to the gates, but held there. A trail of people wound its way around tombstones and monuments. Behind a stone crypt emerged and old man, ragged and torn. Grieving with the Greek mask of tragedy across his face. I squinted and looked closer, adjusting my glasses. Then I gripped the cold iron hard between my fists, the blood pumping to my knuckles.

It was him. The cage-maker! I'd found him here. How strange was this? Could I be dreaming? My heart skipped. I looked around to find Gladys, but all I saw was a sea of dark and sullen faces. Where was she?

I could not find her anywhere. Perhaps this was the funeral of an old friend of François', someone with whom his granddaughter was not acquainted.

"François!" I called, though he could not hear me. Perhaps I'd not opened my mouth wide enough to be heard over the shuffling of steps. Or perhaps in his grief, he could no longer answer to his name.

François, April 3, 1913, New Orleans

With the warm bayou sun illuminating every crevice, I ran my fingers along the marble and thought, *there are things in life a man should not see.* The death of his granddaughter. Not only once but twice. It was an abomination to the soul. And hard as I tried to shut my eyes and squeeze it from my mind, the stone remained a cold reminder before me of so many days gone wrong.

Where had it started? I wondered. The priests at St. Louis Cathedral would trace it back to original sin, all the way to Eden and a rebellious soul, but where, I wondered, had it begun for me? For *my* family?

I made my way slowly to the steps of a neighboring tomb and lowered myself down with my cypress cane. *Trace it back,* I thought. *What is the lineage of your disaster?*

I watched my son Felix as he wiped his entire face with his handkerchief and put an arm around his son-in-law Walter. Had he murdered again? Had my son murdered another? And if not, was it hell enough to be capable of believing such a thing of your own son?

So much death and sadness. Life in this family was as fleeting as time itself, and yet, I was still here to see the bitter ends.

Perhaps it all began with you, François.

A chill rose up my body. I turned to see where the voice had come from, but no living face was turned on me. I had never been one for ghosts, though I lived in a town that honored and celebrated them nearly as much, if not more, than the living. New Orleans loved its yearly bacchanals and macabre parades for long deceased gods. It thrived on spirits, constantly conjuring them.

The fault lies with me? My face fell, and my broken heart fluttered. *I've done nothing but try to do right in my lifetime. I've used the gifts God gave me, tried never to harm a soul,* I told myself.

"But you mingled with her and her money," said the voice. This time I realized it was my own mouth uttering the wicked and wounding truth.

Yes. That was it. Had I never met Madame Saloy, had I never made that cursed cage for her, there would be no money to fight over, and my granddaughters would not be lying in the relentless womb of St. Roch, waiting to emerge at the second coming. I would never have loved and mourned. There would be no tears.

Sometimes the greatest evil lies in the most innocuous of decisions.

"I said yes," I said, as the realization formed in my mind. My glassy eyes stared past the statues and back into my history. I could see myself clearly now, a younger man standing in my studio, diligently working at my craft, building birdcages, unsuspecting. I could hear her voice when she first came to me. Her delight when I took her commission and sold my soul.

In an instant, as if flying through the air of time, I could see everything that had transpired over the many years to follow—the weddings, the births, the burials, the suffering—all of it had its nativity in the moment I said yes.

"Is it too late to go back and change my mind?" I whispered to the air, to the universe, to God if he was still listening. A haunting *yesssssss* hissed around me in the breeze as the crows flew, and I sat still, damned and watching my dwindling family quietly mourn my own mistakes.

I left their faces and took in the visage of the Reynaud tomb. I'd bought it for myself, yet I was on the wrong side of the marble—the living side. I looked down at my feet, shoes once shined now dusty from where I stood on Trinity Walk. Did the Trinity walk here, indeed? Did the Father himself carve and bequeath these tombs? Did the Holy Spirit fill these cavernous stone vases that adorned the steps, or was it pushed out by the flowers of grief? Feeling faint and the need for a miracle, I stumbled back toward the wrought iron gate that bore the name of Saint Roch. I could have escaped perhaps, but there was some place I needed to go.

No one noticed as I made my way to the small chapel. I paused a moment at the Christ figure hanging there on the cross. And then through the doors Saint Roch welcomed me into the chapel and up to the altar, his eternal companions beside him, a dog and the statue of a woman who seemed conflicted, as if she wanted to leave but couldn't.

I leaned my cane upon the altar and grabbed a pencil and scrap of paper. I tried to focus. What could I possibly pray for? That the child would come back? That her sister and mother would also rise from the tomb?

The pencil began to scratch. *Me libérer,* I wrote slowly. *Release me.* I blinked and took a breath. It was hard to swallow. Finally, slowly, I scratched out a barely legible, *Sortie de ma famille. Let my family go.* Then I felt the blood leaving me.

With crumpled note in my palm, I stumbled into an archway where artificial limbs of the healed adorned every square inch of chipping plaster. Cast-off crutches and stone replicas of hands, feet and ears of those who had witnessed their miracles, received answers to their prayers, both abhorred me and filled me with hope. I pictured the people walking again, hearing again. I pictured my vibrant granddaughter, Gladys, wrapping her arms around my neck and kissing my rough cheek. "*Grand-père, je t'aime.*" I would never hear her words again. I pictured her now, lying still for all of eternity. When I could take it no longer, I closed my eyes and slumped, toppling to the ground before anyone could save me.

Before I could wonder if God had heard my prayer.

Y. R. Le Monnier, M.D.

I'd watched François walk toward the chapel, and so I entered the gates of St. Roch, hoping no one would mind my barging in on so personal an affair as a funeral. My desire to speak to Gladys at this point was palpable, and served as my excuse for poor etiquette. I passed the Christ figure and entered the chapel looking about me for François. I did not see him. Passing the altar, I turned toward a little room where odd prosthetics hung akimbo on the walls.

Something caught my eye.

I looked down. He was sprawled on the ground.

I do not remember hitting the floor, but I was on him, ear over his heart in a split second. No, François. No! I could not panic. I needed to bring him back.

"François, my friend, it's me. Dr. Le Monnier. I'm here. Let me help you!"

I put my ear to his heart but heard nothing but a very faint murmur. I felt for his breath, but there was nothing. I looked in his eyes. They were still open, those dark eyes which had seen so much pain, loved so deeply. They belonged to a reckless genius who had been passionate about everything he did in life. I waved my hand in front of them. Nothing. No movement. No response.

"You cannot go!" I said, taking his hand in mine. He was grasping something. I opened his fingers and took out a scrap of paper.

Sortie de ma famille, it read.

"Release your family. Yes, François, that's why I'm here! I know a way to release you all!"

A labored breath rumbled from his chest, and then . . . It could not be. The cage-maker was dead?

The cage-maker was dead.

I felt a part of me die with him, spread out there, cold on the floor. The part that somehow lived vicariously through his confessions.

"It's over," I said softly. "Be at peace, my friend." Then I leaned down in his ear and spoke every scripture I could remember to help him in his passage, the Lord's Prayer and lo, though I walk through the valley of the shadow of death, I will fear no evil . . .

I sat there with him for a moment, stunned, before I realized I needed to tell someone in his group. I couldn't bear the thought of compounding the grief of the mourners by the tombs, but there was no getting around it.

Slowly, quietly, I made my way past the Christ figure, trying to search out the right face, a sensible one not prone to excitability or melodrama. It was then that I saw her, an old woman in a black veil. She would have seen her share of death in her days and it would have lost its horror. But something about her was familiar. I moved closer to get a better look and as I did, it was she who recognized me.

"Dr. Le Monnier," she said.

I came closer still for I could not see her face.

"Yes?" I said. I moved to within inches of her, and that's when I realized who it was. Madeline Pons.

I wanted nothing to do with her. This took me off guard to such an extent that I wanted to flee. I turned to look for another face, a male, and there by the tomb was none other than Felix Reynaud, François' son. If there were two people on the face of the earth that I never wanted to see again, it was these two, and yet, here I was before them.

I could not escape. Felix seemed the least of two evils.

"Mr. Reynaud," I called out. Madeline was still at my side. "Mr. Reynaud, may I have a moment with you?"

His eyes squinted and hardened when he saw me. "What are you doing here?" he hissed. "I told you never to set foot in my saloon again."

"I assure you, I did not intend to come, and I am quite sorry for barreling into such a solemn event, but . . . forgive me." I approached the cold man and leaned in to whisper. "Your father. I'm sorry, but it appears he . . . please, go quickly into the chapel. There." I pointed and watched as Felix moved passed me. I knew what he would find. I closed my eyes. I would not wish such a sight on my worst enemy, and yet, this is what was I serving him.

"What is it?" said Madeline.

"I . . ." I shook my head. She would know soon enough. "François Reynaud is gone. He . . ."

"He's dead?" she asked.

I nodded.

The old woman seemed to sway back, and I reached out and put my arm around her, not thinking about my disdain for her. I walked her slowly to a bench and as we sat down, I could hear the commotion beginning. Felix had found his father, no doubt, and now the mourners were beginning to catch wind of his death.

"He couldn't take it," said Madeline, mostly to herself. "He couldn't bear another death. Especially not another granddaughter."

"Another granddaughter?"

Madeline sat motionless, gazing through sheer blackness at me. Slowly, she lifted her veil and I saw her red, wet eyes, ancient marbles, fading in a spider web of lines. "You do not know whose funeral this is?" she asked me.

I looked around me. I thought for a moment. François had come. Madeline had come. Felix had come. I saw a young man taking a tiny bundle from a woman and holding it, cradling it, like a baby in his arms.

The blood drained from my head, and I felt I might fade. I knew before she said the word.

"Gladys."

"No." I shook my head. "No. No. It cannot be."

"I'm sorry you didn't know. Did you know the girl?"

I was still shaking my head, unable to comprehend what was happening. I was too late! I'd been too long tarrying at my book and had not done enough to stop this madness! I grabbed at my hair and held on to it tightly. I clenched my teeth. "No," I whimpered.

And then I cried. For the first time since my Eulalie had passed, I could not contain my emotion. Gladys was dead. François was dead. I was in a dream, a nightmare. This was all unreal. It could not be happening. This was a cruel joke.

She had come to me, Carmelite. She had come to me, Gladys.

"Gladys Reynaud?" I said. "François' granddaughter? The one who—"

"The one who eloped and just had a baby girl, yes."

"But I don't understand," I pleaded. "She was just with me, in my plantation home. She was there, not two days ago. How did she die? This cannot be!"

Madeline looked at me for a moment, studying me. "She could not have been with you two days ago."

"Oh, but she was. She came to me, asking for help, just as her sister had done before her. And I had finally come up with a solution for her. I cannot believe I am too late!" I pulled at my collar, for I felt I might suffocate.

"Dr. Le Monnier, I'm not sure of your state of mind. I understand you may be upset." She leaned in and whispered coarsely, "Be careful, or they'll threaten to put you away, too. But you do know Gladys died on Saturday, two days after she had given birth. She could not have visited you for she died that very morning. You see, it's impossible."

Terror struck me with a vengeance I'd never experienced. I thought back, my mind racing. I stood and walked to the tomb. I looked at the inscription, REYNAUD. I saw the names printed beneath it. CARMELITE KURUCAR 1890–1907. GLADYS MAESTRI 1897–1913.

My knees buckled.

I didn't believe in ghosts.

I didn't believe in ghosts.

I was losing my mind. I was going insane. My greatest fear was happening. I'd often felt that insanity was a disease that might wipe its grime upon me like mildew crawling up the walls of the Le Monnier mansion. I was deteriorating. My life was ending.

I did not believe in ghosts.

I did not believe in curses.

I did not believe in ghosts who spoke of curses!

I stumbled as I remembered her face, remembered the sound of her humming and her adornment of the Saloy birdcage.

I was beginning to think that the curse on this family was real. I was beginning to think that I, too, had somehow succumbed to it. Yes, it had found me!

New Orleans Item, April 23, 1913

GRANDFATHER SUES FOR SAKE OF BABY
CONTESTS WILL OF HIS DAUGHTER
TALE OF LOVE AND SORROW IS REVEALED

Y. R. Le Monnier, M.D.

It was only a matter of days before the battle began. Felix Reynaud was again coming after his daughter's fortune, and this time, he was using the media to do his dirty work. There was a large article in the *New Orleans Item* with photos of Gladys, her husband Walter, and her father, Felix, himself. He'd been interviewed at length and was playing on the sympathies of would-be jurors.

The photo of young Gladys at her wedding celebration was too much for me to bear. It was her. I was sure of it. Though I'd never met the girl, her spirit had appeared to me, looking exactly as she had in life. I'd been fooled. I was permanently off-balance now, feeling the need to sit much more often, not trusting that the chair was really there. What if I were imagining it? My sense of reality had been altered. If anyone found out, they might very well have proof to put me away as I had done to so many before.

Gladys, from what I gathered in the paper, had properly drawn up a will several months before her death and before giving birth to Pauline, signing over all of her fortune to her husband, Walter. Now, I had to view this in relation to all the other evidence I'd known about her. Gladys had watched her mother die and leave all of the money to her children. She'd watched her older sister, Carmelite, die, who left no will at all, leaving the money up for grabs. And here, Gladys had made a conscious decision to leave the money to her husband, knowing a child was on the way. Was it her way of protecting the child from the money? Of making sure there could be no battle from her father? And yet, what good had it done? The man was going to come after it no matter what.

And how had she died? Her death certificate read, Uraemic Puerperal Eclampsia, an awful end exacerbated by pregnancy in which the body fills with poison.

With poison.

Might it have been a murder instead staged to look like a natural death? Might it have been Felix once again or could it have been Gladys' husband? Again, the maddening ambiguity. I imagined myself marching down to the Continental Saloon. I imagined giving Felix Reynaud a piece of my mind, telling him that I suspected his sinister hand in the death of poor innocent Gladys. I watched his face redden as it had before when I accused him of killing his other daughter Carmelite. I remember the way he had turned things on me, made it look as if by circumstantial evidence, I could have killed her myself. Might he not do the same here? Not with Gladys, of course, but with the cage-maker, François, his father? I was the one who found him dead in the chapel at St. Roch's. Circumstantially, I could have killed him, and no one would have known. Isn't this what Felix would throw in my face if I were to point the finger at him? And how, then, would I be able to retaliate?

I could not. And so I could not venture to Continental Saloon. Another murder would have taken place with no trace, no suspect except the Grim Reaper himself and the cruel hand of Fate.

What could I do?

Yes, perhaps Gladys had been a ghost. If, with a scientific reasoning, one might view this as fact, strange as it was, one might be able to get past the bewilderment of it and see that the girl had made her wishes very clear to me. She did not want the cursed money to fall into her daughter's hands. She would rather it go to Walter, her husband, who had stolen her youth, and perhaps her life. She would rather it fall upon him, this curse.

I needed to speak some sense into Felix's ears. I needed him to understand this curse, assuming he was no murderer. If he was a loving father as his article made him out to be, wanting only the best for his granddaughter, then he might be persuaded to let the money go.

But I needed help. There was no one else to turn to.

I rang the doorbell of the large white house on Esplanade. I could see through the floor to ceiling windows that the house was quiet, with no one roaming about. The black woman I'd met years earlier approached and opened to me. Charity was showing her age more and stooped. How long had she served Madeline Pons? How much of her life had she given to her? What of her own life? Her own children?

"Dr. Le Monnier to see Mrs. Pons," I told her.

I wondered at the state in which I would find her. Would she be in her childlike state of which I had read in the papers, or would her brain be sharp and shrewd as she'd shown me when she tricked me out of my birthright, the Le Monnier mansion? How was it that this trickster had become my last resort?

She came out looking much the part of an infirmed grandmother, wearing a long white gown with ruffles at the shoulders, her white hair pinned up, her feet bearing slippers. Long gone was the gold house coat that spoke of wealth and power.

Her housemaid sat her down in front of a small fire where she stuck her feet out and turned to me with puffed face.

"I brought you something," I told her. I held out the box that had been found in the secret panel of the birdcage. "You must have given me the cage without knowing it was in there."

"No, I knew it was there," she told me.

So it was the cunning Madeline Pons after all before me. She surely could play the part of dowdy old maid.

"So you wanted me to have the jewels?"

"They were my mother's passed on from her mother. It was the one thing of value she had to offer. I didn't want it. I wanted to be rid of it."

"And therefore, I assume you knew her diary was in the cage also."

She was quiet for a moment. Then she nodded. She reached over and rang a little brass bell beside her, and her maid came to call. "Charity, some tea for us, please. It may be a while."

"Of course," she said, and went off to make herself busy. When the tea had been poured and cups were in our hands, Madeline told me that she had a story to tell. That there was more to their story than anyone knew. That for some strange reason, she felt I was the one to share her confession. That she was dying, and it was time.

The good doctor sipped and waited for her to begin.

In the words of Madeline Carcano Pons as told to Y. R. Le Monnier, M.D., in her home on Esplanade, New Orleans, 1913

In 1853, my father died. I was only ten years old. He was not around very often, as he spent his days and nights out fishing, but I loved the times he would come home and lift me up in his arms, swinging me around and around. My nostrils filled with the odor of dead fish. The smell of dead fish, to me, was love.

My mother became restless after Papa died. My brother Antonio and sister Carma were quite a bit older than me, and one day, Mother left me with them. She said she was going to Bay St. Louis to take care of some business matters for Papa. She was gone for over a week, and each of us became worried that something had happened to her.

Nothing did happen, and she returned to us eventually. But she was different somehow. There was a new look on her face, perhaps not happier, but not quite as sad. It was almost as if a tiny bit of hope had crawled back over her since Papa had died. She didn't talk about her trip, just got on with the mending of our clothes and the cooking of our meals. Antonio was our bread-winner now, and spent every waking hour at work.

Years later, at our brother's funeral, my mother broke down and wept bitterly. I'd not remembered her crying this way even when Papa died. It scared me and my sister, so Carma begged her to stay with her for a few days. Neither of us wanted her to be alone in her little apartment.

One morning, I checked in on them. Bertrand was at work, and the help had been sent away on errands. I found Mother and Carma sitting quietly in the study, nary a word between them.

I leaned down and kissed Mother. She smelled of fresh powder, the color of her hair. "How are you feeling?" I asked her.

She nodded and attempted a smile. She pulled me down to her and squeezed my hand. I looked over to my sister. The back of her hand covered her mouth as she stared out the window.

"Is everything all right, Carma? How are we doing today?"

"Fine. Yes," she said. "Would you like some coffee? I've a fresh pot."

I pushed to stand, but mother held onto my hand. "I've got something to tell you," she said weakly. "I've already told your sister."

A steel ball formed in the pit of me. She turned her body to face mine and stared into my eyes. I saw the lines of all her years traced on either side of her face. "I love you," she said. "Do you know this? I've spent my whole life trying to do what was best for you and your sister, your brother."

"She's got another family," Carma blurted out. "In Cuba."

"What?"

"It's true," said Mother. "I'm so sorry, I—I was married once, before I met your father."

"This can't be." I took my hand out of hers and rubbed it. I could not make sense of this. My mother and father had lived in New Orleans all of their lives, had they not?

"But it is true. Madeline, I'm sorry I never told you before, but Antonio wouldn't allow me to speak of it. I have to tell you now. I have two daughters in Cuba. You have two sisters you've never met."

I stood up and walked over to the coffee. I poured a shaky cup and tasted the bitter chicory. I swallowed and turned around. "Mother, I—"

"Are you angry? Your sister's quite angry with me."

"No, no, I'm not angry, I'm just confused. Hurt, that you felt you couldn't tell us. This . . . this changes everything."

"No, it changes nothing. I am still your mother."

"But why now? If you've held your secret this long, why speak up now? We were perfectly happy not knowing any of this."

My mother got up slowly and moved over to the sofa where Carma was sitting. She pushed in close to her and took her limp hand, pressing it up against her lips. "You remember years ago, after your father died? I left to go to Bay St. Louis for many days. Well, I went to Cuba instead, for the first time since I had left. Your father and I, we met and fell in love in Cuba. And when I left, my children stayed there. I'd not seen them in so many years. I . . . I wanted to see them again." She began to cry. "I'd suffered with losing them for such a long time, I couldn't bear it any longer." I watched as she rubbed the back of my sister's hand. "Can you imagine losing a child and then one day being able to see them alive again?"

I looked at my sister and she at me. Pain ripped through us both, down our foreheads and into our eyes. We blinked and looked away.

"They were not thrilled to see me. There was no warm welcome for Mother in Havana. But I did get to meet my grandchildren."

I count it as a small miracle, but for only a moment, I was able to leave my own heartbreak and stand looking out from behind my mother's eyes. I felt her suffering over the loss of her children, her grandchildren. Carma had lost both of her children. I had lost my only son, Bertrand. In this way, I understood my mother's sadness, so I went to her and knelt down. I placed my head on her lap, and she rubbed my hair until she stopped crying. Then she got up and went to her bedroom. When she returned she handed me a book. I opened the faded white leather and saw that it was my mother's diary.

"Terrible things have happened to this family," she said to us. "And I am at the root of it all. You deserve to know. I cannot ask you to forgive me." Mother left us on the sofa with the diary between us. Then she walked back to the bedroom on leaden feet. She stayed there in bed for the rest of the day while Carma and I read her secrets.

From the Diary of Dolores Morales, Havana, Cuba, Monday, August 23, 1829

Dear Diary,

This morning I rolled over and off of Antonio's arm. I sat up slowly on the edge of the bed and listened to the falling rain outside my window.

I breathed in deeply the fragrance of melted wax and smoldering fire. The heat would surely be turning to steam outside and I'd have some relief. A cool respite. Antonio stirred and after a quiet moment, I felt a single fingertip drawing down my back. I tingled.

"Something's bothering you," he said.

My head flinched but I didn't yet turn around. I was formulating the right words but they tasted awkward and wrong. Was there any proper way to say what I had to say?

"There will be . . . we're having . . . a child," I said. No, that had come out very poorly. I turned to look at Antonio. As a fisherman, Antonio spent his days in the sun, and his skin was deep and dark. I noticed something else in his face at the moment, a pink glow beneath that darkness. Was he angry? No, Antonio could never be angry over this, unless he thought—

His face erupted suddenly, and his eyebrows rose to the sky. Antonio inhaled as if coming up for air and held onto my lower back. I felt fragile for a moment and considered the possibility I might actually break.

"We're having a baby?" Antonio whispered. Then he swallowed, and I melted with love for this man. I leaned back and lay my head down on the pillow while Antonio cradled my head, tracing the lines of my hair. I could feel his pulse quicken in his arms, his breath heavy on my cheek.

"We'll be married," he said, suddenly serious.

I closed my eyes. I stiffened and pressed myself back up, pushing him aside. I moved over to the window and watched as lightning filled the sky. I hated leaving Antonio just feet away, but I needed a little distance.

"You will marry me, won't you, *amore?*"

"You and I both know we cannot marry," I said.

"No. It's not true. He'll divorce you. And then you and I—"

"He will not and we will not," I said. I leaned against the wall and felt the edge of a picture frame brush my shoulder. It was of the Virgin Mary of the Immaculate Conception. "I have spoken to Juan already. He will not divorce me."

Antonio burst from the bed and paced now, a beast encaged, enraged. I hoped my next words would settle the matter. "We'll leave here, Antonio. We'll leave this place, and you and I will be together just as you want. Just as I want."

"Leave here? But—how—we have no money . . ."

I took my time and walked slowly, seductively over to Antonio who had stopped pacing and was now clenching his fists. His dark hair had fallen into his eyes. I watched those eyes. I watched them watching my every move, every muscle. I was, after all, trained in the way of flamenco and knew the power of the smallest flick of my wrists, my elbows. I stood there a moment, inches away from him, perfectly aware of my presence, and paused to hear his intake of breath. Then I pressed myself into his chest and looked deep in his troubled brown eyes. I bit my lip, then began smiling. "We leave tomorrow," I whispered. "We have tickets for New Orleans. We're going to America, my love. Together we're going. We'll have a fresh, new start there."

Antonio was a mixture of confusion and ecstasy and lifted me off my feet, inhaling me. He set me down gently when he remembered my condition. Antonio was a simple man. He loved me. The details of the how and why he was leaving wouldn't enter his mind. He was getting what he'd wanted for two years now, his Dolores, and now our child. I knew it wouldn't bother him that I was still married legally to a man in Havana. I knew it wouldn't bother him the way it would gnaw away at me that I was leaving my children, beloved children, behind. That my heart was ripped apart and would never be mended. But these were the sacrifices some women had to make to have love and to be loved, truly. Sacrifice and gain—it was simply the way of the world.

From the Diary of Dolores Morales, Havana, Cuba, Wednesday, August 25, 1829

Dear Diary,

I held on to the rail and lifted my foot. I was inches away from freedom. I set it back down suddenly and breathed in deeply. It wouldn't be an easy transition, I knew. *Moving never is,* my mother had told me when we left Madrid to come to the tobacco farm in Havana, half a world away. I remembered the look on my mother's face, a mixture of relief and fear when she had seen the beauty of the land and the mix of the people in Cuba. *Moving is just a way of life,* my mother had said. *Your father has a wonderful opportunity, and there, we will make our home. We'll be together, and that is all a home needs—for people who love each other to be together.* Even at that early age, I knew my mother wasn't convinced of their move to Cuba—she was merely trying to talk herself into the virtue of following her husband.

At this moment I was trying to do the same; to talk myself into believing that this move from Cuba to America was the right thing to do, the best thing to do. For me, there was no other choice really. It was the only thing I could do. I took small comfort in knowing I wouldn't be doing it all alone. But only small comfort.

"Look up to the sky, *mi amore*." I could feel the low rumble of Antonio's voice in my chest. "You see the sun and how the faded moon still watches? In a few days, you and I will be looking at that moon together, but from the shores of New Orleans." He turned me to him and brushed a stray hair behind my ear. "It will be the very same sun, *mi amore*. The same moon. And you and I will be together forever. You'll see. The sun will shine in New Orleans just as it does here. Even brighter from what I've heard."

I loved the Italian people I'd met in Cuba because of their passion for life, and I loved this Italian, Antonio, because he was passionate about me. He was an optimist, too. A romantic. I knew Antonio was trying to make this easier on me, that he was describing the brightness, the light of the sun, but all I could think about was the heat of it. It was desperately hot in Havana. I sincerely hoped the sun didn't shine brighter in New Orleans. I spent my days fanning my chest with the same fan my father had given me for my ninth birthday, just before we boarded the ship to Havana. It was black lace and very grown up for a girl that age. Now, the black lace fit me well, and it was worn from twenty years' use.

I fanned myself, staving off thoughts of little Concepcion and Magdelena. They would be running into the arms of Juan or maybe Zula by now, clambering at their feet for breakfast. It was more than I could bear, so I shut it out to survive.

Havana was hot steam from a kettle. In Mass on Sundays, instead of hearing the priest speak, I would look toward the windows and imagine that hell was certainly as hot as it was here. Hotter even. The thought made me dizzy and desperate to run.

I was a woman in love, and love should make one hot with passion, Antonio would tell me in the quiet of our secret place, but right now, Havana was hot as Hades, and I couldn't breathe.

Yes. I fanned faster and felt a slight breeze. I would go to America. Surely I could find relief from this heat there.

Antonio's strong hands fit around my small waist. It was cinched tight in my corset, hiding the life that was growing there. I was dressed modestly on this day, my first of our American adventure. I stepped—or had Antonio pushed me?—onto the deck of the Philadelphia. A seaman took my hand and caught my eye, glancing at me a little too long. I was a beautiful woman, I knew this, even dressed so modestly with my long black hair tucked in my bonnet, barely to be seen. I knew the power I had, but I couldn't care less. I forgot in this moment how beautiful I was, how I could turn the head of any man I set my sights on. In this moment with the seaman looking at me and Antonio's hands around my waist, I felt in the pit of my stomach a sickness.

He knows, I thought to myself. *Everyone in Havana knows about me. I have no choice but to leave.*

When we arrived in the port of New Orleans, I was quite sea-sick. I lifted my head up and wiped my mouth with a handkerchief. Antonio's arm was around me, and I tried to take comfort in that. I was missing my babies, and wondering what I had done. What had I done? How could I have left? How could I live without them? Had I been hypnotized? Temporarily insane?

I swear, there was a dark cloud hanging over the entire city of New Orleans, and it filled me with a sense of dread. Antonio saw it too, but chose to look at the silver lining, at the sun which shone on top of the darkness. "You see that, my love? We can see the whole city from here. Look at all the buildings, all the people. Our lives are waiting to begin as soon as we step off this boat. He smiled and kissed my cheek and helped me onto the dock. As soon as I set foot, a woman passed by who looked at me. She was ancient and black as indigo with a cigar dangling from her lips. She stood selling flowers from a cup. "Flowah fa da lady?" she said to Antonio. He beamed at the chance to show a romantic gesture, and I'm sure he felt it was a good omen on our future together. But he didn't see the way she winked at me as he handed me the daisies. And I don't think he heard her say, "Be careful. Sin come with a curse," in the same scratchy voice as the old mulatto slave had done in Cuba. It was strange; it was almost as if it were the same person in two places at once. A chill went up my spine and a dread filled my belly where I was sure my unborn child could feel it. It seemed deep enough and dark enough to haunt us for generations to come.

Madeline

My sister, Carma, and I, were mortified by our mother's betrayal. She had betrayed her first husband. She had betrayed her poor daughters in Cuba. And with her lies she had betrayed us and our children, three of whom were now dead.

She was convinced she was cursed. That the old slave in Cuba had cursed her and her offspring. She convinced us of this and through tears explained that each time one of our children died, she felt directly responsible for it. That our brother, Antonio's, death, his unexplained collapse in the street in front of his house, was due to this curse.

Although upset, Carma was much more good-hearted than I was, and pleaded with Mother that this was not true. That Carma herself had cursed her children when she chose a life of wealth with Bertrand instead of heeding the call to follow God and become a Carmelite nun. That Antonio had lived hard and drank hard, and it was this that stole his life from him. But I took her at her word. Mother had cursed us all, and my only son had perished because of it. My love for her turned to hatred in those moments. I wanted to be rid of her, to be free of her. I wished I'd been born into some other family.

My heart turned to stone.

In the days and weeks following Antonio's death, it became clear to me that to fight fire, one must use fire. I spoke to my sister about curses. I convinced her that what our mother had said was true—that the old slave woman, probably through some ancient African ritual, had summoned darkness to follow our mother and the generations after her. I told her that I knew of a man in a house on Bayou Road who might be able to release us from such a curse. That I'd met him years earlier after my husband had died and was needing money. I'd answered an ad in the paper for good luck talismans. I met him at his home. I danced with him. Soon after, I'd been able to open my own crockery shop.

Yes, it's true. I lied in court. I had partaken of the services of voodou ministers. Of course, I lied. Look who my mother was.

I convinced my sister that the only way to free our family from this curse was to perform a counter spell. But we would need a talisman, something that represented our family. I looked about and spied the birdcage, the huge replica of the mansion in which my sister lived, the one which made me burn with envy. I hated that cage. It was a garish reminder that my sister had so much and I, so little.

I convinced her that the birdcage was just the thing we needed to free us. Eventually she succumbed to my pressure. While Bertrand was out gambling or cavorting with god-knew-who, we had the cage hauled down the stairs and into the carriage. We carried it solemnly to Bayou Street. Carma was frightened, I knew. I convinced her that this cage, with the love that had been poured into it—yes, I told her I knew all about the cage-maker's feelings toward her, that anyone with two eyes could see how smitten he was—that this cage born of love would be the perfect antidote to evil upon us.

It was the goodness of the cage-maker which won her over. She believed in him. She believed in his love for her. She believed it was pure enough to go against any dark forces.

The house on Bayou Street was more run down than I had remembered it. No longer was the ballroom grand, but dark and smelled of mildew. Yet, the Negro Leblanc did not look as if he had aged at all. Many years had gone by, and it seemed he was getting even younger, more virulent, stronger, with intense blue eyes that sent chills down my spine.

The blood of chickens was involved in the ritual; at least, he told us it was the blood of chickens. Carma and I held hands and a crucifix as he summoned spirits from the underworld and chanted to undo the curse of the Cuban slave on our family. When it was over, he did say that the spell might not be one-hundred percent effective. That he could not be sure which spirits the old woman had summoned.

Shaken, Carma was eager to leave the house as quickly as she could. I told her to go wait in the carriage as I paid Leblanc.

But this is where my secret lies. I've not told another soul of it. But now, death is near, so I'm telling you.

Leblanc was clear that the spell might not work, and in fact, might do more harm than good if it failed. He told me that the curse might come back on us tenfold, if he was unsuccessful. I had but a moment to think. I could not bear losing another child. I asked him, "If you were to perform a spell that was to put every bit of curse onto my sister's house, and not on my family, is this something you could do?"

I told you, by this point, my heart had turned to stone.

Leblanc said there was a way. Since he already had the birdcage, an exact replica of my sister's home, that this sort of conjuring would have greater success. I paid him the money and turned my head as he spoke his evil over the cage. As I turned bad fortune away from me and poured it onto my sister's head.

She never knew. In fact when her husband, Bertrand, died a month later on New Year's Eve, she was convinced the spell had backfired, that it hadn't been enough to remove the curse of the Cuban woman. But when Carma herself died a few months after that, I knew that my spell had had its effect.

And now I was poised to take over her money. Nothing was going to stop me from this. Not the State of Louisiana. Not heirs from Cuba. Not God himself.

I would get was I was due.

Y. R. Le Monnier, M.D.

I sat motionless as I watched the old woman. She had cursed her sister herself. She had cursed the cage, which she had given to me. She had cursed the home, the mansion on Royal Street which bore my name.

She had cursed me.

I blinked, unable to move.

I thought back on my dead Eulalie. I thought back further to my sick, dying son. I don't think I moved, but my spirit lurched at the old woman, choking her, choking the life out of her.

She sat there as a dead woman, looking at me. I stared back at her.

This was a moment to make a man. Each man had one, a moment in which he chose what his character would be, what his destiny would be.

I made my choice. I would no longer be under any curse.

"I need your help," I told her.

"You need my help? Did you not hear what I just told you, Dr. Le Monnier? Do you realize what I've done to my sister? Yes, the spell gave me more wealth than I could ever imagine. Yes, my children are alive and well, but don't you see? I damned myself. I sit before you, a woman damned. I have money. I have a large house and many properties. I have old age. But I have nothing. No one loves me, and I trust no one. My own children and grandchildren don't see a woman before them, they see an inheritance. Don't you see?"

"I do see. I see that you need to be free."

"Don't be naïve. There's no freeing me. I made my bed."

"I disagree."

"Were you not at the funeral of poor little Gladys? Or of her grandfather, François? Is it not clear to you that I cursed the cage-maker when I used his cage? All of this is because of me, you see. I am my mother's daughter. You, yourself, Dr. Le Monnier, with your involvement with this family, were cursed the first time you encountered one of us. You are doomed, as are we all."

224

"I cannot speak for you," I told Madeline. "but I need to speak for Gladys. She wanted her daughter to have none of the money. She understood its curse, even though she succumbed to it. There is still time. I want you to pull your influence with her father, Felix. I want you to tell him the truth. I want you to tell him what you've told me here, and then I want you to tell him this: *There is a way to be free of the curse.*" I pulled out a book from my coat pocket. It was a tattered Bible, one which Eulalie read each night before bed.

"It says here in Leviticus that a man or beast or property may be consecrated as holy and devoted to the Lord. That once it is devoted, it cannot be redeemed or sold, for it is holy before the Lord." I closed the book. "I've figure out a way to end this. The money needs to be given to the Lord. And the house, the Le Monnier mansion, needs to be consecrated."

"Felix is the owner of the house."

"I realize this."

"And he wants his daughter's money. He will make sure he gets it, along with having some trickle to his granddaughter so that he'll appear a doting guardian."

"But I think he would change his mind if he heard this coming from you."

Madeline set her teacup down and folded her arms as if she'd gotten a chill. The fire still blazed at her feet.

"No one will hear this from me. Do you understand? They will put me away faster than I can sneeze, Dr. Le Monnier. I have nothing. I have nothing but this house to keep me warm before death, and after that, I shall have other things to keep me warm."

"Then perhaps you can save your very soul. Give your house to the Lord. Let him undo your curse. Give God all your money, and your children will have nothing to fight over. There is still time for you, Madeline."

"Why are you being so kind to me?" She asked me, eyes squinting. "I do not deserve your care. I gave you the cursed birdcage. I attempted to heap this family curse upon your head, just as I did with my sister."

"You did, yes," I said. "But you see, I have no heirs. I have no child, no wife. I have nothing left to lose. You took it all. I can choose to be angry, or from here, the curse can die with me."

Charity, the housekeeper, came to us and asked if we would be needing any more tea. Madeline said no, but did not dismiss her. It was clear that I was the one being dismissed.

225

"Please consider what I've suggested, Madeline," I said, standing. Charity handed me my coat and hat. "It's not too late. For any of us."

She did not speak, but I prayed that I got through to her. I walked to the door and stood there a moment. Finally, I turned back. "One last question," I said. "Have you any word about Andrew Reynaud? How is he faring in prison?"

"He's ill," she said. "The last I heard he's caught pneumonia. He'll probably die there in prison. It's the same fate for each of us."

New Orleans Item, 1915

Mrs. Marie Madeline Pons, wealthy widow who died Friday morning and over whose fortune her family has engaged in bitter legal battles.

Y. R. Le Monnier, M.D.

On Christmas Eve, 1913, just nine months after his youngest sister died, Andrew Reynaud stepped off the Mississippi Valley train from Baton Rouge onto Carrollton Avenue beside another life-termer who'd gotten parole. "Jim," he said. "We're all right now. We can walk."

They were free men. Finally free.

After hearing that Andrew was ill in prison, I called in some favors with a gentleman on the parole board. He had served in the war, and I needed only convince him of the marble memorial I'd had made that now stood permanently at Shiloh commemorating the sacrifices of the Crescent Light Regiment from New Orleans. He rewarded my benevolence with an interview with Andrew and another with the board. I convinced them this time that his case should be brought before the parole board. It was a quiet affair. The newspapers were not quite aware of it.

Andrew stepped down onto the street, and I was waiting there for him with a warm coat and a fresh cup of coffee. He was gaunt but looking slightly better than he had the last time. He'd been convinced he'd never step foot in New Orleans again.

"Welcome home," I told him. "You're a changed man now. Things will be different."

I'd told him I'd have a carriage pick him up, but he insisted on walking. Said he'd count each footstep as a blessing as if walking on sacred ground. He'd been dead and was now alive again. "I don't deserve this," he told me. "It's grace. I walk along these sidewalks and storefronts knowing I was a dead man. You cannot know how grateful I am."

We passed women who ignored us, but Andrew's eyes lit up as he saw them. "I haven't seen a woman in years," he told me. He was still a young man, and soon those desires would reawaken.

"Be careful or they'll be your downfall." We spoke of methods to stay away from women and drink, of steering clear of the houses of sin. We spoke of spending more time in God's house, how it would protect him from falling again.

Andrew seemed eager to hear me. I believed that he was sincere and wanted to make a fresh start.

Which is why I handed him the keys before I led him into the front door of my home on North Galvez. I'd cleaned it up, cleared and replanted the garden for him.

"What are you doing?" he asked me.

"This is your house," I said. "I've no need for it any longer. I'm quite happy at Shiloh."

"But I can't take your house from you. Let me buy it. I've still plenty of money."

"Oh, but you can't," I told him. "That which has been consecrated to the Lord is holy and cannot be sold or redeemed. This is my gift to you. On one condition."

Over a meal of beef tips in gravy, after he'd bathed and shaved and was feeling human again, I explained to him that I did believe in his curse. Finally. It had taken me a long difficult while to understand, but I did now. Fully. I explained to him the history of his family's disaster. Of his great grandmother, Dolores's betrayal. Of his great-aunt Madeline's. He tried several times to stop eating but I begged him to continue. He would need his strength. I was about to convince him to do something that was completely foreign to him. Something he'd never been taught nor had he seen modeled. I was about to convince him to give sacrificially every cent he'd ever inherited. That only then would he be free from the curse and from the lure of drink and women.

It didn't take much convincing. The next morning, after a good night's rest in his new home, Andrew roused me and handed me a cup of coffee. His eyes were ablaze with hope and tears of gratitude. It was Christmas morning after all.

"I want you to go with me," he said.

"Where are we going?" I asked him, rubbing the sleep from my eyes.

"To do something I should have done a long time ago. I only wish I'd done this before Carmelite and Gladys had to die. But I'm doing it now. It's not too late for me. I've been given a second chance. I see that now."

Watching Andrew handing the notes over to the sisters of Our Lady of Victory, I couldn't have been more proud if he'd been my very own son. In a way, I thought of him as my own son. His father never came around. He fought for Glady's money but her husband kept it. Gladys had given it to him, after all, in a legal will, fully knowing a child was coming. The courts had no choice but to honor it. But Walter didn't want the child when he met a new wife. And Felix would only have put her away as he'd done with Gladys.

So after Walter remarried and had his own daughter, little Pauline went to live with her uncle. Andrew.

I pulled my coat around me and walked slowly, hand on rail, down the few steps behind my house. Shiloh had been good to me. She had been my peace, after all. She let me finish my book, let me have my say about the war. But I did not care for the accolades. It was the writing of the book, the making of it, or its making of me, which was important.

I rarely went to New Orleans anymore. Andrew and Pauline were no longer there. He learned how to be a mechanic and took the girl to Chicago, where he met a young woman and married her. He had a child of his own now, two girls to look after. He enjoyed very much being a father.

In his letters, which he sent me weekly (and I opened immediately!), it sounded as if they were happy and healthy and doing well, eeking out an honest living together. He had put his past behind him. He had put the thoughts of his former wealth and shame behind him. He was faithful to his wife. He lived the days of a blessed man. Any curse which ever held him had been broken.

I'd like to say I had a small part in that, but I was the one who was blessed. The boy loved me. It is all I'd ever needed, the love of a child. I looked to the sky and saw gray clouds. The sun was behind them, so full and white, I could look upon it with no problem at all. It did not hurt my eyes. I could look upon heaven's glory those days and it did me no damage at all.

The birdcage still sat there between two glory maples. It had housed more than a few pairs of birds over the years, but now there was a sweet pair of turtle doves who were busy rearranging their nests. They wanted it just right when their children came, just as their parents did before them and those from the generation before. They cooed and fluffed and came and went as they pleased, unaware of the sacrifices of those who came before them, those who cleansed the house and filled it with God's mercy. Some torn pages of Dolores' diary now lined the cage and caught their droppings.

It made me happy to listen to the flutter of wings. I anticipated the tiny white eggs that would make their appearance in the spring. I would count them when they arrived. I would bless each one. And I would sit there in peace for another day, waiting with hopeful anticipation for more good news from Chicago—from the son, not of my blood, but of my heart, and of his little girls so blessed along with him.

Dear Doctor Le Monnier,

We're coming to New Orleans for an extended visit. If you'll have us, we'd like to stay with you at Shiloh. I've missed you as you must have noticed from all of my letters. Chicago has been good to us, but it does not feel like home. Home, I am beginning to understand, is not so much a place from the past, but a destiny. I'm looking forward to coming home. We've much to talk about and a great future to plan. Now that my father is gone, I feel that New Orleans may once again welcome a Reynaud. I hope so. Three weeks from Tuesday next we'll see you. Pauline, especially, is ready to give you a big hug.

Andrew

He must have gotten my clippings from his sister, Viola's, and his father's obituaries. They died only three months apart, the girl to go first. Felix went from complications of tuberculosis, but I had no idea what took young Viola. God only knew. But it was over now.

I went back indoors with my blood stirring. I looked about me. So much to do! I was eager to clean out the rugs and the curtains, and I'd wash the linens for the guest rooms upstairs. But first . . . I headed for the small table which held a lampstand. I struck a match and held out the flame. I lit a candle each day for those who were gone—for Eulalie and little René, for the Saloys and the cage-maker, for the two young brides Carmelite and her sister Gladys, and even for the dreadful Madeline Pons. Only God knew, in his mystery and wonder, what happened in each heart before they left this earthly place. God have mercy on each and every soul. I was heir to them all and would keep mass and vigil in that place until I, myself, was no longer able.

This was not my curse, but a blessed duty which I performed willingly day after day on behalf of those who left before me.

I blew out the match and watched as the lights burned and flickered. The smoke went up in tiny wafts and swirls together with each move I made. I breathed in deeply the smell of flint and beeswax, and then exhaled with anticipation.

There was peace there, finally, at Shiloh. And much to do. So much more to do.

Dr. Yves René Le Monnier (Papa)

My little Pauline

Letter from Y. R. Le Monnier, M.D.
to Pauline Maestri, April 3, 1927

Dearest Pauline,

Let me share with you that most amazing day in 1918.

On the day you came to stay with me at Shiloh, you ran to me, your little spritely self, all long dark curls and your mother's sweet eyes. "Papa!" you squealed as you wrapped your arms around my neck, and I lifted you from the floor, twirling round and round. You were so small for five years old, just a doll in the folds of your frilly frock. I squeezed you tightly so you'd know I loved you, then held you away from me so I could get a better look.

"My, how you've grown."

Your uncle came just feet away.

"Andrew."

"Doc." I wished he wouldn't call me this. There should be some less clinical word for our relationship, but I'm afraid "Father" held none of the usual warm connotations for him. He reached out his hand, and I grabbed it, holding it firmly, then he pulled me to him, embracing me with something deeper than friendship.

"I brought you something," he said.

"For me? From Chicago?"

He smiled and walked to the front porch where I followed him. He led me down the stairs and over to a carriage where I saw your aunt Mabel still sitting with little Isabelle. They looked as if they were holding in a great secret. I kissed both the girls then spied something large in the back, covered in a blanket. My heart stopped.

"It's not another birdcage, is it?" I asked tentatively.

"No, no," he laughed. "I don't think I have my grandfather's skill for that. I do, however, think he passed something down to me. Well, we'll see what you think."

I was filled with giddy joy as I wondered what my dear Andrew had done. I looked at him, and he at me. "Well?" he said. "Are you ready to see it?"

I could not speak, but perhaps nodded. I was smiling. As if on cue, you came and ran up into my arms again. You were perched on my hip. Andrew reached his hand over and his sleeve rose up. I saw something there on his forearm. A tattoo. A number.

"What's this?" I asked him.

He brushed it off as unimportant. "It was my number at Angola," he said. He could see the horror on my face, and added, "Don't worry, I put it there. I don't ever want to forget how far I've come. It's a good thing, really."

"Okay," I said. I believed him. I had to.

Andrew began to tug at the blanket, and you jumped up and down on my hip as if I was your horse.

"Is it wonderful?" I asked you.

You nodded and continued to buck, so I placed you on the ground and moved in closer. When the blanket slipped off, I was left there, struck with a beauty I had never known. A large black wrought iron monogram sat before me with the curvaceous letters *YLM.*

"I—how did you get this? The railing from the Le Monnier mansion?" I was dumbfounded and could not get my words to come out right.

"He made it," said Mabel.

I looked at Andrew and held my heart. "Made? You . . . how did you do it? It's identical to my grandfather's railing."

"It's what I wanted to speak to you about," he said. "I've discovered a have a knack for drawing and iron work. I know it's not much, but I figured there would be a lot more need in New Orleans with its gates and fences."

"Yes. Yes!" I said. I was looking at this child with wonder and awe. He was his grandfather's progeny after all. I'd inherited the cage-maker's family. I was overcome at the moment with gratitude over my good fortune that François ever set foot in my office. Simply overcome with it all.

"It's spectacular, Andrew. I don't know what to say. Truly. What a gift."

"I owe you much more than this."

"You owe me nothing. Do you understand? But this . . ." I looked around at my plantation house and up to the second floor balcony. "This is beyond what I could have imagined. How did you know it would mean so much to me?"

"I pay attention," he said, "when it comes to someone I care about."

I threw my arm around his shoulder and pointed to the railing. "There. Do you think you can work it in there?"

"Exactly what I had in mind," he said. Then we all headed into the house, you and your cousin Isabelle laughing and bringing joy into it, the likes of which it had not seen in some months. For a moment, I caught myself wondering if this happiness was real, if Andrew and you and the others were truly before me, then I stopped myself from agonizing. I watched as

Andrew and his wife settled in and went to the kitchen to put on some supper. I was reminded that another Great War raged on the other side of the world, but mine, I realized, had ended in victory.

I looked to my lampstand with the candles that are still burning and saw the ones lit for Eulalie and little René. My heart no longer broke with wishing my family could see the moment. Instead it swelled with knowing—they were already here.

I love you, sweet Pauline. Always remember that. Although not my blood, you are my family. Some familial collisions are rife with trouble and drama, and some, if you look hard enough, are forceful enough to spark new life. So it was with the cage-maker and me.

If you have read all this, I am terribly sorry, but I am already gone. What will you do with your inheritance? What choices will you make for you and your progeny?

All my love,

Dr. Yves René Le Monnier (Papa)

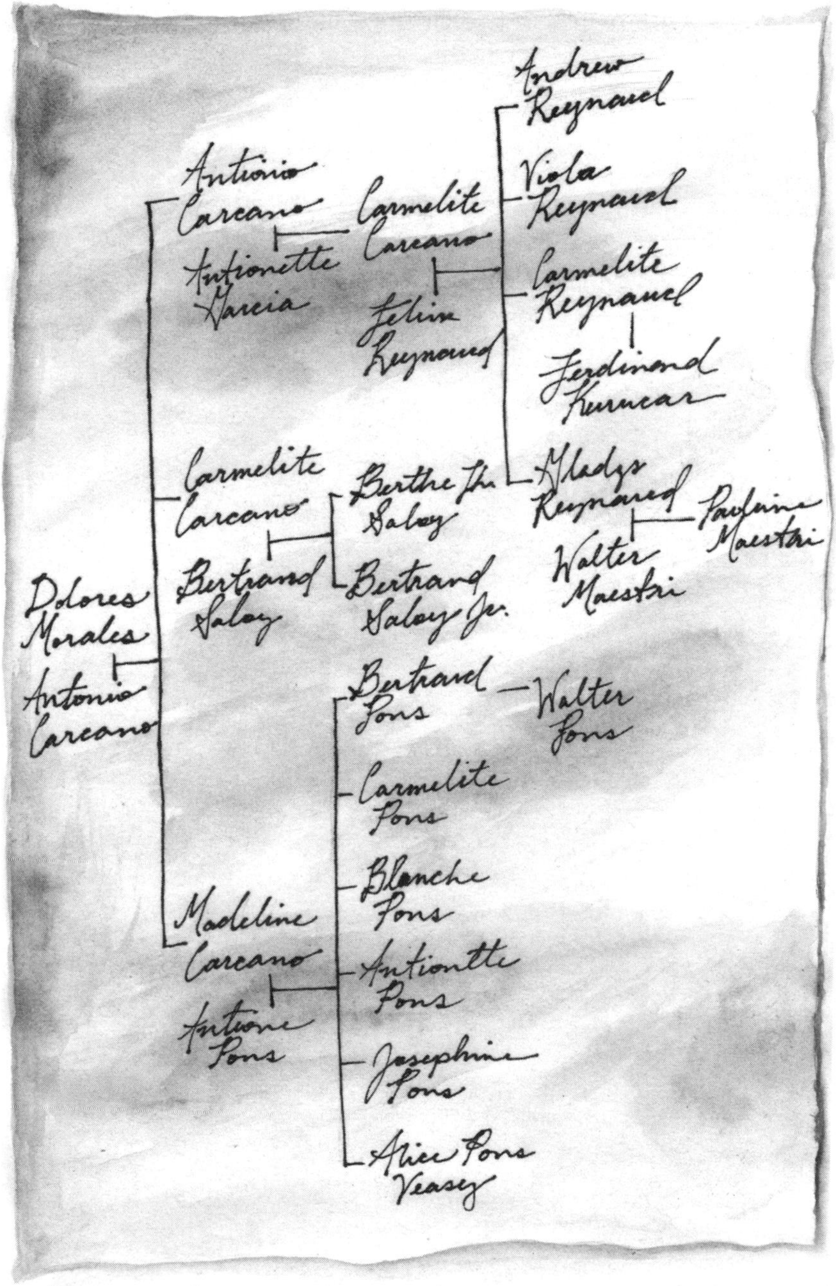

Pauline's bloodline by Y. R. Le Monnier, M.D.

Addendum: General Beauregard at Shiloh

BY Y. R. LE MONNIER, M.D.

THE GRAHAM PRESS. 430–32 COMMON ST., N.O. LA. 1913

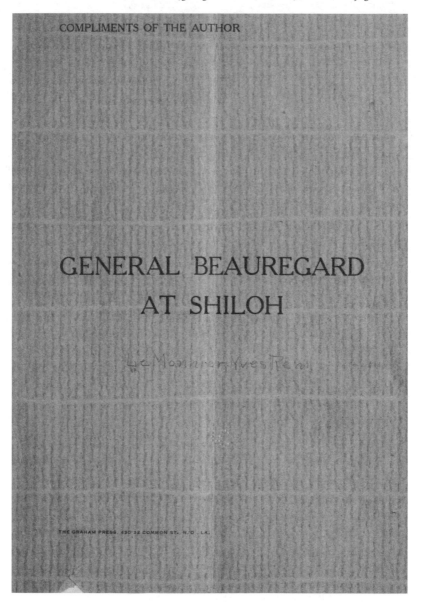

COMPLIMENTS OF THE AUTHOR

GENERAL BEAUREGARD AT SHILOH

THE GRAHAM PRESS. 430-32 COMMON ST., N.O., LA.

PREFACE

GENERAL BEAUREGARD AT SHILOH,

SUNDAY, APRIL 6, 1862.

Having been an active participant in the famous campaign of
Shiloh, from beginning to end, desirous of establishing a correct
record of the maneuvering of General Beauregard at that battle,
during the first day's fight, Sunday, April 6, 1862, I submit the
following pages, the result of honest researches from official documents and other means at my disposal, my desire being naught
but a knowledge of the truth of history and its dissemination for
the sake of our children, the honest student of history and the future generations, avoiding all namby-pamby.

Y. R. LE MONNIER, M. D.,

*Ex-Private, Company B, Crescent Regiment, Louisiana Infantry,
Ponds' Brigade, Ruggles Division, Bragg's Corps, Army of the
Mississippi.*

New Orleans, La., October, 1913.

New Orleans, LA

Dear Granddaughter,

I know not your name. These damnable lawyers have kept this from me all these years. Imagine, knowing you have a granddaughter somewhere in the world, blood of your blood, yet no way to reach her.

I imagine you do know how this feels. Perhaps better than I. How many times must you have wondered about your mother and father? How many tears have you cried, thinking of your abandonment? They tell me you went to a loving couple. I have held onto this truth for decades. I do not know about you, but God willing, you know about me now. About us. About your history.

When 'Papa,' Dr. Le Monnier, died and gifted me my inheritance in the form of a birdcage and a mass of ancestral research, I finally learned about my mother, Gladys's demise. My father Andrew, who was actually my uncle, loved me yet never spoke of my mother nor any of our family. I learned about the curse that corrupted our lineage. I read the research and mourned. It struck me with such dark force that I swore I would never tell my own children about it. Perhaps ignorance was the way to beat the thing.

My daughter, Elise, your mother, never knew anything about her roots. And I watched with horror as she succumbed to the same fate as those who had come before her.

Elise began drinking at an early age. She began to disappear from home for days on end. I could do nothing to reach her. She came home one day, nearly eight months pregnant. I did not know who the father was, who your father was, and I suspect my daughter may not have known either.

We had agreed that the baby would live with me. That I would raise her. You. But a week after you were born, Elise took you and disappeared. She arranged for a closed adoption, and I never saw you again. Nor her.

Oh, how I loved you. I have lived for nearly 100 years and have remembered your face and the way it felt to hold you. Each year, my heart breaking anew.

My daughter died from an overdose soon after she gave you up. You can imagine my grief. My daughter and my granddaughter, gone. I have plotted to tell you all about your ancestry and so worked the cage into my will. The lawyers would be forced to find you. If you're reading this, you have found the hidden documents. You have learned the truth about your family tree. That and my undying love are all I can give you in this life. May knowing the truth protect you from it. May knowing you are loved allow you to love more.

Your loving grandmother,

Pauline Maestri Stroop

Blog post, ReVive or DIY Trying, July 4

CELEBRATING FREEDOM

Last Independence Day, I celebrated with you by painting a hopeless mid-century table with a red, white, and blue theme. Remember this photo? There I am, holding the sparklers, all content and ignorant, not knowing anything about my true past. Was I happier then? Maybe. Maybe not.

I've been working on reviving my inheritance, the birdcage, for a month now. By far, it's been the most transformational time of my life. I've learned nearly everything about my adoption. I know who my grandmother was, who my mother was, and how I was given up. I suppose I'll never understand why.

And then my most amazing parents came back from overseas, and I finally sat down with them and showed them what I'd inherited from New Orleans. My mother got teary-eyed and my father went stoic. They told me they knew nothing about my birth mother except for one fact they've never shared with me . . . before now.

My birth mother had me when she was only fifteen.

People, I HAD KELSEY WHEN I WAS ONLY 16!

Like mother, like daughter? Has my whole life been predestined because of the blood in my veins? And what about Kelsey? She's turning 14 next month! God help us!

Needless to say, I've made a decision. In the spirit of freedom on this Independence Day, I have a very special offer for you, my faithful readers:

FREE TO A GOOD HOME

This 150-year-old hand-crafted French birdcage is a masterpiece of New Orleans architecture.

Cost: PRICELESS

It's been lovingly restored by my own hand and would look perfect in your home or sun porch. Seriously, people, FREE to a good home, one

KICKASS ANTIQUE BIRDCAGE. I've had it appraised, and it's worth a pretty penny, so if you insist on paying me for it, DON'T! SEND THE MONEY TO YOUR FAVORITE CHARITY. Not to me, please.

Will there be anything in the secret compartment, you ask? Good question. My gut tells me some things are better left hidden, but my heart tells me to hold onto the research of my family tree and share it with Kelsey at the right time. Everyone deserves to know the truth about their heritage, no matter how difficult it is.

Comment sweetly for a chance to win, and happy Independence Day.

Trish

PS. The Birdcage to go "as-is." No returns. EVER. Buyer beware.

Author's Note

Dear Reader,

I, too, love a good story, which is why I got hooked on this one. When researching my own family history in New Orleans, I ran across a great-grandfather who was a birdcage maker at 47 St. Ann Street and another great-granduncle who married a young heiress named Carmelite. She died only nine months later, and I found I could not stop digging until I knew the truth of her demise. Was her husband, my ancestor, Ferdinand, involved in any way, or did she die naturally? And why had they eloped when she was only fifteen years old?

I began to find Louisiana Supreme Court cases detailing a complex mystery of love, fortune, and deceit. I stumbled upon a money trail and followed it all the way back to an adulteress in Havana. Heir after heir of this great New Orleans wealth met with death or disaster soon after receiving the inheritance. There was talk of voodou. A young murderer spoke of a curse on his money. And when the younger sister died after eloping only a year before, just as her sister had done, I watched as her father again went to court in search of the money. So you see, I had to keep going, although I didn't know what I would or even hoped to find.

I needed a way to tell this web of a multigenerational story, and after two years of research, in a most unusual way—he'd been there under my eyes the whole time—he came to me, Dr. Le Monnier. He was a Civil War veteran and the city physician in charge of the insane asylum. I'd been drawn to his records for years, yet it wasn't until the day I read his name at the top of the ledger, that I made the connection. His family had built the Le Monnier mansion on Royal Street, the same house the Saloys owned—the same house owned later by my great-granduncle's mother-in-law, Carmelite.

One day, after receiving some death certificates in the mail, I started to piece together that there might be some medical link. The causes of death appeared to be similar. I did an internet search and found that this particular kidney disease was not passed down in families. Over and over, I read the same thing . . . until I went a little further. There was one voice who claimed that there was a genetic link, Dr. Anthony Bleyer. I found him at Wake Forest Baptist Health. I sent him an email in May 2013, with the smallest chance he might be able to shed light on this family tree. To my surprise, he was interested, asked me to call him, and to have his secretary page him if he was teaching. My timing was beyond coincidental, he told me. He had only just the day before published the discovery of a gene that could connect my mystery. Yes, a genetic kidney disease may have killed each young heir. Or it could have been lead poisoning. Or something else more sinister, I thought.

Although this book is completely fictional, there are some parts, places and people inspired by reality. None of the houses mentioned in this book is "cursed," and none of the people was actually involved in any voodoo or curse-making. There was an article that mentioned Madeline's dancing at the house on Bayou Road, and Andrew did claim that there was a curse on his fortune, but that is the extent of it. The rest of the story was completely fictional. Alas, there is no actual birdcage, and, sadly, my beloved François is simply a figment of my grand imagination. In the end, I'm afraid one is still left to wonder about the deaths of Carmelite and her sisters. Was it possible some generational curse followed the money? Was their father bent on retrieving their inheritance and somehow involved in their deaths? Or did they suffer from some genetic disease that has only been discovered 100 years later? This, I am sorry to say, is not a case so easily closed. And I suspect I will wonder about and search for years to come for what truly happened to this rich New Orleans family, and to the souls that captured mine.

May God, in His mercy, grant each of them peace.

Nicole

Acknowledgments

Writing this seventh novel was, by far, the longest and most intense experience of my career. Much historical research went in to this project, and I would like to acknowledge with gratitude the following entities: *The Times-Picayune*, *The New Orleans Item*, Louisiana Secretary of State/ Vital Records, New Orleans Public Library City Archives, The Library of Congress, *The Southern Reporter* and *Louisiana Reports* by West Publishing Company. Some articles were used for research and others taken mostly verbatim, including a section on the king's physician from *Memoirs of Marie Antoinetta, Vol. III* by Joseph Weber, 1812. I would also like to thank my writing and praying friends, Dianne Miley, Dorothy McFalls, and Shellie Rushing Tomlinson. Thank you for encouraging me to persevere to publication.

To my family, I appreciate your sweet support and understanding that "Mom's a writer." It's not the easiest occupation I could have chosen, but it's one that that brings me great joy. And last, I am so grateful to Jonathan Haupt and Pat Conroy and the entire talented and caring crew of Story River Books, an imprint of the University of South Carolina Press. To Jonathan, you've believed in me and this story all along and championed it through the rigorous process of acceptance. Thank you for your guidance, for making the book even better, and for letting me tinker with illustrating, my other love. And to the one and only, the beloved and late Pat Conroy, if I could tell you just one more time, "Thank you for everything you've done," I would. Eternal thanks.